REWRITING ADAM

By Connie Mae Inglis

Published by Siretona Creative
www.siretona.com

First Printing—July 2021
Printed in Canada by PageMaster, Edmonton, AB.
Distributed to the trade by The Ingram Book Company.

Cover art: Mykal Inglis
Cover design: Gary Horsman

Titling font: Batangas
Text font: Palatino (paperback)
Text font: Candara (large print)

ISBN 978-1-988983-15-8 (paperback)
ISBN 978-1-988983-32-5 (large print)
ISBN 978-1-988983-16-5 (ebook)

I find Connie Mae Inglis's book a refreshing story of freedom and healing. The message of hope and compassion for people struggling with the impossibilities of life, the questions that are not easily answered, and the answers that are looking for satisfying questions, pours forth in her delightful, imaginative, and redemptive novel, *Rewriting Adam*.

NICOLA MACCAMERON, author of the *Leoshine* Series
www.leoshine.micandpen.com

A struggle with addiction, a failed marriage, and the longing to make things right for a child's sake are just a few of the things that pull at the heartstrings in this well-written novel of failure and redemption. Ms. Inglis pulls you in, leads you into an imaginary world of wonder, and makes you want to stand up and cheer as the story comes to its satisfying conclusion.

MARCIA LAYCOCK, award winning
Canadian author and speaker
www.marcialeelaycock.com

With hints of the literary and artfully composed, Connie Mae Inglis's extraordinary attention to sensory details transport the reader to every location including her parallel universe, which is both believable and fantastical. Simply put, *Rewriting Adam* is a beautiful read.

TRACY KRAUSS, best-selling author and playwright
https://tracykrauss.com

Rewriting Adam explodes with sensory experiences. The sights, smells, and tastes of Chiang Mai come through vivid and true, even if Ethan is too numb to appreciate them. At the end of each chapter, I just want to keep going. At bedtime, my husband said, "It must be a good book because you've been holed up in the bedroom for hours." That's right, down a hole and into another world. This book is something like traveling out of the silent planet to Perelandra, but with an edge. Pain and awkwardness produce a constant discord; unceasing, jolting brakes on an uncomfortable night train. Yet a harmony of peace and hope wafts on the air, getting stronger as the night train travels toward morning. Toward awakening.

ELISSA IKEDA, PhD

Dedication

To Douglas Maxton Inglis
—my hubby, my love, my faithful support.
You believed in me and loved my crazy imagination
long before I put one word of this novel
down on paper.
Thank you.

Epigraph

Come as you are, as you were,
As I want you to be
As a friend, as a friend,
As an old memory …

—Kurt Cobain, "Come As You Are."

Preface

Inspiration for this novel came from four sources, like the four cardinal directions of a compass rose, intersecting in this novel:

1. My love of all things science fiction, and speculative fiction in general. Ever since I was old enough to read, I had a fascination with this genre. Even back then, I was dreaming about other worlds and writing about funny-looking Martians. It was my happy place.

2. Our years as a family living in Thailand and working in Southeast Asia. Cultures are fascinating and beautiful. They deserve to be celebrated in words. Thus, here is where my protagonist begins his journey. But not just that. I focus specifically on one language group—the Khimsha* people. As we spent time with these people, I fell in love with their stories, their legends of origin and their unique cultural ways. I wanted to give the world a taste of who they are. I wanted the world to fall in love with them too.

3. Creation and the Garden of Eden, the opening story of the Biblical narrative. As a follower of Jesus, I know this story well. It too is beautiful. It also feeds my imagination and my mind says, "What if this?" or "What if that?" My sci-fi mind took one of those "what ifs" and turned it into a

whole new world—a parallel universe where my protagonist finds himself in his search for answers. Oh how I enjoyed developing this world. May you enjoy it too!

4. A number of years ago, a young man entered my fairly-sheltered world, unannounced. He was angry and hard, and so unrelatable. And yet, I saw a tenderness beneath his tough exterior. When I learned of his dysfunctional, lonely, and painful upbringing, my heart ached for him. It aches for him still. This novel is for him, as an offering of hope. But not just for him. It's for all the broken, hurting people in this world who have lost hope. May my words offer restoration and hope. And may you remember that you are never alone.

Connie Mae Inglis
Edmonton 2021

*pseudonym

PRELUDE—Ethan's Song

Trapped on the mainline
Point a to point z fighting time;
Incessant click-clacking noises
Of all the choices,
Forced upon my life.

Endless nights of endless stations
And empty faces,
Myopic masses can't see, can't hear,
Me
Screaming.
Screaming behind
Handle-less doors.

I'm a prisoner, a stranger,
Banished—unbonded.
Help me; save me;
Unlock the doors.

'Cause I'm trapped between the stations,
A stinking tramp
Without a destination,
Without a home,
Dreaming of rescue from travel alone.
Do eyes of hope seek to find me?
To offer rest from loss and pain?
The tunnel's deep and night envelopes
A guiding light I seek in vain;
The stations pass like hidden doorways
I'm locked within. No stop. No home.
No rest from pain—my destination.
O destined I to travel on.

Lone destiny; I find no home.

CHAPTER ONE

Tender shoot of a child needing
warmth and shelter and
gentle care
left,
to fight the elements
alone.

Wind whips and sleet stings
without nurture and
loving hands
bent,
to find a crutch
alone.

Addictions replace healthy
sustenance and hope and
discovered love
withers,
from pain and fear
alone.

"He was always trouble," his
estranged mother sneers
in disgust, unstable,
crippled,
she too is lost
alone.

> His life gnarled and knotted
> he fakes a carefree
> smile, but at
> night,
> he cries silently
> alone.

HE JERKED AWAKE. One lone man, fighting an invisible contender that wouldn't stay down.

"Noooo!" he whispered to the empty room, his heart beating double time on a bass drum. Despite the tropical heat, his body trembled with a clammy sweat. He pulled the sheet up under his chin and curled into a fetal position, thankful for escape, again.

He knew the nightmare well: His mother entering his room, announcing that she's leaving, moving out, but instead of sadness, her voice expresses controlled excitement, and when she turns to leave, he sees a toothy grin on her face. Suddenly, he's transported to a long, planked train platform, one from the wild, wild west. His mother peeks around the corner of a dilapidated station, that same grin on her face. Her green eyes glaze over, her long auburn hair turning thin and stringy, as she transforms into a zombie-like apparition, her mouth spread wide with vampire teeth, her filmy gown draped loosely around her. He screams in horror, yet no sound comes out. He turns and runs. On and on. Forever running. Yet the doppelgänger's creepy laugh just keeps getting closer and closer. In blind desperation, he leaps down onto the tracks, hoping to lose her among the rail cars. Instead, he finds himself falling, ever falling, never landing. Then he wakes up.

He squeezed his eyes tight against the image. Why did his mother keep haunting him? What happened to his happy dreams? Did he have happy dreams? He did! He knew he did. In an attempt to disengage his thoughts, he focused on the click, click, clicking of the old floor fan. What time was it? He forced his eyes open and looked at the clock on the wall through the mangled mess of shoulder length hair covering his face. 11:00 o'clock. He needed a drink. That was a lie. What he really needed was food.

* * *

It was noon by the time he left his room to walk out to the busy street of this foreign city. Finding an empty table at the sidewalk eatery closest to his guesthouse, he ordered a cola and reached for the tattered menu, the gaudy pink flowers of the plastic tablecloth jumping out at him. Pink. His daughter Cassie loved pink. The thought made him smile. For a few minutes he allowed images of her to enter his mind—old memories from happier days. His smile began to spread. But then an image of Jill, his ex-wife, burst in. His skin prickled. *Stop!*

Betrayers! Both his mother, who haunted his nights, and his ex-wife, who haunted his days. Ten days of Thailand's oriental beauty and he still couldn't shake either of them. He pounded his fist on the flimsy, metal table, rattling the aluminum box of communal forks and spoons resting on one end. Embarrassed, he raked back his blonde hair, his sky-blue eyes landing on the tattoo inside his left forearm: COME AS YOU ARE. Four words. Nothing else. He scoffed at the words. *I'm here but nobody cares.* He looked around … still a stranger in a strange land. Gripping the cola bottle, he moved his fingers up and down the condensation, plunking out a mocking tune: "A pri-so-ner. A stra-an-ger."

His stomach growled, disregarding his misery glut. The tables around him began filling up—just like they'd be doing at hundreds of other street stalls camped along thousands of cracked sidewalks in Thailand's second-largest city, Chiang Mai.

How ironic, he thought, to be surrounded by all these people in the "land of smiles." He watched the pedestrians maneuver effortlessly around the ad hoc arrangement of eatery tables blocking the sidewalk, smiles on their faces, while he himself couldn't smile. Thoughts of last night returned.

"Running from your past will kill you inside." Jill, as his new bride, had advised this the first time she witnessed him wake in a panic after one of his nightmares, her hazel eyes blatantly fearful, bulging out of her girlish, creamy skin. "You need help."

"Yes, I need help," he'd replied, thinking she'd be his help, his savior. Didn't happen. She turned out to be Jill the Jilter.

He shook the thoughts away and returned to the menu, the foreign curls and angles of Thai script stretching in one long stream, labeling faded photos of local dishes. *Another simple choice to make.* Since arriving in Chiang Mai just over a week ago, he'd eaten lunch at this little street café every day, enthralled by the endless variety of dishes. Thinking himself a foodie, ever since his brief employment as a chef, he made a game of guessing the ingredients from the photos and then judging to see if they matched the actual dishes. So far, the cook was rackin' up the points.

The noonday sun beating down on his back was a welcome change from the biting cold he'd come from. "Canadian prairie winters are the worst, especially when you're trying to drive nails into the walls of half-built condos," he'd told his server a few days ago. She nodded slightly without reply, pretending to understand his lazy foreign tongue but in reality, she, like all the servers, understood little when the conversation veered away from food. *She is "saving face."* He knew it was a Thai cultural value from reading about it in one of his travel books. Accepting that she didn't want to embarrass him or herself, he forced himself to remain calm. *I can swear a stream of colorful words without offending a soul.* Funny at first, but then an inner ache tipped his emotional balance. He had no one to share his joke with. But did that matter? His mind said it didn't. *This journey you're on is yours, and yours alone.* His heart remained restless, suspect.

"What you like today, Et-dan?" His actual name, Ethan, sounded so exotic rolling off the slender girl's tongue. He had mentioned his name only once and soon all the servers knew it. After correcting their pronunciation several times, he gave up, realizing that most Thai people could not imitate the "th" sound. He sighed. Even in his name he was not himself.

He pointed at a picture. *"Pad khrapao muu,"* she responded, the lilt of Thai tones playing on her vowels, so opposite to the harsh consonants of English. *"Aw pet mai kha?"* He had heard this question before. In fact, he had heard it with every meal and now understood. Translation: Do you want it spicy? On day one he said yes, but then hated himself with each burning, sweat-inducing bite. On day two he used his thumb and forefinger to indicate a little bit. Still too hot. On day three he just said no and found the spice to be exactly to his liking. Each server, however, still asked the question, no matter how many times he said no.

"Pad khrapao muu." He muttered to himself. *Why did those words stir a memory?* He wondered if maybe Jill had fixed this dish for him. She had made him Thai food, but he'd never bothered to learn the names of the dishes.

"My favorite."

The fluent English disrupted his thoughts. Was the comment directed at him? Uncertain if he had heard correctly over the endless traffic just a few feet away, he turned to the man looking at him from the next table.

"What you just ordered. It's my favorite." The man grinned. "Think I'll order that, too. Tryin' out different stalls."

Ethan nodded and watched him order the dish and an orange soda, fearlessly competent in his use of Thai. He even made the young server laugh. Ethan's curiosity piqued but, not wanting to stare, he sized the man up out of the corner of his eye: thirty-ish, muscular. Ethan noticed a slight curl in his short hair, a fitting match for his dark, olive skin. Congenial face. Friendly enough, but Ethan had little interest in making friends. *Friends never stay friends.*

"Had it before?" The man looked at Ethan.

"Huh?"

"This dish. Have you had it before?"

Ethan's internal thoughts usurped any verbal response, leaving the man hanging. *Have I had it before?* He remembered Jill standing over the large wok on the stove in their cozy apartment, laughing over his coughing spells as she stir-fried little hot chili peppers in spattering oil as she made the Thai food. "Comfort food," she would call it, "because it reminds me of home." Thailand, this place so opposite of all things Canadian, had been her home for thirteen years. He looked to the street, attempting to envision this "home" through Jill's eyes. A few teenage girls passed by in their crisp, matching red and white school uniforms; one of them looked at him and they turned to each other and giggled behind their long, silky hair. Ethan ignored them, his gaze on the spewing motorcycles weaving in and out of spotless BMWs and gleaming Toyotas. The motorcycles inched their way forward like a dancing Chinese dragon sputtering noisy fireworks, ready to take off when the intersection light turned green, the drivers all trying to get ahead in their own way on their little 100 cc bikes.

"Trapped on the mainline; Point a to point z, fighting time ..." *Song lyrics? Where'd they come from?* Ethan knew they belonged to a song he'd written at the age of thirteen, when his home life, his world, had spiraled downward. Though the initial lines referred to riding a train, somehow his mind connected the slow, relentless passing of Thai traffic to train cars. Not a good connection for his mood. Trying to avoid the melancholia, he shifted his eyes to the shoeless girl in dirty rags approaching with chains of fresh jasmine flowers. She raised her spindly arms to everyone she passed, most ignoring her dark, pleading eyes. Ethan smiled. Though knowing the money would only go to an adult handler, he couldn't deny her beseeching face and, pulling a ten-baht coin out of his pocket, he stretched out his hand for the girl to notice. She hesitated in her approach and then swiftly exchanged the coin for a ring of fragrance adorned with a red ribbon. Bowing, she scooted away, enveloped in the moving crowd.

"Nice," his neighbor said quietly.

Still hesitant to make full eye contact, Ethan silently returned to his drink, anxious for his meal to arrive. Within seconds his server appeared, placing a sizzling plate of food in front of him, along with the condiment foursome that he came to expect as part of every Thai meal: Sugar. Fish sauce. Vinegar infused with mini, sliced peppers. Dried chilies. He looked at his dish: a crispy, fried egg over ground pork full of bok choy, basil leaves, and a few chopped peppers, all on a bed of fragrant rice. He half-smiled, pleased that it actually did look like the picture on the menu. "The streak continues," he mumbled, thinking about the cook.

"Sorry?" A question definitely aimed at Ethan.

"Oh. Nothing really." He dropped his eyes to his plate. "I've been playing this game with the cook's dishes—seeing if what I get looks like the pic on the menu."

"Huh. How's he doin'?"

"What?"

"The cook. How's he doin'?"

"He's headin' for the Hart Trophy."

"The Hart Trophy?"

"Hockey term. A team's MVP. This dish. It looks just like the one in the menu. And just as I remember it." He said those last words without thinking. *This is the dish Jill made me, more than once, with lots of pungent basil and a fried egg on top.* He remembered the fried egg. Thought it weird, but after his first blended bite of mellow yolk and spicy pork, he changed his mind. The egg made the dish.

"The egg makes the dish. But then if you've eaten it in the past, you'd know that."

Without thinking Ethan replied. "Yeah, my wife, uh my ex, used to make it for me."

"Sorry, man."

"What?" Ethan finally looked up.

"The whole ex-wife thing. Sorry."

"It's all good." Ethan tried to sound convincing. "You married?" *Why am I making conversation?* And suddenly he found himself sharing his table as the man slid onto the stool across from him.

"No. Never been. But I've seen enough."

"Right." Ethan smirked.

"No, I'm not talking about my relationships. What I mean is, I've seen enough marriages shot to hell, even in my own family."

"Hell," Ethan repeated. *Endless nights of endless stations / And empty faces.* Lyrics from that same song besieged his mind again.

"Cross-cultural marriages, having a Thai wife, that's a whole 'nother story."

"Huh? Oh, no man, she wasn't Thai. Canadian. But grew up here."

"Oh. I just assumed if she was cooking Thai, that she was Thai. Canadian, ehhhhhh?" He stretched out the expression. Ethan rolled his eyes, but the stranger moved on. "Don't know many ex-pats who actually grew up here. She have lots of stories? She learn to speak Thai?"

"Some." Ethan wasn't interested in talking about Jill and her ex-pat life. A few stories came to mind from the many photos at her parents' place, but she probably had way more tales than she ever told him. After a few, she'd picked up on Ethan's lack of interest and stopped talking about life in Thailand. Soon she stopped talking about a lot of things. Their love, if it was love at all, grew cold. *Endless nights of endless stations / And empty faces!*

"Yeah, stories to tell." The man shifted on the stool. "Travel stories. I've got a few of my own. Many ways a man can get into trouble, especially in this city. Too many choices, too many easy choices with all the pretty young things to capture your attention. Gotta learn quickly to keep your hands to yourself." He paused. "Butt loads of danger otherwise."

Ethan's respect for the man rose. "I hear ya. Got caught

off guard by a *tuk-tuk* driver my second day here. Took me down a risqué side street. Red light district style. Guess he thought I'd like it. I—I couldn't sleep that night." He leaned into the straw bubbling up from his warm soda, needing to wash down the building urge to hurl. Images of young girls still cropped up in his mind. Girls that hadn't looked much older than his daughter. The thought made him sick.

The stranger across from him simply nodded. "Janus, by the way. My name, it's Janus." He put out his hand.

Ethan took it, out of Canadian politeness. "Janice?"

"I know." Janus seemed undeterred by Ethan's questioning look. "A girl's name, right? I get that all the time. It's actually Jan-us, with a u. My mother was into Roman and Greek mythology. She thought my birth would change things for her—new beginnings or some such illogic. You think names decide destiny?"

Ethan remained silent. In his mind, he was thinking about his name: Ethan Conrad Adam. Nothing to give away his own mother's issues. *When she chose my name, had she even thought about it, about me?*

Ethan stabbed the egg with his fork. "I'm not here to think, just to eat."

"No problem." Janus nodded but didn't go back to his table. Instead, he turned to the street and watched the people passing by. Ethan spread runny yolk over the aromatic minced pork and basil, then mixed in the rice. Each steamy spoonful reminded him that this dish was his favorite too. However, still uncertain about this guy with the curious name, Ethan had no desire to vocalize his thoughts. Admittedly, he did find the interaction in English refreshing.

After a minute of silence, Janus's dish arrived. When

he spooned additional dried chilies over it, Ethan gawked in silence.

Janus grinned. "Yeah, I know. It's already spicy. Guess I've been here long enough to need an extra kick. You'll get there, too, if you stay."

"Don't know."

Janus looked up from his plate.

"I don't know how long I'm staying. My boss gave me some extra time off, after …" Ethan stopped himself and coughed slightly, the potency of Janus's dish suddenly burning in his throat. He took a long drink, rethinking his words. "Uh, been here just over a week. Have a one-month tourist visa. Not even sure if I'll travel outside Chiang Mai. Just not sure."

"Ah, the tourist life." Janus swooshed his spoon through the air. With eyes back on his food, and totally oblivious that the spoon passed mere inches from Ethan's face, he continued. "You finding what you're looking for?"

"Huh?" Ethan felt a sudden tightness in his stomach. *What am I looking for? What was the opposite of betrayal? Peace? Or something more? Hope? Dare he say love?*

Janus looked up, one eyebrow raised. "As a tourist. Are you enjoying the sights and sounds of the city? Isn't that why you're in Chiang Mai?"

"Oh, that." Ethan relaxed his shoulders. "Sure. I guess."

"Now I'm curious." Janus put down his spoon and took a swig from his bottle. "So why *are* you here?"

"Uh, long story."

Janus simply raised both eyebrows and waited.

Ethan cleared his throat. "Guess I'm on a hunt." Janus leaned in. Ethan clarified. "A hunt for answers."

"Answers, huh? That's vague. Vague and mysterious." Janus gave Ethan a crooked grin and added, "Thought maybe you'd say a hunt for treasure."

"Treasure?" *Who is this guy?* The knots in Ethan's stomach tightened further. He forced out a long, slow, breath. He turned the question back on the intruder, unable to control his mocking tone. "What about you? Are *you* here for treasure?"

Janus guffawed, a little too loudly. "Treasure? Not …" He stopped and shifted in his chair. "No, a work trip," he said, "though right now I'm in waiting mode. Not treasure," he repeated, with eyes glazed and mouth open, like he was calculating how much to say, as if it somehow mattered to him. Ethan waited, but didn't probe. Janus quietly returned to his dish.

Ethan suddenly wished for lunch to be done. Janus must've thought so, too, because while still chewing his last bite, he pulled a fifty baht note out of his pocket and tucked it under his plate.

"That should cover it." He smacked his rough hands down on the table, bounced up, and looked at the sky. "Well, I'm late. Maybe I'll be back. Cook makes a mean *khrapao*. And, oh," he pulled something out of his pocket, "here's my card, in case …" He paused. "Let's just say, in case you're hunting for something more, down a different rabbit hole." With that, he was gone, lost in the crowd.

What the … Ethan sat, bewildered. *No time to even respond.* He looked at the card: Eden Archaeology; Janus McGinnis PhD, Archaeology and Expeditions. *I just had lunch with an archaeologist?* He shook his head. His skin tingled in the uneasiness. Why? Did it have something to do with the mention of treasure? And why the rabbit hole reference? He noticed the web address at the bottom of the card and determined to check it out.

CHAPTER TWO

"Wakey, wakey, little one,
Wakey, wakey, night is done."

Ethan woke with a start, the little jingle that Jill would sing to their daughter bouncing off the walls of his mind. *Was that in my dream or was someone ... ?* He wrenched his body over, up onto his elbow. The pounding in his head killed the moment. The two bottles on the bedside table reminded him that his only companion for the night was the local whiskey and cola he'd bought at the convenience store around the corner, the whiskey bottle now empty, the soda barely touched.

"Bad choice." He moaned, despite the friend he found in the hangover. Maybe he moaned because of the memory in his dream. Even the alcohol couldn't snuff out his past with Jill. He fell back onto the unforgiving mattress and growled a long, loud streak of expletives. The release was consoling. He turned on his side and lay there motionless, trying to calm the relentless waves crashing in his brain. The floor fan clicked and swayed back and forth, back and forth.

The bedside phone rang, sour notes laughing at his condition. "Hello." He grunted into the receiver.

"Good morning, Mr. Adam. This is your wake-up call as you requested." The voice sounded robotic, the English a little too enunciated, a little too perfect.

"Okay." He hung up and turned over. The bright sun snuck in between the frosted glass slats of the jalousie windows. It beckoned him, but he was imprisoned by the emotional angst of yesterday's excursion, like Gulliver tied down by the Lilliputians of his mind, still unsettled as to what it was about yesterday that constrained him.

He'd visited Jill's high school, Khwam Rak International, which catered mostly to expatriate families. Too afraid to enter the school grounds upon arrival, he'd crossed the street to a little coffee shop, wishing for something strong to deaden his nerves. Once stoked on caffeine, he crossed the street. At the gate, the Thai guard had him sign in and wait. Soon an older expat man, wearing a dress shirt and tie, came out. When Ethan explained his connection with the Sands family, and that he merely wanted a tour, the principal welcomed him up to the office.

The Thai receptionist asked him to sign in with a smile. "Who did you say you knew?"

"Jill. Jill Sands—with siblings too."

"Oh, the Sands family. Yes, nice people. The children attended many years. And the mom volunteered regularly." She said it as if on best-friend terms with the whole family. "In fact, one of the teachers here now was in the same class as Jill, I think. Maybe she's free. I'm sure she'd love to give you a personal tour and catch up."

Catch up? Catch up? What the hell? Ethan flipped the visitor lanyard over his head, all the while thinking about excusing himself and fleeing the scene, but when he looked up, the receptionist had disappeared down the hall, seeking out this "old friend" of Jill's.

Walking over to a large window overlooking an outdoor

swimming pool, he sighed. *Oh to disappear under the water's surface.* He closed his eyes and plucked a tune on the side of his pant leg to calm himself. Seconds later, his daydream was interrupted by a bubbly young woman with a captivating southern accent.

"Hi, I'm Emily. Nice to meet a friend of Jill's." Her head tilted from side-to-side as she talked. "You should've brought her with you. It would've been great to see her again." She laughed freely, stretching out her hand.

Mechanically, Ethan gave a quiet "hi" and a handshake, all the while wondering how much Emily knew about Jill's life the last few years. His racing mind relaxed when he learned that they hadn't been in the same grade and that, while they'd been close in elementary school, by the end of junior high, they'd gone their separate ways, had different friends.

"Kind of sad really." Emily seemed content to converse in the echoing foyer. "And funny how you can be so close to someone and then one day realize that you're not. Choices we all make, I guess." She took a deep breath, but when Ethan gave no response, she continued. "Jill was unique. Really smart but didn't hesitate to push the limits on the rules." Emily half-laughed. "Drove some of the teachers nuts."

"Sounds about right." *That's my Jilly. Wait? My Jilly? Did I really think that?*

"Weird too." Emily babbled on, not like a drowsy brook but like whitewater rapids. Though interested, Ethan had a prickling urge to dash out, scared he would slip up and embarrass himself.

"She had this uncanny ability to read people, like, to sense their emotional state. Maybe it had something to do with that evil clown she kept seeing in her bedroom when she was younger, like an evil spirit that haunted her night after night." Emily stopped talking.

Ethan looked at her, almost seeing the haunting lingering in her eyes. Focusing only on the goose bumps climbing up the back of his neck, he remained silent.

"Wow. Sorry. She's probably over that by now, I suppose. I guess I remember 'cause we were closest during that time and she shared all that with me. Kinda scary and made Jill more skeptical of others. Most people didn't know."

Right. Like me. Jilted again.

"Here, let me show you something." Emily turned down one of the spacious hallways, her short, dark hair bobbing with each step, reminding Ethan of the familiar magpies of home. Smiling at the thought, he almost walked right into her when she turned abruptly in front of a piece of art hanging above them on the wall. Catching himself, Ethan turned and looked at a twenty-by-sixteen-inch acrylic of very non-Van Gogh sunflowers.

"This is one of Jill's paintings from art class. Dark, like all her pieces." Emily stopped talking. She seemed mesmerized, perhaps by a memory, or perhaps by the strokes of thick, muted, paint.

Ethan shifted, his mind drifting to the distant sound of children playing outside.

Finally shaking her head and blinking her eyes tightly, Emily continued. "I remember the art teacher, Mrs. Bowditch, chastising Jill for always painting in dark themes with bleak colors. She even painted a creepy clown once. Ooo, gives me the willies just thinking about it." Emily shuddered. "But for this painting, Mrs. Bowditch had asked her to paint something bright and sunny for a change, like flowers. Jill conceded, starting with happy yellows and oranges but by the time she finished, the sunflowers in her painting were faded and dead." She stepped up to the painting, pointing to the top left corner. "And yet, there's life—you can see it in the light and shadows where the sun's rays stream in. Captivating." Emily paused. "And somehow redemptive." She turned from the painting. "Anyway, that was Jill in high school, always making a statement about life in her art."

* * *

Now, in the quietness, Ethan thought about the paintings Jill had put up in their condo. They were dark. All of them. He'd never thought about that until yesterday.

Ethan opened his eyes and stared at the water-stained ceiling. He realized what disturbed him about that conversation with Emily. He'd learned things about Jill that he'd never known. A memory surfaced to answer why. He hadn't liked hearing about Jill's past life, how good everything was, how perfect and beautiful, when his own past had been so horrible, so cruel, and ugly. He'd shut her down, keeping her from sharing anything, good or bad. *But that was her choice.* He gave a slight nod. *She could've still shared that ugly stuff, so I didn't feel like the only screw up.* In the back of his mind, he knew his response was unsatisfactory, but he had no desire to dwell on it further.

"Wakey, wakey." The words resurfaced. Enough gloom and doom. He kicked off the rough, sun-bleached sheet and sat up, the day's heat already permeating the room. Popping open the plastic bottle by his bed, he choked down two pain killers. Despite the headache, he knew he had to do something, or his thoughts would keep haunting him.

Naked, he shuffled his feet along the cool parquet floor to

the desk. Pawing a few strings of hair off his face, he blinked a few times, trying to read a list on a loose sheet of paper resting on the desk. He picked it up, but the words remained blurry. Pressing his eyes deep into their sockets and rubbing his right temple, he looked back at the beckoning bed. "No," he half-shouted, refocusing on the paper. "Places to visit in Chiang Mai." He fingered down the list, almost second-guessing his decision to visit the "old stomping grounds" of Jill and her family.

"Mengrai University," he said aloud. "I wonder where that is from here?"

The owners of the guesthouse would know, but he also knew that their guidance would be nonsensical. Ethan often felt like the conned fool when it came to asking Thais for directions, thinking that behind their smiles they were intentionally trying to deceive. Then another foreigner explained to him that Thai people don't think in Western grid patterns but rather in concentric circles around well-known *wats*, or temples. It didn't matter who it was, the shop owners, the tuk-tuk drivers, or the traffic policemen, they all viewed the world from that vantage point. Finding a decent map in a bookstore helped, yet when Ethan showed a number of public transportation drivers where he wanted to go on the map, they still couldn't recognize the destination points. Some of them would finally figure it out but others would just drive away, both parties frustrated.

Ethan had never thought of map reading as a learned skill. In fact, there were a lot of norms in his Canadian culture that he'd presumed universal, until he came here. Something as simple as vehicles driving on the left-hand side of the road rather than the right spilled over to influence street walking. Ethan now looked right, then left when crossing a road and he'd learned to shift left instead of right out of politeness when passing someone on the sidewalk. He also tried to keep his toes from pointing directly at another person when sitting so that he wasn't thought of as rude. Jill had never talked about any of this. And why would she? He probably would've brushed it off as empty chatter.

When he stepped out of his room into the open walkway, the trumpeting traffic one block over grated on his still-throbbing head. Needing peace, he glanced down over metal bars to a small garden of tranquility, thankful for the Thais' appreciation of aesthetics. Despite the random shapes and sizes of pots, there was a certain Zen in the plant clusters and flower choices that surrounded a small round pool filled with pink lotus flowers. He closed his eyes, knowing he'd lost such inner tranquility long ago. Now aware that his sweaty fingers were opening and closing on the railing, he opened his eyes, shook out his hands, and walked away. His fingers began to tighten again at the sight of the unfamiliar woman sitting at the front desk. She put on her smile and he pulled a map out of his back pocket, hoping for easy communication. It didn't happen.

Fortunately, a fellow tourist walking through the foyer knew the way to the university. Ethan made a point of giving a smile and nod to the receptionist, and then he headed out of the narrow side road to catch a *tuk-tuk*, his Thai cheatsheet in hand. Flagging down the motorized three-wheeler was easy, bartering for fares not so much, thus, the need for his piece of paper.

The *tuk-tuk* driver who stopped for him offered him a good price, no bartering needed, maybe because it was the hottest time of day and customers were scarce. While Ethan's eyes focused on the little amulet on the dusty dash, dancing to some muffled, Thai ditty on the radio, his thoughts drifted back to a memory … Jill's mom saying something about Jill being the best barterer, how she always stood her ground. "She should've been a lawyer," Jill's mom had said. *Don't I know it.*

Thoughts of the custody battle for their daughter and all that time in court surfaced. Jill had been ruthless. "Vixen." He muttered the word, though deep down he knew the truth. He had taken her to court when she had wanted to settle outside the system. *Her fault. She tricked me.*

He arrived at the university entrance sweaty and irritable, though thankful he'd put his hair in a ponytail. Finding the linguistics department on the campus proved a challenge, however. Nobody understood the word "linguistics," a word too obscure for his small English/Thai dictionary. After ordering a slushy lime shake at the outdoor food court, the elderly man behind the counter motioned with his hand to a table of young foreigners, all linguistic students, getting up from their lunch.

"It's at the far end of the campus," one of the female students said when Ethan asked for directions. "Just come with us."

"Thanks." Ethan took up the rear. Swishing the straw around in the ice remnants of his drink, he listened to the students chat about some visitor who'd come to the department. He paid little attention, his mind still in a fog. When he stepped through the door of the main building, he couldn't believe who he saw. There, in front of one of the office desks, sat his "friendly neighborhood" archaeologist, Janus McGinnis.

Janus turned and gave Ethan an easy smile and nod. Ethan, on the other hand, remained stunned, questions running through his head. *Him? Here? An archaeologist asking about linguistics? Has he been following me? Is it me he's asking about?* Checking his ridiculous thoughts, Ethan's mind switched to the conversation on the walk across campus. The students had been referring to Janus McGinnis; he was the mysterious visitor to the linguistics department.

"Ethan. Hello again." Janus's relaxed demeanor eased a bit of Ethan's tenseness. "Fancy meeting you here. Must be providential, you and me here at the same time."

"Yeah, well, maybe." Ethan half-smiled.

"What do you mean, maybe. This is great." Janus wiggled in his chair, like an over-spirited schoolboy, the kind Ethan could never figure out.

On the other hand, the only thing Ethan wanted to do was to inquire about the work Jill's father had been doing, without any hoopla. Back when he and Jill were still together, Ethan had had a number of engaging conversations with Jill's dad about helping the underprivileged minority language groups in Myanmar, specifically one Shan group, if he remembered correctly. He was sure that someone in the department would have more details. Now his plans were thwarted by Janus's presence.

"This is my friend Ethan." Janus addressed the bearded, elderly man behind the desk.

Ethan only stared in response.

"Welcome. I'm Rick. Rick Sparman, department head." The man stood and put out his large hand. "So you're friends with Mr. McGinnis. Are you Canadian, too?"

Janus gave an easy shrug. Ethan had forgotten to check out Janus's website. *Duped again.*

"Yes, yes, I am." Ethan stepped up to take Rick's hand,

pretending to ignore Janus's cocksure look. "I'm just visiting Chiang Mai and knew someone who taught here. Thought I'd check it out."

"Sure. Have a seat." Rick motioned to the chair next to Janus, returning to his chair and clasping his hands over his portly midriff. "I'm usually not free to chat but … schedule glitch. So, who is it you knew?"

"Ben Sands. He taught here, right? And worked with a language group in Myanmar? A Shan group, I think?"

"Ben. Of course, I know him. We worked together for years. Great guy. How do you know him? Were you a student of his in Canada? I know he taught there too."

"No, not a student." Ethan knew he had to tell the truth if he wanted information in return. "Actually, I was married to his daughter, Jill. We're divorced now."

"Oh." The corners of Rick's mouth took a downturn. "I'm truly sorry to hear that."

"Yeah, thanks." Ethan was surprised by the empathy. *Breathe.* "But—but I appreciated Ben. He talked a lot about his work with a group in Myanmar. Really interesting. Now that I'm in Southeast Asia, I was curious about learning more."

"Well, I'm surprised that Janus didn't fill you in, as a *friend* and all."

Ethan was glad he'd told the truth. He sensed that Rick had a keen ability to read people.

"New friends." Janus seemed unperturbed. "We met just a few days ago. He had no idea I would be here today. In fact, he might be asking about the same area that I am. Could be?"

Rick looked at Janus. "Well, I thought you were asking about an area in Kachin State, way up north around Myitkyina. At least, those are the files I gave you to look at."

Rick turned his focus to Ethan. "On the other hand, Ethan is asking about the Shan group that Ben works with." Rick hesitated. "Although now that I think about it, Ben's group isn't in Shan state. Long history lesson there but I remember now; they settled further north in Kachin state, pockets of them among different language groups." Rick leaned back in his chair, scratching his peppered beard. "So, I guess that means your searches are similar."

"Now you've really got me curious." Janus chimed in before Ethan could reply.

With the pain killers Ethan had taken wearing off, the hammer was starting to pound on the anvil in his head again. He sank down into his chair, both exhausted and overwhelmed by Janus's intensity. *I give up. The lonely bystander once again. I guess I'll have to come back another day. And who gives a crap? It's not like I have anything else to do.* Ethan wondered where the closest convenience store might be. Then, remembering the alcohol ban from two until five o'clock, he looked at his watch. Two fifteen. *Farang! What a ridiculous law.*

"You interested in looking at this?" Janus's words pulled him back to reality.

"What?"

"Did you want to look at this?" Janus dropped a document into Ethan's lap. "It's a legend, a myth, about the beginnings of the language group that Ben Sands works with. It's been written by a young Khimsha woman named Myint Myint Than, as told to her by her grandfather."

Blank stare.

Janus continued. "Well, this is exactly what I've been looking for. It might be a myth but there is historic value and insight here. And I think it just might be the direction I need for my trek into that area."

Picking up the story, Ethan sagged back in his chair. His eyes drifted to the words on the page. Through the fog, their meaning took shape, dragging him into a new world.

CHAPTER THREE

Once upon a time,
The world was in its prime;
Gold and silver, precious stones
Rained down and all seemed fine.
'Til jealous greed brought pain and death,
Alas! Man's paradigm.

*Long ago a precious tree appeared near the Nam Kyo River in what
is now northern Myanmar. It was an iron tree, one hundred and fifty
feet in diameter and twelve miles high. This tree had five branches
that stretched north, south, east, west, and upward. The branch that
stretched to the east was made of rubies. Even the leaves, fruit, and
flowers were rubies. The branch that stretched south was gold with
leaves, fruit, and flowers of gold. The west branch was bronze and everything on it was bronze. The branch that stretched to the north was
silver with leaves, fruit, and flowers of silver. And finally, the upward branch was made of jade with leaves, fruit, and flowers of jade.*

*When the wind blew, all the precious fruit, flowers, seeds, and
leaves fell with the wind, and when they hit one another they made
a beautiful sound like a melody. This melody sang to the race of
people that lived under the tree. It told them of their ancestral line—
how they came from a hermit and a half-woman, half-bird creature
named Keang Na Lee.*

The people called this land Khimsha Lone and it was ruled by four brothers. The oldest two brothers ruled the northern kingdom and this area spread north from the Nam Kyo river to the mountains. The oldest brothers gave the kingdom south of Nam Kyo river to their youngest two brothers to rule.

Because the precious tree was located in the northern kingdom, the older brothers enjoyed the riches from this tree. The two younger brothers requested some of the treasure from the tree but the oldest two were greedy and not merciful. They said, "The treasure from this precious tree is ours because of our good deeds in our past lives. Your concern is not our concern. If the tree begins to grow in your kingdom, then you can enjoy its riches."

The two younger brothers became very angry and attacked the northern kingdom with sticks, knives, spears, and arrows. Many soldiers in both armies died, but the army of the older brothers was stronger, and the younger brothers returned home defeated. Their anger now turned to hatred and all they could think about was killing their older brothers so that they could have the precious tree to themselves. And so they devised a plan.

They knew of a powerful king in a neighboring kingdom within China. So the younger brothers sent a delegation of heroes loaded with gifts to speak to this king, asking for his help to defeat their brothers. This king agreed and sent two large armies to Khimsha Lone.

When the two older brothers heard of the coming armies, they were frightened. But one of the Chinese military leaders wrote a letter to the older brothers telling them not to worry, that they were not coming to fight, but to negotiate. The older brothers believed the letter so that when they were later invited to the southern kingdom for negotiations, they went. The older brothers traveled down the Nam Kyo river to the southern kingdom but before they even reached the meeting place, they were ambushed by the Chinese armies and were killed.

So Khimsha Lone again became one kingdom. However, it was not under the power of the younger brothers, but the Chinese king. One of the military leaders, Lao Swan, became ruler of the kingdom and appointed the younger brothers as lords, giving them some authority but not full rulership. Lao Swan ruled fairly and justly, so there was peace in the land. And every year a large tax of precious goods was sent back to China from the wealthy Khimsha Lone kingdom.

Because of the precious tree, the people prospered. They were healthy and happy and lived long lives. In the markets they sold their leaves and fruits and flowers made of gold and silver and jade and rubies. News spread far and wide about the precious tree and foreigners came from miles around to trade with the Khimsha Lone people.

Ethan stopped reading, conscious of the only sound in the room—the hum of the air conditioner. He flipped ahead. Four more pages. He looked up. Rick had returned to some documents on his desk, but Janus was staring at him like a giddy child.

"So, what do you think? Exciting stuff." Janus's eyes twinkled. Rick looked up and rolled his chair away from his desk.

"Well, I didn't read it all."

"How far'd ya get? Did you read about the jealous sorcerer sending an elephant-sized black bird that started eating people?"

"Uhh, nope. Maybe later." Ethan looked at Rick. "*If* I can keep this copy. Is that okay?"

Rick nodded. "By all means. We have more. Just promise you won't reproduce it or share it with anyone."

"No problem there." Ethan laughed to himself.

"I can't believe you didn't read it all." Janus shook his

head, the smile gone from his face. "Especially the ending. You gotta read the ending. It's unusual."

"Alright. Another time." Ethan folded the papers lengthwise and tucked them into his back pocket. "Sounds like the kind of fairytale my daughter would like, if it had pictures."

"Yes, legends from this part of the world are like that. This one offers a unique picture of the Khimsha people." Rick closed the folder on his desk and held it up. "This file is full of such legends … stories that had only been passed down orally. These oral traditions do matter to the people." He paused. "Ethan, I have many files about the Khimsha. Would you like to see other linguistic work that Ben did?" Rick swiveled his chair around to face the wide metal filing cabinet behind him.

Before Ethan could reply, Janus cut in, rising from the chair, the pitch of his voice rising with him. "Captivating! The first written account of a story that has been passed down from generation to generation orally. A compelling rabbit hole, for sure. I am definitely interested."

What's with him and rabbit holes? Ethan found the reference distracting. He knew Rick was waiting for his answer but he had none to give. He'd always prided himself in being self-taught, self-made, but in this area of study he could not compete. His leg began to twitch. *Why didn't I do more research?* His guesthouse didn't have wifi—his choice—but he could've found another source. Thoughts of his guesthouse reminded him of the unfinished bottle of whiskey on his bedside table.

"So Janus, how does this interest an archaeologist?" Rick turned to Janus.

Janus pulled a card out of the side pocket of his cargo shorts and handed it to Rick. "My card. I'm doing survey work for possible digs. Little has been done in Northern Myanmar.

Rarely approved, from what I've read. But times are changing, right? I want to get in there before anyone else does."

"Understandable. Perhaps the time is right."

"If I get in, I'll need contact with a group that's lived in that area a long time." Janus reached over to pick up the myth document and waved it around. "This folktale tells me Khimsha is such a group." He turned to Ethan. "Just imagine the discoveries a dig might uncover in the exact spot where that precious tree grew. You never know." He plopped back in his chair. "You never know," he repeated and stopped talking, though by his faraway look, Ethan knew Janus's mind was still speeding ahead like a European Velaro train.

Ethan had forgotten what that kind of passion was like, that adrenalin rush of pure energy. He had that once, as a hockey player in junior high. The thrill of the game, hearing the "ping" of the puck hitting the iron bar at the back of the net. But then an illegal check from the side tore up his knee, ripping away his passion, too. He stared at Janus with a mix of jealousy and further respect. *Oh, to be passionate again.*

Satisfied with Janus's response, Rick shifted the questioning back to Ethan. "So, is it the Khimsha you were curious about? Because of Ben's connection?"

"Right. Khimsha." Ethan sighed, exhausted. "Honestly, I'm not sure."

"Well …" Rick relaxed back in his chair, looking at both of them. "You might consider talking to Ben himself. He'll be here in about a month, at least that's what I heard. He usually returns to the area once a year to meet with the nationals he works with. If you're still here, he could help you."

"Good to know." Janus nodded. "I might follow up on that if I'm around, though I'd like to be gone by then."

"Yeah, thanks." Ethan knew he wouldn't follow up on the option. He had a strained relationship with his ex-father-in-law ever since Jill walked out with their daughter. *Too bad, because Ben and I did get along. I really liked having a dad. But then she severed the connection, betraying me with all her accusations, convincing Ben to take her side.*

He's a prisoner, a stranger, / Banished—unbonded. Lyrics from that same song interrupted Ethan's thoughts again. He forced the door shut to the room in his mind that bulged with bad memories. He looked up at the clock, rose abruptly, and forced a smile. "Looks like time's getting away on me. Need to catch a *tuk-tuk* before traffic gets too crazy. Thanks, Rick, for all your help." He put out his hand and Rick rose to respond. "And sorry." Ethan felt the sweat of his palm against Rick's cool grip and pulled away. "I, I guess I wasn't too prepared with the right questions. Maybe I'll be back, if that's okay. I'll know better then, so thanks again."

"Sure. You're welcome anytime. I'm not always here, but my assistant usually is. I'll let her know that you might return."

"Yes, Rick, thanks."

Janus popped up as if following Ethan's cue. "Your information has given me direction. I think I'll be heading out, too." He turned to Ethan. "Can I share that *tuk-tuk* with you? Think I'm headed to the same part of the city."

"Uh, okay." Ethan shrugged.

"Glad I could help you both and maybe I'll see you again." Rick gave a slight wave and turned back to the documents on his desk.

The two of them stepped out the door. The afternoon rains had left behind heavy humidity and intensifying heat. The two zigzagged around the muddy puddles that spilled over the road's potholes, not looking like students at all. All the Thai students they passed wore the required attire: the young girls in their tight white blouses and even tighter black skirts, with their silky, raven hair; the guys in their long-sleeved white dress shirts and black slacks, all with that slight bagginess at the ankles. Ethan figured he and Janus must look like an odd couple, even for foreigners. Himself: tall, lanky, in clean designer jeans, with freckling skin and a blonde ponytail. Janus: shorter yet brawny, in well-worn shorts and t-shirt, with tanned skin and a crew cut fade, shouldering a hiker's backpack with ease.

After circling the open-air gymnasium, they stepped up on a narrow sidewalk, walking single file with Janus in the rear.

"A daughter. That's the first I heard you mention a daughter, though I'm not surprised," Janus said, breaking the silence.

"What? When did I mention my daughter? And … and why aren't you surprised?"

"Well, you mentioned that your daughter would like the Khimsha story, 'if it had pictures'. Remember?"

"Oh right, I guess I did say that."

"And I'm not surprised because of the attention you gave that little street girl the other day over lunch—an act of kindness when most people weren't even acknowledging her existence. Would she have been your daughter's age?"

"Yeah." Ethan was surprised Janus had made that connection when he hadn't. "Yeah, my daughter's five, almost six. And I mentioned her because she loves fairy tales. At least I think she still does."

"You don't know?"

"Well, after Jill left, I didn't see my daughter much. It was too"—he wanted to swear but swallowed the word down—

"too hard to spend time with her and then leave her again."

"Tough choice."

"Yeah, well, my ex sure didn't understand." He didn't dare finish the story, the part about him drowning his sorrows in alcohol. By the time he changed his mind about wanting to spend time with his daughter Cassie, the alcohol had taken over.

They walked in silence past the outdoor food court and over a narrow bridge, Ethan deep in a past conversation with Jill: "Figures," Jill had said. "Should call you the running man. And what about Cassie? Have you even thought about her in all of this?" He hadn't answered.

"Are you a hiker?"

Ethan stopped so abruptly that Janus almost knocked him over. "That question came out of left field." Ethan half-turned back.

"Sorry, man. I just noticed your hiking boots. Very high-end."

Ethan laughed, kicking out one foot. "I guess you know your hiking gear if you recognized quality from behind."

"That's my job, sort of. When you do as much trekking as I do, you gotta have good footwear. I learned that the hard way with my first hike in the Rockies."

"Yeah, hiking the Rockies does require good boots. Wait. What?" Ethan turned around, now walking backward. "You've hiked the Rockies?"

"Yup. Lots of times, ever since I was a kid."

"Of course you have." Ethan mocked. "And thanks by the way, for springing that whole 'fellow Canadian' thing on me back there with Rick." He turned back around.

"Yeah, sorry. You should've seen the look on your face. Guess I made the assumption from your hockey comments.

Plus, you said your ex-wife was Canadian. Me, being Canadian, s'pose that wasn't obvious."

Ethan thought back to their lunch. He remembered their conversation as being minimal. "No. Not obvious." Ethan didn't like being the butt of someone else's joke, so he changed the subject. "But yes, in answer to your question about hiking. I've done my share. After rehab from a torn ACL, I started hiking a lot. Loved heading out to the Rockies to hike the trails. I stopped for a while. New wife, new baby, and all. But started again this past summer. Sometimes, when my ex wanted to be extra kind"—*and when I'd show up sober*—"I'd get to take my daughter."

"Your daughter, huh? You changed your mind about seeing her?"

"Yeah, after a while. Turns out she loves the outdoors." Ethan had no intention of divulging the truth of the story with Janus.

"Cathartic, perhaps?"

Ethan took a couple of short steps and stopped. "What?"

"The hiking. Was it cathartic?"

"Cathartic. I s'pose. Sort of."

Janus cocked his head. "You okay?"

Ethan cleared his throat and continued walking.

Seemingly undeterred, Janus just kept talking. "I've done some here, outside the city." As they turned up the road to the Superhighway, Janus pointed to the old, low-lying mountains in the west. "Lots of tourists go trekking in those mountains, although they're nothing like the Canadian Rockies. Still, it's good." He looked at Ethan. "You done any hiking here?"

"No, man. I haven't. Might not be a bad idea though. I could use some catharsis."

"We should go sometime. You and me. Don't know how long I'll be in waiting mode, and I need to stay in shape." Janus grinned. "Plus, you've got the right boots."

"Um, I guess so. Yeah, sure. My daughter would think it badass if I hiked in Thailand." Ethan thought about Cassie and their hikes together, sometimes out to the Rockies, sometimes just in the Edmonton river valley. She surprised him with her tenacity and fearlessness, braving some steep climbs. He was proud of her. Did he ever tell her so?

"Watch out!" Janus's voice pulled him out of his daydream. Ethan leaped off the road's edge to avoid an oncoming motorbike, landing on his backside in rain-drenched weeds and gravel.

"*Farang,*" Ethan yelled as the motorcycle zoomed by, oblivious to the near miss.

Janus watched it careen down a side road and then turned, extending his arm out to Ethan. "You okay?"

Head down in embarrassment, Ethan didn't move.

"So, why did you call her a *farang? She's* not the foreigner. *You* are," Janus said.

"Duh." Ethan pulled himself up.

"Though she did drive like a first-time foreigner." Janus smiled and repeated. "Sure you're okay, Mr. *Farang*?"

"I'm not laughing." Ethan wiped his muddy palms on his now-wet jeans.

"Okay, okay." Janus put on a straight face and turned to the road. "But can you explain why you used *that* word as a cuss? It sounded like the Thai word for 'foreigner'."

Ethan sighed. "Alright. Here's the short version, since I've already talked about Cassie."

"Shoot."

"Well, I used to swear a lot. And I mean, a *lot*. Thanks to my mother. She swore *all* the time. Her habit became my habit. I, I just couldn't help it. And nobody ever corrected me, especially in the blue-collar construction world. Nobody, that is, until Cassie came along, and Jill challenged me on it. Said it would rub off on our daughter."

"I s'pose that's true."

"Well, I didn't get it at first. I mean, what two-year-old swears, right? But one spring day I had Cassie out in the yard and the tires on her little car became so caked with mud, it wouldn't budge. So, what did she do? She kicked it with her little red boot and started saying the f-word over and over again. She was, well, she was a little me. I just stood there in shock. And Jill? Well, she just gave me that I-told-you-so look and reprimanded Cassie for using bad words."

"Kids are mimickers, all right. But that doesn't explain the *farang* word."

"Yeah well, later that evening, Jill broached my swearing issue. I knew I had to change, and not just the f-word. Lots of words which, unfortunately, still come out at times. But such a drastic change? How? I'd been swearing most of my life. In jest, Jill started spouting off all the words starting with 'f' she could think of—to replace that one word for starters. When she blurted out the word, *farang*, I stopped her, refusing to believe that was a word. She laughed and explained what the word meant. At first we joked about that becoming my replacement word. But the longer I thought about it, the more I liked the idea. So, that's how the Thai word, *farang*, became part of my vocabulary. The change took a lot of work, to be that intentional. And, at the time, I never thought I'd be visiting Thailand."

Janus didn't reply.

"Satisfied?" Ethan had to raise his voice, competing with the three lanes of congested, cacophonous traffic before them, as they approached the Superhighway's access road.

"More than." Janus yelled back. "Your determination to change for your daughter is impressive. Not many dads would do that."

Ethan turned to face Janus. "My determination to change?" Ethan hadn't thought about it quite like that. He had only promised himself that he wouldn't parent like he'd been parented.

"Yeah, sounds like you seriously altered your vocab. Cutting out the swearing. It's almost like you had to learn a new language."

"Huh." He *had* done it, for Cassie. His working buddies had even noticed his toned-down speech. They didn't get it. He hadn't cared. Easy choice at the time.

Still deep in thought, he turned to the road, keeping an eye out for *tuk-tuks*. Each time he saw one coming, he stuck out his hand, fingers down, but in early rush hour each one was occupied, the driver refusing eye contact. Out of the corner of his eye, Ethan noticed Janus extend his arm downward, signaling a yellow *songtaew*, a totally different form of public transportation than a *tuk-tuk*.

"Change of plans." Janus shouted as the truck approached, passengers already compressed tightly along the bench seats in the truck box like the bellows of a resting accordion.

"How's a *farang* going to fit in there?"

"Good one," Janus mouthed with a wide grin. He walked over to the driver and said a few words. Then, grabbing the metal bar that jutted out for standing passengers, he swung up onto the back platform already occupied by a couple of Thai boys. As the *songtaew* sputtered its displeasure, Janus twisted his head around. "Don't forget our hike." Ethan nodded and watched the smoking *songtaew* join the vehicle parade.

CHAPTER FOUR

Broken shards of cultures past,
Silenced by time and earth,
Beckon one to the quest,
the test of the pit,
the fire in the dig,
the passion
in the excavation of life.

Broken shards of familial past,
Locked away by mind and heart,
Paralyze; the other hears no quest,
runs from the test,
hides from the fire,
no passion
in the tell of life.

"Can you turn that up?" Ethan shouted at the elderly woman hunched over in her chair, his staccato voice waking her from a deep sleep. Though he'd been coming to this internet café for a week now, these were his first words to this woman.

Sitting up and rubbing her eyes, she stared blankly at an anxious Ethan leaning over the counter, pointing to a small television bolted to the concrete wall above her.

"The TV. Can you turn up the volume?" Ethan repeated.

Rattling something in Thai, she stood up and turned to

the television, her frame too petite to reach the knobs. Despite the foreign tongue of the two news announcers, the images displayed behind them provided Ethan with enough information to follow the gist of the story: something about a passenger train derailment in the Himalayan Mountains of Tibet.

"Trains." Ethan whispered the word, his body shivering despite the late-afternoon heat.

The television station obviously had no discretion, displaying severed body parts of men, women, and children strewn along the torn-up tracks, an occasional mangy dog already enjoying the spoils. Ethan swallowed hard, the sight inducing an uncontrollable urge to heave. He turned away.

"Never mind," he muttered to the woman and returned to his computer in the far corner.

He sat there for a long time, staring at the screen, willing away the churning whirlpool in his stomach. The news alert returned to an uber-dramatic soap opera and, in the back of his mind, Ethan heard the acting voice of a teenage girl crying, screaming, hurling dishes. Overkill. And yet in the moment, he wished he could be that girl, venting his emotions at the childhood memories resurfacing at the mention of a train. Only not just any train, but a disaster of twisted steel, broken glass, and death.

"I hate trains." Ethan mouthed the words at his own reflection in the blank screen. His right leg twitched again. He forced it down with both hands.

He needed a coffee, but he wouldn't find it here. Leaving his belongings, he nodded to the woman at the counter, and walked just a few doors down to a local coffee shop. Once the caffeine kicked in, he looked over his notes. Hiking information mostly, but also thoughts jotted down from googling

Eden Archaeology and Janus McGinnis, PhD. A professional website, with what appeared to be a strong financial backing. *But why the lack of information on Janus's current trip?* That reminded Ethan of something else: Janus's odd mention of treasure in their first conversation. What was Janus's *real* reason for doing a survey in northern Myanmar? Ethan shuddered in his chair, then shook his head. He knew speculating was not healthy.

Maybe checking out the topography of northern Myanmar would provide some answers. He signed back in on the computer. An email had arrived. It was from Jill.

With the new information Emily had given Ethan about Jill's childhood and her "creepy clown" dreams, Ethan had emailed Jill with his questions: Why hadn't she told him? And if she'd experienced and worked through those nightmares, why couldn't she have helped him with his? And been more understanding of his drinking? In some small way, Ethan hoped this email would be the beginning of healing for their relationship. Instead, her reply widened the rift.

Ethan,

I'm not sure what you want me to say to this. Do you want me to verify Emily's story? If so, then yes, it's true. Did it frighten me? Yes, for years. Sometimes still. But that's where the comparison with your nightmares end. What I experienced was not a nightmare. No! I was wide awake, listening to that evil clown jeering at me. Nightmarish, yes, but real.

When we were together, your nightmares did remind me of my own pain. Maybe I could've been more empathetic. But you shut me out of what was going on. I knew you needed outside help. I was willing to walk through it with you, but your issues were

beyond me. I gave up when you said you could get past it by yourself. Fine. Now you have another thing to get past on your own with the divorce and the court case settlement. Perhaps you think that travelling to Chiang Mai will somehow soften things between us. I won't know the answer to that until you return, because the underlying issue is still your drinking. Can you admit it's an addiction, Ethan? If you're still depending on alcohol to get you through your days, then nothing will change on my end. No matter how much you try to connect with my past, I still won't let you see Cassie. At this point, you are NOT good for her. Do you get it? I hope so.
Until then, please don't email me again.
Jill.

Ethan dropped his head on the table, too exhausted to be angry, hope slipping through his fingers. He knew she was right. He'd always tried to do things on his own, to prove himself, especially when it came to his addiction. Sometimes he'd stay sober for months. Yet, he always crashed. *You're weak.* His mother's voice shrieked in his head. *A no-good alkie.* Once a term he'd used to describe her. A warm tear trickled down his cheek. He sat up instantly, swiping his face with the back of his hand, squeezing his eyes open and closed. *Pull yourself together, Ethan. Stop wallowing in self-pity. Take action. Action? Is that what Jill wants?* He bolted up, not caring when the plastic chair toppled over. "Hike time. Is that enough action for you?" He spit out the words, just above a whisper.

The room started spinning. Too much caffeine without any food. Couldn't hike until he'd eaten. "Stupid, Ethan. Real stupid." He shoved all his notes into his backpack, paid for his internet time, and stepped out onto the sidewalk, knowing where he'd find his favorite khao soi vendor.

Served almost immediately, he took his large melamine bowl of steaming soup, along with the toppings, to an empty table. Ignoring the usual condiments, he topped the soup with plenty of crunchy noodles, pickled cabbage, red onion, and lime. He grabbed some chopsticks and a spoon and dug in, peeling tender slices of chicken off his drumstick and then slurping the egg noodles bathed in the rich coconut curry broth, being careful not to splash on his white t-shirt. He remembered Jill's words, "You need a lobster bib for eating khao soi." He smiled briefly and then enjoyed every heavenly spoonful. With new energy, he decided to walk down to Warorot market for some fruit.

Somehow he took a wrong turn and found himself down a narrow street. He stopped after passing a few shops, for there, nestled between a small Indian restaurant and a nightclub, sat a guitar shop, the guitars hanging systematically in the front window. A guitar shop? He tried the door. Locked. Odd for this time of day. Cupping his hands around his eyes, he peered in. More guitars, though none electric. An excitement mounted in his stomach, the earlier angst falling away. Why hadn't he looked for this kind of store on day one of his arrival? He considered his cash flow. His dad had given him a pretty good chunk of money. Early inheritance, he had said. Maybe he could afford to spend some of it on a guitar—or even a ukulele. He could buy a cheaper one and just give it away when he left Thailand. His mind raced with possibilities as he headed back towards the market.

His exuberance heightened his senses. In the market, the colors of patterned cotton and silk reams seemed bolder. The pyramids of red and green rambutan fruit seemed brighter, fuzzier. The large basins of spicy red, green, and yellow curry paste smelled more pungent. He did a slow 360, drinking in the atmosphere of what Jill called, "the Market System," each stall contributing their small effort to create a giant kaleidoscope of pleasure. He smiled as he maneuvered his way through the maze, picking up a paper bag of crispy-battered bananas, and then a tray of segmented pomelo. He wandered over to the Ping River to find a bench away from the activity. He broke open the plastic wrap covering the pomelo and shoved a whole slice into his mouth. The citrusy juice dripped down his chin. The combination of tart and sweet had quickly made pomelo Ethan's favorite fruit. He'd probably never eat grapefruit again.

His eyes turned to the river. The muddy, silt-ridden water swirled along the concrete barrier beneath him, gliding on to the Gulf of Thailand, its final destination. *Even the river knows where it's going. Where am I going?*

And with that, the angst returned. He bit his tongue to hold back the swear coming out and returned to thoughts of guitars. *Should I buy one?* He took a bite of warm banana and shook his head as if it were a Magic 8-Ball, hoping an answer would float to the top. Perhaps he shouldn't veer from his original plan. Janus or no Janus, a hike would be the better choice. Then like déjà vu, Janus appeared, parking himself beside Ethan, an open bag of dried mango in his hand.

"Hi. Long time, no see. How's it goin'?" Janus's casual confidence always took Ethan by surprise.

"Well, hey. Doin' okay, man." Ethan tried to sound upbeat, focusing his thoughts on hikes rather than trains. "Thought I'd go hiking. After what you said, I started liking the idea again."

"Great. Yeah, sorry 'bout that. I thought we'd have trekked

a few trails by now." His apology seemed genuine. "But do you remember how I changed my plans while we were waiting for that *tuk-tuk* outside the university? I didn't have time to explain then, but I got a message on my phone while standing there that redirected me."

"Huh."

"But in a good way. Wanna hear about it?"

"Sure. Why not? Care for a banana?" Ethan passed the bag of crunchy strips to Janus.

"Sure. Trade ya for a mango strip." Janus turned his bag to Ethan.

"Thanks, but I'll pass on the mango. Tastes too much like peaches."

"Not a good thing? Everybody likes peaches." Janus stuck his hand in the bag of bananas, pulling out a few pieces. "There's something about these, though." He grinned and took a large bite. "So good."

Ethan smiled. "I know the travel books said to be careful about local foods but these"—he pulled one out of the bag for himself—"these greasy buggers, I can't resist."

Janus laughed loudly. "I've eaten food in way iffier places than Chiang Mai without any problems. I think my stomach's made of concrete." He gave his gut a shallow punch.

"So far so good for me, too." Ethan downed the last banana.

"Anyway, the message on my phone was from the Myanmar consulate."

"Oh?" Ethan tried to sound interested, the news irrelevant to him. Still, he couldn't deny that the spirited tone of Janus's voice pulled at him.

"Yup." Janus almost jumped off the concrete bench. "My documents were finally processed." Ethan said nothing. Janus continued in his charged tone. "Do you know what that means?" Janus leaned back, arms spread wide. "It means my survey is approved. It means I'm heading up to Kachin state. It means—it means I'm finally going somewhere." Janus tilted his head up into the sunshine and closed his eyes, as if he was breathing in life for the first time.

"I'm happy for ya." Ethan stared at the joy on Janus's face. *When will my turn come?* The niggling voice in his head replied. *Never! Remember, you're just a stinking tramp without a destination!* Ethan squirmed. The leg twitching returned.

Janus turned to Ethan, excitement dancing in his eyes. "So, that's what I've been doing. Getting paperwork in order, getting a tourist visa, making sure I have the gear I need. It always takes longer than you think."

Ethan turned his eyes back to the swift-flowing water. It seemed to be laughing at him and his last week of stagnation. "Wouldn't know, I guess."

"Well, maybe that could change." Janus's eyes smiled.

Ethan pressed his leg down and cocked his head at Janus. "Huh?"

"You say you want to get back into hiking?"

"Tryin'."

"Well, how about one loooong hike, into a world of unknowns?"

"What? Your cryptic talk is so … weird." Ethan smashed the empty paper bag into a small ball and pitched it into the garbage barrel a few meters away. "So what're you sayin'?"

"You. Me. A guide. Trekking in northern Myanmar. Precisely in the area where the Khimsha live, if I remember that conversation with Rick Sparman correctly."

"Khimsha. Right." Ethan thought Janus would've moved

on in his search for survey possibilities. "Wait." Ethan's eyes popped out. "Are you asking *me* to join you on your trip? I'm just a blue-collar dude. Know nothing about surveys. I—"

"Okay." Janus held up both hands, palms out. "Just hear me out. I've had time to think about it and I know you could do this. It's a survey. Just taking readings and soil samples and such. Plus, getting coordinates for future digs. Hopefully, anyway." He paused. "But really, there'll be more trekking than anything else since that area is pretty much untouched."

Ethan stared at the river once again, his mind swirling with, then against, the current. *This is crazy; yes, it is. But you could do this; no, you can't. Prove something to yourself; you're a loser with nothing to prove. Prove something to Jill; you'll fail again. Make a choice; I can't choose.* His head throbbed.

Ethan closed his eyes, then turned to Janus. "What you're asking, well, it sounds like you just need a second person. Isn't there anyone else, with at least some experience?"

"I'll let you in on a secret," Janus said. "Being an archaeologist isn't as glorious as it sounds. It's a lot of trekking and clearing undergrowth, a little bit of digging and then more trekking. You've probably got more experience than some of my fellow graduates."

"Huh." A slow train of possibility began moving in Ethan's stomach.

"And you're right," Janus continued, "about needing a second man. I did have a partner at first. Arrived with me. But he didn't like the waiting game. Got bored and then made some bad choices that got him into trouble. Bummer for me, and for him, I guess. I sent him home."

"Guess I could say that's *faranged*-up." Ethan laughed at his use of the word.

"Yeah, I guess you could, because it was." Janus tilted his head. "But maybe not for you, at least not today." He nodded. "Luck's on your side. 'Cause he left his survey gear behind. I thought maybe he'd return but, nope. Haven't heard a thing."

"Huh." The debate continued in Ethan's head but the train began to pick up speed. Maybe he needed this.

"Well, think about it. But I can't give you much time. If you say 'yes,' then we've got to get you the right papers for Myanmar a-sap." Janus slapped his knees and stood up. "Doesn't take long, only a couple of workdays. We could even get a day trek in as a warmup. That is, if you're interested."

"When do you need to know?"

"Tomorrow evening, if possible. Sorry 'bout that. Not much time. But either you're in or you're out. Not complicated." Janus pulled another card out of his pocket. "Here's another card, with my cell number on the back this time. Call me. If I don't hear from you, I'll just assume your answer is no." He gave Ethan a pat on the back and turned toward the street.

"Okay. Tomorrow. Thanks, man," Ethan said in a daze. Janus was already out of earshot. *Were thanks in order? Thanks for what?* Alone again, Ethan stared at the phone number. *Was this for real? Did Janus really invite him on a survey trek into Myanmar?*

Ethan had a decision to make—and not a small one.

CHAPTER FIVE

Fill me, I will quench your thirst,
Spin me, I will keep you warm,
Blow in me, I will play music,
Eat me, I will heal you,
Bind me, I will shelter you,
Bend me, I will not break,
Strong as iron, thin as paper,
A tree but not a tree.
What am I?

Ethan sat for a few minutes, wondering what to do next. It was too late in the day to hike. He'd leave that for tomorrow morning. Make his decision then.

He headed back to the guesthouse. With dusk settling on the city, Ethan watched the shop owners close up their stores. The ones with glass window storefronts pulled rattling metal, crisscrossing gates across the entire store. Others, like his internet café, pulled corrugated metal doors down from the top of the door frame and hooked them into the concrete floor with a ring and a padlock. It reminded Ethan of manual garage doors back in Canada, but without the lock.

At the same time, food carts on wheels jangled out from seemingly nowhere, dishes already prepared. Ethan stopped at one and picked up some Thai-style barbequed chicken and sticky rice to eat in his room.

As he dipped balls of sticky rice into sweet chili sauce back in his room, he noticed the folktale document sitting on his desk. He hadn't finished it. Curious about Janus's reference to some bewitched black bird, he flipped to the last couple of pages and began to read:

Because of the bewitched black bird, many people left the area. There were those, however, that were too old to leave. Family members of the aged willingly stayed to take care of their parents and grandparents, believing that no danger would come to those people with good hearts. But if they died, they would die with their parents and they were okay with that.

Other people talked of leaving but they also wanted to remove the bird rather than fleeing. They went to the king to ask for counsel. The king and his officers said, "We know this bird has found its home in our precious tree. Perhaps if the tree no longer existed, the bird would leave and our kingdom would be saved. It is true that we have developed and prospered because of this one tree but thousands of our citizens are dead. Is not life more important than wealth? So, for our life and our kingdom, we must throw away this precious tree." The people agreed.

So the king appointed four heroes of the kingdom to take down the tree. These brave men sneaked under the precious tree, unseen by the big bird now living in the tree, and started four fires around its base. Then the citizens carried charcoal by boat to the tree to keep the fires burning day and night. Because the iron trunk was so hard and so wide, the melting process was slow. After seven days and nights, the tree began sloping to the south and then finally fell to the ground. The whole kingdom shook and a violent voice like an earthquake was heard throughout the land.

The silver branch broke in many pieces that became a silver mountain where later people dug for silver. This mountain exists on the way from Putao to Nwa Meung. The ruby branch fell to the southeast and later people dug for rubies in that area. The jade branch fell to the southwest and later people dug for jade in that area.

When the tree began to fall, the big bird was frightened and flew up into the sky. However, there was a large flat rock not far from the village and it rested there and continued to disturb the people. But the people were not discouraged. They could see the place where the bird rested, so they devised a new plan. They cut down a tall tree to make a large bow and a long arrow. The bow and arrow was so large that it took one hundred heroes to lift it up.

They then cut down the trees marking the arrow's path toward the bird resting on the rock. The one hundred heroes then lifted the bow and arrow and waited. They waited for a few days and finally the bird returned with a wild boar in its beak. While the bird ate the boar, the one hundred waiting heroes shot the arrow. The arrow hit deeply into the heart of the bird and out its back. The bird was surprised and tried to fly away. It only flew as far as the upper Nam Kyo river where it fell into the water, unconscious. As it was floating down the river, it hit a large boulder and woke up. It was filled with new strength and flew up out of the water. But again it did not get far and fell at a place called Na Lyian. There it died at once.

The people came out of their houses cheering and then went to see the dead bird. They decided to have a celebration with a large feast at the spot where the bird lay. Some of the people began beating the bird in anger. And in their anger they decided to roast its meat and eat it. Those who did so later became ghosts because the bird had been evil. The others knew that the bird was evil and they tried to stop those who were eating the bird but they could not because of the all-consuming anger. After the celebration, people who had left the kingdom, returned. And even though they no longer had the precious tree, the people lived in peace once again.

Maybe not such a great fairy tale for kids, after all. He shivered thinking about the ghost reference. It sounded like one of his nightmares. Maybe his mother was a ghost. He brushed the pages away and burst out laughing.

And yet … maybe his mother *was* possessed in some way. She did seem to turn evil overnight, at least that's how he remembered it from the night she just up and left.

And now look at you. His mother's voice. *You left too. You're weak, like your father.*

"Stop!" Ethan jerked up, taking the plate with him. Chicken bones and chili sauce splayed across the floor. "Awe, hell." He turned away from the mess and walked out the door.

The wrought-iron bench beside the garden below beckoned him. A good place to decompress. In the quiet, he closed his eyes, all the while caressing the still-warm iron slats. The scent of night jasmine lingered in the air. He breathed in the sweet fragrance, releasing his anxiety. He forgot about ghosts and began thinking about his dad, Frank. Was it true that he was weak? Ethan knew his mother's words were a lie. After all, *he* was the one who stuck around, taking on the burden of the household and caregiving after she left. And *he* was the one who forgave her two years later. No. His love wasn't weak.

Back when he was 17, Ethan didn't get that. He'd packed up his old '86 Toyota Corona and driven west, no regrets. But, eight years later, when Ethan had invited Frank out to Edmonton to meet little Cassie, their relationship shifted. During the day, Ethan watched Frank dote over Cassie with fatherly tenderness. Late into the night, he and Frank talked man-to-man. Ethan's eyes were opened to the truth about his mother.

"I wanna be like my dad," Ethan whispered. Speaking the words gave him hope. But, could he follow through? Not if he kept running away. His dad had always stuck around. Which brought him full circle back to Janus's invitation. Should he go on the survey? Or was it time to go home?

Home. Elbows on his knees, he propped his head in his hands and groaned. He had a tiny bachelor pad waiting for him, but it was just four empty walls. It wasn't home. Home had no meaning. And that scared him.

He crossed his arms and lowered his head. "Lone destiny, I find no home." He sang the words he'd written as a teenager, holding the last unresolved note. He believed them still. And with the words, his fears grew. Fear of failure, fear of rejection, fear of pushing his daughter away. He didn't choose it. It chose him. When his whole body began to tremble, he jumped up and half-ran to his room, seeking to drown his fears in a bottle.

* * *

A Greater Coucal bird whooping in the large rain tree outside his windows woke him from a dreamless sleep. He moved his head, expecting a headache. Not there. Then he remembered. There'd been little whiskey left in the bottle and thankfully, he hadn't had the energy to go buy more. He rubbed his eyes and sat up, a shiny green iPod slipping off his bare chest. Right. He'd chosen music over alcohol … had even played along on an air guitar. A soothing release. He hummed, and then began singing one of his Nirvana favorites. "Take your time, hurry up / The choice is yours, don't be late."

His hike. He couldn't be late for that. Plus, he had a decision to make. No time to sleep in. He threw off his sheets, put on some light cotton pants, and grabbed a protein bar for breakfast. He wanted to get to the Huay Tung Tao reservoir outside the city in time for a good hike. Tossing other snacks and water into his backpack, along with his map and compass, he headed out the door.

By ten thirty he was standing in front of the Golden Buddha image on the west side of the small lake. Though only ten kilometers out of the city, the air was fresher, the noise pollution almost non-existent. The little huts jutting out into the water along the water's edge were almost all empty. Not a busy day. Studying his map, and with compass in hand, he found the easy-to-follow trailhead heading northwest. *I wonder if Janus knows that I'm pretty good with a compass. There's my first point for the "pros" list. Why else should I go with Janus?*

Gear: check. Funds: check. Thanks to his dad. And he did have the time thanks to a considerate boss who knew about the court fiasco with Jill. But did he want to be gone for another month or more? He should've asked Janus about time commitment and overall cost.

You should've asked more questions. How stupid are you? The deprecatory voice stopped him in his tracks.

No. I won't listen. Not if I want to prove to Jill that I can be a good father.

Ethan gulped some water to boost his confidence and looked around at the unfamiliar vegetation, so different from the Canadian prairies or the Rockies. The forest was mostly deciduous—green, but not as thick as he thought it would be. The only tree he recognized was not even a tree: bamboo, a grass. Whether in clumps, or individual shafts, it always pushed straight up with leaves shooting out only at the top. He rubbed his hand up and down the ringed stalk. Smooth. Cool. Jill loved bamboo—had a little stem of it in a jar on their kitchen counter. He thought it odd, but she said it connected her to home, that it made her strong.

What was it she said? "Bamboo knows how to bend but not break." At the time it made no sense, but now, as he felt the stalk bend with a sudden gust of wind, he understood.

Ethan looked at the sky. Heavy clouds. Rain. He forgot about the rains. *How could you forget? You're so stupid. Add that to your list of "cons."* A memory rose in his mind … one where he and Cassie had been caught by a freak storm in the Rockies. They had found shelter under the low-lying branches of a white spruce. Nothing like that here. But perhaps that semicircle ring of bamboo. That might work. A few raindrops hitting his head, he made a dash for the sheltering sphere. As he tucked himself up against the sturdy stalks, his backpack under him, the wind began to whip through the treetops. The bamboo high above rubbed together like deep-throated wind chimes, but down below, in the shelter, only a light breeze touched his skin. He fidgeted, attempting to get more comfortable on his backpack. Finding a perfect nook for his head, he closed his eyes. The chimes soothed his anxiety. And under their spell, he fell asleep. A deep sleep. And with it, a disturbing dream.

In his dream, he's back in his usual zombie-mother nightmare. But when he jumps off the train platform, he lands in a semi-tropical forest, surrounded by aged green bamboo. He sees a path and instinctually continues running. The trail ends. He stops. Nobody's following him. He turns around and around and around again. He's lost. His only hope is to return the way he came. But when he starts walking, the whole scene changes to a dense jungle of creeping vines, the thick foliage turns the dream dark and ominous. He hesitates but knows he must keep moving.

Without warning, the jungle opens up into blinding sunlight and a luminous pond, clear and glistening, with what looks like rainbows dancing on the surface. Thirst overcomes him and, falling to his knees, he drinks deeply. Lifting his head, he gazes into the pool, and notices the variety of fish swimming mere inches away from him, seemingly unafraid of his intrusion. He stares at the abnormality.

A voice calls his name. Not a familiar voice but one sweet-tempered and young. He looks up and sees a child hovering over the water. She reminds him of Cassie, and yet not Cassie. She's a couple years older, her ebony hair hanging in curls around her kind face, her skin creamy, her eyes violet.

"Peace, Ethan." Her delicate lips don't move, but Ethan hears her voice.

"Help!" Ethan mouths the words but nothing comes out.

"Yes, help. We all need help. So, come. And do not give up hope." Her words enter his thoughts, her voice also like rainbows dancing on the surface of his mind. "Hope will help you make the right choice," she says.

"Choice? What choice? I just need help out of here."

"It's up to you." Her words float in. She turns her head, as if in response to another voice or sound. Then, like windblown smoke, she disappears into a white light in the sky.

Ethan woke, slowly, as if still under the little girl's peaceful charm. It took him a few minutes to realize he'd fallen asleep. The wind persisted, but the clouds had passed with no sign of any downpour, the sun shining brightly, his clothes dry. He looked at his watch. Less than an hour had passed and yet he was completely refreshed.

He reviewed his dream so he'd remember, though he was

sure he'd not forget the girl's confusing words: "We all need help. So, come." Were those words offering *him* help if he'd come or was this *girl* needing his help, so he needed to come? He couldn't tell. And where was he coming to? Did this have something to do with joining Janus on his expedition? The dream offered no answers.

A deep bong from the bamboo high above brought him back to reality. It was getting late. Grabbing his bag, he headed back down the trail, but not before he turned to give his bamboo bed one last look. He wanted to remember. Maybe to tell Jill? Would she listen if it involved bamboo? Maybe not. But Cassie would. *If* he could see her.

Cassie. *She* should be part of his decision-making, not just Jill. After all, it was Cassie who needed a father worthy of her. Maybe Janus's offer was an opportunity to prove himself to *her*. The voice in his head returned. *You'll never prove yourself worthy—of her or of anyone. You're an addict and a loser.*

The words of the little girl in his dream returned. "Peace, Ethan." He let those words linger as he thought about hiking with Cassie, about the strength of her resolve for one so young. *If she can hike Jasper's Whistlers Mountain, then why can't I say yes to Janus? Make a resolution right now to go "cold turkey."* The one line of lyrics came back to him: *The eyes of hope will seek to find him.*

"I can do this." Ethan whispered the words at first, but then he repeated them over and over, louder and louder, until he was yelling them, up and out to the world, joining the wind and the chimes. "I can do this! I can do this!" There may have been no rain, but his cheeks were wet with tears.

He picked up his pace, silent tears still falling. This time he was running toward, instead of running away.

CHAPTER SIX

Addiction. Broken relationships,
broken dreams. A bandage only
prevents awareness. Name it.
Fight for your life—but not
alone. Let Love take
your hand. Do not
resist the
healing
dance.

"I'm in." Ethan called Janus as soon as he got back to the guesthouse. Even by then he'd lost some of his confidence, the "logical" voice in his head telling him that rash decisions only lead to failure.

"Fantastic!" There was that elevated voice again.

"But I got questions."

"Heck. I'd be worried if you didn't. How 'bout a breakfast meeting. That way we'll have the day to get your paperwork going. Say 7:30? You're at Happy Hunting Guesthouse, right?"

"Sounds good, but how …"

"Great. I'll swing by and pick you up."

"Okay." Ethan replied to a silent line, picturing Janus on the other end, ticking one more item off his to-do list.

Ethan tossed and turned all night. He refused the usual alcohol fix before bed, knowing that in a few days he wouldn't even have a choice. *I've got to do this alone.* To encourage himself, he propped up a photo of Cassie on the bedside table. She would be his muse on this adventure. While lying there, staring at her big grin, he decided he'd send Jill an email, letting her know his plans, even though she had said not to. He told himself it was for Cassie's sake, but a small part of him wanted Jill to know too, as if her approval mattered. He shouldn't still care. So why did he?

Cassie's smile greeted him when he opened his eyes. In the morning light, Whistlers Mountain loomed in the photo's background. The memory gave him an instant energy boost. Half an hour later he'd had a shower, packed up his belongings, and was sitting on the guesthouse steps. He plucked a nameless tune on his leg.

Janus sped into the alleyway on a well-worn 100 cc motorcycle that backfired to a halt at Ethan's feet. "Like my rental?" Janus unclasped his fluorescent yellow helmet and hung it on the handlebar. "Got tired of public. It's saved me a butt-load of time."

"Uh, I'm gonna ride on *that,* with *you*?" Ethan's sarcasm was deliberate.

"Sure. Why not? Even got you this." Janus threw Ethan a scuffed-up, silver helmet with a black racing stripe. "You don't wanna trust my driving?"

"Whatever, man. As long as we're not travelling like that across Thailand," Ethan chided. Riding on the back of a motorbike with Janus was almost asking too much.

"Nope. Just around town. Although, I guess that depends on your decision. You think Thailand's the opposite of Canada? Myanmar's a whole 'nother ball game … or should I say, 'rabbit hole'."

Something in Ethan snapped. He had to speak up. "Rabbit hole this and rabbit hole that. In what world does that make sense?"

Wide-eyed, Janus turned to Ethan and half-laughed. "Makes sense in Wonderland."

"Not funny."

"Right." Janus swung his leg over to sit side-saddle. "I have this uncanny attachment to *Alice's Adventures in Wonderland*. The storyline is so much like the life of an archaeologist that I just can't help myself." He paused, then uttered one loud guffaw. "Okay. If I think about it from your perspective, mentioning the rabbit hole at random times is bizarro."

"Yup."

"Would you like me to quote from another character? The Cheshire Cat or The Mad Hatter?" Janus pretended to tip his hat in service.

"Are *you* mad?" Ethan wasn't about to play Janus's game. "You're one strange dude."

"Ha. Yeah. Well, you can blame my mother. Along with her Greek mythology fetish, she loved English classics, preferring Charles Dickens, but the 'we're all mad here' world of Alice's Wonderland enticed me. You do get how it relates to my occupation, don't you?"

"I guess. But … to keep referring to it is more spooky than uncanny."

"Okay, okay. No more mention of rabbit holes."

Ethan doubted that, but he let it go.

"We've got more pressing matters. You've got questions? I've got answers. Let's go get some breakfast."

* * *

"Ironic." Ethan dropped his helmet in the bike's front basket.

"What is?" Janus unbuckled his helmet and balanced it on the handlebar.

"Of all the places you could've picked for breakfast, you chose this one."

Janus's eyes scanned the unassuming café front. "Why? Don't you like this place? I mean, I know it's nothing fancy, but they make a decent bacon and eggs. Good coffee."

"No." Ethan shook his head. "I wouldn't know about that. It's just that, well, yesterday, I noticed that shop for the first time." He pointed to the guitars hanging in the store across the quiet street and then, looking at Janus, he bent his head to one side as if to say, "C'mon. Let's take a look." Before Janus could argue, Ethan had his feet firmly planted in front of the shop, closed once again.

"Guitars." Janus grinned. "*Now* I get it."

"Huh?" Ethan's eyes were glued to the collection.

"Well, I noticed the words of your tattoo the other day. Couldn't place it, 'til now. 'Come as you are.' Nirvana, right?"

Ethan smiled at Janus and turned his inner left arm up to the sun. "Yup."

"You play?" Janus tilted his head to the window.

"Electric. Own a Fender." Ethan looked back at the guitars. "But I'd take one of these for sure. *If* I have enough cash for this trip, that is." Knowing the probability was low, Ethan walked back to the café, and sat down at the first table.

Janus ordered for both of them: two American breakfasts and two hot coffees. "Gotta keep my possible partner happy." He grinned again.

Ethan stared at the spoon balancing between his thumb and index finger, guitars still on his brain.

"So is that a passion of yours? Playing guitar?"

Ethan put the spoon down and tipped back his bamboo chair, toying with the balance. "Well, I love playing guitar. Probably more than you love Alice's Wonderland. But a passion? Not sure." Ethan looked out the window. "Guess I play more out of necessity. But maybe … maybe it *is* a passion." Now he *really* wanted a guitar.

"Out of necessity?" When Ethan didn't respond, Janus switched the question. "Been playing long?"

Turning to Janus, Ethan brought his chair down to earth. "Yup. I was still a kid when my mom taught me the ukulele. She said I was a natural. Taught me 'golden oldies' like 'Mr. Sandman,' and 'Dream a Little Dream of Me'."

"Don't know those songs."

Ethan laughed. "Nor would you want to, really. But as a kid, I loved them. My mom would sing and I would play. Her voice was, well, back then, I thought she had the voice of an angel. Pardon the cliché." When the waitress arrived with their food, Ethan stopped talking.

"So, when did you switch to guitar? Your mom teach you that too?" Janus dug into his plate of food.

Ethan came close to spewing a mouthful of coffee across the table. He grabbed a handful of napkins, embarrassed by his outburst. But he didn't answer the question.

Janus kept eating. Halfway through his eggs, he put down his fork. "Did I say something wrong? Thought I asked a valid question."

Ethan paused from making swirling patterns around his hash browns with his over-easy eggs and looked up. "Sorry. The combo of guitars and my mother … not good, to put it mildly. Too much 'mother' talk and I lose my appetite."

"Well, I get that, sort of. My mother could …"

"No." Ethan dropped his fork, leaned back again, and closed his eyes. The lyrics swept in. *Without a home, / Dreaming of rescue from travel alone.* "No," he repeated, jerking forward, the front legs of the chair coming down hard, scraping loudly on the tile floor. Ignoring the looks from the waitress and the elderly tourists sitting on the far side of the café, Ethan grabbed his cup and swirled the coffee around and around. Janus said nothing.

"No." Ethan kept his eyes on the coffee. "You at least talk about your mother like she cared. Mine? Well mine lived just to destroy my life. She did that well when she disappeared one day without even a good-bye."

"What? That's crazy."

"You got that right." The coffee cup began shaking in Ethan's hand. He put it down and clasped his hands in his lap. By this time his right leg was vibrating like a jumping bean, but he knew he couldn't stop it, any more than he could stop a locomotive without brakes from careening down the rails.

"Sorry. Did she … did you ever find out why?"

Unsure of why Janus cared about the topic, Ethan kept going. He had to finish what he started. "She left with another man. And I? I became 'Blue Eyes Crying in the Rain'."

"Huh?"

"An old Willie Nelson song she'd taught me. Kept playing over 'n over in my head." Ethan's voice cracked. He stared down at both legs now bouncing, and pressed his palms up and down his thighs, trying to get a grip on his emotions. Janus seemed in no hurry. Eventually, Ethan looked up with a long sigh. "Sorry." He cleared his throat. "In the end I smashed my ukulele into pieces. Couldn't take the reminder." He shifted in his chair. "Anyway, my dad somehow knew I needed music and one day he came home with an electric guitar. By then I was listening to heavy metal and grunge, even death metal. Stuff that reflected my pain, I guess."

"Right. So that answers my question about the guitar."

Ethan ignored Janus's comment, his eyes now glued to the sticky, yellow goo on his plate. "But two years later she came back with a vengeance. Like an F5 tornado. The stuff she said. The words she used. Raging at Dad for buying me that guitar. Swearing up and down at me for my music choices, my clothing choices, my friend choices. Blaming Dad for screwing me up. What a joke." Ethan looked at Janus, a crooked smirk on his face. "She had no idea that *she* was the one who screwed me up." He leaned back and closed his eyes.

"Wow. Probably pointless to say sorry. Guess my mother has nothing on yours," Janus said with a light-hearted tone, as if trying to lighten the mood.

"Enough about my mother. Why'd you even ask? I mean, that's not what this breakfast's about."

"Well, you're the one who has questions. And besides, it's not a bad idea to learn more about my partner, right?" Janus grinned. "So, what d'ya wanna know?"

Ethan sat for a minute, trying to remember his questions. Needing more caffeine, he made eye-contact with their waitress and raised his mug. She came immediately with two more cups of the potent brew.

"I'm pretty sure I've got the funds." Ethan stirred two spoons of sugar into his second cup. "It's more the time. Just wondering how long we'll be in Myanmar."

"Honestly, I don't know." Now Janus leaned back in his chair. "Depends on so many things. At the least, a couple of weeks. A month at the most." He leaned into Ethan. "Why does it matter?"

"I ... I guess I didn't want to be away from Cassie for too long."

"Your daughter. Right." Janus seemed to understand.

"Though things are strained with my ex right now, so not sure if it matters." *Why did I add that?*

"Oh?" Janus stirred sugar into his coffee. "Something happen with Cassie?"

"No. Not really." Ethan sighed again. "Okay, I've gotta be honest with you."

"Shoot."

"I emailed Jill a few days ago. Just to touch base. She told me not to email her again until I've worked through some sh—some stuff. That I couldn't see Cassie until I did."

"Stuff, huh?" Janus leaned forward. "Look. We're all working through stuff. Maybe for you this trip could ..."

"What? Heal my pain?" *Stop!*

Janus didn't flinch.

Ethan gripped his mug and sucked in a long breath. In, then out. "Sorry. It's just that, well, she's right." He looked straight at Janus. "I don't wanna talk about it anymore." Ethan slumped back, exhausted. "Hope you're not regretting your decision."

"Not a chance." Janus shot up, his face as carefree as ever. "If there's nothing else, I'll pay up and we'll be off. Got a busy day ahead."

You can do this. A child's voice. Cassie? Could it be? The words were caffeine to his soul.

* * *

Janus wasn't kidding about the day being busy. Photos of different sizes. Visa forms. Line ups. Two trips to the

Myanmar consulate. Ethan became Janus's trained puppy, following instructions without asking questions. Unusual to be completely at the mercy of someone else. Unusual to be trusting someone he hardly knew. Despite Cassie's encouragement, the morning's conversation kept playing over and over in his mind as they whipped in and out of traffic. Why had he talked so much? Janus's questions always seemed to catch him off guard. He didn't know if that was good or bad.

Dropping Ethan off at his guesthouse at the end of the day, Janus opened the main zipper of his backpack. "Here." He handed Ethan a large, soft-cover book. "It's about field archaeology. The sooner you start reading it, the better."

Ethan read the book title out loud: "*Field Archaeologist's Survival Guide,* by Chris Webster." Then he flipped through the pages.

"Not like having a degree but definitely helpful when it comes to fieldwork."

"Thanks." Ethan looked up with a grin, unable to remember the last time anyone gave him anything of significance. "Guess I'll start reading it tonight."

"Good plan." Janus pulled his helmet on. "See ya in the morning." He yelled the words over the stuttering motor, whipped the contesting machine around, and was gone.

* * *

Day two continued with much of the same, though Ethan made a concerted effort to watch and learn. Almost enjoyable.

On the morning of day three he found time to send an email to Jill. He kept it brief, informative, giving her his and Janus's cell phone numbers in case of emergency. He mentioned the area of Myanmar they'd be in and that he hoped to see the Khimsha people, thinking that she would pass the information on to her dad. The need to prove himself to others still held power over him, still controlled his choices. *Will this ever change? Jill doesn't even want to hear from me so who cares what I write?*

He maneuvered the mouse to the "send" icon, then reluctantly pressed down, shooting his message to the other side of the world. He exhaled slowly. It was done.

When Janus called to say Ethan's tourist visa was ready, the day filled up once again. Reality didn't fully sink in for Ethan until the friendly Bangkok Airways travel agent handed him his airline ticket.

"This is really happening." Ethan half-mumbled as the two of them walked out of the cool air-conditioned airport into another muggy post-downpour afternoon.

"Uh. Yeah, it is."

"And tomorrow." Ethan looked down at his ticket. He thought he'd be excited by now. Instead, all he felt was his familiar friend—fear. By the time he looked up, Janus had zipped across the busy corridor of traffic in front of the airport, leaving Ethan behind. Ethan willed himself to the motorcycle, a pounding in his chest and ice in his limbs.

"You okay there?" Janus gave Ethan a long, hard look and changed his tone. "I remember my first survey. Mix of emotions, even though I'd been waiting for that day for a long time. Not like you." Janus held out the second helmet. No response. "Sorry, man. You've had no time to process. I get it. But I know you can do this."

You can do this. A chill ran up Ethan's spine. Then he let his body go. He shoved his helmet on and flipped down the visor, not wanting any more conversation. Janus casually threw his leg over the saddle of the bike without saying another word.

"So, about tomorrow." Janus turned to Ethan as he dismounted the motorcycle at his guesthouse.

"Shoot." Ethan smiled, trying to reassure Janus that he was okay.

"Why don't you come to my guesthouse just before ten. Gives us plenty of time."

"Can do."

"Okay, then. I'm off to return this motorcycle." And once again, Janus shot down the alley on his not-so-trusty steed.

"Yup. Tomorrow." Ethan's whole body shivered. He wondered if he was getting sick. *You are sick.* A response from his mother's voice. He countered it with the probable cure: food. He needed to eat. Dropping his backpack off in his room, he headed back out to the street for one last Thai dish. He chose *phad thai*, opting for something basic, not spicy but still savoury and laden with his favorite shrimp. He used chopsticks, relishing every bite, while watching the evening street life emerge one last time, thinking back to his first meal at this very same table.

Chaotic, he had thought back then, just three weeks ago. But now he didn't think so. He saw method in the seeming madness—cars stopping at intersections, giving room for motorcycles to crawl to the front of the line, vehicles making allowance for illegal roadside stops for food pick-up from rows of food stalls, passengers jumping in and out of tuk-tuks and *songtaews* from any point on the road, and somewhere within the din, karaoke music playing from an unknown source. He could almost feel the rhythm of the city, like a drumbeat that kept the people around him singing and dancing. Still chaos, perhaps, but an almost rhapsodic chaos. Cultural choices that made the Thai's world go 'round. *Who am I to argue with that?*

Ethan returned to his room, wishing for a guitar. *Noodling on a guitar would soothe my mind.* But no guitar. Instead, he headed back to the convenience store for one last bottle of SangSom. The wrong choice, he knew. *But I need to get a good night's sleep. SangSom is good for that.*

Upon returning to his room, Ethan plopped down on the side of the bed and poured a full glass. But as he picked it up with trembling hand, the child's voice returned … *his* child's voice, from the little girl with the sparkle in her blue eyes and the bubbling buoyancy in her step. *I am here with you, Daddy. Don't give up. I'll be with you as you chase that rabbit. It will be the best adventure.* She sounded so near that Ethan scanned the room for her. Though alone, he sensed her spirit there with him, her presence flooding him with peace.

He gazed at the glass in his hand and calmly returned it to the table, the urge washed away with Cassie's words. He turned and, curling up on his bed with his back to the bottle, fell asleep.

CHAPTER SEVEN

On a flight to Mandalay,
Where past and future join to play,
As the sun bears down psychotic on humanity in fray.

Go you now to Mandalay,
Where old hidden cultures lay,
Can't you 'ear their voices calling from Chiang Mai to Mandalay?

"Go you now, you slick surveyors; Go you now to Mandalay!"

Ethan arrived at Sabay Jai guesthouse before ten o-clock the next morning with a newfound confidence. He'd actually made two good choices in a row: one, he said yes to this trek; two, he said no to the alcohol last night.

Janus swooshed the door open before he could knock. Ethan recognized the energy. Controlled, but antsy. For the first time, he almost wanted to reciprocate the exuberance.

"Good morning, Ethan. A glorious day, wouldn't you say?" Standing in the doorway, Janus sucked in a deep breath, as if breathing fresh, clean, Rocky Mountain air.

"Sure?" Ethan turned to look out, curious to know what Janus saw. Just a peek of a hazy, non-descript sky above the dominant concrete jungle of typical three-story buildings, blackened with streaks from high humidity and a hint of green from rainy season mould. Nothing very glorious about it. But then, Ethan knew Janus was not referring to the immediate physical view but to the future of unknown possibilities.

"Yup. A great day. And a long time coming for me." Janus trumpeted, turning back into his room. Ethan stepped in, noticing the packed bags but also the stack of unfamiliar items in one corner.

"This is what we have to divvy up?" Ethan stared at the pile.

"Yup. Everything we need for field survey work." Janus paused. "Pretty much. We can get the rest in-country. And, what we don't need, like the gradiometer," Janus picked up a hard, black case that to Ethan looked almost like a high-end guitar case, "I'm leaving with Rick."

"Rick?"

"Uh, yeah, Dr. Sparman. You know, the linguistics department head at Mengrai? I've been back there a few times. Needed more historical information. Interesting guy. Anyway, he offered storage space."

"Huh. Guess I should've gone back." Perturbed at his past idleness, Ethan shifted his weight from side to side, but Janus appeared too engrossed in his own thoughts to notice.

"All right then, let's do this."

* * *

By the time the two of them arrived at the airport, it was one o'clock. Even the flight seemed to go by quickly as he flipped through the Myanmar travel book that Janus had given him. Some of the tips he read reminded him of Thailand: Remove your shoes at a temple, don't point your toes at a Buddha statue, transactions are all done in cash. But then unique tidbits of information raised his curiosity: Men wear wraparound skirts called *longyis*, women apply a protective yellowish powder to their faces called *thanaka*, U.S. currency is acceptable but any bills that are worn, creased, or marked in any way will be rejected. *Not like Thailand at all.*

What the hell are you doing? You've finally lost your mind. His mother's angry whisper.

Ethan turned to Janus for some diverting conversation but to his dismay Janus had fallen asleep without a sound or a shift in the Asian-sized seat, a hint of a grin still on his face. *Figures.* Ethan almost snorted. *Probably another necessary quality for an archaeologist.*

The voice piped in. *Something you're not.*

Ethan stared back down at the book, unable to focus, relieved when the seatbelt sign came on announcing their descent. *Was Myanmar really going to be that different?* According to Janus, yes. But then, how much did Janus really know? Ethan suddenly felt the fool, again. He knew very little about Janus's pre-planning, assuming it to be based on first-hand experience. But was it? He whispered to the shroud of gray outside the window. "Some rabbit hole."

"You say something?" Janus straightened up and stretched noisily, one of his bulky arms nearly hitting Ethan's head. "Guess I dozed off." Smacking his lips, Janus strained his neck to look out the window. "No turning back now." He looked at Ethan with a sleepy grin.

Ethan said nothing. Instead, he watched the unknown world open up before them as they dipped below the clouds. The image of a wide-open clown's mouth entered Ethan's mind. Problem was, he couldn't tell if the clown was smiling or frowning. Either Janus didn't see Ethan's whole body quiver, or he chose to ignore it. Sitting back in his seat, he rubbed his hands together. "Exciting." He reached for his backpack.

"Guess I'd better pull out our paperwork."

"Paperwork? You mean my passport and visa?" Ethan turned to look at him.

"For you, yeah, but I have a number of forms I have to show the authorities upon arrival. Without them we'd just be the usual tourists going to the usual tourist spots." Janus dug a bright green folder out of his backpack and waved it in Ethan's face. "*This* is what's going to get us into areas no foreigner has been to in a long time. At least, I hope."

"You hope? You mean you still have doubts?"

"Not in the paperwork." Janus sighed. "But I'm not stupid. I know I'm still dealing with government officials, with individuals who don't know who I am, nor should they care. Plus, I've never been to Mandalay, only Yangon." He paused, then added soberly, "No. What I hope is that whoever sees these papers is having a good day and is a forward-thinker. You never know."

"Huh. Never thought about it like that." Ethan considered Janus's explanation. "Makes a person appreciate Canada more, I guess."

"For sure." Janus opened the folder, scrutinizing the first form. Then he perked up. "But I've got a notion that today … well, today I think God's on our side."

"God?" Ethan grunted. "Why bring him into the picture?"

Janus raised his eyebrows. "Um. I don't know. Just an expression. Didn't mean to offend."

Ethan turned, mumbling to the window. "Long story, about God 'n all. Caught me off-guard." His voice turned stern. "Don't know if I want him on my side, today or any day."

"No problem. I get it. Just an old expression my grandma used to say. Not even sure why it popped into my head. Her sayings do that sometimes."

Ethan looked away, not wanting to hear any more. Janus read the cue and went back to his paperwork.

* * *

The Mandalay International Airport confused Ethan. Much of what he had read described the country of Myanmar as poor and primitive, slow in advancement. The modern design of the airport, complete with gleaming Buddhist stupas jutting above the roof line, displayed the opposite. The inside embodied affluence as well. Clean, cool, orderly. *Not much different from other airports*, Ethan thought, until he noticed the large counter of government officials, all of whom seemed eager to examine Janus's paperwork. *Unfamiliar and intimidating.* Janus, on the other hand, didn't appear unnerved, responding without hesitation when they were beckoned to step up to the crowded counter. Ethan watched him answer each question with a quiet and unfazed demeanor, flashing his smile at times. Even after an hour of different officials making phone calls, seeking information, and asking the same questions multiple times, Janus remained unperturbed. Ethan, on the other hand, knew the impatience was building in his belly. He went and sat down. Almost two hours later, the officials stamped their seal of approval on every form.

"Impressive." Ethan nodded after they situated themselves in the back seat of a spotless white taxi.

"Thanks." Janus leaned back. "That went well, actually."

"No shit?" Ethan looked at him. "Well, for someone who doesn't know a word of their language, it sounded like a mad tea party, actually." He grinned.

"Hmm. If I didn't know better, I'd say you're beginning to sound like an archaeologist." Janus laughed. "Time just doesn't hold the same value here. Much like Thailand. If you don't figure that out from the get-go, you'll just offend the nationals. And once you've offended the wrong nationals, you're gonzo." Janus, still smiling, rippled his hand out his half-open window.

"Well, now I'm even more impressed. I've never been a patient man. Guess I better learn."

Janus orated in an odd, deep voice. "Patience produces character, my friend, and character produces hope."

"Huh? Another famous grandma saying?"

"Yup." Janus ignored the sarcasm in Ethan's voice.

"You are one unique dude."

Janus's eyes gleamed. "I'll take that as a compliment."

Ethan turned from him, his eyes on the window, looking but not seeing. He thought about the few positive influences in his life. No grandma. None of his high school teachers. He was too much of a screw up by then. Junior High? Yes, perhaps his history teacher? And his hockey coach? But they never stuck around. Knowing how his thoughts could spiral downward, he dropped the ponderings and focused on the world outside his window.

The clean, concrete world of the airport had been quickly replaced by an alien one, the one in the travel books. Old women, teenagers, little girls, all in assorted, tattered, faded clothes, trudged along the dusty red dirt of the road's edge, bulging mounds of produce or full water pots sitting precariously on their heads. Behind their painted *thanaka* faces, Ethan saw their struggle.

Men too, in cotton dress shirts and checkered *longyis*, were part of the throng, though most pedaled old creaky bicycles in thin, dirty flip-flops, bumping along the broken highway on their way to somewhere, or nowhere, yet without the extra burdens.

It was the little girls that Ethan's eyes revisited. "Cassie." His voice was barely a whisper.

"You say something?" Janus looked up from a folder of papers.

"Huh?" Ethan turned to respond. "Oh, I was just thinking about the kids in this country, especially the girls."

"Yeah?"

"Sad how hard they work. I mean, childhood should be fun, shouldn't it? Mine wasn't perfect. Not even close." Ethan half-snorted. "But it was pretty carefree. Not like this." Ethan returned to his people-watching.

Janus took a moment to look out his window. "There you go. Showing that you care again." He turned to Ethan. "I told you."

Embarrassed by his emotion, Ethan turned his head almost 180 degrees from Janus.

"I think it's *boss*."

"I ..." Ethan looked at Janus and shrugged. "I s'pose that's my daughter's doing. I guess you have your grandma and I have my daughter." He turned back to the window with a smile. *Cassie is with me.* The smile lingered as he studied more of the world outside. Sputtering motorcycles became more frequent as they neared the city center but still few in number compared to Thailand.

The sun began to stretch her long, hazy fingers across the road as dusk approached. Even from inside the taxi Ethan recognized her intense hold on the city. He rolled down his window slightly and stuck his hand out. He was right. Hot.

The taxi pulled up to their hotel, the green concrete face

of it slightly chipped, the pink steps cracked. Behind the large spotless glass doors, the bright fluorescent lights and white walls glared fallaciously. *Where am I?* Ethan thought.

"Here we are." Janus swung one of the bags over his shoulder. "The Jade Hotel. We're only here for one night so don't get comfortable." He winked. "Tomorrow we'll be taking the train up to Myitkyina. That's when the real adventure begins."

"The what?"

"The adventure."

"No, the other thing."

"The train?" Janus turned to face him. "What's wrong, man? It's not like we're getting on a ghost train." He laughed.

Ethan, sensing the blood rushing from his head, slumped down on the bottom step, the concrete edge crumbling slightly under his weight.

"You didn't mention anything about trains." For some reason he'd hoped that once he said yes to Janus's trekking offer, all would go smoothly. *Why can't life deal me a good hand?* He tried to control the inner turmoil. After a minute of silence, Janus sat down beside him.

"I don't *do* trains." Ethan almost spit the words out between clenched teeth.

"Huh?"

"I don't … I can't do trains." A headache began building behind Ethan's eyes. He kicked a piece of broken concrete. It crumbled into little pieces.

Without saying a word, Janus pulled the water bottle from his backpack and stuck it in Ethan's face. Ethan lifted his head, accepted the offering, and took a long drink, focusing on the cold liquid flowing down to offer life, no matter how small.

"Thanks, man." Ethan wiped his mouth.

"You weren't lookin' very good. Thought you were gonna pass out on me."

"Trains. Oh *farang*." Ethan squeezed his eyes shut. *Breathe.* "I just … trains and I don't mesh. More mother crap."

"Right." Janus swiveled his head, peering into the hotel. "Wanna talk? We've got time."

"Not right now." Ethan stood up slowly. "Can we just find our room or rooms or whatever? I could use a nap, maybe a shower if they have one. That'll help."

"Sure. But we'll have to talk about it at some point. Not much for travel options."

Ethan remained silent as they climbed the four flights of stairs to their room, knowing that Janus needed the issue settled. How quickly could he travel through his childhood, resolve his phobia, and come out the other end willing to step foot on a train? Siderodromophobia—the medical term for it. He had looked it up years before, though never admitted that he had it.

They were almost at their room when Ethan let out a loud guffaw.

Janus turned, his eyes questioning.

"I'm not crazy. Don't worry. I'm just a *farang*, thinking about the rabbit hole, your rabbit hole, that I've agreed to, forcing me to get on that train." Ethan waited for Janus's response. None came. "I know. You question my phobia. Hell, so do I."

Janus opened the door to their room: two beds, narrower than twins, a small table with a retro lamp in between, an old, faded mirror above a low-lying table in the corner next to the unpainted door into the tiny bathroom with the typical squatting toilet.

Ethan tossed his backpack onto the bed. "Think I've changed my mind." He turned away. "I'm going for a walk."

"You sure?" Janus looked surprised. "Want some company?"

"No. No, I've got enough company up here." Ethan pointed to his head. "Got things I need to clear. By myself."

"Gotcha."

Ethan walked out the door, thankful that Janus hadn't pressed the issue. He couldn't admit that what he really hoped to find was some strong drink to drown his fear, and pain. *Loser.* His mother's voice returned. With no energy to argue, Janus's words popped into his head: *I think God's on our side.* He snickered. *Where was God now?*

CHAPTER EIGHT

The world so lost in dark of night,
Such deep despair, no break, no sight;
But lo—in Eastern sky so slight
The glimpse of dawn, the hope of light.

Ethan's body rocked back and forth, more jerky than gentle. Assuring himself that the motion was merely part of his dream world, he sank into its rhythm. Something about it felt familiar. And yet not. *How peculiar.* The broken click-clack slowed and his nose picked up a nasty combination of excrement and potent chilies. With a tickle building in his throat, he coughed and, for the first time, opened his eyes.

"What the ..." Like a tightly wound rubber band, he snapped up off the thinly padded seat. As he turned to face Janus, the train car jolted beneath him. His attempt to brace himself by spread-eagling his legs failed. His head spun. His world turned black. Feeling himself falling into darkness, he slumped back onto the bench, his shoulder blades pressing into the unforgiving wooden slats, causing further pain to his already aching body. He clamped his eyes shut. *Pain. Focus on the pain.* "Trains. I can't ... phobia." He moaned. "I told you."

"Guess I forced your hand." There was no regret in Janus's voice.

Ethan bent over and put his head between his knees. "*Farang* on the whole thing." He grunted between shallow breaths.

Janus ignored Ethan's word choice. "I bet you don't even remember last night?"

Ethan couldn't speak. *Re-focus. Think about something else.* Ethan tried to remember the previous night. He'd gone out with a specific target in mind. He remembered hitting the bull's-eye when he stumbled upon a dark, obscure drinking establishment along an uninviting sewage canal. That's where his memory stopped. He shook his head. "No."

"I woke up at two, your bed still empty. Not good in Mandalay. Much like Chiang Mai. So I went out looking for you." The calmness in Janus's voice helped to ease Ethan's mind, though he said nothing. Janus continued. "Two hours later I returned to find you curled up against the outside door of the guesthouse. Curled up and drunk, I might add, unaware of where you were or how you got there. What I'd like to know is why?"

Ethan heard the tension rise in Janus's voice. He knew he had to respond. Janus deserved that. With his head still between his knees, he forced the words out. "Were you not listening? When I talked about my mother?"

"Huh?"

"You heard me."

"Well, you *did* mutter something about your mother last night. So what's the train connection? You've only told me about ukuleles and guitars and ... and abandonment."

Silence.

"Okay, let's just leave it for now." Janus sighed. "But you should know, this morning, when I had to pack up all the gear as well as your personal stuff, I was *this* close to leaving you behind." Bending over, Janus forced his thumb and forefinger into Ethan's face.

Ethan opened his eyes, his blurred vision seeing no space between the two digits.

"If it wasn't for …" Janus stopped, the abruptness noticeable even to Ethan. "Well, let's just say I'm pretty sure there's an unknown guardian that's got your back."

"A guardian? More like a witch." Ethan spewed out the last word. "You don't get it."

"Try me." Janus waited. "I listened the first time 'round, remember?"

Janus's words swirled around in Ethan's head, as if someone were stirring them in a black cauldron over twisting flames of fire. Ignoring Janus's question, he pressed his thumbs into his temples.

"I do expect an explanation. If you want to continue working with me, that is."

"Yeah. I'm trying." Ethan struggled with every word. "Really. Just, just get me out of this … this horror movie."

"You mean the train you've been on for almost nine hours?"

When Janus stuck his wrist into Ethan's face, he shoved it away. "It's almost five-thirty." Janus looked at his watch. "Which reminds me." He opened his backpack and pulled out a round, wrapped item. "The conductor came back for a chat a few hours ago. Think he just wanted to practice his English. But he gave each of us one of these."

Raising his head, Ethan opened his eyes just enough to watch Janus open the cellophane, revealing a flattened burger.

"He called it a Dik Mac." Janus burst out laughing and lifted the bun top to reveal a blackened, shriveled piece of something, hardly burger looking, the smell repulsive. Ethan bent over once again, controlling the urge to hurl.

Janus continued, ignoring Ethan's response. "I gave mine

away to some kids running alongside the train at one of our five hundred stops. I think they needed it more than me." He re-sealed the malodor and shoved it back into his pack. "Guess I'll be giving this one away, too. Just wanted you to see it." He chortled.

"Get—me—off—this—train," Ethan repeated through clenched teeth.

"Ethan. I can't. We won't get to Myitkyina 'til the morning."

Uncontrollable expletives erupted out of Ethan, like a wolf howling to the wind. Then dropping his head back between his knees again, he forced his thumbs deeper into his temples. It hurt, but he needed the distraction to keep from entering full panic mode. *Focus on the pain. Focus on the pain.* He repeated the words over and over in his head, his thumbs digging down deeper.

He whimpered.

"I can't pretend to understand your dilemma." Janus's voice softened. "But you should be aware that there are other people in this train car."

Ethan muttered quiet expletives to the floor, now aware of the rows behind them.

"Food might help. I've got …"

"No. No food. Trust me." Sweat began forming on Ethan's forehead. "Got anything stronger in that bag of yours?"

Janus opened the zipper wider, digging to the bottom for something. "It'll be dark soon, which may help. But here." He offered Ethan two large pain killers. "See if these'll do anything for you." Ethan accepted them without question, swallowing without water.

"Too bad there's no music in here. From what you've said maybe …"

"What did you say?"

"I said, too bad ..."

"No, I heard you the first time." Fighting back the vertigo, Ethan lifted his head, sensing a possible escape from the dark pit he was now swirling in.

"What?" Janus stared wide-eyed.

"Music. You mentioned music."

"So? Like I said, there *is* no music."

"There might be." Ethan's voice began to build again. "I might have brought ... oh, just grab my backpack, and open up the small pouch on the left side." He turned to Janus. "Please."

Janus just stared at him, looking concerned.

"C'mon. Thought you wanted to help." Ethan forced himself up on his feet.

Janus jumped up, grabbed Ethan's upper arms, and lowered him back down, effortlessly.

"I got this. Sorry." He pulled Ethan's pack down from the metal rack above their heads and dropped it to the car floor. Sitting down, he began scouring the pockets for the correct one, without a break in his talk. "You surprised me is all. After all your nonsensical ramblings last night, I thought you'd gone off the deep end again. Ah, here we are." Unzipping the pocket, he pulled out an iPod, the ear buds wrapped neatly around it.

"An iPod, huh? I haven't seen one of these in years." He toyed with it in his hands. "Got any good tunes on here?"

Ethan ignored the question. He snatched the device, slowly untangled the white cord with shaky hands, and stuck the buds in his ears. He wiped his sticky brow with the front of his t-shirt, leaving a streak of dirt behind. Then, pressing a button on the little lifesaver, he leaned back on the hard, slat backing and closed his eyes. Immediately the floaty voice of Black Sabbath's Ozzy Osbourne in "Zeitgeist" drowned out the train's incessant clickety clack. And as the sun began to melt beneath the foliage-wild and palm-tree-dotted land-scape, the combination of the music and the painkillers took over. Ethan's body relaxed. Hoping Janus's focus had shifted elsewhere, he opened his eyes. Under the greying blanket of night, Janus strained to read his folder of notes. Ethan smiled at the man's tenacity, both with work and their friendship. He focused on the song lyrics and nodded off.

* * *

Ethan woke before dawn, yet the sky whispered with an expectancy that sunrise was coming. "Come," he whispered. The word reminded him of his ebony girl dream. With his iPod dead, his left leg started to dance up and down. Almost instinctually, Janus woke up, smacking his lips and stretching his arms high above his head.

"Good morning, almost." The words were half-whispered.

Ethan imagined Janus smiling. "Good? Really? Hopefully morning soon." Ethan shifted in his seat, the sudden, sharp pain in his tailbone causing him to wince. *Focus on the pain.*

"Well, these last two days will soon be a memory, though I'm not sure how much you'll remember anyway." Janus shook his head.

Ethan kept his thoughts on his aching back. A tiny corner of his mind wanted to be told what he couldn't remember, though he could probably guess. Ethan's fears returned, this time as Thing 1 and Thing 2 in *The Cat in the Hat* books. With sneering grins, they raced around in his mind, spilling and crashing and making a mess. The thought of Cassie broke into his thoughts. She loved those books. *Cassie.* The memory of her sitting on his lap as they read together placated his anxiousness. He stood up, staying steady against the jerking motion of the car, and walked slowly to the door five feet in front of them.

"What're you doing?" Janus bolted up. "If you think I'm gonna let you jump off ..."

"Not jumping." Ethan focused on the door. He fumbled through the doorway and crouched down on the first of three steps, clinging to the railing, all the while mumbling, "Cassie, Cassie, Cassie." Janus followed, and after fifteen minutes, returned to his seat.

Even before the train came to a complete stop, Ethan leapt off and almost ran to the far edge of the platform. He bent over, his body shaking once again.

Within seconds, Janus came scrambling over to Ethan, carrying half the equipment. "We've got to get all this unloaded before the train takes off again." He piled items around Ethan, fighting for space amid the throng of scrambling passengers, pushy vendors, clucking chickens, and public transportation workers looking for their next patron. He looked up at Ethan. "You stay here and guard our stuff while I get it off the car. I'm not sure how prevalent thieving is in this country, but we can't afford to lose anything."

Ethan nodded, relieved that his assistance wasn't required. He collapsed onto one of the bags and looked at his watch: 7:00 a.m. Part of him wished to return to Happy Hunting Guesthouse, away from this nightmare and this train station. Part of him really wanted a drink. But part of him was proud ... proud that he'd overcome. He'd made it. All by himself.

Smiling, he took a long drink from his water bottle, still

dehydrated from the alcohol. And, after almost two days without a shower, he was a saltlick. The perpetual heat prevailed, yet the air was slightly cooler here than in Mandalay. He escaped the foreign din by closing his burning eyes, mulling over past conversations with Janus about Myanmar. His partner really had done his homework in preparation for this trip. Ethan's brain had quickly become saturated. Information in, information out. How had Janus retained it all? It was almost inhuman. He laughed internally at how ridiculous that sounded. Still, it did put Ethan to shame, especially when he thought about how little he knew about Chiang Mai after being there for over three weeks. *I'm a prisoner, a stranger / Banished—unbonded.* Lyrics from his childhood returned, reminding him of his own pitiful life. He'd wasted the last few months. He moped around for two months after the court case ruling regarding custody of Cassie, and before he left Edmonton. So why had he chosen Chiang Mai, knowing Jill's history in that city? He still didn't know, but something about the connection had tugged at his soul.

And here you are. And I am here too. Cassie's voice returned. Her words energized him.

Out of nowhere, he got an uneasy feeling that he was being watched. And wasn't he supposed to be keeping an eye on the equipment? Forcing his eyes open, he jerked into a sitting position, his forehead almost colliding with the upside-down face leaning over him—a questioning face with onyx eyes, straight, bowl-cut black hair and a dark complexion.

Ethan stumbled up and stepped back. Before him stood what looked like a boy, yet by his crisp white shirt and a purple and green plaid *longyi*, Ethan assumed he was a young man.

"Are you Mr. Janus McGinnis? I am pleased to meet you."

The man grinned and put out his right hand, cupping the right elbow in his left palm in the culturally appropriate form.

"Er, no," Ethan stuttered. His initial misgivings appeased by the man's smiling eyes, Ethan stepped forward and shook the man's hand. "But I am travelling with him." At that moment Janus hopped off the train with the last of the equipment. "Here comes Janus now." Ethan pointed and when the man turned toward Janus, Ethan raised his eyebrows at him, turned his pointing hand to the man, and shrugged his shoulders.

Janus scurried across the platform, darting around passengers, boxes, and chickens, placed the equipment down, and offered the man his hand. "Hello, I am Janus. And this is Ethan."

"I am pleased to meet you, Mr. Janus and Mr. Et-dan." The Asian pronunciation made Ethan smile. "I am Barnabas."

"Barnabas?" Ethan half-shouted, holding back the desire to make a joke.

"Yes. It is my Christian name." He seemed unaware of Ethan's rude tone. "My Khimsha name is Sai Hkam Leng, but I prefer to be called Barnabas."

"Barnabas works for me." Janus smiled. "I'm actually surprised to see you. I didn't hear back from you or anyone from the trekking guide company, so I wasn't sure if there'd be someone waiting for us here or not." He turned to Ethan. "Ethan, Barnabas will be our guide for the duration of our trip."

"Right." Ethan looked at Barnabas and managed a pleasant nod, pretending to know what was going on, questions bouncing around in his head. *Was I supposed to know this? Did Janus tell me about a guide somewhere in all that information he spouted off to me? Or is this just Janus being Janus again?* Ethan blocked out the negativity to focus on the now.

"Yes, sorry, Mr. Janus," Barnabas said. "The internet in the north does not always work well. But my office did receive your request. I am grateful for the work." He bowed slightly.

"Well, I was just happy to learn that we could hire a Khimsha guide. What're the odds of that happening, right Ethan?" Janus gave Ethan a wink, though Ethan didn't acknowledge it. His mind went immediately to the thought of emailing Jill with this information. Would it interest her enough to email him back?

"What do you think, Ethan?" Janus's words broke into his thoughts.

"Huh?"

"We're going to check in with the government officials and then Barnabas'll go out to the street to find us a motorized tricycle. He didn't realize we'd have so much equipment. But between that and his motorcycle, he figures we can all get to his house."

"Well, you have a better idea of how much … Wait. His house? We're staying with him?"

"I guess." Janus had a puzzled look on his face. Ethan had never seen that look before. "I know. A bit unusual to our way of thinking. But the Burmese are known for their hospitality. We shouldn't be surprised." Janus's confident demeanor returned. "Cultures are fascinating, aren't they?" He started grabbing equipment, not giving Ethan a chance to reply. "Guess I'll start taking gear out to the street." He yelled back as he disappeared into the crowd. "Good ol' Barney might be waiting for us."

Barney? Barney! Ethan laughed for the first time in days. He thought of the three of them trekking the jungle. Barney, the purple and green dinosaur, followed by his companions,

Janus the Roman god of beginnings and Et-dan the wanderer. Like Huck Finn, rafting down an endless river of unknowns. What a threesome.

By the time they reached Barnabas's house, Ethan thought he'd just travelled the whole North Saskatchewan River, his senses in overload. They passed emaciated, fly-covered oxen pulling makeshift carts burdened with precarious loads, some of them controlled by children that looked Cassie's age. They veered around an abundance of squeaking, dusty trishaws, also heavy with passengers and market loads. They inched through a growing crowd gathered around a large mud-pasted lorry truck half off the road, the back wheel stuck in a sunken pothole that looked like the mouth of an old well. Janus and Ethan grinned at each other as they watched a few men trying to pull it out with oxen.

Ethan didn't need the travel books to tell him the economic situation of the people of Kachin State: Poor. *Do the people themselves know it?* Ethan wondered.

All the people they passed offered large smiles to the pale-faced foreigners bumping along, their trishaw raising crimson dust. Some of the little kids even chased them, laughing and shouting as they tried to keep up. Ethan waved back, wishing he still had some of the White Rabbit milk candy he'd bought in Thailand.

Barnabas's home sat on a small, fenced plot at the edge of town, a typical stilted bamboo and rattan house worn gray by heat and rain. A couple of chickens roamed the hard-packed ground and a dirty black pig, tethered under the house, let out a grunt.

"My apologies. My house is not big. But this is the best place for your equipment. I have a room to keep it safe."

Barnabas took as many bags as he could and ascended like a gazelle up the precarious-looking ladder to the doorway. He returned within seconds for another load, not allowing Janus or Ethan to help.

"It's their cultural way, I think," Janus whispered to Ethan. The only thing the two could do was stand and watch Barnabas move deftly up and down.

"Good," Barnabas said after four trips. "You can come up now. My wife has prepared a meal for you. She wants to meet the friends of Ben Sands."

What the … Did I hear right? Ethan turned to Janus and scowled, certain that Janus knew of the Ben connection.

"These are quite the steps." Janus ignored Ethan's stares. "Narrow for our boots." Standing with both his feet balancing on the bottom rung, he bounced up and down, the step bending with his weight. "Oh the beauty of bamboo."

Too perturbed to engage in the conversation, Ethan waited for Janus to reach the top landing before he ventured up, keeping his eyes focused on his feet.

The petite woman just inside the doorway bowed low and long as Janus and Ethan entered the dim room. After Ethan's eyes adjusted, he noticed the top of a baby's head peeking out from the bright pink sling on her back.

Ethan's thoughts shifted to a memory, a time when Cassie was a newborn, sleeping peacefully on Jill's breast, wrapped in a soft pink sling. He smiled at the scene before him, then the corners of his mouth turned down, thinking about his own loss.

Barnabas placed his hand on his wife's elbow and spoke gently to her in a foreign tongue that sounded a lot like Thai. The woman bowed and backed away slowly. Then turning, she disappeared into a side room, baby sleeping quietly as she went about her work.

Was I ever that soft-spoken with Jill? Ethan shook his head as if trying to get out of a hypnotic trance. *Don't be stupid. She's the one who did you wrong.*

"That is my wife Lydia, and our daughter, Anna. My wife is shy and embarrassed because she cannot speak English." Barnabas smiled. "But she is honored to have you in our home."

"Tell her thank you." Janus smiled back. "The honor is all ours. I'm sure she worked hard to prepare food for us, especially with a baby." Ethan nodded.

"Thank you. Please sit." Barnabas motioned to two cushions surrounding a low table steaming with freshly made dishes.

Ethan's stomach growled. For the first time in two days, he was hungry. While he struggled to slide cross-legged up to the table, Barnabas scooped large mounds of rice onto each of their plates. He then picked up a dish of ground meat, red with spice and the aroma of curry.

"It's okay." Janus reached for the dish. "You are a good host Barnabas, but Ethan and I can serve ourselves. Thank you." Barnabas gave up the bowl and Ethan breathed a sigh of relief, unsure how much spice his stomach could take at this point.

"Of course." Barnabas sat down across from them. "I have forgotten. It has been a while since I have been with Westerners." He bowed his head and began speaking aloud in his foreign tongue. Janus and Ethan looked at each other and then at their food, waiting in silence. After Barnabas finished with an "Amen," he quietly began spooning smaller mounds of food from each bowl, placing it on his rice, like ice-cream toppings, unaware of the awkwardness.

Janus and Ethan did the same.

"I hope to see Mr. Ben when he comes, although I have not heard when that will be. Do you know, Mr. Janus?" Barnabas looked directly into Janus's face.

Busted! Ethan smiled to himself.

"Sorry." Janus shrugged. "I don't. And in truth, we aren't exactly friends."

Barnabas's eyebrows went up. "But that is not what your email said. I do not understand."

"Our relationship is only a professional one. My apologies if I didn't explain myself. It's actually Ethan who knows Ben personally." Ethan shot Janus a look of displeasure but when Barnabas turned to him for answers, Ethan responded cordially.

"Yes, I do know Ben, but haven't had any contact with him for quite a while now." Ethan's answer satisfied Barnabas, at least for now.

"I thought you worked with him." Barnabas spooned an oily sauce full of hot pepper seeds over his food. "Mr. Ben has been a good friend to me and the Khimsha people. Without him, we would not have the Bible in our language. The Bible changed my life forever."

"How?" Janus seemed unfazed by the nature of Ben's work.

"It shames me to say I was addicted to heroin, as so many Khimsha men are. My father left me a small piece of land. I chose to grow opium poppies to feed my addiction. I became a cruel and angry man." Barnabas looked to the doorway that his wife had disappeared through. "My wife put up with a lot. It shames me still." He bowed his head and mumbled something.

Ethan squirmed on his hard cushion.

"So what's the connection with Ben Sands?" Janus ignored Barnabas's personal story.

"Well, five years ago a Khimsha leader named David came to me and asked if I would help him. I had gone to university for two years, and he needed a Khimsha man with some education. He said he would pay me to read something and tell him if I understood it, whether it was good Khimsha writing. I did not know that I was reading the Bible in my language. But as soon as I started reading it, I knew it was different than anything I had ever read before."

"And Ben Sands?" Janus cocked his head.

"Well, Mr. Ben had helped David translate what I was reading. I kept reading whatever they translated and soon it changed my heart. I knew I no longer wanted opium. I wanted what the Bible offered."

Neither Janus nor Ethan wanted to ask what that was, but Barnabas continued. "Peace and hope. Two things I had been searching for and I did not even know it."

"Peace? Hope? Have you ... ?" Everything inside Ethan wanted to ask Barnabas if he'd ever dreamed about a girl coming down from the sky. How ludicrous that sounded. Seeing that both Barnabas and Janus were staring at him, he shook his head. "Forget it. Sorry." He took a bite of food.

"Well, it's true we're all searching for something." Janus broke the silence and turned back to Barnabas. "Me, I've got my own search going on. Of course, that's why I hired you. But ..." He paused. "There might be more to my search than what I mentioned in my email."

Ethan controlled the urge to swear, though he did stare at Janus for a long time. Maybe Janus *wasn't* being completely honest with him about the goal of this trip. Yet here he was.

"Yes, of course. We will talk more tomorrow." Barnabas's

voice was steady, unquestioning. "How impolite of me to talk about my life when you are here for work."

"Not impolite at all. I asked," Janus said.

"Well, after eating I will take you to your hotel." Barnabas smiled again.

"Hotel. Right." Janus pretended to know the plan.

"I wanted you to know your equipment was safe. And to offer you a simple meal. I also have a gift for each of you." Without waiting for a response, Barnabas rose and went into the kitchen. Ethan looked at Janus. Janus simply shrugged and went back to his food.

Five minutes later Barnabas returned with a tray of unusual containers. "These are cups made from bamboo. And used for hot drink." He placed one in front of both Ethan and Janus. "My gift is not a fancy one but it is unique to the Khimsha people." Barnabas sat back down and stretched out his hand. "Please, enjoy the green tea and take the cup back with you to Canada."

"Thank you, Barnabas." Janus bowed slightly. "We are honored to receive this gift."

"I thank you too, Barnabas." Ethan picked up the carved-out bamboo mug, the surface cool despite the hot tea inside. His thoughts immediately went to Jill. Oh how she'd love this. The smooth surface. The detail in the woven handle. He shook his head.

"I hope the tea will help you sleep." Barnabas smiled. "I have travelled on that train. It is tiring."

"Tiring? That's not the word *I'd* use for it." Ethan chortled. Barnabas nodded, but didn't drop his smile. Ethan said nothing. He couldn't read this guy, always smiling. He thought of a new name for him: Smiley Barney.

"Sorry, Barnabas." Janus came to his rescue. "We can't imagine what it's like to live in such poverty." He paused. "But you can help us, and we can help you so that's good, isn't it?"

"Yes." Barnabas gave a slight bow. "It is good. And I am thankful for the work."

The unease in the pit of Ethan's stomach didn't go away, even after he and Janus left in a trishaw. Thankfully for Ethan, the two of them sat facing opposite directions in the sidecar; Janus faced forward, and Ethan faced the traffic following behind them. He wanted to think, not converse. *What had Janus been talking about? What was he really searching for?* Again, he realized how little he knew about Janus.

And then there was Barnabas. A puzzling man as well. Despite his one phobia, Ethan thought he was pretty good at coming across self-assured, like he had it all together, but Barnabas seemed to look right through all that with his warm smile and calm disposition. That mention of peace and hope. Is that what it was? Was it connected to his dream? But there was more. Jill had also talked a lot about hope. An unseen hope. Weird.

Without warning, another voice broke into his thoughts, the bitter voice of his mother. *Get ahold of yourself you stupid boy. It's all nonsense.* Her words stung. *Yeah, nonsense.* He sighed into the darkness, anxious to curl up in a real bed and forget about the last two days.

Then he remembered the email possibility, hoping that the mention of Barnabas and his unusual gift, might soften Jill's hostile view of him. Hope. That word again. He didn't know what it meant. But he liked it.

CHAPTER NINE

"Fear is the mind-killer"
The root of the pain
Twisting cognition
From sane to insane.

Suspicions and questions
Shadows of night
Hell on the pathway
Eclipsing the light.

Yet "hope springs eternal"
For those who will choose
For king, pope or beggar
With nothing to lose.

And peace can come gently
Releasing the mind
A dove of compassion
For all of mankind.

So cast off the ghostlings
Fear's befouling stains;
Trust in the pure love
That enfolds and sustains.

Janus and Barnabas spent the next day and a half planning the
treks and whittling the supplies down to a minimum. Accept-

ing the all-too-familiar outsider status, Ethan kept to himself. He wandered the main market, initially intrigued by the varieties of fish living in the Ayerwaddy River. He even kept a lookout for guitar shops but found none. With kyat, Burmese currency, in his pocket, he bought a hand of small bananas, found a quiet spot on some rocks along the river, and sat down to watch the boat traffic, particularly intrigued by the long-tailed boats that spewed water high and far behind their sterns. How different this place was compared to Canada.

A bit homesick, he decided to go touch base with his "partner." When he barged into the meeting room unannounced, both Janus and Barnabas stopped in mid-conversation and looked at Ethan with sheepish faces. Quickly, their faces relaxed, but the awkward silence remained. Ethan pretended not to notice, remained for a few minutes and then left. But the expressions on their faces lingered in his thoughts.

He needed a distraction. Walking past a small concrete building, the front shaded by a large awning, he almost missed the English sign: Internet Café. He turned around, ducked his head under the faded awning and sat down at one of the few available computers. He decided to try writing Jill. He knew she'd probably not respond but he needed to do something to settle the homesick blues. Somehow he hoped that she'd at least share his adventures with Cassie, so he wrote simply, describing the unique sights and sounds and smells of Myanmar and then telling her about this friend of her grandpa's that he'd met.

As he wrote, a gnawing question kept repeating in his head: "What does Jill really want to know?" He knew. She wanted answers about his alcohol addiction. Could he offer her anything? Some hint of hope? But that would mean admitting she was right. Maybe she was, but why give her the satisfaction of knowing it? He slumped down in the plastic chair, suddenly so tired. How long could he fight the truth? For a while he just sat there, staring at the screen, as the comings and goings of people swirled around him, their tonal language a foreign song that frolicked about with no effect on his frame of mind.

Don't give up hope, Daddy. Cassie's voice broke into his suspended thoughts. Sighing deeply, he sat up. If he wanted Jill to reply, he had to give her something. He rewrote his closing paragraph six or seven times, not sure how much to say, finally coming up with this:

Don't worry. There's no alcohol on this trip. I'm not needing it. I hope you can give me the benefit of the doubt.

He debated about the last line but with all the recent talk about hope, he thought it a good word to use. He pressed "send," not expecting much in return.

Despite the time change, Jill replied almost immediately. Ethan sat riveted to the screen, oblivious to the surrounding din, his eyes widening as he read:

Hi Ethan.

If you're being truthful with me, then I guess it's a start. You've been down this road before, however, so I'm not holding my breath. Clever of you to use the word "hope." I'm still a sucker for that word. That being said, don't expect me to reply to more emails. And I'm not sure if I'll share your stories with Cassie. Gotta think about that.

Guess I do owe you a response to one of your previous emails regarding your conversation with Emily and my "haunting." Not something I like to remember but here goes:

It started soon after we moved to Chiang Mai as a family. I guess I was ten or eleven at the time. We were renting an older house with jalousie windows. Many nights for a long time, months, maybe years, an evil creature would arrive through one of the window slats and would sit at the end of my bed, haunting me with its macabre laugh. My child-mind described it as a creepy, frightening clown with sharp tusk-like teeth and hypnotizing eyes; later I realized it was a character from Thai mythology called a Yak Demon. I'm sure you saw statues of them in Chiang Mai, as guardians of the temples. I didn't know any of that. I only felt the evilness of it as it leered at me, with a laugh so sinister, so spine-chilling, that I was afraid to sleep. And the worst part of it was, nobody else could see it. I was alone in my nightmare. Even my parents didn't believe me at first. Once they did, the only thing that put me to sleep was my dad's singing of old hymns. Looking back, I think the house was haunted—and I was the recipient of the haunting. Good thing we moved after four years, though the image lingered in my mind long after that. Those were four years from hell—and still not something I like to talk about.

Jill's email stopped there. A cold chill crawled up Ethan's back. A couple of months ago he would have mocked such an irrational story, calling it unscientific drivel, never connecting it to the personal encounter in his own grim nightmares.

Ethan had watched staunch Buddhists spend much time appeasing the bad spirits with offerings at the temple, while honoring the good spirits and ancestors by doing good deeds. Merit-making, they called it. He didn't realize their belief system had been rubbing off on him until he read Jill's story. Instead of scoffing, he empathized, and accepted her story.

But then he began thinking about his own mother night-mare. His skin prickled. His heart began to race. His body began to sweat. He knew what that meant—his body telling him he needed a drink.

Don't give in. You're stronger than you think, Daddy. Cassie's compassionate voice chimed in. But could her words over-power his craving? He hoped so. And there was that "hope" word again. Cassie's hope in him. His heartbeat lessened. He released his breath, slowly.

Others can help. We all need help.

"What?" He looked behind him. Nobody there. *Others? What others?* The voice said no more, but he recognized the one line from his dream. He clung to Cassie's words of hope and went back to the hotel. He needed a nice, hot shower.

* * *

By the time they boarded their plane to Putao the follow-ing afternoon, Ethan had bought himself a small journal to keep record of his adventures. He imagined sharing his stories with Cassie. Sitting in his seat, he checked the side pouch of his pants for the little notebook and stubby pencil. Still there.

The flatlands built as the shadows cast by the late after-noon sun stretched longer and wider. Upon their descent into Putao, the same drab rooftops appeared, though fewer in number than Myitkyina. The travel guides touted Putao as a tourist destination and trekking hot spot. Ethan wondered why until he exited the plane and did a visual three-sixty. The snow-capped Himalayan mountains lay hazy in the north while lush foothills fingered down protecting the fertile val-ley on either side. The cooler temperatures confirmed the higher elevation. He welcomed the coolness and the sight of jagged peaks.

"Almost like home." Janus spoke from behind him.

"I agree, and it's good. Other than the soil being red and the harvested crops being rice, you'd think we were in the foothills of the Rockies."

"And the fresh, cool air." They both took a deep breath. "Isn't it great to be alive?" Janus let out an exuberant laugh. "And it's now our world to survey, starting tomorrow. You ready?"

"Hell, yeah."

"Hell?" Janus walked away. "I think this is heaven." He turned back and spread out his arms, then continued on his way.

Heaven? Ethan looked around. Though the natural beauty might be considered Eden-like, the decrepit wooden wagon piled high with baggage being pulled by workers in tattered uniforms and flip flops contradicted Janus's statement. *No heaven here.* He sighed.

* * *

"You will be spending the night with a Khimsha friend of mine," Barnabas said after they checked in with the local authorities. "Sorry. It could not be helped because of your late trekking inquiry. The guesthouses had no vacancies. Do not worry. It is safe."

"No problem." Janus thanked him.

That night, while lying on a cot, the waning gibbous moon filtering through the slatted door, Ethan thought about Barnabas's comment. *It is safe. Safe? Safe from what?* A picture entered his mind, the image of two creatures sneering at him: Jill's creepy clown and his own howling doppelgänger. Is that what he needed to fear? A grunt from one of the pigs below them pulled him back to reality.

"Tuh." He spit out the word, disgusted at his own thoughts. *Ridiculous!* Still, Ethan decided that at some point in their trek, he'd ask Barnabas what he meant.

After a dreamless sleep, the morning arrived arrayed in late October mist. Typical for the area according to Barnabas, but Ethan hadn't expected such cold dampness.

"Chilly. Just like the northwest." Janus rubbed his crossed arms while they waited for breakfast. In broken English, their host encouraged them to walk the few blocks to the morning market before eating. There they could find warmer clothing. They each bought a light down-filled jacket, though the sleeves stopped half-way between their elbows and their wrists. They both laughed, Ethan slightly embarrassed, but not Janus. "Practicality over fashion."

Over breakfast of assorted greens and thinly sliced beef in a clear broth, Janus finally briefed Ethan on the plan. First trek was just two days in, to a small village south and east of Putao called Machanbaw. Janus wasn't sure how many days they'd stay there.

"Depends what we find. We'll drive for the first part of the trek, piggybacking with another group. Then, finally, I'll get to put my training into action." Janus pumped his fist. "And once I start digging test pits, I'll be busy mapping and recording. What d'ya say? Wanna help with the digging? The rest is up to me, pretty much."

"Sure." Ethan nodded. "Whatever you need."

"That's the spirit." Janus looked up from his food. "So then—maybe once I get a system down you can do more in that area. I was hoping you'd offer to help because I could use you in another way."

"Oh?" Ethan said, less assuredly.

"As you know, digging test pits is a fairly random activity. I can dig in what I think is an accurate spot only to find nothing.

I might be educated, but it's the locals who are the experts."

"So?"

"You see," Janus continued, "the Khimsha have always been an oral culture. That means their stories are just passed down through word of mouth, not through writing such as what we read back in Chiang Mai."

"Again, so?"

"So then talking to the local people and hearing their stories, their history, could give us further insight into possible dig areas." Janus leaned back.

Ethan said nothing. He just stared at Janus, his brow furrowed.

Janus finally spelled it out. "I was hoping you'd be my ears in the villages while I'm doing the grunt work. Barnabas said he'd be happy to work with you, be your translator. And if you hear anything of interest, you could write it down."

"You mean suddenly become an anthropologist?" Ethan sat up straight. "Sounds extreme. And, in case you haven't noticed, I'm not the greatest communicator." Ethan knew that was a mild assessment. Jill would say his communication skills were in the negative.

"Well, really, Barnabas will be doing much of the work. He knows people. You just gotta trust that he'll find the right people to ask is all. I'm pretty sure you can do that."

Ethan bit his tongue. His left leg started to bounce.

Janus sighed. "Your choice. But …"

"I'll do it, okay?" Ethan grunted the words. "But could you give a guy a bit of a heads-up next time? I don't like surprises."

"Got it. And thanks. This'll really help me. And Barnabas is a great guy. In fact, if there's opportunity, maybe you could just pick his brain, ask him about the history of the area." Janus looked at his watch. "Speaking of Barney, he's meeting us at the trekking office. We'd better get going." He pushed back his rickety chair and voiced his thank-you to their hostess.

Ethan looked down at his food. Only half eaten, but his stomach was in knots. And his appetite was gone.

* * *

Heading east, they bounced along a pot-holed dirt road in the box of an old half-ton truck with six other trekkers. Only eight kilometers but it took them an hour. Ethan sat on his backpack. Even then, he felt like one of Cassie's rag dolls by the time they reached the Malikha River.

"We will wait here for a long tail boat to take us to Kaung-mulone village." Barnabas put their gear in a pile by the water's edge and sat down. Janus, his nose in his folder of notes, said nothing.

Ethan focused not on the famous, shimmering white and gold pagoda jutting up from the village, but on the crystal-clear river. It looked so inviting that he took off his boots and socks and waded into the icy waters that flowed down from the Himalayan mountains. It reminded him of the Rockies of home and that was good.

In the narrow boat, Janus could hardly sit still. He twitched about, a permanent smile on his face. The boat had hardly touched land when he hopped off, swinging on his gear at the same time. Ethan and Barnabas scrambled to keep up. Instantly, Janus became a bloodhound, sniffing out archaeological potential, along the river's edge, near the two-thousand-year-old pagoda, in every unique dip or hill along their path.

The three paused often as Barnabas expounded on some historical tidbit. In response, Janus jotted down possible test pit sites for their trek back to Putao. Initially, Ethan and

Barnabas watched Janus's every move, curious in the hunt, but without a trained eye, Ethan lost interest and decided to simply enjoy the hike. Soon, Barnabas joined him. The two walked side-by-side on a level stretch of the trail, heading to Namkham village.

"Can … can I ask you a question?" Ethan decided it was time to begin the task Janus asked of him at breakfast, though he wasn't even sure where to start.

"Yes, Mr. Et-dan, what would you like to know?" Barnabas's black eyes sparkled.

"Well, first, you can just call me Ethan. We are co-workers, after all." Ethan smiled as Barnabas reciprocated with a small nod.

"So, yesterday, when you commented that the house we were staying in was safe, what did you mean? Is there some construction flaw in a Khimsha house that makes them unsafe? Or does it have to do with some sort of civil unrest in the area that we don't know about?"

"No, no, Et-dan." Barnabas shook his head. "The Khimsha build strong houses. And we live in peace in Putao. No fighting with anyone."

"Then what?" Ethan asked. They walked another fifty meters, Barnabas deep in thought.

"Do you believe in ghosts, Mr. Et-dan?" Barnabas eyed him.

"Ghosts?" The blood drained from Ethan's face. "I … I'm not sure. You mean like the white-robed creatures that try to scare the living?" He flittered his fingers through the air.

Barnabas didn't catch the humor. "No. I have been told that ghosts in your culture are not the same as ghosts in our culture. The word we use, *baseu,* does not translate into English."

"O-kay." Ethan drew out the syllables, his voice shaky.

Barnabas sighed. "I am sorry. I am not explaining well."

He made some unusual clucking sounds in his mouth and continued. "Mr. Janus told me you read a story at Mengrai University about our history, a story about the giant tree full of riches and of the black bird that our ancestors killed."

"Yes. Like a fairy tale." Then Ethan remembered. "Oh right. The mention of ghosts. Not how fairy tales end in our culture." The harrowing face from his reoccurring nightmare flashed through his mind. "Not how they end," he repeated.

"Well, then it is not a fairy tale. For us, it explains the beginning of ghosts in our culture. How they came to be. Ever since that time, there have been ghosts living among the Khimsha."

Ethan stopped in his tracks, the goose bumps creeping up his arms. "You mean now? In this day and age? Ghosts? That can't be. It's, it's … more rabbit-hole madness." Ethan blurted, knowing Barnabas wouldn't understand. Then he made the connection in his head. "Are you trying to tell me that there were ghosts, or something you say are ghosts, in our house last night? Haunting us?" With each word, Ethan's voice rose, his vocal cords tightened, as Jill's evil clown and his mother's ghoulish zombie entered his thoughts again.

"No, sorry, no." Barnabas shook his head hard and waved his hands. "I knew you would be safe because your host is a friend of mine, and a God-believer. He is not a ghost and his house does not have ghosts. That is what I meant."

"You mean our host *could* have been a ghost?" Ethan barked. "But there was nothing ghost-like about him. He looked like you and me." This time the hairs on Ethan's neck prickled. "Ghosts in the daylight." Lightheaded, he stumbled back, daunting thoughts swirling in his mind. His calves hit the mossy rock behind him and he slumped down, his head dropping to the familiar position between his knees. "I don't feel so good."

"Sorry, Mr. Et-dan. My English is not so good. I do not have the right words." Barnabas took a few steps toward him. Ethan stuck out his arm abruptly, stopping Barnabas in his tracks.

"Hey!" At that moment, Janus came bounding out of the dense forest behind Ethan. Like a frightened rabbit, Ethan leapt to his feet. His world turning black, he tripped on a root jutting up through the dirt, and landed in a heap behind Barnabas.

"Was it something I said?" Janus joked. He changed his tune when he noticed Barnabas's stoic face. "What's going on?" Barnabas looked at Ethan.

Both embarrassed and afraid, Ethan said nothing. His pulse pounded in his ears and he clenched his eyes tight, wishing he were somewhere far, far away and hoping both Janus and Barnabas would simply walk away. In the back of his mind he knew Janus, Mr. Inquisitive, wouldn't let it go.

"I am sorry, Mr. Janus." Barnabas broke the silence. "I was trying to explain ghosts in our culture to Mr. Et-dan. I am afraid I did not do so well."

"Ahh, right." Janus nodded. "The word 'ghost' doesn't mean the same thing to you as it does to us. Took me awhile to get my head around that concept too." Stepping over to Ethan, Janus pulled out Ethan's water bottle and shoved it into his face. "Here. This'll help."

Ethan took a long swig. Though the water was lukewarm, he appreciated its restorative flow. His taut muscles relaxed. He slumped over.

"Tell you what." Janus peered at him. "When we get to our stopping point for the night, I've got something for you to read."

"What's more reading gonna do?" Ethan pressed his fingers into his temples.

Janus didn't reply but neither did he move.

Ethan sighed. "Hauntings at every turn." He put his hands down and looked up, into Janus's perplexed face. "Yes, you heard right. No matter where I go, how far I run, I can't get away from them." He put his face in his hands. Janus and Barnabas remained silent. Ethan raked his hands through his hair. "Zombies. Demons. And now a whole tribe of ghosts? That we're staying with?" Ethan paused. "I'm so tired." Even the bamboo stalk eventually breaks. "Too much." He whispered into his hands. "Too many surprises."

"C'mon," Janus slid his arm under Ethan's. Then another arm lifted him from the other side. "Some food and more water will help."

Ethan didn't fight it. He didn't have the strength.

By the time they arrived at their lunch destination, Ethan was walking on his own. They sat around a rough-hewn wooden table outside a little hut. The sunshine-warmed wood massaged Ethan's skin.

Ethan nodded at both Janus and Barnabas. "Thanks." And he meant it.

CHAPTER TEN

Choose young man,
Choose: Mother or Father;
Mother/son bond rises—then falls in
Her abandonment; A black veil of home-unsweet-
Home shifts to birth pains as phobia
Floods the forgotten home-
Fires burn fear.

Food in his belly revived Ethan, at least enough to keep hiking. Still wobbly on his feet, and sure he'd fall any second, he remained silent all afternoon. They followed the Malikha River, passing through numerous small villages. Barnabas knew everyone and everyone knew Barnabas. A hyped Janus used these connections to engage the villagers and ask questions.

Afraid that they might be ghosts, Ethan ignored them all as faceless people talking language gibberish. Refocusing his thoughts, he started humming his old song, but the lyrics came with it and that made him sad. *No stop. No home / No rest from pain.* No help. He turned to nature but even the beauty of the many clear-trickling streams and vivid green vines hanging from above, bursting with violet morning glory flowers, could not invigorate his spirit.

He battled in mind over the idea of ghosts existing the way Barnabas described. How could ghosts exist as real people? And what did that mean when it came to all the supernatural? Were there good ghosts or just bad ghosts? There had to be some opposing force, didn't there? A good force? What did that look like? The questions without answers kept coming. He wondered if Barnabas had any answers.

Then Ethan remembered past conversations with Jill, because Jill believed in that good force as God, her divine God. At one time he thought he believed. He wanted to. But he still had questions he never voiced. And now, he had more questions. *If God is good, how did I end up here, alone? No, God does not exist; ghosts do not exist. I choose to not believe in any of it.* He lowered his head, still alone … and stuck in the empty chasm of his own soul.

As they approached Namkham village, their day's destination, Ethan became distracted by the fields of planted trees … orchards of what looked like oranges and grapefruit.

"What the …" Ethan turned to Barnabas with big eyes. "You have citrus trees growing here? In the middle of nowhere?"

Barnabas laughed. "You noticed. Yes. And they are delicious, though not yet ripe." He stopped and turned to Ethan. "They were introduced to this area by missionaries in the 1930's. The Suli family we will stay with tonight have many trees."

"A Suli family? Not Khimsha?" Ethan was glad. No ghosts.

They ate a flavorful but not spicy evening meal on a wide wooden veranda, surrounded by grapefruit trees. Ethan breathed the air deeply, sure he could smell their tangy sweetness. They watched the sun slip away quickly behind the low mountain range. Darkness arrived, with no long dusk period like on the Canadian prairies in the summer, so the three of them moved inside, sitting on mats around a fire pit centered in the main room that would eventually become their sleeping quarters. That and a few candles placed around the perimeter were their only light. The crackling fire staved off the mountain-dewy chill.

Ethan watched the flames dance, wishing they would glide through his body and soothe his cold bones. Janus settled onto the cushion beside him with a folder in hand.

"You interested?" Janus opened the folder. "Got this copy from Rick back at Mengrai U."

Ethan read the title: "Ghosts in the World of the Khimsha."

"Don't think so man." He turned back to the fire. "Had enough …"

"Look." Janus pushed the folder back to him. "Knowledge is power, especially when it comes to the supernatural. The more you know about it, the less you'll fear it."

"Fear it?" *They see my fear.* Ethan's hand, resting open across the folder, began to shake. He made a fist, then let it go. "*Farang!*" He glared at Janus. "Do you really wanna know why this … this … paranormal focus is freaking me out so much?" Ethan spewed out the words, the promise of a confession, before he had a chance to contain them. They were now wild broncos free from the corral of his subconscious, and his dream world.

"We're listening." Janus sat up, put the folder on his lap, and crossed his legs.

Ethan took a deep breath, exhaling slowly. *No turning back from this rabbit hole now.* "Okay, guess I owe you. It'll explain my fear of trains, too." Ethan cleared his throat, trying to shake off the jitters. "Bet you thought I'd forgotten, huh? That I wouldn't remember my promise to explain my drunken behavior that night in Mandalay?"

"Honestly? I didn't know. Would've brought it up eventually, but glad I don't have to." He looked at Barnabas. "We had a rough ride on the train. Guess that's all you need to know. Don't think either of us want to relive those forty-eight hours."

"Damn right." Ethan kept his eyes on the fire, the flames slowly shrinking in front of him, the embers sucking the life down into their shifting glow. His dry, pasty mouth, his pounding temples, his shaky sweating hands, his whole body fought against his choice to talk. He'd told Jill part of the story, but never all of it. He wasn't even sure where to start.

"Something more about your mother?" Janus leaned in, as if sensing Ethan's uncertainty.

"More about my mother." Ethan grunted the words. "So much more." And then, under the protection of passive shadows, another story from the past spilled out of him, unclogging and releasing more of the sludge and stinking garbage that had been building up for years.

"That night she left. She came into my bedroom to say her usual goodnight. All sweet. Said she was going to the corner store for some smokes, and then she was gone. Like a ghost." Ethan paused, his mind trying to decipher between reality and nightmare. "Initially I was just angry at Dad. I blamed him, of course. Finally, out of desperation, I think, he told me that Mom had not only left me, left us, but that she'd emptied their bank account and run off, not just with any other man but with one of his co-workers. A fellow train engineer, of all things. She just hitched a ride with him on the train that night, a train bound for the east coast. And here's the ironic thing—Dad considered this guy a friend. Ha! Some friend. A friend of betrayal, if that's a thing." Ethan watched the phantasmical embers, his mind torn between stopping and staying the course. As he sucked in another breath, a puzzling calmness came over him.

"She made a choice, and we suffered the consequences. *That's* when I smashed the ukulele."

"Ukulele?" Barnabas said. "I do not know."

"It's like a small guitar, though tuned differently," Janus said and then added, "Ethan's mom had taught him to play." Janus turned to Ethan. "Keep going."

"I want to say I hated her." Ethan clenched both his fists, releasing them slowly. "And yet I still loved her." He finally looked up, his two comrades mere outlines by then. "It wasn't until after she left that I saw how much my dad had loved her too. It destroyed him. But I was just a kid. I couldn't do anything. Well, except struggle with guilt, like her leaving was somehow my fault." Ethan shivered, remembering all those nights of watching his dad drink himself into oblivion, of how he began to mimic those ways, sneaking sips from his dad's bottle, making sure his older sister didn't see him, hating the taste but liking how it numbed all his emotions.

"No kid should have to carry such a burden." Janus's voice was low.

"It was hell, a hell I couldn't navigate. A hell that mutated into a fear of trains."

"Trains. Ri-i-i-ght." Janus leaned forward and stirred the coals with a metal poker.

"The next time my dad took me to the train yard, I had a full-blown panic attack. We were standing beside the engine and all I could think about was what my mom had done. When my dad told me to hop on board I crumpled to the ground. So I've been told. Guess I was so scared that I fainted. Dad took me home. I woke up in my bed."

"Did he ever take you to the hospital?"

"My dad?" Ethan laughed. "No. Not his way." He shifted

on his cushion. "I think … I think he was in denial. I don't know. We never talked about it, but neither did he ever take me back to the train yard. You could say we came to an unspoken agreement."

"That's good. I guess."

Ethan appreciated the empathy. "Yeah, I guess. But it didn't stop the nightmares."

"Nightmares, Mr. Et-dan?" Barnabas leaned in.

"Yeah. Like bad dreams, really bad dreams. I have a recurring one. Of my mother. She starts out normal, gentle and kind, how she was before her betrayal, and then suddenly she's a grunting, zombie-like, ghostly creature chasing me across a train platform."

"A ghost." Barnabas sucked in his breath. "Then, Mr. Et-dan, you do know of ghosts." Ethan looked at Barnabas. His eyes were now eerie orange orbs in the flames' reflection.

"Yes. Yes, I do." Ethan's body spasmed in saying those chilling words. "At least in the dream world. But you talk about them in the physical world. And that, *that* just feeds my fear."

"Yes, ghosts should be feared." Barnabas whispered, as if not wanting the dead to hear.

Ethan focused on his own breathing. Inhale. Relax. Exhale. Relax. As if in the distance, he heard a quiet conversation in a foreign tongue between Barnabas and their host. Someone placed a few logs on the coals, stirring the embers to ignite fire and warmth.

Barnabas shuffled through his pack. Then, like the robin's song after a long, cold winter, the sweet, mellow notes of a bamboo flute accompanied the flames dancing up to the ceiling. Barnabas played a tune so familiar, yet so lost to Ethan. He searched his mind for a connection. *Jill. Jill used to sing that song to Cassie, sometimes at bedtime, but more often when Cassie was sick or in pain. Jill would rock our baby girl back and forth, back and forth, either singing or humming this tune. What was it?*

Barnabas played the tune over and over again until even the flames relaxed. Finally, the music stopped. "Do you know this song, Mr. Et-dan? 'Jesus Loves Me.' The first song Mrs. Ben taught me. I play it for my baby at home. Do you think she hears it now?"

Ethan smiled. *Of course.* He knew the first line. *Jesus loves me this I know.* The words reminded him of Cassie, and that brought comfort to his unsettled heart.

"Thank you, Barnabas." Ethan managed a smile a few minutes later. Then he gave Janus a tenuous grin. "You can read your ghost stories now. I'm ready."

Janus smiled back. "Okay, then." He picked up the folder but paused. "Your story explains a lot. Thanks."

Ethan kept his eyes on the fire.

"And I like that despite all that torment, your curiosity got the better of you."

"My curiosity?" A memory floated into his thoughts … a memory of his mother, the kind and loving one. *"You're always so curious,"* she had said. *"Your teacher says the same."*

"Yeah." Janus continued. "I mean, why else would you come to Myanmar, in search of finding something in the un-known, like Alice following the rabbit? Isn't that curiosity?"

"Huh. Curiosity. Maybe." Ethan thought about the girl in his dream who mentioned help, but he wasn't interested in telling any more stories. "Curiosity," he repeated. "Probably not my driving force but there nonetheless." He looked at the flames, little tongues of curiosity, seeking, licking the wood, then shooting up to taste the air, the surrounding world.

Janus glanced at Barnabas who just shrugged. "How 'bout if I read these narratives out loud? Should lessen the creepiness of it all."

"Yeah. Okay." Ethan sat up a bit, bolstered by Janus's words.

Janus stretched his legs out in front of him. "All right." He grabbed the flashlight conveniently found in his anorak pocket and flipped over the title page. "Okay, so the first page is just background—the Khimsha's basic definition. Then we get into some nice freak …" He stopped, remembering his audience, and began to read.

CHAPTER ELEVEN

Once along a jungle pathway, bamboo heavy, blocking sun's ray,
Traveller needing rest and beckoning home hearth,
presses t'ward the call,
   Danger comes so unsuspecting, in human form, veiled presenting,
Shadowed stalking unrelenting, weary traveller trapped to fall,
Danger bites, addiction's power, death feeds slowly from the fall—
   Fear the ghost. Fear—one and all.

Ghosts in the World of the Khimsha Shan
<u>*Connecting Ghosts to the Khimsha Myth of the Giant Black Bird*</u>
Ghosts only appeared in the Khimsha culture after people killed and ate the meat of the mythological giant bird. Those people who initially ate the meat of this bird would return to the killing site daily and would continue eating the bird meat. As time went on, these people became obsessed with meat only from that giant bird, leading to addiction.

After depleting the bird meat, these people began to believe that its meat had been so sweet and delicious because the bird had eaten human flesh for so long. They wondered if human flesh would be just as succulent. They first tested their theory by visiting cemeteries at night, eating the flesh of dead humans, discovering that yes, human flesh tasted similar to the bird's flesh. Gradually some of these people evolved into ghosts that would not only seek dead flesh of humans but also live flesh of humans, first the flesh of children but eventually their addiction intensified until they began to bite, kill, and eat humans of all ages.

That is how ghosts evolved and that is why ghosts only like human meat. It satisfies their innermost desires—not just their physical urges but also their desire for power in consuming the human spirit and soul.

"Wait." Ethan looked at Barnabas. "The giant bird and ghosts. That's what you were trying to connect this afternoon, wasn't it Barnabas?"

"Yes, Mr. Et-dan. This explanation is good. Do you understand better now?"

"Understand, yes. Believe? That's a whole 'nother story."

"We shall see," Janus chided, then kept reading.

Description of Ghosts

Throughout the places where the Khimsha live, especially in the villages, ghosts are a real and daily trepid thing. Through the years, the Khimsha have become convinced that ghosts are real physical people due to eyewitness accounts of physical manifestations, such as eating, playing, singing, and fighting with humans. Yet ghosts often possess certain malformations, such as extremely small stature (two feet tall), severe ugliness, or even intense, desirous beauty.

"What?" Ethan's mouth gaped open. "Did I hear right? A beautiful girl could be a ghost? Ghosts are malformed. Ghosts can be ugly. Sure. But beautiful? I've never heard *that* before."

"Not just beautiful, Mr. Et-dan, but … but, I think the term would be sexy or maybe irresistible." Barnabas looked at Janus. "Is that correct?"

"Good words." Janus smiled. "Provocative works too.

The stories definitely give that impression."

"Well, guess I better not pay attention to any *provocative* women in the next couple of weeks, huh." Ethan laughed. A chill, like an electric shock, passed through his body.

Janus and Barnabas remained silent.

"Guess I'll keep reading," Janus said after a minute.

Ghosts can do strange, supernatural things, such as squeeze through holes that are physically too small for them or transform themselves into animals or inanimate objects. In all cases, they can move in and out of these forms.

A ghost's ambition is to cast evil on humans, either for some past wrong done to them or their family, or because they think they deserve to be better than humans, especially if they are ghosts as a result of their heritage. They want to be human but because that's impossible for them, they oppress humans. Their aim is to become more powerful than humans and then lord that power over them. With each successful incident of frightening or harming a human, ghosts gain power.

Often ghosts scare a person just enough to snatch up their spirit in that split second of fright. Once their spirit is in the grasp of the host, the person is without consciousness or self-awareness. They are like zombies (although not vicious). Once in this form, the person is easy to kill and devour, though generally the intent is to kill the person slowly, often by biting. Evidence of death may be physical, such as a cut by a knife, or non-physical, where there is no apparent external reason for death. Ghosts sometimes consume the entire body, but sometimes they leave parts of the body as a scare tactic, letting people know that ghosts are wandering about.

Ghosts often appear as normal human beings by day but become ghosts at night. So by day, ghosts can be your friend, your neighbor, or your co-worker, but at night they lurk in the forest scaring and haunting and causing unexplained deaths.

Janus paused and looked over at Ethan. "Okay, so far?"

"Well, that answers the question I had for Barnabas, the one about the place where we stayed." Ethan looked at Barnabas. "How you said it was 'safe'?"

Barnabas nodded. "Safe. Yes."

"Again, I hear what you're saying. But that doesn't mean I accept it. Really. I mean, whose information is this? Anyone could've made this stuff up."

"Ironic." Janus stared at the paper in his hands.

"What is?" Ethan shifted awkwardly on his cushion.

"You asked for testimony. I've got it. Real stories by real people. How'd you know?"

Ethan said nothing. Janus went back to reading.

<u>*Testimonials*</u>

1. (A personal story told by a Khimsha man named Kyaw Win)
When I was about five years old living in the village of Putao, my friends and I would play in the yard, pretending to dig wells and draw water. We would make the wells out of milk cartons and use sticks and string to hoist the water up using small plastic cups. We did this over and over again, all the while singing happy songs.

One night in bed, after playing like this all day, I heard voices and humming, exactly the same way my friends and I had done during the day. Then I heard footsteps and the sounds of cutting and assembling of milk carton wells exactly the same as we had done as we played. I also heard the sounds of water being poured into the milk cartons. These sounds continued as if adults were playing our games in the dark right outside my window. I was curious and wanted to go to the window to take a peek.

Suddenly, my mother rushed into the room and told me to hide under my blanket. She heard the same loud and distinct sounds and told me that ghosts were making those sounds. I wanted to look out and watch but my mother said, "No, no! They will see you and bite you and you will die." I couldn't sleep at all. All I could do was listen in fear all night long to the ghosts outside, mimicking children's play.

I still believe that ghosts are real because I wasn't the only one hearing the sounds. My mother heard them, too. Also, nobody would dare go out and play like that at night to scare others. Only ghosts would do that.

2. (A personal story told by a young Khimsha man named Ai) When Ai was fifteen years old he attended a school in Hokho Village of Putao Township. He studied his lessons at his teacher's house, a common occurrence for school children. At night, Ai and his friends liked to hang out outside the teacher's house that backed up against a thick bamboo forest.

When Ai was young, his mother told him that ghosts like to loiter around houses close to the forest. Ai himself had never seen or heard any ghosts so he doubted whether ghosts actually existed. At the time of this story, Ai had long forgotten about ghosts and his mother's stories.

One school night four of the boys snuck out, even though their teacher told them not to. They also didn't care that it was winter and snowing, and even though the moon was out they could only see two feet in front of them. They walked some distance from the house but upon returning, there were two paths to take, a shortcut and a main path. Ai's friends wanted to return on the main path that was far and long, but Ai wanted to take the shortcut even though it ran through the dark forest and crossed a stream. Ai didn't want to be shamed by showing fear in front of his friends, so he proudly stated that he was taking the shortcut. Alone.

Ai set off, in total darkness, without any thought of ghosts. Soon he heard footsteps and twigs snapping alongside him as if his friends were walking with him (not behind him as if he was being followed). When Ai spoke out nobody replied, and again all he heard was someone walking. When he finally approached his teacher's house, he walked quietly so as not to wake her. He slowly opened the gate so it wouldn't creak and carefully looked around to make sure no one was with him or following him. When he arrived at the door he found it locked so he decided to climb into his room through the window he had intentionally left unlocked. Unfortunately, the window into Ai's bedroom was high up and difficult to reach, so he had to climb up onto a large pile of firewood in order to get in. It took some struggling but he was finally able to pull himself through the window and into his room. He lit a candle, checked the four corners of his room and then crawled into bed, putting out the light.

After a few minutes, Ai heard familiar sounds. When he listened he realized they were the same sounds he had made in climbing up to the window—the same wood falling in exactly the same way, the same footsteps fumbling for footing on the logs. He didn't imagine them, they were real. Then he heard the very same sounds he had made when climbing in the window. The hand grabbing the sill, the small struggling grunts to get through. The sounds were so real that it was obvious that someone was there, coming in.

Suddenly Ai lost consciousness, as if on the verge of falling asleep and unaware of anything. Then he was startled awake by the sound of a large snake hissing near his bed. He quickly grabbed the machete near his bed, swinging it back and forth at the noise of the snake, succeeding only to wedge the blade into his bed frame. Then he got up, lit his candle and looked around. Nothing. He called his teacher who just scolded him for sneaking out.

After that, Ai began believing in ghosts.

"How many of these stories are there?" Ethan interrupted. "'Cause really, that's all they are, just stories that could've been concocted in someone's wild imagination." Ethan could hear Barnabas suck in air from across the room.

"Mr. Et-dan." Ethan heard the unusual lack of peace in Barnabas's voice. "Please listen. I know the men who wrote these stories, and they are true. These men would not lie. They are good and honest men. Why do you doubt?"

Why do I doubt? Ethan fought back the desire to strike out from a closet full of caustic memories. Out of respect, he chose to say nothing.

Janus spoke up. "Barnabas, why don't you give Ethan one of your personal accounts? I know you have them."

"I can, Mr. Janus." Barnabas glanced at Ethan. "Are you sure? My English is not good."

"I think it's good enough to get your story across." Janus nodded. Then, turning to Ethan, he asked, "Is that okay Ethan?"

"Sure." Ethan sighed. "Why the … yeah, why not?"

Janus clicked off the flashlight and slipped the file back into its folder. They sat in silence for at least half a minute.

Barnabas began. "For a time when I was younger, I did much fishing. We lived in Putaung in Putao Township, but at night I would go fish in Panlai, another village. I would net fish along a stream that joined the two towns. Always, when I came to the bridge near Putaung, I would stop and go home.

One night the fishing was not good and so I decided to walk home early. It was a moonless night and very cold." Barnabas paused here and, picking up his cup, slurped noisily.

"When I got to the main path, I heard footsteps. They

sounded labored, like someone was carrying something heavy. I was surprised. Nobody ever travelled that path at night. I stopped to listen more. Then I hid in the bushes and looked in the direction of the sound. And there I saw the dark outline of very tall, lanky man carrying another man over his shoulder. The man over his shoulder was drooping as if he were dead."

"Was he? Dead, I mean?" Ethan had come to trust Barnabas. His story wasn't just words on a page.

"Well, I waited and watched as they came closer. I even held my breath because I did not want the man to see me. Something about him made me so afraid." Barnabas paused. "Fear can be very painful. I have never known cold like that."

"I know that fear, believe me."

Barnabas looked up from the fire and, despite the shadows from the dying embers, Ethan could see compassion. "I believe you, Mr. Et-dan. And for that, I am sorry." Barnabas locked eyes with Ethan. Ethan turned away.

Barnabas continued. "And in answer to your question, Mr. Et-dan, the man was very dead. But there is more. I knew the dead man. He was a friend of mine in Panlai."

"No shit?" Ethan looked at Janus who smiled slightly and nodded his head.

"You haven't heard the best part, yet. If you wanna call it that," Janus said. "Barnabas?" Both Janus and Ethan turned back to the Khimsha man.

"Yes, there is more." Barnabas shifted his *longgyi* to cover more of his crossed legs. "I sat there shaking for a long time after the man walked by. So cold. So evil. I rose and stumbled, my legs wobbly. I did not wish to be heard or seen, so I walked slowly and quietly, all the while thinking about my friend in Panlai. I decided I would go see him in the morning because I knew that something was wrong."

"That's an understatement," Ethan gibed. Barnabas again paused briefly.

"The next day, I found my friend very sick in bed."

"Wait. He wasn't dead?" Ethan asked.

"No, just very sick. He could not even talk. His family had no idea what happened. The *sarli*, what you would call the witch doctor, came to see him but he said he could do nothing, that my friend had been bitten. But I had seen him just a few days before, working in the market. He was healthy and happy. On that day, we had a short conversation and then I left. I had no idea that he would soon be dead."

"So, you're saying that that frightening man was a ghost? And he bit your friend?" Ethan frowned.

"Not a real, physical bite but, yes, I know he was a ghost. The evil coldness was true and I feared for my life. Yes, the fear was very real." Barnabas stopped and, for a minute, the only sound was the dying fire, the bright orange embers now glowing like amber jewels.

"You can't deny Barnabas's story, Ethan," Janus finally said.

Ethan kept his eyes on the erratic coals, reminding him of his own thoughts, a vagarious chaos of questions, but none he chose to voice.

"You okay?" Janus leaned toward him.

"Honestly?" Ethan didn't know what to say. "Honestly, I think my brain's about to explode. This trek, dig, whatever, it's more than I bargained for." He stopped there.

"Mr. Et-dan. You should know that I no longer fear the ghosts of these stories. The fear is gone. I hope for you, too, that your fears can be taken away."

In the quiet, Barnabas pulled out his flute and played that same song, sweet and soothing. The reminder of Cassie quieted Ethan's confused mind and returned his focus back on why he joined this adventure to begin with. When the music stopped, Ethan offered Barnabas a smile.

CHAPTER TWELVE

Jungle fogs and drips,
a dome of dirty batting,
suffocating weight.
Paralyzed. Who will pull back
the blanket of tears and fears?

Ethan lay awake long into the night, shifting on the hard, coconut-frond mattress just three inches off the floor, listening to the loud breathing and occasional snorting coming from Janus's bed across the room. He thought about Cassie—her playful laugh, her love of adventure. After finally falling asleep, Ethan drifted into his dream world.

He was running, not from his zombie-mother, but this time from a ghost. He recognized the oppressive jungle from a previous dream. Ravens taunted him from above. In desperation he called out to his trekking buddies, but the night air remained silent in response. He called out to family, his mother, his father, his sister, but nothing. He called out to Jill and Cassie. Nothing. He stumbled along, tripping on unseen roots and rocks, yelling out the names of everyone he ever knew … friends from school, acquaintances from work, even his ex-father and mother-in-law. Nothing.

The jungle opened up to the pond from his previous dream. The sun's reflection on the surface blinded his eyes. He fell back. And again, the ebony girl floated down from the sky.

"Peace," she said again without moving her lips.

Ethan sat up. "Help. I'm lost."

"Yes, help will come. Do not give up hope." Again, her words drifted into his mind like a soothing melody. "You are not lost. You only need to choose the way of hope. Do not run from it. Come to it." She took flight, up and away. As she did so, the foreboding jungle became bright with sunlight, the ravens' squawks now delightful bird twitters.

Ethan jerked awake to the rooster crowing from under the house before the first hint of light. His heart pounded. His head ached. Sweat covered his body despite the air's frosty chill.

"Not again," he moaned. He was told repetitious dreams mean something but this one made little sense. He fought back silent tears. *Boys don't cry. Get a grip and stop being such a wuss.* His mother's voice. The words buzzed around in his head, stinging his spirit.

Another voice broke in. *I am here, still with you. Take courage.*

Ethan couldn't tell if it was Cassie's voice or the voice of the ebony girl in his dream.

"Who are you?" he asked in his mind. No reply. Instead, his body tingled with energy and a forgotten vigor. With the sensation came an idea. Since his dream included a ghost, perhaps Barnabas could help. Perhaps *he* could explain his dream.

When the host came into the room to stoke the fire to begin the day, Ethan made a choice. He'd talk to Barnabas. But he'd also temper his emotions and think of Cassie and her love of life. He didn't want yesterday's events to fester in his mind. He just needed to focus on helping Janus. Jill would like that. And Cassie would beam, proud of her daddy.

* * *

Ethan was the first one out in the yard, ready to go, undeterred by the damp morning mist. Barnabas looked surprised to see him so chipper.

"You look better today, Mr. Et-dan."

"Thanks. Thanks for noticing." Ethan grinned and rubbed his hands together. "I'm ready to face the day. No repeat of yesterday."

"I am glad." Barnabas opened the gate. "Are you coming?"

"Nope. I'll wait for Janus. Thanks." Barnabas turned down the path and Ethan leaned up against the bamboo fence. Janus appeared a few seconds later, his eyes glued to his clipboard.

"Which way today, boss?" Ethan bounced up to Janus.

"Huh?" Janus looked up, oblivious to Ethan's eager presence. "Oh, well, that's easy enough. We just keep following the river south. Barnabas knows." Barely taking his eyes off his clipboard, he motioned with one hand to their guide, already up the rocky trail.

Ethan looked over his shoulder. "Whaddya got there, anyway?"

"What?" Janus said. "Oh. Maps. Just maps. Mine that I did yesterday for possible test spots but also one hand-drawn by Ben Sands."

"Oh?"

"But then, he wasn't an archaeologist so I guess I wouldn't expect it to be too precise." Janus turned the clipboard. "Yet, something seems off." He looked at the map, thinking out loud. "What he drew is not what he told me."

"What did you say?" Ethan's ears perked up.

"Huh?"

Ethan planted his feet in front of Janus and put his hands

on his hips. "What did you just say? I'm sure you said, 'What he drew is not what he told me.'" Ethan's suspicions were off and running wild once again. "What the hell? I thought you didn't know Ben. Isn't that what you told Barnabas?"

"You're twisting my ..."

"Don't want to hear it." Ethan stared at him, fists clenched, fighting to keep them at his sides. "Guess I shouldn't be surprised." He swung around and stomped off, his anger churning, arms stretched wide, his voice yelling. "What kind of psycho circus is this, anyway? Why the secrecy? The rabbit hole ridiculousness? Not a rabbit hole. Just a psycho circus." He marched right past Barnabas who had paused on the side of the path, eyes big, mouth wide open. Half a minute later Ethan heard a response.

"Mr. Et-dan. Mr. Et-dan."

Barnabas. Not Janus. Ethan ignored the calls.

Barnabas finally caught up to him, his shorter legs doing double time. "Mr. Et-dan. Are you okay?" He seemed unafraid of Ethan's outburst.

"Whaddya think? Liar. He's a liar. He's been lying to me the whole time. He's probably lied about everything. Maybe ... maybe he's not even an archaeologist." Ethan stopped abruptly, towering over Barnabas. "So no, I'm not okay." He returned to his fast pace down the winding path. "Leave. Me. Alone." He disappeared into the hanging clouds.

With sound enhanced by the fog, Ethan could hear Barnabas's light footsteps about fifteen feet behind him. They were soon joined by Janus's longer strides. Ethan had no problem overhearing their conversation, though they spoke in hushed tones.

Janus spoke first. "You okay? He kinda let you have it."

"Yes, Mr. Janus, I am okay." There was a pause. "I am just sad for him. He was so happy this morning. Now he is not."

"Yeah, I know. He's had a hard life. We just have to be patient."

"Patience. Yes. Many have been patient with me. I can be patient."

"Stop talking about me as if you know me." Ethan did a 180. Walking backwards, he added, "But maybe you *do* know all about me. At least everything Ben knew. Thanks for the lies." Turning back up the path, he stopped and looked up into the mist. "And thanks for the betrayal. My dream fulfilled. Ha!" He screamed to every relationship in his life and picked up his pace.

"You don't want to be walking alone in this weather." Janus's yell didn't faze him. He kept walking.

"But don't worry. We'll keep our eyes on the red maple leaf of your backpack."

Ethan ignored the comment. He needed to stay focused on his pace. His legs began to burn. He slowed down, wishing his leg muscles could keep up with the thoughts in his brain, unable to block out the conversation going on behind him.

This time Barnabas spoke first. "Perhaps I could try to talk to him about his daughter. Because I have a daughter too. Would he listen?"

"Possibly. He does love his daughter. Seems she's the only one who matters to him." After a couple of minutes, Janus continued. "Funny, but perhaps you, Barnabas, have more in common with Ethan than I do."

"I do not know, but having a daughter is good, is it not?"

"Yes, yes it is."

Focusing on a lengthy verbal response in his mind, Ethan

stumbled over a sharp rock, quickly self-corrected and then stopped. He needed water.

"It is good you stopped," Barnabas said, as the two of them caught up. "There is a bridge just around the next bend."

"A bridge? So what?" Ethan wasn't ready to play nice.

"You will see." Barnabas took the lead. Janus just shrugged his shoulders at Ethan and followed. Ethan took up the rear, now hearing the sound of rushing water ahead.

The fog dissipated just as they reached a narrow, rickety bridge hanging twenty feet above a wide river. Though the swift, rock-riddled water looked perilous, the bridge looked even more so. It consisted of bamboo poles, only two or three wide, strapped together, and then lashed end-to-end, stretching across the river. A single fraying rope stretched loosely above the bamboo for a railing. Ethan sucked in air. He needed to watch and learn from Barnabas.

"Okay. I get it. You're in charge here," Ethan conceded and glared at Janus.

In silence, Barnabas stepped out onto the bridge with no hesitation. "Just keep your eyes on the back of my head." He glanced over his shoulder. "Bamboo is stronger than you think."

Ethan let out a long breath. Bamboo knows how to bend but not break, he remembered.

The misty dampness still clung to the smooth poles and rope. Ethan shuffled along, aware that Barnabas's slow advancement was for their sakes. His smaller, nimble feet never hesitated. Ethan's heart was pounding like a hammer on an anvil by the time they reached the bridge's end. He knew he should stop, catch his breath, but he didn't want to talk. He stepped off the bridge and kept right on walking.

When his feet began to burn, Ethan slowed his pace. He replayed his morning conversation with Janus in his head once again. Why did he doubt others so much? *But tunnels deep and dark envelope.* He hated the bombardment of song lyrics. "I'm. Not. Listening." He spewed the words out in a half-whisper.

He heard footsteps coming up behind him. "Ethan. Please, listen." It was Janus. "I know you're upset but have you forgotten? I have a survey job to do. I need ..."

Ethan swung around, wanting to lash out. Somehow, he found the energy to stop himself.

Breathe, Daddy, Breathe. Cassie.

"I ... I'm having a hard time trusting you, after this morning." He turned and kept on walking.

"Then let's talk about it." Janus caught up and remained beside him.

"I'm not ready to hear your weaving of lies into truths. At least not yet." Ethan shifted his pack and picked up his pace, leaving Janus behind.

"Mr. Et-dan." Barnabas had been following a few paces back. "Mr. Et-dan. There is a pagoda up ahead. On your left. We will stop there, by the river."

Ethan didn't respond.

"Mr. Et-dan?"

"Okay Barnabas," Ethan said. "Thanks."

Soon Ethan saw the golden spire of the pagoda shimmering high above the tree line in the distance. He exhaled slowly, knowing that stopping meant conversing, yet he needed the break.

Forty-five minutes later, Ethan slipped off his backpack and slumped down on a lip of grass just above the fine, white sand of the riverbank. How serenely the water flowed at this spot, almost silently, a stark contrast to farther upstream, and to the questions still swirling in his mind. Janus and Barnabas settled twenty feet away and disturbed him only long enough to bring him a plate of food, a hot grilled fish laden with spices sitting on top of a bed of rice. Ethan grabbed his spoon and dug in, wondering briefly how and where Barnabas came up with something so delicious.

He sat, mesmerized by a group of old men panning for gold along the river's edge. Barnabas had talked about them days ago. Now, as he ate, Ethan watched them filling their pans, and then dumping the mixture of soil and water down a tilted, concave sluice propped up with a trio of bamboo poles. Ethan wondered what motivated them. Did they ever strike it rich?

His food finished, he looked over at his companions. Janus was gone, leaving Barnabas alone to clean up. When Barnabas saw Ethan look his way, he grabbed his flute from his backpack and walked over.

Without saying a word, Barnabas sat down beside him and began playing a tune, one that Ethan had never heard. He began softly, the melancholic trills rising and falling as if following the motion of the river, then ending in long, dissonate notes. Barnabas put the flute in his lap.

More relaxed, Ethan broke the silence. "Another song for your daughter?"

"Maybe. It's a Khimsha song that tells a story. Almost all of them do."

"Our songs do too, in a way." Ethan thought about the song he wrote as an angry, teenage boy, full of tritones. "The devil's interval," his guitar teacher called them. Fitting way to sing about his mother's betrayal.

"You must write songs, then?" Barnabas offered Ethan his toothy smile.

"A few." Ethan didn't want to focus on the song in his thoughts. "I've never tried playing a flute, but I play guitar." *Why did I offer that information?*

"And ukulele." Barnabas's eyes became gentle pools in the river's reflection. "You know then, Mr. Et-dan, how music can make you happy or sad, angry or at peace."

"Yes. Yes, I do." Ethan said no more, his eyes focused solely on the clear-flowing water.

Barnabas continued. "The song is about a young Khimsha father who is forced to leave his village and go to war—a war he does not believe in. He does not want to go but knows that if he does not, his wife and newborn daughter will be killed for his treason. So he goes and he fights hard for his wife and daughter. Finally, the war is over, and he returns home only to find his village has been burned to the ground, all the people gone. He spends the rest of his life searching for his wife and daughter, but he never finds them. In the end, he dies heartbroken."

Ethan understood. Struggling to fight back tears, he sniffled. "Wow, you sure know how to cheer a guy up." He turned away.

"Sometimes it is easy to forget what matters. How do you say in English? Your perspective is lost?" Barnabas looked over at the prospectors. "Like those men. I knew one who was so obsessed with finding gold that he never went home to see his family. He did not eat, or even sleep. One morning the other men came down to the river and found his body, face-down in the water, right over there." Barnabas pointed to a spot just a few meters from them. "His body just quit from exhaustion."

"You're just full of stories, aren't you?"

"In our culture, stories always mean more, Mr. Et-dan. Sometimes we need stories to help us make right choices. Sometimes they help us get through life. They give us hope. Life is not easy for the Khimsha people. Sometimes stories are all we have."

"And what about dreams. Do they mean more?"

Barnabas's black eyes narrowed under his scrunched brow. "Please explain."

"Last night, I had a dream. Sort of reoccurring. Had a ghost in it, probably because of all those ghost stories last night. Anyway, I was hoping you'd know what it meant."

"Ahhh." Barnabas nodded. "I understand, though I am not a dream interpreter."

"A dream interpreter? That's a thing?"

"Yes, in our culture it is. Do you not have them?"

"Nope. At least not that I'm aware of."

"I do not wish to offend but to me that sounds backwards."

"Backwards? Funny, but I won't argue. There's probably lots backwards about my culture." Ethan kicked the sand. "But what about this dream interpreter? Are they everywhere?"

"That depends on the village. But everyone knows their local dream interpreter." Barnabas twirled the flute between his palms. "I do believe, Mr. Et-dan, that there is an elderly woman in Machanbaw village who could explain your dream. If that is what you want."

"Didn't I just say that?"

"Yes." Barnabas turned to Ethan, his familiar smile gone. "But remember how I said stories mean more?"

"Sure."

"Well, you need to be aware that dreams mean more too, Mr. Et-dan. You may hear things you do not want to hear."

"You coming?" Janus had returned but kept his distance.

"Yes, Mr. Janus." Barnabas stood.

Ethan didn't move.

Barnabas looked down at him. "You have one day to decide. Until then …" Barnabas paused. "Until then, perhaps we could listen to Mr. Janus's story."

Ethan cursed under his breath. "Janus's story. A make-believe one, I bet."

"I do not know Janus well, but he is a good man. As are you." Barnabas kept his eyes on Ethan. "He is your friend. Please choose to listen to him. Friends give us hope."

"My friend?" Ethan picked up a pebble and whipped it far out into the river. "He chose to lie to me, and you think he's still my friend?" He paused. "Not sure we ever were friends."

"Then my heart aches, for both you and for him." Without waiting for a response, Barnabas turned and walked slowly back to his supplies.

Ethan rubbed his throbbing temples. *I need help to make right choices. Who will help me?* Picking up a stick, he began drawing lines in the sand, waiting for an answer. No response. He rose with a sigh, gave a dispassionate nod to Janus and Barnabas, and the three of them continued down the same trail, leaving the picturesque panorama behind them.

CHAPTER THIRTEEN

We are but puzzle
pieces,
unnumbered
snippets of
a whole—outer
frame finished,
flaunting finality yet
bordering inner
confusion,
hole sections of
yin and yang—
vacancy.

We are but puzzle
pieces,
in need of
other
intervention.

It was a damp night. The three of them sat closer to their central fire pit in another bamboo hut in another small village. All their clothes now carried the slight scent of smoke but Ethan didn't mind. The familiarity consoled him.

"I'm ready to hear your story." Ethan stared right at Janus. Janus looked back with wide-eyed innocence. "My story?"

"You're kidding." Ethan was not backing down. "You

know. How you met Ben?"

"Right." Janus smiled. "I can do that. Not that exciting, and not that secretive."

"Let me be the judge of that." Ethan caught his tone and looked at Barnabas. Barnabas smiled back. "That is, if you don't mind."

"Okay." Janus sat up and crossed his legs. "Well, it started in the summer after I graduated from the University of Alberta. I worked on campus doing landscape maintenance. That summer the Linguistics Department held a week-long international conference on campus. Curious about the connection between archaeology and linguistics, more from a cultural viewpoint, I decided to slip in on one of the sessions over lunch. Rather randomly, I ended up in Ben Sands's lecture on the language and culture of a small group of people living in northern Myanmar. The Khimsha."

"What're the odds." Ethan couldn't keep the mocking tone out of his voice.

"I know, right? And while I appreciated the lecture, I was actually more intrigued with Ben himself. What made him tick. So, after everyone but Ben cleared out of the lecture hall, I went down to the front and asked him outright what motivated his passion. Turns out it was his religious beliefs. And you know what? I wasn't even surprised by his answer. It reminded me of my grandmother."

"Your grandmother? What's the connection there?"

"Well, I had a devout grandmother. She was a staunch Catholic who spent hours helping others. Working in soup kitchens, serving the helpless and homeless, knitting them scarves and toques for cold winter nights. And when she wasn't doing that, she was sewing dresses for little girls in

Africa who had nothing. Granddad thought all her actions were such a waste of her time and his hard-earned money, but she was a stubborn woman and followed her own way. I've always thought I was like her."

"How's that?" It seemed Ethan was finally getting a glimpse into the real Janus, even though he'd veered off on a tangent, away from any connection with Ben.

"Her stubbornness, I guess. And desire to do her own thing. Maybe 'cause as a young school kid I spent lots of time with her. My dad travelled a lot for work. And my mom, well, with her degree in psychology, she worked odd hours helping clients, so I'd be at Grandma's a lot. We'd gallivant around the city by bus, dropping off cookies or other goodies at this shelter or that home. Sometimes we'd walk to the post office with a box of newly sewn dresses. But the best part about all that was the stories she would tell me, stories about characters named David and Goliath, and Samson, and Jonah. My favorite was about Adam and Eve and the Garden of Eden, how they did something bad and were banished, so that the garden became hidden, guarded by an angel with a flaming sword. As a boy, I asked lots of questions about the Garden of Eden because I really liked swords." At this point Janus swished his arm about as if he were wielding a sword. "Anyway, I loved her fairy tales."

"Fairy tales?" Barnabas jumped in. "Are these not stories from the Bible?"

"Yeah, well, Grandma didn't tell me that 'til I was nine or ten. Suddenly they became real stories because Grandma said so. Peculiar how a child can believe anything if the information comes from someone they trust."

"Don't I know it." Ethan nodded. "Grandmothers. Mothers. Trust is overrated."

"Perhaps, though I'd never trade that time spent with my grandma. She fed my inquisitive mind when nobody else could. And even though she passed away when I was twelve, I think it's because of her that I became an archaeologist."

"Her effect on you was good." Barnabas's eyes gleamed.

Ethan didn't buy it. "You mean you're here 'cuz of those stories? Right."

"Valid point." Janus agreed. "She also told me stories of her family's past, stories told her by her mother, though they didn't interest me much. At least, not till university. As I said, Grandma wasn't around anymore, so I asked my mother. She knew nothing. Nothing of these stories. No written documents from her mother. So, the stories died with Grandma."

"What does that have to do with your choice to become an archaeologist?"

"Right. Well, turns out Grandma's mother was born somewhere in the foothills of the Himalayas."

"Oy." Barnabas blurted the reactionary response so typical in Asia. "Could she have come from northern Myanmar? Do you know her family name?"

"I don't know anything, Barney." Janus's voice sounded surprisingly melancholic. "Like I said, I didn't listen well to those stories. Of course, as a boy, I remember something about a war and fighting. Her parents took her and fled over the mountains to escape. They got on a ship somewhere and left their past behind. I liked the adventure of it all. But that's it."

Barnabas swerved his head back and forth. "It is unfortunate that those stories are lost. Such stories are vital to the Khimsha culture."

"I get that. At least now I do." Janus nodded. "When I

plied my mother further, the info she gave was about the grandfather *she* knew. Step-grandfather, I guess. From northern Ontario somewhere. A small mining town. Don't know what happened to Grandma's real father. Maybe he didn't even get on that ship. Or died over the ocean. Who knows? My mother doesn't."

"I get it." Ethan finally spoke up.

"You have a similar story?" Janus asked.

"No, I get why you're so obsessed with this part of the world. Why you're here."

"Yup. Two reasons for me, I guess. That's why I had to go talk to Ben that day. Between my heritage questions and Grandma's stories about the Garden of Eden, I couldn't help myself. Obsession unearthed, you could say." Janus laughed at his archaeology joke. When the other two didn't respond he kept going. "And while all my academic studies in the sciences made a Garden of Eden sound preposterous, for some reason I couldn't shake my grandma's beliefs. I retained a reticent interest in this garden, reading books and articles on it in my free time. History books about this area of the world too. But then graduate studies hit. Free time went out the window."

"Sounds legit." Ethan tilted his head. "But then how'd you end up here?"

"Well, I retained the heritage interest, for sure. But it wasn't until I read that legend about the Khimsha and their beginnings in Rick Sparman's office at Mengrai U, that I thought again about the Garden of Eden. Do you see the possible connection?" Janus paused, taking a sip of lukewarm green tea from the chipped teacup resting beside him on the slatted floor.

"Eden Archaeology. That's where you got your name

from." Ethan smirked. "Kinda cheesy."

Janus shrugged. "Maybe. But I liked the connection to my grandma. Couldn't think of a better name."

It all sounded believable to Ethan. "And Ben?"

"Ben. Right. You need that question answered." Janus cleared his throat. "Well, during my graduate studies, I travelled extensively, mostly as a surveyor for future archaeological digs. I sought out unique, uncharted areas to survey with the hope of discovering something new and exciting, and worth pursuing. I had checked out Myanmar back then, but it appeared off-limits. That is, until I graduated. The country was opening up and the timing to do survey work seemed perfect. That's when I first arrived in Chiang Mai, attempting to interact with the Myanmar government, hoping to receive access into their north. Without personal connections, I failed miserably." Janus stopped and, reaching for the metal poker, played with the fire. The flames burst higher and he continued. "I thought my dream was over. But then, one day, out of nowhere, Ben's name popped into my head. Ben and his work in northern Myanmar. I knew he'd help me if I could get in touch with him. So I hunted down his academic contact info online and sent him an email. Kind of a last-ditch effort for me."

"Just like that, huh?" Ethan said.

"Pretty much. I really was desperate. Know what that's like?"

"Think you know the answer to that."

Janus's mouth twitched. "Still, when Ben replied, I was shocked. And believe it or not, he remembered me from that summer conference and how direct I was with my questions. Anyway, he readily connected me with his contacts in Yangon. His help has been invaluable."

"That sounds like the Ben I know." Ethan nodded.

"Well, then it shouldn't surprise you that the Ben you know mentioned your name to me after my partner headed back to Canada, leaving me high and dry."

Ethan's eyebrows went up.

"Thought you'd like that." Janus grinned. "Ben was the one who told me you were in Chiang Mai. Gave me a description and everything."

"Huh. That *is* a surprise." While Ethan liked the notion, he was bothered by another thought. "So, why didn't you tell me this from the get-go? Why the secret?"

"Guess I just wasn't sure how you'd react to the Ben connection after hearing you talk about your ex-wife. I heard the pain in your voice."

"Pain." Ethan lowered his head and pulled his arms in tight. "You got that right. I ..." He stopped in mid-thought. *Self preservation.*

"Again, sorry." Janus shifted on his thin mat. "But getting back to Ben, he did mention that you were a hiker."

"Really?" Ethan forced a smile, but he couldn't look up.

"Yup. So, I just kept on the lookout for you, checking out the usual tourist hotspots. Did you ever frequent any of them?"

"Huh?" Ethan did a quick shake of his head and looked at Janus. "On occasion, I guess. Tended to stick to myself."

"Right. That's why I couldn't believe my luck when I saw you that day, eating lunch alone at that little random food stall. Your blonde ponytail a white sail in a dark sea. All I could think of was *mission accomplished.* But then I had to somehow persuade you to join me."

"Is that why you followed me around? Even to the university?" Ethan didn't like the thought of being spied on.

"No." Janus laughed. "That meeting was actually not planned. But it did encourage me to keep pursuing you. No, that day I was on a mission, searching for the perfect area in northern Myanmar to survey. And when I read that Khimsha myth about their ancestors migrating to the land of the one tree that produced precious metals and stones, I knew I'd found what I was looking for, where I wanted to trek. It sounded so Garden of Eden-ish." Janus paused, deep in thought. "Anyway, you'll never guess who was connected with this Khimsha group?"

"Ben, of course." Ethan couldn't help but grin.

"Yup. So I contacted him again, first by email but eventually via phone calls, asking about the area around Putao where the Khimsha lived. Ben was great. He offered insight, full of helpful information. He even emailed me a hand-drawn map of the area, something I couldn't find anywhere."

"The hand-drawn map," Ethan muttered.

"Yeah. That's what I was studying this morning when you lashed out in a frenetic tirade." Janus stopped and took another sip of tea.

"You done now?" Ethan asked, already sorry for his morning actions.

"Pretty much. That's how I know Ben Sands." Janus looked directly at Ethan. "Do you get it, Ethan? That when I met him, I really had no idea who he was? Or his connection to you? It was just business. I saw no reason to explain all that." He paused. "Guess I was wrong."

Ethan cleared his throat, thankful for the shadows. "Guess an apology's in order, for this morning's overreaction. So, sorry, though some honesty on your part might've been nice."

"I get it." Janus turned, the reflection of the red embers

dancing erratically on his dark pupils. "So, let me be honest right now."

"I'm ready." Ethan squirmed.

"Honestly, I didn't think you'd say yes to my proposition."

"What? No lie?"

"No lie. Ask Barnabas." Janus looked at Barnabas and he nodded in agreement. Janus continued. "Remember when you walked in on us in Myityina? That's exactly when I was telling Barney here my initial hunch about you. Timing couldn't have been worse."

"That's for damn sure." Ethan rearranged his pillow and stuck his stiff legs out to the side. "And thanks, thanks for the vote of confidence. Yours and Ben's it seems."

"Ben's?"

"Well, you must've got your doubting Thomas perspective from somewhere."

Barnabas leaned forward and looked Ethan directly in the eye. "No. That is not the Mr. Ben I know." Strong words from Barnabas. Ethan held his tongue.

"I have worked with Mr. Ben. He is a kind man who cares about people. He cared for me when I needed help."

Really? Is that supposed to help me? Ethan's inner voice reacted. *Where was he when I needed help? When his daughter walked out on me? Taking Cassie with her?* "Perhaps that's how you know him, Barnabas. Seems he helps everyone, everyone but me. Can't remember the last time he helped me."

"Well, Ethan, you could try a month ago," Janus countered. "Ben gave me your name, remember? And, he also mentioned your strong work ethic, that you are very capable. Seems that once you put your mind to something, you do it. I would agree with him."

Heat began to rise in Ethan's cheeks. "You know that flattery will get you nowhere." He pseudo-laughed.

"Ben also told me you've been struggling since your marriage ended." Janus looked right at him. "But Ethan, I think he mentioned you to me because he *is* on your side. He was worried about you and thought that this survey adventure might help you find what you're looking for. No betrayal, Ethan, only concern."

He's bullshitting you. His mother's voice.

See, you're not alone. Grandpa does care, just like I do. Cassie's voice.

I need a bottle of SangSom! Ethan's head hurt.

"There's something else Ben said about you, too, Ethan. You listening?"

Ethan blinked his eyes, trying to clear his mind. "Shoot."

"Well, at the time I didn't get it, but I do now, at least partially, now that I know you a bit more. He said he was impressed with your effort to be a good dad to your daughter, despite your past."

"He really said that? You're not just making this up?"

Janus chuckled. "Couldn't if I tried."

"That was all he said? No talk about my anger issues, my alcohol issues, my supposed attachment disorder issues?" The information tumbled out before he could close his mouth.

"Uh." Janus scratched the stubble forming on his chin. "No. He didn't mention any of those things. Should he have?"

"He …" Ethan stopped, clenched his fists, and pressed them into the cushion. "I'm just sick of being analyzed like … like some foreign mold growing in a Petri dish."

"Well, nobody here's judging you." Janus chuckled. "Heck, I'm up to my eyeballs in survey analysis. I don't have time for judging. I'm just trying to find my own Garden of Eden, remember?" He drew quotation marks in the air around "Garden of Eden" and laughed.

Ethan thought about the last five weeks. "Sorry." He sighed. "I mean it. I've been an idiot from the get-go." He knew both men deserved more, but Ethan couldn't give more. He looked at Barnabas and forced a smile. The black eyes smiled back in their usual peaceful way.

Janus's eyes also showed no condemnation. But neither did they reflect peace. Ethan stared at him, his brow furrowed.

Janus looked away. "So. Call it even Steven?"

"Huh?"

"Even Steven. You know. You told me something from your childhood and dreams and now I've told you something about my childhood, and my dreams."

"Sure, man." Ethan looked at Barnabas and cleared his throat. "There's something else I'd …"

"Well then," Janus said, smacking his lips and stretching his arms above his head, "let's call it a night."

Either Janus hadn't heard him or didn't want any more questions. Ethan couldn't tell. He decided any conversation about hunting down the dream interpreter could wait until tomorrow.

"Tomorrow's the end of the line at Machanbaw. I'm pretty sure I'll have a few test pit sites around that village. Been told there's an interesting rock formation in the area, too, and a possible cave."

"A cave? You want to survey a cave?" Ethan thought that odd.

"Yeah. I still can't get that Khimsha myth out of my head. You know, the felling of the tree, the death of the large bird on the top of a large rock."

"So?" Ethan still didn't see the connection.

"Well, maybe this rock formation is that rock? Maybe we'll find something that substantiates their story?"

"Like treasure?" Ethan remembered Janus's word.

Janus mouth gaped open. He squirmed. "Treasure? Why do you say that?"

Ethan smiled. That's the response he was hoping for. "Hey. You're the one who mentioned it when we first met. Not me."

"I did? Huh." Janus shrugged his shoulders. "Well, an archaeologists' treasure isn't what you think. So yeah, treasure in the rock formation. Treasure in the cave. Guess I'm just curious, that's all. Nothing wrong with that, is there?"

"No." Ethan decided to agree. "Nothing wrong with that." But the churning uneasiness in the pit of his stomach kept him awake late into the night.

CHAPTER FOURTEEN

For the first time since their arrival in Myanmar, the morning arrived ablaze with sunshine, golden rays slivering through the walls of worn thatch as they packed up for the day's trek.

"A good sign." Janus smiled as they began their hike to Machanbaw. Ethan didn't see it that way. While he appreciated the early warmth, he thought it archaic to call it a sign. Plus, he still questioned Janus's motivation behind searching for a cave.

"So, tell me more about this rock formation."

"Well." Janus's voice raised to an excited pitch. "It's what the locals call the 'stone dragon.' Story goes, this dragon was once alive and it fed on people. Sound familiar?"

"Well, yeah, but that's typical for a dragon. And it's a dragon, not some giant bird."

"True enough. But the story still piques my interest." Conversation over.

They took a narrow, machete-hewn trail, following the shoreline of the river, although they often lost sight of it through the dense, broad-leafed foliage. For the first time, Ethan actually noticed the singsong of birds serenading them down the path. He smiled, remembering how much Cassie liked birds.

"Watch out for snakes, Mr. Et-dan." Barnabas yelled from a few meters behind him.

"Snakes?" Ethan shouted, high stepping over a sleek, reptilian-shaped object that stretched in front of him. Instant adrenaline rush. He looked back. Not a snake. Just a root jutting out of the soft soil. He stopped and bent over to settle his beating heart.

"There are many on this trail." Barnabas caught up to Ethan. "And leeches, too, when the bamboo and trees are so thick and wet."

"Thanks for the warning." Ethan grunted. "First ghosts. Then snakes. What next?" He didn't expect an answer.

"Sorry, Mr. Et-dan." Barnabas put his hand under Ethan's elbow. "I noted that you were not watching your steps."

"You noted?" Ethan straightened up, pulled his arm in, and took a deep breath. "Guess you're right. I was watching the birds. First time I've noticed how noisy they are … and unique. So many of them have such vibrant and interesting markings." He shifted the weight of his backpack and headed back up the path, wanting to catch Janus.

"You know birds?" Barnabas pulled up beside Ethan, the path now wider.

"Crazy, right?" Ethan grinned. "It's 'cause of my daughter. *She* likes birds, so when I'm with her I try to appreciate her world."

"You are a good father."

"Thanks." Ethan straightened up and smiled. "Anyway, I thought I could record the names of some birds here and then Cassie and I could look them up when I get home. She'd like that. You know names?"

"Yes." Barnabas frowned a bit. "But not in English. In Khimsha or Burmese maybe."

"Right. Got it. I'll try to keep their images up here." Grinning, Ethan tapped his head. "Scribble down the info later. Meanwhile, I will watch my step *and* watch for birds."

"Good." Barnabas looked ahead. "At least the way is shorter today."

Barnabas was right. They arrived at Machanbaw after an hour, without any interruption from Janus stopping to map out possible test pit sites. And no time to talk to him about visiting a dream interpreter.

"I'll start surveying from here." Janus walked into the clearing surrounding the village. "But I'd like to check out that rock formation before we do anything else. All game?" He didn't wait for a response. "I think it's this way." He pointed to a path to their left. "Am I right, Barney?"

"Yes, Mr. Janus. You are right." Barnabas offered Ethan a weak smile and took the lead.

The path narrowed as they began weaving up and down through the jungle, the eastern mountain range slowly closing in on them. Half an hour later, the forest opened up to a three-hundred-foot-long rock outcrop jutting up from the ground, as if it had been a forgotten plaything of the gods. If Ethan used his imagination, he could see the dragon shape, but it wasn't obvious. They climbed up to a ledge skirting the head of the dragon, its fury lost by the presence of burned incense sticks and crusted candle wax surrounding a small golden shrine.

"One man's bad luck is another man's good fortune, I guess." Ethan snickered. "I don't get it. Why would anyone worship a creature that is historically evil?" Ethan looked at Barnabas for an answer.

Barnabas seemed eager to explain. "They do not come to worship it. They use it to fight bad karma. The killing of the dragon became a symbol of power and strength. It became good karma."

"Still, trusting in a petrified dragon is ludicrous."

"Is not everyone searching for something or someone to trust in, Mr Et-dan? Trusting in Buddhism is just one way. I trusted in it once but found no hope. Now I trust in the God of the Bible."

"I know. Ben's God." Ethan spat out the words like venom. "I tried that. But never again. Nothing on this earth's gonna change my mind."

Barnabas turned slowly to Ethan. "So, then, what do you trust in?"

"Me? We-e-ell ..." Ethan stood up straight. "I'd say just me. I trust in me. Nobody else." Ethan thumped his chest, attempting to boost his own confidence.

"Oy!" Barnabas voiced his surprise, looked away, and shook his head. It was a moment or two before he turned back. "Is it okay if I do not agree?"

"What do you mean?"

"I see you trusting Mr. Janus, and me."

"How's that?"

"You trusted Mr. Janus enough to come with him to Myanmar. You trust both of us as we hike. You may even trust the dream interpreter." Barnabas clucked. "I know this journey has not been easy for you. And yet, you are still here. You are following, and learning."

"I …" Now Ethan turned away, unnerved by the truth in Barnabas' evaluation.

"How tired you must be." Barnabas's voice was compassionate.

The words hit Ethan hard. Nobody had ever revealed so much truth in so few words.

Barnabas wrinkled his brow. "Are you also searching for something?"

Am I searching for something? Yes. Searching for a way to prove to Jill that he could be a good father. Searching for answers to his alcoholism. Searching for that illusive world of hope.

Needing a distraction, Ethan walked over to a shelf of rock covered in yellow wax, the candles long since burned out. His fingertips caressed the smooth surface, the wax soft from the warming sun. Breaking off a piece, he rolled it gently in his hands, the counterclockwise motion soothing his angst.

"Yes, Barnabas, perhaps I am. But … but it's a journey only I can trek. Alone."

"I hear what you are saying, Mr. Et-dan, but you are never really alone."

Goose bumps prickled up Ethan's arms.

"Hey!" Janus yelled, sticking his head out from behind a

jog in the rocks. "I hate to break up your little philosophical discussion, but I think I've found a way down to where the cave entrance is supposed to be. C'mon."

Ethan raised his eyebrows at Barnabas and gave a shrug. They came to the edge of a precipice in time to watch a red backpack slide down a narrow spiraling lip of rock. Both followed without question. The sunlight disappeared, hidden by a carpet of vines and an overhang of damp, mossy rocks. Janus was nowhere to be seen.

"Over here." A voice shot out from a stygian void, then a beam of light. "I think this is it." Ethan and Barnabas slipped on their headlamps and walked into the darkness.

"Watch your step. It's slippery."

Ethan crouched along, his light a mere spindle of revelation. The path inclined slightly and then the rocks became dry and jagged.

"You can stand up now," he heard Janus say. Ethan adjusted his lamp toward the ceiling, now eight feet above them, thick with a blanket of black cocoons.

"Bats." Ethan's yell bounced off the walls.

The colony took flight, streaming down at them. All three men fell to the ground, evading the onslaught, attentive to the explosive whirl and woosh of wings veering past their heads and out toward the entryway.

Ethan lay with his face on the rock, his headlamp gone. He spewed a mouthful of aged cave and rich expletives.

"Sorry," Janus said. "Thought you'd recognize the smell. Forgot you wouldn't know." He stood up, shaking dirt and bat droppings off his clothes. "Caves have bats."

"*Farang*," Ethan shouted, making sure Janus heard him. He began groping over the sea of bat guano pellets for his headlamp.

Janus remained focused on his obsession. "Well, now that we're alone, we can figure out if there are more openings from here." By Janus's beam of light, Ethan could tell he was already searching just above the cave floor. "Just pick a wall." Janus waved his hand. "And scan it slowly."

"An opening?" Ethan disliked the sound of that, but he couldn't argue. Without warning, invisible hands reached into his throat and clamped off his esophagus. Fighting for breath, he sat up on his haunches, his screams lost in an empty wheeze. The nausea hit him, churning his stomach like a giant turbine rivaling the normal flow of things.

"Yeah." Janus's voice was steady, unaware of Ethan's predicament. "Big or small, it doesn't matter. Could even be in the floor so be careful."

"Help! Help!" Nobody seemed to hear Ethan's voiceless cries. His head began to throb, a low rumble. Only the rumbling was not coming from his head but from the cave floor. The rocks beneath Ethan quivered like jumping beans, then rippled like ocean waves.

"Earthquake!" Ethan heard Barnabas shout above what sounded like a locomotive bearing down on them. "We must go."

"You got it." Janus scrambled for the exit. "C'mon, Ethan."

He was unable to answer.

"Ethan," Janus called, again, and then again. "Where are you, Ethan?" His voice became more and more desperate.

Ethan mouthed silent words as his breathing shallowed, his whole body sucked into a tornado of pain. Then without warning, the cave gave way under him and he began sliding. Down. Down. Down.

Ethan plunged into oblivion, a frenetic flail dancer at the mercy of nature, still fighting to catch his breath. The chute beneath him turned slick as he accelerated into a black, timeless hole. His body turned numb, then bouyant, then simply odd. *Maintain your self-awareness. Gain control.* The only thing he could control was his reaction to this … this … reality? Unconsciousness? Dream? *What is this?* He had no answers, his dreams of late so real.

Like a puck gliding on an airhockey table, he descended for what felt like hours. The tight squeeze on his airways released. He sucked in a breath. Then another. He was alive! The pain behind his eyes. The swirling in his stomach. It was all gone. The music theme from "The Twilight Zone" entered his head. *Cut it out!* He didn't like where this dream was going.

His falling slowed—or so he thought. The slide shifted to an easy rocking. Just at that stage where he could sense a lulling sleep, the tunnel began filling with water.

His body jerked, from his pseudo-sleep. He tried to sit up, almost spun upside down, and then remembered where he was. The water under him flowed cool and fresh. Was that a pinhole of light up ahead? Or were his rods and cones playing tricks on him?

Slowly the pinhole grew, and soft light streamed up, if it was up at all. A resonant churning replaced the low rumble and he found himself out of the chute and free-falling with a cascading waterfall into a deep pool of effervescence, his body plummeting but not touching bottom.

Ethan's body hung almost weightlessly a foot off the bottom, the law of gravity seemingly subverted. The smooth stones covering the pool floor appeared to be lit by an inner light source, like multi-colored fairy lights. With no thought for his oxygen need, Ethan hovered there, captivated by the beauty. Slowly a woman's face appeared among the rocks, a vague, swirling, alluring face. Completely captivated by her glowing emerald eyes, Ethan watched her hair swirl around her face. But then her features shifted to a grotesque apparition of ink and shadows with angry ash eyes and fanged teeth.

Completely unhinged by the hideous contortion, Ethan opened his mouth and screamed. His desperate cries only led to gulping water, a life-threatening amount and he knew it. He kicked hard in the direction of a more promising light source.

The light grew until he broke the water's surface. He sucked in air. Life. Spotting the closest bank, he backstroked frantically in that direction, his eyes closed to calm himself. *Janus. Barnabas. Where are they?* He opened his eyes, focusing on the waterfall, expecting to see two more tumbling bodies. None came. He was alone, all alone. *I need to wake from this dream. Why haven't I?* In his dreams, falling always ended with jerking awake.

When his head scraped the sandy bottom of the pond's edge, Ethan turned and crawled up onto the lush grass, glistening with tiny droplets of waterfall spray. Closing his eyes, he rolled over and spread-eagled his body on the green blanket. He shook from the inside out, as if releasing all the tension from his body and his mind. Each limb, each appendage, had been asleep his whole life, but now each nerve was waking up to a much-anticipated morning.

Did he hear music? For a brief second he thought he did, and then it was gone. He flexed his fingers, swiveled his head, wiggled his toes. Nothing broken. He rotated his ankles inside his waterlogged boots. All good

Opening his eyes, he looked straight up into thousands of delicate, slender leaves fluttering on pendulous branches. He sucked in a breath and reached up, splaying his fingers across the leaves.

He knew this tree well. The weeping willow. As a child, Ethan would hide away under one in the corner of his yard. It had always been his place of peace and protection. He lay there, spellbound by the tiny fingers of sunlight bending in and out of the fluttering leaves. *What is this place?* He slipped out from under the tree and, remembering about his boots and socks, he rolled up his pant legs, freed up his feet, and eased them back into the tingly water. Small goldfish darted about just inches from his toes. *What the …* He looked up. *This pool. I know this pool, the one from my dream, with the ghost and the ebony girl. I must be dreaming.*

Though the pool was the same, the surrounding vegetation had changed. Gone was the menacing jungle and in its place, along with the one weeping willow, grew poplar, birch, spruce, and pine from the boreal plains of Alberta. The foreboding vines and blackened orchids had been replaced by fescue grasses, wild roses, and buttercups.

Nothing else was similar. Everything had a luster that Ethan couldn't explain, as if someone had washed the whole world with a translucent layer of metallic paint. Not really gold, nor silver, but more like a rainbow of reflective twinkling. Yet not quite. Words failed him.

He expected that, at any minute, the little girl with the jet-black hair would come floating down from the sky. The sky. Even the blue of the sky scintillated as if in a permanent state of aurora borealis.

What? Where? How?

A baritone voice trumpeted from behind him. "Welcome."

Ethan vaulted up, his body twisting. He lost his footing,

stumbled, and fell backwards, wet all over again. Not wishing to show his embarrassment, Ethan half-lifted his face and stuttered, "Wh-who are you?"

"Welcome." The man smiled. "My name is Malachi. Welcome to Eden."

CHAPTER FIFTEEN

Swollen rain droplet
Clinging to delicate web;
Storm erupts! Time shifts
To timeless, word to wordless,
Sense to non-sense.

Ethan couldn't believe his ears. Forgetting his angst, forgetting his crab-walk position in the middle of a pool of water, forgetting the glistening fish darting around his sprawled arms, he dwelt on one word and one word alone. Eden. *Had he heard right? He was in Eden? Janus's Eden?* In Ethan's mind this dream had taken a twisted turn from odd to completely bizarro. *C'mon, Ethan, wake up. Wake up!*

"Can I help you out of the water?" Malachi extended his hand.

"Huh?" Ethan glanced Malachi's way. *Do I want this apparition to touch me?* "No. Don't want your help. No," he repeated and wobbled up, sloshing his way onto the shore.

"I did not mean to startle you." Malachi peered at him. "I thought you would have heard my arrival."

"Heard your arrival? Over the booming waterfall? There's no way in h ..." The word froze in his throat when he looked into Malachi's eyes, as if looking into the innocence of a young child, yet physically the man appeared to be in his thirties.

"In your mind? Were you not made aware of my entrance into your perimeter space?" Malachi spoke slowly, as though searching for the right words.

"My perimeter space? Ha. I think it's *your* mind that's left the building." Ethan smiled at his own cleverness. Malachi's expression did not change. "Well, I guess if you're asking me what I think you're asking me, then the answer is 'no.' No, I didn't feel you sneak up on me." Ethan emphasized the word "feel."

"Hmm." Malachi's questioning brow unwrinkled. "Well, then I apologize to you. Sorry."

"It's okay, man. I'm just a little shaken up. This dream is beyond confusing."

Malachi didn't reply. His piercing blue eyes took on a far-away look. He was of average height, well-proportioned, and muscular, a full, well-kept beard hiding what looked like a prominent chin. He appeared not much older than Ethan, except for his eyes. His eyes were that of a sage, commanding and wise. The oddest part about him was his loosely fitted tunic made of a gauzy material that reflected the colors of his surroundings, almost as if you could see through it. And yet not.

"Oh, you think this is a dream." Malachi nodded. "Please excuse me if I do not always understand. Your words can have multiple meanings and I do not always get the gist of the … of what, I think you would call 'figurative speech'."

"Figurative speech?" Ethan suddenly remembered Janus's reference to the rabbit hole in Alice's Wonderland world. *That must be it. I must have fallen down that rabbit hole in my dream.* "Okay. Sure. Well then, of course, my figurative speech has you confused. Maybe if I talked like the Mad Hatter you'd catch on." Ethan laughed at the joke. Again, Malachi just stood there with the same innocent smile on his face.

"Who are you again?" Ethan thought he might as well attempt to view this dream world through Alice's looking glass.

"As I said, my name is Malachi, and this," he stretched his arms out wide, "is Eden."

Ethan arched his eyebrows. "Huh. Not names I recognize from Lewis Carroll's world."

"Lewis Carroll?"

"Yeah, you know, the author of *Alice's Adventures in Wonderland*? Don't tell me you've never heard of that book?"

Again Malachi's eyes glazed over briefly. "I believe it is an imaginative narrative." He turned to Ethan. "Am I correct in this conclusion?"

"Sure. Sure you are."

"Thank you." Malachi lifted his eyes to the sky.

"Huh? Thank you? What the hell's going on?"

"Again, my apologies. Your speech and references are more difficult to comprehend than I thought. I am ill-prepared to converse it seems."

"Ill-prepared? What's with the funny talk? So outdated."

"Precisely. That is what I am trying to say. I 'talk funny'." Malachi grinned, his perfect teeth pearls of white. "The use of language obscures meaning."

"Now I'm lost. Are we just talking in circles?" More and more Ethan was sure he *had* fallen down a rabbit hole. "But you still didn't answer my question. You said thank you."

"Yes, I did."

"To whom? There's nobody here but you and me. Wait." Ethan took one step toward Malachi and looked at the side of his head. "Are you wearing an earpiece?"

"An earpiece? Could you please define that word?"

"Yes, I *can* define that word." Ethan's voice began to vibrate in agitation. When Malachi kept smiling, Ethan shook his head and answered his question. "Well, it's a device you put in your ear so that someone can communicate with you using radio waves that travel through air. In other words, you can hear them talking to you."

Malachi cocked his head. "Interesting."

"What is? An earpiece? What century are you living in?" Ethan realized that Malachi had distracted him from his original question.

"No." Malachi gave his head a quick shake. "I find it interesting that you need an earpiece to communicate with others. Melody gave me general information about your kind, but I still have so much to learn."

"Melody?" Ethan latched on to the name. *Now we're getting somewhere.* "Is that who you're talking to? Now who the heck's this Melody and why's she feeding you info about me?" The anxiety began to swirl in Ethan's stomach. He swallowed hard.

Again, Malachi turned his head away for just a few seconds before he replied. "I said, 'about your kind.' I was not referring to you specifically. And yes, I am communicating with Melody, but I am not yet sure how to explain in words who *she* is. I did not realize how difficult this would be, trying to use words."

"So much talk about words. Words are words. That's how communication happens."

"Perhaps that is true in the world you came from," Malachi shook his head, "but this is not that world."

"I was right. I am right." Ethan stumbled backward to the water's edge. "How'd my mind come up with a dream like this? And when will it end?" Ethan pinched the skin of his forearm tightly in an attempt to wake himself. The pain had no effect, a mere mosquito bite. "This dream is getting weirder by the minute." He bent over, his hands on his thighs, his dripping hair falling in strands around his face.

Malachi leaned toward him. "I believe you are experiencing fear."

"Ha! You think? Phobic nightmares are my specialty, it seems." Ethan raised his head.

"Phobic nightmares? Phobic nightmares." Malachi turned his head a notch to the right. "Again, my comprehension skills are lacking. I can offer you serenity and hope, even courage, all in opposition to the ... the disharmony."

His tender voice did help calm Ethan's hammering heart. "Just give me a minute. I'll be okay. Just gotta remind myself that this is all a dream. Then I can just play along."

Malachi waited in silence.

Ethan took a few deep breaths and stood up, forcing a half-smile. "I'm good."

"Then I think we should return home."

"Home?"

"Home. My home. Is that not a word you understand?"

"Understand? Yes. Connect with? Not sure. Seems I've been ... oh, never mind." Not a topic Ethan wished to discuss and, thankfully, Malachi didn't press him.

"I can offer you some dry clothes and something to eat, perhaps? I am a gifted cook." Malachi turned away from Ethan. "Then we will both be more prepared to converse." Malachi pointed to a wide, grassy walkway, one that Ethan could swear wasn't there a minute ago.

For the first time, Ethan looked beyond his immediate

surroundings and sucked in a breath, wide-eyed and sure he'd just stepped into a painting like the ones from Jill's "Impressionist Art" calendar that once hung in their kitchen.

Beyond the pond lay a wide valley, the waterfall a final spill from the rocky valley wall, although the mountain range behind the falls rose gently. Nothing like the Rockies. Looking down the path, scattered trees stood tall, pristine, the floor below dotted with dancing blue flax and orange lilies. Nothing that unusual.

No, it was the palette of color that shocked all his senses, boldly vibrant to the eye, on the verge of singing in his ears, an ambrosial aroma in his nostrils. Opening his mouth and half-sticking out his tongue, he swore he could taste the air. Almost like gulping cold, refreshing water on a hot day. But more. Even his skin twitched with new life. A warm breeze lifted the leaves on the trees, as if singing them alive in four-part harmony. The leaves shimmered in response, much like the silver poplars on the prairies, only it seemed these leaves were talking, whispering his name. Goose bumps once again, but he couldn't look away.

"Let us depart." Malachi's voice brought Ethan back to "Earth." Side-by-side they walked down the shaded path, Ethan still sloshing along noisily in his water-logged hiking garb, his bare feet massaged by the soft, humus-like soil. Malachi ambled in near silence in his loosely sashed tunic and leather sandals. On occasion, Ethan looked at Malachi out of the corner of his eye. Malachi didn't seem to notice, a permanent smile chiseled on his bronzed face.

The tree clusters thinned and opened up to a full sweep of lush golden fields swaying in a light wind. The sensuous, enigmatic wonder displayed before Ethan weighed him down and yet also filled him with a lightness of spirit and soul. Under the full force of the sun's stirring warmth, the air became more alive, if that were even possible. Ethan gave up trying to find words to describe his surroundings. He inhaled slowly, the musty smell of earth tingling in his nostrils, the sweet harmonies of original bird songs dancing on his eardrums. He swept his right hand over the velvety pink peonies now lining the trail. Like the ones in his ex-mother-in-law's garden, yet more fragrant. It was as if he was awakening from years of Rip Van Winkle sleep.

Malachi hummed a tune. Ethan listened and, although he didn't recognize the song, he appreciated its cadence.

The fields came to a distinct end on the edge of a town of log cabins. The houses wound for miles along a lazy river. But these were not simple settlements. In fact, they were nothing like Ethan had ever seen before, each building unique in shape and size, each entranceway crowned with an intricate carving hewn into the archway, each door prismatic, reflecting a distinct hue. *Impressive. Where did my subconscious come up with these ideas?*

Malachi stopped humming. "My house is close by, since I spend my days in the fields."

Ethan said nothing. They walked past a few houses, each with its own gate, although not really a gate because none of the yards had dividing fences, making a gate pointless. But rather, each yard front had a large ornamental arbor covered in various flowers and vines.

Malachi turned, ducked below the trailing bell-shaped flowers of one of them, and continued along a pebbled path lined with recognizable purple and yellow-faced pansies guiding them up onto a wide porch stretching around the house front.

"My wife Seshat is not here." Malachi clicked open the front door. "She is at work. Work. We do not name it that. I think 'service' would be more applicable."

"Service. Right." Ethan smiled, still surprised at the creativity of his own imagination.

"As I said earlier, cooking is one of my gifts, so I do most of it in our home." *There was that word again.* Shaking the thought off, Ethan followed Malachi through the house and out the back to a large outdoor kitchen complete with a long charcoal grill and a well-used stone oven.

"This is your kitchen?" For such a stylish building, Ethan had expected a modern kitchen complete with all the latest stainless-steel appliances and gadgets. "I think my mind is playing tricks on me." Ethan scanned the room. "This is not what I expected it would create."

"Hmm." Malachi stepped down to the terra-cotta brick patio laid in an intricate herringbone pattern, the bricks softened with age. Ethan could appreciate such skillful work. "Melody gave me an idea of your world." Malachi stood at the grill. "But more like a sense of it. I could not fully comprehend the word pictures that floated into my mind. Machines that would emit hot brew and heat cold food. Untranslatable images, I think." He turned away from the grill where he had been re-igniting the coals with a familiar ease. "But I guess that explains your dilemma, does it not?"

His clothes already dry from the sun, Ethan settled into one of the many over-stuffed chairs that surrounded a large table of rich mahogany, also skillfully carved and embossed with slender veins of burnished metal. *Is that gold?* Trying not to be distracted by the foreign surroundings, Ethan went right back to the question he had asked back at the pool. "So, can you tell me who this Melody person is? I mean, now that we're here?"

"Melody. Yes. I hope my definition can satisfy you." Malachi removed a bowl of pre-cut vegetables from what looked like an ice-chest, tossing them onto the grill with one hand, while cracking two eggs into them with the other. He sprinkled it all with items from small wooden bowls lined up alongside the grill top, wiped his hands on a florid, woven towel he'd wrapped around his waist, and sat down across from Ethan.

Ethan found Malachi's ease of movement mesmerizing. In fact, everything in this dream mesmerized him, including the vibrancy of unidentifiable colors and the shimmering that still permeated it all, the grass and trees, the sky and clouds, even the logs of the house.

"Are you communicating with someone?" Malachi asked.

"Huh?" Ethan returned to the present conversation. "No. Why'd you ask that? I was just deep in thought."

"Oh, well your facial expression reminded me of a person who is conversing with someone not in sight."

"You mean someone invisible?"

"No, I mean someone not in visual range, like someone in the house for instance."

"Well, we can't do that without talking or, I guess, phone texting." Ethan finally clued in. "Wait. You mean you can do that? As in telepathy? As in talking to someone who's not right here? Like, say, your wife?"

"Yes." Malachi nodded as though to say, of course.

"No shit. Fascinating. Can't do that in the real world. The dream world, well, that's another story, I guess."

"That explains much, for both me and you." Malachi smiled. "But now that I know you at least can define telepathy, however simple, explaining Melody's means of communication will not be as difficult."

"Shoot." Ethan was anxious to hear Malachi's explanation.

Malachi paused for those typical few seconds, then smiled. "Oh, you are asking me to go ahead and explain. Your colloquialisms discompose me." He rose from his chair, pulling two tall hand-blown glasses from a shelf above the grill, filling them with water from a large casket. "I apologize for my inadequate hosting." He placed a glass in front of Ethan. "Your visit is unprecedented, but I sensed your thirst."

Ethan gave Malachi a puzzled look, then realized that he was right. "I am thirsty." He guzzled the whole glass.

Malachi picked up Ethan's glass. "Allow me to continue." He poured him another. "Melody. You made reference to her as a person. She is that, and yet not."

"Oh?" The concept of ghosts still lingered in Ethan's mind.

"For one, she is neither a she nor a he."

"Transgender? In Eden?" Ethan smiled. "That's boss."

Malachi drifted off for a second, the wrinkles on his brow becoming a familiar sight for Ethan. Then he looked at Ethan again. "I must be honest. I am easily distracted by your argot."

"My argot? What the heck's that?"

"Oh dear." Malachi sighed. "Incorrect word. I simply meant, by the way you talk. But," Malachi smiled, "but this too helps me explain how we communicate."

"Explain away."

"So, you used the word 'transgender.' I am not familiar with that word. But even before I had formed a question in my mind about its definition, Melody heard my questioning spirit, aware that I had no past knowledge of that word. So, even while I was searching for the right connection in my neural pathways, she began filling my mind with relatable terms."

"Seriously? From the little I've read on neural networks, that's crazy." Ever the skeptic, Ethan remembered, *this is but a dream.*

"Well, that is not the full story because words only divulge partial information."

"Huh?" The aroma rising from the grill provoked hunger pangs that overpowered any other thoughts. He took a deep breath, hoping he'd remember every aspect of this world.

"Enough. You are hungry. And I need to remember what it is like to be young to this world. Something I have not been for many ages. I also accept that you need time. Again, a concept indefinable for us." Malachi got up from his chair, walked over to the grill, gripped a long-handled spatula and scooped all the roasted vegetables onto a long, wooden platter.

"You can read my mind, can't you?" Ethan eyes were glued to the sizzling morsels.

"I would not call it 'reading.' Again, that involves words. Nothing is that specific." Malachi placed the tray in front of Ethan, handing him a silver spoon. "It is more a sound in my head. I hear your state. I have already learned that your emotions are closely connected to your physical condition, things like thirst and hunger. Yet, this learning, and what Melody divulges, is not done in words. Rather, she transposes it into a musical note or bar or whole tune, to explain the meaning behind your words. Not the most adequate answer, but the best I can offer."

Ethan looked up from his plate, swallowing his first bite. "Music that speaks. I get that. *And* in a melody," he added, pleased with his play on words. Again, Malachi didn't get the joke, but Ethan didn't care. His thoughts were on the food. The tastes played on his tongue like a rave of electronic beats. He stared at each spoonful. It was the most delicious dish he'd ever eaten.

Malachi made himself a plate, a playful grin on his face. Then he sat down across from Ethan. "You know, I am learning in this, too, learning about humanity in your world."

"Really." The sarcasm in Ethan's only word between bites was lost on Malachi. Ethan concluded that Melody chose not to translate his tone.

"Yes, I am learning that emotions seem to control much of what you say and do. Many of them are so, so off-key."

Ethan stopped chewing.

"Would you say that is a fair assessment?" Malachi's tone was innocuous.

Within seconds, Ethan watched Malachi's expression shift from one of intensity to one of joy and lightness. He stood up and, turning his whole body toward the side of the house, laughed.

That's rude. And annoying. This dream is toying with my mind. Ethan's eyes followed Malachi's, unsure of what to expect. From around the corner a young girl burst into Ethan's dream world, her long, black curls bouncing off her slight shoulders, her violet eyes shining with delight, as she skipped up to Malachi and gave him a big hug.

Ethan's jaw dropped. His spoon dropped. He squeezed his eyes shut and then slowly re-opened them. *It's her. The girl in my dream, calling me to come, and offering peace and hope.* "Ebony."

CHAPTER SIXTEEN

Loss from leaving,
Life of lament.
Look.
Linger.
Learn.
Listen.
A new song approaches.

Not acknowledging Ethan's whisper, or even his presence, Malachi and the girl Ethan called "Ebony" stood there looking at each other, the girl's hands dancing about. Their facial expressions played through a series of emotional movements. The girl half-twirled her torso back and forth, the colors of her tunic coming alive in the sun's splendor. His dream had not been long, but Ethan stood by his belief that the two girls were one and the same.

Aware he'd been staring, Ethan straightened up in his chair and returned to his platter.

Ten minutes later, the girl turned to Ethan. "Hello." She hesitated. "Daddy tells me you are our guest."

"I … I guess."

After more awkward silence, at least in Ethan's mind, she turned to her daddy, giggled, and ran up the back stairs and into the house.

"What was that?" Ethan asked, forgetting all about his dream connection.

"Pardon?"

"Your joke. Were you making fun of me? Telepathically? Because I'm *not* telepathic?"

Malachi looked wide-eyed at Ethan. "No Ethan." He turned to give Ethan his full attention, his eyes softening.

Is that pity? I don't want anyone's pity.

"Again, I am sorry." Malachi sat down to finish his lunch. "I did not realize that you might consider our behavior to be inharmonious. My daughter and I were communicating about her morning at," he paused, "at what you would call school." Malachi's eyes twinkled. "She told me a story about her friend who brought her pet lamb to school because today the lesson was on sheep-herding. But the lamb did not take very well to the excitement of the children, resulting in pandemonium. Must have been a funny scene." Malachi chuckled. "And then I asked her to say hello to you. With words. I reminded her of your … your uniqueness."

"You *reminded* her?" Ethan asked, not liking the implication of that word. "Does that mean she already knew about me?"

"Yes, a little. Does that surprise you?"

"What do you think?"

Malachi gave Ethan a puzzled look. "Sarcasm. A new word. Out of tune."

Ethan laughed. "Out of tune. Yeah. Why not? This whole dream is."

Malachi smiled. "In answer to your previous question, Melody informed me of your soon arrival and asked if I would be your guide, a mediator, if you will. Knowing it would affect my family, we mused over the possibility. So yes, she knew."

"You mused over the possibility?" Ethan shook his head. "I think you should've practiced your word choices. Or did Melody make you do that, too? I mean, your daughter didn't seem too sure of herself."

Though Malachi's eyes rested on Ethan, he took on that faraway look once again. It both unnerved and intrigued Ethan.

"We actually did practice, as you called it, though obviously not enough. But you should know that Melody never forces decisions on us. The choice is ours."

"And boy, did you make the wrong one." Ethan raised his glass in a scoffing cheer.

Malachi ignored the cynicism and replied to Ethan's prior comment. "And yes, speaking is more laborious for the children. Gimmel hesitated, perhaps in having to use words or perhaps because in her mind, she cannot grasp your uniqueness, so I told her she could go. But then to make her laugh I mentioned that she needed to be careful when they study ornithology because Rufus would cause even more pandemonium than a lamb. I love her laugh."

"Rufus? Gimmel?" Ethan blurted the words, trying to control the uneasy emotions rising in his stomach.

"Sorry. Again. My words do assume that you have a context in your mind. I think you are going to become quite weary of my apologies."

"Believe me," Ethan sighed, "I'm just as frickin' frustrated as you."

"I perceive that." Malachi rested his spoon on his now-empty platter. "Rufus is Gimmel's pet raven and, as you may have surmised, Gimmel is my daughter. She thought my joke funny. You, however, did not. Your response sounded dissonant, paranoid, I think, is the word you might use. Have you no peace?"

Ethan didn't answer, the question too personal. *Why am I surrounded by people who ask about my inner self? Always scratching away at what they see on the outside, even in my dreams? I am so tired.*

Malachi stopped the questioning and began clearing away the dishes. "You have been given an abundance of information. Your mind must be weary." He picked up the platter. "Perhaps what you require is a rest. We have a room for you upstairs. Or, perhaps a river walk would be more beneficial. The path winds through the whole town. Following it will make it easy for you to return home."

"Home?" Ethan said, his mind racing. *Perhaps if I follow the river, this dream will end, and I can really get home. But then, where is home for this farang?*

"Well, I meant back here, to this home."

"Right." Ethan sighed. *Are these more tricks of my subconscious? Maybe I should rest. Maybe if I fell asleep here, I would wake up back in Myanmar. But then, maybe it's the river trail that will get me back. Another choice. Why so many choices? All alone in my choices. C'mon, Ethan, decide!* He sat quietly, wishing someone else would choose for him.

"Responsibility can be a scary thing."

Ethan frowned. "You reading my mind again?" He gritted his teeth.

"No." Malachi raised his eyebrows. "Again, Melody is offering me conceptual chords with a specific emotional baseline. She knows your needs. Be encouraged."

"Enough." Ethan barked the word, pressing his hands firmly on the table, and rising abruptly from his chair. Forcing his anger down, he fell back into the chair. "I've had enough, enough of this dream." The anxiety constricting his throat, he quaffed the last of his water, and, without thinking, slammed the glass down on the table. "Just, just show me to that room. I need to lie down."

* * *

Ethan spent most of the afternoon trying to get back to that elusive place he called home, though he knew it was more like "ground zero." He did fall asleep, sprawled out on the softest, down-filled mattress he had ever lain on. His dreams, however, only made him more anxious. He found himself back in reality, having an out-of-body experience, hovering over a surreal vignette of people in his life: Cassie crying, with Jill, tears in her own eyes, holding her close; Janus and Barnabas hunched over on small wooden chairs, all in a cold, foreign room, heads down, and then Ben arriving, not saying a word.

The oddest part for Ethan was the presence of an unknown man, a man standing off in the corner watching each person, also teary-eyed, his arms bent out at the elbows, his palms facing the room as if pushing against an invisible wall, yet his stance was one of strength and tranquility. Ethan hovered above, calling names, waving his arms frantically. No response, his presence merely phantasmal.

He woke. His heart beat like a bullet train, the twisted sheets damp with sweat. *Is a dream within a dream possible?* He lay there for a while, gaining composure. Turning his head, he noticed a note scrawled on the bedside table.

Here is a fresh change of clothes for you: a tunic, a sash, and some sandals. Seshat also thought you might wish to refresh your skin, so I have provided you with a towel. The water room is on the main floor. I also am sorry for not being present to tend to your needs. I am out in the fields examining the grain. Salutations, Malachi.

"Salutations." Ethan mocked. *Archaic, even in his writing.* He tossed the note across the room. He didn't like it when others predicted his needs. Still, Malachi was right. He sighed, grabbed the towel, and headed downstairs.

After a refreshing shower, he made a conscious decision to put on the awkward tunic. In his plan to go for a walk, he preferred anonymity to questioning stares. The weightless material slipped over his head with silky ease, the sash a perfect length. The sandals, too, were comfortable though a little long. A bright pink band to pull back his hair completed the ensemble. He laughed at how silly he must look, like a glimmering prophet of old, though he found no mirrors to support his assumption. He had also hoped to shave, his facial hair beginning to itch, but found no razors. He wondered if all the men in Eden had thick facial hair like Malachi.

The lightly-pebbled path just outside Malachi's house followed the unassuming river. It reminded Ethan more of the Bow River that flowed through Calgary, than the North Saskatchewan that ran through Edmonton. This river's banks were low, its water semi-opaque. It looked deep. As he walked, he passed a number of people, most of them in groups. They all appeared human, offering him easy smiles and friendly nods, like small-town Saskatchewanians. He was half-expecting a forced conversation about the weather, the crops, or hockey. One of them, a young woman with flowing auburn hair, even looked familiar, though he couldn't connect her with anyone from his past. Maybe it was her backpack, which looked like a military tactical pack, that he somehow remembered. Or maybe it was more her city-dweller aloofness. He couldn't figure it out.

The more people he passed, the more he wondered if they

were all using their psyche voices on him. He liked the term psyche. A good word for this dream's telepathic language.

In the end, the walk proved fruitless, just like his sleep. He remained in Eden, unable to find any hint of a rabbit-hole return to reality. *Why is this happening? Why can't I get home?*

He returned to Malachi's house, hoping to find a beer in the fridge or something harder in the cupboards. Nothing. He sighed. Relieved.

Unable to sit still, he snooped about, searching for a television or a stereo system or even a guitar to distract him, anything to fill the pervading silence. Even the usual voices arguing in his head remained silent. He needed something to fill the void yet found nothing.

As if in answer to his need, a soft classical piano piece entered his thoughts, sounding somewhat like Beethoven's "Moonlight Sonata," one of the songs that Jill used to play to soothe Cassie. But the note progressions had been tweaked. As the music grew, a serene presence filled Ethan's mind, then said softly, *"I am here—in your silence."* His inner senses somehow awakened, he inhaled the scent of night jasmine from his guesthouse's garden in Chiang Mai; he tasted the pungent basil of his favorite *khrapao* at the back of his tongue; he heard the distant rumble of an approaching prairie thunderstorm; he felt Cassie's small, warm hand curl up in his. Ethan caught himself opening and closing his hand. Freaked out by the whole experience, he half-ran out the front door, needing to get away from the house. Not knowing where to go, he headed for the fields, hoping to find Malachi.

The fields stretched on for miles. Fearing he might get lost, Ethan stopped searching after an hour. Then an idea came to him. He'd return to the pool of water he landed in and from there try to find some way back up the waterfall, back into the cave, back to Earth. He remembered the path, his anticipation and excitement building with each step. *This is the way home.*

His own song lyrics barreled down on him: "*Without a destination, / Without a home.*" Fiercely upsetting words. *Is that where he was going to end up? No destination? No home?* He began jogging, hoping to empty his mind of all thought. Once he saw a section of the pond, a reflection of twinkling silver in the distance, he picked up his pace but even before reaching the shoreline, he braked, stumbling forward as if his feet had hit a concrete curb. His waterfall had disappeared. It was gone. Completely gone. The dry cliff had left no indication of a porthole. None. His connection to the real world had disappeared.

Dazed, Ethan staggered to the water's edge and sat down, sticking his feet in the cool water, sandals and all. His mind hissed with anxious static. He still believed Eden to be a dream world, yet he was powerless against the dream. It was taking over reality. *Help. I need help.*

The same euphonic piano notes rose above the noise. His skin tingled at the awareness of an invisible presence, though not a ghostly one. No, this one brought peace and stillness. It made him want to release his fear in tears. He fought them back, half-expecting to hear his mother's voice of reprimand but hoping to hear Cassie's voice of encouragement. Nothing. No one came to offer advice, compelling him to choose one way or another, one emotion over another. No. He alone had to choose his responses to these circumstances, in silence.

And yet the music lingered, barely audible. *Please, whoever, whatever, you are, no more silence.* His reply was inaudible. He guffawed thinking about who he'd been trying to communicate with. He wanted to hide, so he crept under the weeping willow and leaned back on the tree, his skin cool against the smooth, warm bark. He stretched his legs to enjoy the cushion of grass.

The tune followed him and, in the quiet, Ethan began sensing these words. *"I am Melody, your halcyon."*

"Melody." Ethan tipped his head. "Malachi's Melody?"

"Yes, that is who I am, to all, not just Malachi." Her words serenaded through his mind on the notes of the sonata, tranquil and melodic. *"Silence is your choice."*

What? Seriously? That is not what Ethan needed to hear. *How is silence my choice? I've never had a choice. Stop the lies!*

Instantly, the voice, the melody, the peace, vanished from his mind. In the strained moment, Ethan's whole being became a chasm of bottomless, emptiness. An emptiness he'd never known before. He closed his eyes, his hands clutching the grass.

"She contacted you." Malachi's voice broke in from the other side of the wall of leaves, a blasting bugle compared to Melody's soothing softness.

Ethan chose not to speak.

"I am confused by your discord."

"My discord?" Ethan spewed, half-opening his eyes.

Malachi dipped under the branches and sat down at Ethan's knees, placing a basket of produce beside him. Ethan, conscious of his minimal clothing, tucked the tunic under his knees, though Malachi didn't seem to notice or care.

"She will return. You need not fear." Malachi handed Ethan a bright yellow, perfectly shaped apple. Ethan accepted the offer, Golden Delicious being his favorite.

"How do you know?" Ethan leaned forward. "And who's to say I want her to return?" He took a bite of the apple. Never had he tasted an apple so crisp, so bursting with flavor. Catching the juice dripping down his chin, he stared at the piece of fruit in his hand, wondering if it really was an apple.

Malachi laughed, full and hearty, his white teeth a bold contrast under his black mustache. "Thought you'd like that. My preference also. Like a symphony in the mouth. And yes, that is a simile. I composed that one while walking down the path."

Ethan couldn't help but notice how proud Malachi looked. "Funny." Ethan frowned. "How difficult forming figures of speech can be for you." He took another bite. "And yet, you didn't answer my question about Melody."

"That is true, Ethan. Simply know that once Melody has found a connecting network, no matter how fine the thread, she will always return. Her pursuit of our minds is relentless." Malachi gave Ethan a big smile. "You will see."

"That sounds like coercion."

"Coercion. Again, your thoughts appear to be so, so inharmonious."

"Inharmonious?" Ethan sat up. "You wanna hear about inharmonious?"

"No, Ethan, I do not." Malachi shook his head. "I am aware of your grim past."

"You're aware?" Ethan snorted. "Don't tell me. Melody. Am I right?"

"Yes, but again, not the specifics. I hear sour, jarring noise coming from murky, lifeless shadows, and the stench of broken relationships."

"Enough," Ethan interrupted. "Unless you're trying to depress me."

Malachi dropped his eyes. "You are right, Ethan. I cannot imagine what life has been like for you. I meant no harm.

There is much I still do not understand."

"Okay." Ethan took a deep breath. "I just don't like talking about it."

"From what I have learned, your world sounds so harsh. Without peace. Remember that you, too, are foreign to us. Do you think an arrival like yours is a regular occurrence?" Malachi gave Ethan a look of curiosity. "It is not. As far as I know, you are the first." Ethan remained quiet. Malachi continued. "And as far as Melody is concerned, she does not coerce. You cried out to her, so she came. You told her to leave, so she left. She will never impose, though she is always listening for our call. In that she is relentless."

Ethan replayed his conversation with Melody in his mind, realizing that Malachi spoke truth. He had called out for help and she did leave when he commanded her to. "You are right." Ethan nodded, with reservation.

"She is also mysterious."

"Mysterious? Even to you?"

"Does that worry you? Not being able to define her or her plans?" Malachi cocked his head, as if searching Ethan's face for the answer. "From what I have learned of your world, I thought you would appreciate a good mystery. Is it not like one of those novels you mentioned previously?"

"Sure, but that's fiction. In reality, I'm not a fan of mysteries."

"Peculiar, you are. Maybe that is why you have not asked the one question I expected you would ask straightaway."

Choking on the large chunk of apple in his mouth, Ethan began coughing uncontrollably.

Malachi pulled out a waterskin from his basket and handed it to him. "My apologies. I did not intend to so disrupt your enjoyment of the apple."

Ethan took a swig of water and wiped his chin. "You definitely disrupted my enjoyment." He pitched the apple core into the pond from under the tree.

Malachi's eyebrows flew up.

"What?" Ethan scoffed. "It's a fruit. It's biodegradable."

Malachi said nothing.

"So, what's the question I *should've* already asked?" When Malachi opened his mouth to answer, Ethan stuck his open palm in Malachi's face. "Oh, let me guess. I bet it's the same as Alice's. It's 'Who in the world am I?' Am I right? Is that the question?"

Gazing up into the flittering branches, Malachi sighed. "I am not accustomed to how you relate. Such relationship discord. My heart has an unfamiliar sadness." Closing his eyes, he began humming a tune. Ethan, now ashamed of his childish behavior, lowered his head.

"Sorry, man." Ethan choked it out, his eyes focused on the blades of grass, each sparkling with their own color. "Can we try this again? I really *am* curious about the question."

"Why?" Malachi said gently. "The question is 'Why'? Why are you here? All mankind needs meaning and purpose. At least in Eden we do. Is this also true for you? If so, what is it?"

The blood drained from Ethan's face. He had no idea why he was here. Or why this dream wouldn't end. Perhaps this wasn't a dream … that he was supposed to be here. He wished he could answer Malachi's question, as much for Malachi as for himself. "I—I have no idea."

Malachi's face remained serene. "I have asked Melody this question. However, in her mystery, she has not revealed the answer. No matter. I am content in the waiting." His eyes began to sparkle. "So, it remains a mystery. One that will be revealed. Of that I am sure." He winked, slapping his hands on his knees. Then, wrapping one arm around his basket, he pivoted gracefully out from Ethan's hiding place.

Ethan scrambled after him, struggling to crawl out in his twisted tunic.

Malachi was already sauntering up the path back to town.

Ethan caught up. "You're sure? How can you be so confident, so 'chillaxed,' as my daughter would say?"

"Simple. A lifetime of learning and seeing. And," Malachi turned to Ethan, "trusting." Remembering the betrayal of trust from his past, Ethan looked away.

"Do not fear, my friend."

Friend? Malachi considers me a friend?

"Trusting." Malachi smiled. "One of the scribes brought a book to the house for you. It will offer further explanation. It is what you call a history book, composed specifically for you."

"For me? Is my presence here that significant?" Ethan couldn't help but wonder what these Edenites expected from him, if anything. The thought of becoming some sort of hero sounded laughable. *If only they knew the real me.* He anticipated a headache, but none came.

"Know this, Ethan. You are vital. Important to all of us, for good."

"What? You mean like a hero?"

Malachi stopped, and, ignoring Ethan's question, turned his face to the sun with eyes closed. He smiled and opened his eyes. "Your role is also somehow connected to your life back in your world." He returned to walking.

Ethan's jaw dropped at Malachi's mention of the link between his world and Eden. "That's it?" He scrambled to catch up again. "That's all you're gonna give me?"

"That is all I know. Does it not provide hope?" Malachi began humming that same tune, swinging the basket slightly, lost in a place of complete contentment. Ethan, however, struggled with Malachi's statements. A hero role? That somehow connects to home? But then wasn't he hoping to become a hero for Cassie when he agreed to go with Janus to Myanmar? Wasn't he somehow still on that journey? Ethan's pace slowed, the responsibility of fulfilling his role dragging him down, not a monkey but a chest-pounding gorilla on his back. If Malachi "read" his mind's image, he ignored it.

"Nobody is home yet." Malachi waved toward the house. "I put the book beside your bed. You can peruse it now if you like, while I prepare food."

"Thanks." Ethan shuffled up the stairs, exhausted. He opened the door to his room and there on the bedside table lay the book, thick, leather-bound, the edges gilded with gold. He took off his sandals and, propping himself up with multiple pillows on the freshly made bed, he opened the book and began to read.

This is the mystery we hold to be true. For in the beginning, the Composer was. From eternity to eternity he was and is and will always be …

CHAPTER SEVENTEEN

You can lose me; you can find me,
Race against or get behind me.
I can ripen; I can fly,
I can march or I can die.
I am money; I'm a thief,
I'm a teacher; I'm a reef.
All humanity is trapped inside me,
Searching for roads that lead outside me.
What am I?

Ethan spent most of the next week alone in his room, partly out of interest in reading about Eden's history, but also partly out of denial, doubting his purpose, and unwilling to foster deeper relationships, still hoping Eden to be a dream, afraid of the repercussions if it wasn't.

The book became a good distraction. It piqued his interest, especially in the similarity between Eden's history and the history of his Earth, with a surprising connection to the Bible. At least, what he remembered about it, from his short time with Jill. Growing up, Ethan knew nothing about the Bible or the God of the Bible. In fact, the only God-related words he knew were curses gushing from his mother's mouth. Those last few years at home before he moved out, Ethan had learned to swear with the best of them—a gift bestowed on him all too easily. *The things my mother taught me. Thanks Mom!*

No answer. He sighed.

Ethan thought of his "Bible" memories, most of them centering around the storybooks Jill would read to Cassie before bed, much like the way Janus's grandma told Janus stories from the Bible. Coincidence? Ethan didn't know. But he *did* know that Cassie loved the creation story the most, with the lights and all the animals, especially birds. Sometimes even Ethan would read her that story as a gesture of love. The stories stuck in his head. That's how he came to recognize similar themes between the two writings: an eternal, omnipotent being creating the universe, a garden with a tree of life and a tree of the knowledge of good and evil, the arrival of a man and woman who give names to the rest of creation, the paradoxical presence of good and evil.

Ethan also noticed definite differences, attributing most of them to one overarching choice made in the first few pages of his reading, a choice that redirected the course of Eden's history in all the pages after it. The woman, whom Ethan related to Eve, denied the serpent's questioning words and, refusing to eat from the tree of the knowledge of good and evil, chose to eat from the tree of life. It was a decision she'd made on her own because the fruit enticed all her senses. Then no more mention of a serpent. What happened to the serpent in this world?

It was the thought of these Edenites being eternal beings that dominated his thinking. Could that be true? If so, how old would Malachi be? Or even Gimmel? Ethan read slowly, carefully, looking for answers, not just answers to the "How" in getting home, but also answers to Malachi's "Why?" question. Clues to the answers eluded him.

He read in the morning and he read at night. He read while drifting off to sleep, always hoping for change, always waking to the same four walls, his questions and uneasiness mounting. He spent his afternoons pursuing that same hope, but not with reading. Donning his tunic and sandals, he went for long walks, mulling over questions, always crossing paths with people but never smiling or looking them in the eye, thinking that the civil thing to do, since he didn't know what to say. And every day he ended up at the familiar pond of water, wishing for the reappearance of the waterfall. It never came.

At the pond he'd tried to find a path up the rocky crag but the dense vegetation prohibited any forward progress. In defeat, he'd sit on the water's edge and watch the gleaming fish dart around his ankles. On occasion, if he bent his head too close to the water, a fish would jump above the water's surface, splashing his face, as if offering him a gift of refreshment. It made him smile, if only briefly.

A couple of times he thought he was being watched. Once he was sure he saw someone looking at him through a grove of trees, a flash of something, or someone, that didn't quite match the landscape. The eerie unease made him think of Lewis Carroll's Cheshire Cat character, with the ability to appear and disappear.

A snippet of dialogue between Alice and the cat popped into his head. When Alice asked him which road to take, the cat replied, "Where do you want to go?" When Alice didn't know, the cat said, "Then, it doesn't really matter, does it?" Goose bumps began crawling up Ethan's arms, hitting the back of his neck. When his whole body trembled, he turned, and practically ran back to the house. He had no interest in meeting up with anything close to the Cheshire Cat.

With each passing day, however, he began to wonder if maybe Malachi was right. Maybe there was a reason for his presence in Eden. And maybe the fulfillment of this reason would get him home. It sounded ridiculous yet he found solace in it.

On the morning of the seventh day, Ethan decided he needed a change.

"I see you have the book with you today," Malachi said as he poured Ethan a full mug of quasi-coffee. "Any reason in particular?"

"Thought I'd read outside today."

"Are you finding what you are seeking?"

"What I'm seeking?" Ethan picked up the mug. "Still not sure. Haven't forgotten what you said, though, about why I'm here."

Malachi smiled. "Perfect day to apricate, especially now that the sun's warmth has removed the heavy dew."

Apricate? Ethan opened his mouth. *No, I don't need to know.* He turned and headed out the back door.

"Enjoy the day's song." Ethan did not acknowledge Malachi's cheesy remark as the screen door swung shut behind him. He walked to the edge of the backyard. There, nestled under a wide-spanning peach tree, he found one of the comfy chairs and a small table, as if he were expected. He sat down, stretched out his legs, put his head back on the cushion and closed his eyes. Such a peaceful spot. For the first time, thoughts of being a hero danced happily across his mind like bright notes on a musical staff.

But then the aroma of sweet peaches sucked him into an ugly memory. He returned to a vivid image of newly bought peaches, bruised, mushy, and spoiled, all over the back seat of his Mazda Rx-8. Rather than slowing down, he had accelerated upon reaching the Park Bridge that rose high above Kicking

Horse Pass in British Columbia. The passenger's side-mirror had smashed against the concrete barrier as the car swerved over too far, almost careening Jill, baby Cassie, and himself down into the rocky gorge below. He remembered Jill's first words after he pulled over, her voice shaky: "Stop making stupid choices. You've got a family to think about." She had walked a crying baby around the rest area while he cleaned up the box of peaches as best he could. Refusing to converse, she spent the rest of the trip in the back seat with Cassie. Her words stung like vinegar on an open wound.

"Go away," he yelled to the memory. Just when he was beginning to consider his hero role in Eden as a way to get home. Home was a good place, wasn't it? This memory said otherwise. He remembered. Jill had been right. Which made him question his ability to be a good father to Cassie, once again. *Does it even matter?* He knew it did. He still wanted to get home and try. He thumped the book down on the table, sending it toppling—book, mug, and all. Jerking up with hands clenched, he left the mess and started walking. Where? It didn't matter.

Circling around a tall hedge of trees, he came upon Gimmel and two other girls walking toward him, each with a different animal. Gimmel with her raven, another girl with a lamb, and another with a large cat. *A cougar perhaps?* Ethan couldn't tell. He forgot about the previous incident and looked at the animals. The combination puzzled him.

"Ethan!" Gimmel squealed upon seeing him. She began skipping, with Rufus like a bobbing parrot on her shoulder.

"H-Hi." Ethan was still unsure about the approaching feline. Gimmel ran up, about to hug him, and then she stopped, seeing Ethan's eyes focused on the cat.

"Is all okay?" There were little wrinkles on her forehead.

"I ..." Ethan paused. "Your friend has a pet cougar?"

"Oh." She looked at the cat. "You mean Prancer? Belinda's panther? Do you want to meet him? And Kinky, the lamb?" She grabbed Ethan's hand, fighting his resistance. The two mammals came together as if wanting to be greeted. Gimmel, seeming to accept Ethan's uncertainty, put her hand out and both animals began licking it, no carnivorous desire in the panther and no hesitation in the lamb. "It tickles." Her eyes lit up.

"Huh. Is ... is that normal?" Ethan asked, believing he could speak freely. *Little girls I can trust. Maybe Gimmel can answer all my questions.*

"What? That it tickles?" Gimmel's forehead crinkled again.

"Umm, no. I mean, isn't the lamb afraid that the panther will eat it?"

The three girls looked at each other and giggled. Ethan wanted to turn and walk away. Then he remembered Cassie and her friends laughing over the silliest of things and he relaxed. Gimmel took his hand once more, putting his palm out. The two creatures began licking it as well. Instinctively, Ethan pulled back. The two animals stepped forward and continued, almost as if they recognized Ethan's inner curiosity. He forced himself to remain still.

"You're right, Gimmel. It does tickle."

"Where you come from do panthers eat sheep?" Gimmel's eyes widened."

"Yes, yes they do." The girls gasped. "We have carnivores and herbivores, predators and prey. That's the simplified version anyway."

The three stood looking at each other with puzzled faces.

By their nods and hand gestures, Ethan could tell they were in conversation. Ethan wished he could eavesdrop on their little talk. He waited, wondering what their next question would be. Gimmel turned to Ethan.

"Did the Composer make them that way?"

"The Composer?" Ethan had read about this character in Eden's book of history but had his own questions about who he was. And not just the Composer, but a man named Lyric as well. Along with Melody, Ethan wondered if these three main characters even existed in his world.

"The Composer created the animals." Gimmel leaned in. "Did he in your world?"

"Oh." Ethan took a moment to let the definition sink in. "Of course. The Composer." The girls waited. He didn't know what to say, but neither did he want to brush them off.

"Well, to answer your question, my world is complicated. Lots of different people believe in lots of different things. And who's to say who's right and who's wrong?" By the girls' faces, Ethan could tell his answer accomplished nothing. "In my world …" *Did I just say, "in my world"? Like Alice?* Ethan cleared his throat. "From my perspective, the existence of a Composer, and his involvement, is, well, questionable. Is he real? Is he a myth? Is he just hocus-pocus? Who's to say?"

"Hocus-pocus?"

"Girls?" Malachi's voice broke in from behind him. "Is this where you should be?"

Gimmel peaked around Ethan to see her father. "But Daddy …"

"No excuses. I believe you were on your way to the Casswell farm, were you not? For husbandry training?"

"Yes, Daddy." Gimmel dropped her head. The other two

girls nodded. The three simply turned and walked off, their animals following. Just as they began crossing a large meadow dotted with yellow goldenrod, Gimmel turned and gave Ethan a wave. He waved back.

"Thanks." Ethan looked at Malachi.

Malachi gave him a quizzical look. "Do not thank me. Thank Melody. She communicated to me that you were in an unpleasant position, though she did not share specifics. Being surrounded by three mirthful girls did not appear dangerous."

"You'd be surprised. Kids are pretty honest. And ask tough questions, sometimes." Ethan took one last look at the girls. "Though I did enjoy their mirth, as you called it."

Malachi smiled. "And now Gimmel's friends will have a story to tell their families at the dinner table tonight. Delightful."

"Delightful? Is that what my presence is to you Edenites? Delightful?"

"I did not m ..."

"Forget it." Ethan didn't wish to discuss the conversation he had with the girls. "I'm sure I've caused enough disruption in your workday, so I'll just go on my usual walk and be back later." Ethan marched off in the opposite direction of the girls.

"I will await your presence at dinner." Malachi's raised voice was still annoyingly cheery. With no change in his stride, Ethan flapped an arm in response.

* * *

While finishing up some notes in his journal before dinner that evening, Ethan heard the plunk-plunk sound of a familiar instrument coming up from the main floor. He dropped his pencil in mid-sentence, slipped on his sandals, and took the stairs two at a time. There, perched on the edge of a big willow-woven chair, sat Gimmel, a ukulele in her hands. Startled by Ethan's abruptness, the whole family stopped what they were doing and looked at him.

"Is everything satisfactory?" Malachi asked.

Ethan, ignoring Malachi's question, just stared at the ukulele. "You play?" He looked at Gimmel.

"I am trying." Gimmel huffed, sneaking a look at her mother and then putting the ukulele on her lap. "I am in a school band. We have a, a concert soon. My mentor, umm, teacher, said I should practice."

"Gimmel." Seshat wiped her wet hands on her gingham apron. She stepped around the large island of a hard, unfamiliar wood, espresso in color, and ran her fingers through her own brunette curls. "I do not think practice time is over." She looked at Ethan with a smile. "Her teacher … that is me." Then she looked back at Gimmel, still smiling. "I think she thinks her teacher is asking the impossible."

Gimmel's protruding bottom lip showed her displeasure. Still, she picked up the ukulele and began strumming, her small fingers fighting to press the right strings.

"This is awesome-sauce." Ethan laughed at his word choice. Cassie's expression.

"What?" Seshat asked.

"Sorry. I mean, the fact that Gimmel plays ukulele *and* that you're her teacher. I'm just surprised. Why didn't you say anything?"

Seshat and Malachi looked at each other.

"I … We did not even think about it," Seshat said.

Malachi put his pairing knife down. "We assumed you knew. Everyone plays a musical instrument here. It is part of our expression, a gift given to us at the time of Enlightenment." Malachi walked over and sat down beside Ethan. "Is it not the same in your world?

"Not a chance. Lots of people don't play. Not their thing. And there's no gift-giving, as you call it, though there is natural ability."

"Hmm." Malachi tilted his head.

"So, where've you been hiding your instruments? I've checked every room, never saw a hint of anything musical." He looked at Malachi. "Got a guitar kicking around by chance?"

"No, no guitars." Seshat caught on to Ethan's words before Malachi. "I play the violin and Malachi plays the harmonica. At least, I think that is what you would call it."

"Really?" Ethan's excitement surged. Maybe someone would have a guitar he could play. "So, where are they? Your instruments, I mean?"

"Well, because I teach," Seshat said, "I keep mine at school. Malachi stores his in the bedroom."

Ethan wanted to grab the ukulele and dance around the room with it. Finally. Something he enjoyed, something he was good at. He couldn't resist squeezing in beside Gimmel in the chair. "Can I give it a go?"

Gimmel grinned and then looked at her mom.

"Of course, Ethan." Seshat smiled. "Of course you may play."

So, while Seshat and Malachi returned to dinner preparation, Ethan serenaded them with old tunes, his long-term memory feeding his fingers with precision. Gimmel plopped down on the floor in front of him and clapped along. At one point she got up and twirled around the room, singing "la-la-las" to the tunes. After a few songs, however, Ethan's memory went down the wrong rabbit hole and he remembered his mother's connection with the ukulele. Halfway through

"Take Me Home, Country Roads," he stopped, unable to continue. He quietly returned the ukulele to its case. "I think …" He cleared his throat. "I think it must be dinner time." Nobody questioned his sudden change in demeanor, though Ethan could tell Gimmel wanted to.

Seshat nodded. "Almost."

Needing a distraction, Ethan sat back and watched the camaraderie in the kitchen. Seshat worked confidently alongside Malachi, yet she always maintained humility, deferring to his knowledge. Though not as exuberant as Malachi, she smiled lovingly at Gimmel, now skipping about setting the table, her sulkiness gone. Ethan smiled too.

"Getting there." Seshat grinned at him. She struggled less with her use of words, conversing with an ease that always relaxed him. When he asked her why, she paused, then smiled. "Probably because I am a teacher."

To Ethan, Seshat engaged in her world with a balance of self-reliance and grace that contradicted all his preconceived ideas about women. He hesitated to interact with her at first, not desiring any sexual enticement since she was attractive and since she appeared to be his age, but in the end he looked at her more as a mother figure, as if he was in some sort of Freudian experiment. After a few evenings of reading, he understood why. Despite her looks, Seshat was probably hundreds, maybe even thousands of years older than he was. Still guided by his own cultural norms, he had yet to ask her age, hoping the topic would surface in casual conversation.

Gimmel returned to her usual chipmunk-chatter during dinner, happy to talk about the events of the day. Ethan had noticed that her fight with the ukulele was not her first display of moodiness. The more he interacted with her, the more he noticed her questions, too, like a seeker who didn't have the same self-assurance as the adults. In that way he connected with a brooding side of her that he didn't find anywhere else in this world. She was more real to him, a questioner of life and its struggles. And although he didn't ask about it, he could tell that Gimmel knew it, too. She, however, seemed more nervous about it than comforted by it.

As well, Gimmel's presence in his dream back in northern Myanmar gave Ethan hope that their two worlds really were connected, as Malachi had alluded to. *Is she part of the reason I'm here? To be her hero?* Remembering how he'd failed Cassie in that department made him want to run away.

"Would you like to do that?" Seshat's question broke into Ethan's thought-world.

"Huh?"

"Gimmel asked if you would come to our music class and play some of your songs."

"My songs?" Ethan thought about the only song he'd ever written, not one he wished to share.

Sheshat tipped her head. "Songs from your world. The ones you were just playing. I know all the children would enjoy it."

"Ple-e-e-ease." Gimmel's puppy-dog eyes reminded Ethan so much of Cassie he couldn't say no, despite his reservations.

"Okay. Sure. Guess I'd be your show-and-tell." Ethan smiled.

"Yay!" Gimmel squealed, jumping out of her chair and circling the table to give Ethan a hug around his neck. "I think I love show-and-tell."

Ethan laughed, patting her slender arm.

"Gimmel," Seshat said. "I do not think Ethan needs to be attacked. Come sit."

"It's okay." Ethan liked the reminder of Cassie's hugs.

Gimmel returned to her chair, merely picking at her food, her chatter on high speed. Ethan went to bed that night more excited about playing guitar than anything else.

"Eden definitely has its perks." Ethan grinned at Malachi the next morning, still thinking about locating a guitar. "However, your coffee is definitely *not* one of them." He raised his mug in a mocking toast, expecting Malachi to get the joke since he seemed to be getting better at reading Ethan's subtle humor. He placed his mug back down on the island, pulled out a well-worn wooden stool, and sat down.

"No. Not coffee." Malachi returned the smile. "It's a blend of roasted grains and chicory. Coffee beans are one commodity we do not grow." He walked to the window, looking out on the fields of grain. "Hmm. We have brought in other crops before. Perhaps we should try coffee."

"How many?"

"How many what?"

"How many new crops have you brought in? And how long ago?" Ethan asked, hoping to use the question as a springboard in his search for other answers, forgetting that Melody would inform Malachi of Ethan's underlying need.

"You are wondering how old this world is, and how old Seshat and I are." Malachi gave a slight grin. "To be honest, I thought you would have asked those questions sooner."

"Yeah, well, where I come from asking questions about age is taboo."

"Taboo? Ah yes, forbidden." Malachi nodded his head. "Well, our world is the same age as yours so then you tell me how old our worlds are."

"I don't know. Does anybody?"

"Oh?"

"It's a debate. All that old-earth, young-earth crap, which, by the way, I didn't know existed until I met my ex-wife's father. He had his own ideas on the topic, so I studied up on it."

"And?"

"Don't remember. Guess I wasn't that interested. With each advancement in technology, it seems our world is getting older and older." Ethan laughed. "As far as the debate goes, both sides insist they are right. I thought such dogma was just bull, er, baloney. But now that I'm here, maybe I should've thought about it more. You know, the age of Earth and all."

"What a curious people you are, debating over such a minor issue."

"Minor? What?"

"Sorry. I am not trying to offend. I forget that you come from a time-conscious world. Time is irrelevant here."

"Irrelevant?" Ethan shook his head. "If I didn't know you, I'd be offended. It's like you're calling my time-conscious world irrelevant."

"No. Not at all. I am speaking only of my world." Malachi cocked his head. "Are you struggling to grasp the concept?"

"Huh?"

"The notes of Melody's song began to become inharmonious. I must admit, nobody in this world would find your distress relatable."

Ethan wrapped his fingers tightly around his earthenware mug, trying to stay grounded.

"No need to fear, Ethan. We do measure time in a way, mostly according to the rising and the setting of the sun. And we have seasons that repeat to constitute what you would call a year. This measuring matters more to the pre-epiphany ones, like Gimmel, but after that, all of time blends into eternity."

Ethan stared into his muddy drink without saying a word, trying to process this new information and the term "pre-epiphany." Malachi, who'd been standing at the window, pulled out the stool kitty-corner to him and sat down.

"None of this should surprise you if you have been reading the book I gave you."

"You know I have." Ethan cleared his throat, trying to control his shaky voice. "I just thought it all metaphorical, like some author's interpretation of your past. You know, historical fiction."

"Historical fiction." Malachi paused. "Ah, based on history but not completely true."

"Right."

"Are all your people like you?"

"Huh?" This time Ethan really had no idea what Malachi meant.

"Do all your people question truth?"

Sensing no malice in Malachi's voice, Ethan answered the best he knew how. "It's not that we question truth. More like we interpret it individually. You know, 'If what you believe works for you, then go for it.'"

"So there is no standard?" The concept seemed to surprise Malachi.

"Sure there is, but like I said, it's for the individual. Nothin' wrong with that is there?" Ethan attempted an ever-fleeting confidence.

"But no higher truth or moral code?"

Ethan heard the apprehension in Malachi's voice. A jolt of cold air, like an electric shock, disrupted the warm, almost caressing aura of peace he had come to accept as the norm in the house. Malachi hummed a bit of his familiar song and the serenity returned.

"That must be a lonely existence, each person isolated, their relationships off-key." Malachi gave his head a slight shake. "But it does explain some of your actions."

"My actions? Oh f …" Ethan stopped. For the first time, he recognized how his own negativity affected the room's harmony. *How is this possible?*

"Please. I am not wishing to offend, but sometimes your actions clash with this world. I guess you would use the words 'abnormal' or 'uncustomary.'"

"Seriously? I've been trying to fit in, to go unnoticed."

"Hmm. Fitting in and going unnoticed are not synonymous here. The tunic and sandals help but your actions give away your foreign identity." Malachi's tone was matter of fact. Ethan could tell he was choosing his words carefully. "Your unfriendliness, your uneasiness around others, as if in self-protection, is noticeable."

"You think?" Ethan mocked. "I'm the foreigner *with* the inharmonious past? Remember?"

"Yes. I know. Your actions are no surprise to me. But Melody has not chosen to share your past with the whole community. They do know that you are from another world, but she has not revealed much more than that to them. She knows that your privacy is important to you."

"Is that so wrong?"

"The concept is so foreign, so antithetical, to life here that I cannot even address the thought. In this world, life is always about relationship. It is what we live for and it ties in this our purpose. Firstly, the individual lives in harmony with nature. But se …"

"Wait." Ethan put two and two together in his head. "Is that what's going on in your house? Is there some sort of 'harmony' in the air? I think I just figured it out. Except …" Ethan looked down, his eyes resting on the words of his tattoo: Come As You Are. *Don't I wish!* He sighed. "My presence here has really disrupted that, hasn't it? For all three of you?"

"Not disrupted. All is good, Ethan. We knew." Malachi smiled. "We knew also that Melody promised an extra measure of peace and patience. An added gift, if you will."

"Huh." Ethan looked around the room. "So, she's the one that fills this place with peace?" He looked at Malachi and half-grinned. "I'm sure you've needed a bigger dose than you thought." Then another idea popped into Ethan's head. "So, does that affect speech too?" Malachi tilted his head. "You know, the words we use." No response. Ethan looked up at the ceiling and huffed. "My words." He spread his hands out. "My biting words. Swearing, we call it. It's being altered somehow. I mean, it even grates on me to hear it. I don't get it."

"Oh-h-h." Malachi nodded his head. "The swearing. Yes, that is Melody's presence. Her song brings peace. Again, I could not predict her effect on you."

"And cravings? Does she curb cravings?"

"Cravings? I do not know …"

"You know, addictions." Ethan cringed inside, surprised that he had the courage to mention the word.

"Addictions. Hmmm."

Ethan watched Malachi's eyes glaze over but then open wide with surprise. "Addictions. Do you have addictions?"

"Surprise, surprise." Ethan bobbled his head. "Not uncommon in my world. Though here, I don't know. The cravings aren't the same, which is weird."

"I am sorry. It appears I still have much to learn about how different you are."

"Right." Ethan leaned back and sighed. "Ever the abnormal one. To be honest, the idea's getting old." He leaned forward. "Can we talk about something else?"

"Yes, I have been waiting for your questions. I believe that the more of our world you observe, the closer we will come to knowing why you are here."

Ethan wasn't sure where to even start. The list seemed daunting, unbearably so. *What is pre-epiphany? Who is the Composer? How does he know anything about my world? And how old are these people?* More questions than answers. *I just want to get out of here, but not out there with those people. I want to go … I want to go home.* He missed his world, his privacy, his anonymity. He even missed his messed up relationships.

"Remember, Ethan, you have a purpose here. For us. For yourself. That is truth. Trust it."

Trust it? Can I? It had been so long. Janus and Barnabas came to mind. He had just started trusting them when …

Malachi put his hand on Ethan's forearm. Ethan pulled back instantly, splashing his drink all over Malachi in the process.

"Sh … shoot." Ethan jolted up out of the chair.

"It is no problem, Ethan. I startled you." Malachi walked over to a bowl of soapy water on a little stand near the table and grabbed a wet cloth. "I simply wish to assist you in your learning, as your friend." He put the cloth down. "I have an idea. How about you come out to the fields with me today? I will show you what I do, and we can continue this conversation."

Ethan sat back down, head lowered, as Malachi cleaned up the table. *How does he take my stupid actions and turn them into encouragement? Without a hint of frustration?* Malachi's ways were totally opposite of his own. For the first time in a long time, he was truly sorry for his biting words and unkindness.

Ethan couldn't make eye contact. "Sorry, Malachi. I get it."

Malachi said nothing. After five minutes of silence Ethan spoke again. "I think you're right. I'll go with you, pull my weight around here since you're feeding me." He lifted his head, giving Malachi a slight smile.

"Good. Very good." Malachi stood. "I have been wanting to ask, but Melody gave me the word 'patience.' She is wise." He gave Ethan a knowing wink.

"Yeah, right." His sarcasm made him wince.

"And you will have the opportunity to meet the others I work with."

"The others?" Ethan's doubt returned.

"Harmony. We live and work in harmony, remember?"

"Right. Harmony. I do need harmony." Ethan closed his eyes and breathed in deeply. On the intake Melody's sonata floated in as if to say, "*I can give that to you.*"

CHAPTER EIGHTEEN

Oh forsaken, one,
maneuvering
the maze
of life—
you were not made for
the solo flight,
an instinctive individual,
but for
the group noun,
the V-shaped skein
of nurturing numbers,
of companionship,
of harmony.
Oh forsaken, cast off the one—
join the throng.

In their short walk to the fields, Ethan listened for more thoughts from Melody, but none came. Yet, her presence lingered, calming him with that scent of night jasmine, and completely distracting him from asking questions.

They stopped at the edge of a field where a group of men had begun harvesting a crop of wheat, their muscular arms whipping back and forth, back and forth, with large swishing scythes, their actions effortless, the sound rhythmical and hypnotizing. The two of them watched for a few minutes and then as if mere cogs in some giant mechanical engine, the workers stopped en masse and looked over at Malachi.

"Good morning." Malachi waved. "My intention was not to disrupt your rhythm. I only wished to introduce Ethan to you, the young man visiting Eden."

Visiting? Visiting sounded good.

Malachi put his hand on Ethan's shoulder. Some of the men nodded with welcoming smiles. However, Ethan couldn't help but notice two on the far side that looked at each other and turned their backs. Within seconds their heads turned to look at Malachi. Ethan let out a surprised, "Whoa." The two were obviously younger than the others, closer to his age, something he hadn't expected. Plus, their faces revealed that look he'd seen in Gimmel. Anguish. Anger? Fear? Both? Ethan couldn't tell.

"Visiting, perhaps to deceive." The one on the left spoke. his eyes boring into Ethan. Malachi raised his hand abruptly without a word. The young man looked away.

Together, the two took a few slow steps toward Malachi, their agitation affecting everything Ethan found unique about Eden. The tingling dance of harmony within nature became a funeral dirge. The ground under Ethan's feet quivered as if in silent sobs, causing him to almost lose his bearings. The fluorescent glimmering air that even Ethan had grown accustomed to, separated and scattered in hiding. A foreign chill replaced the warm breeze. The whole scene dulled as if in sadness, or pain. Dulled until it was Earth-like. Malachi and the two appeared in intense conversation, the young men's faces still brooding. Malachi's remained steady. Ethan's fear churned ever so slowly in the pit of his stomach. His throat tightened. He tapped the fingers of his right hand along the side of his tunic. Remembering the thermos attached to his sash, he unclipped it and took a long swig. It helped to focus on something else. On cue, a happy memory swooped in. The day he and Cassie had hiked up Mt. Fairview. He'd been so proud of her. His mind quieted but his fingers clutched white around the thermos.

Nobody spoke for what seemed like forever. The cool breeze remained. Ethan watched as the older ones began to move, altering their positions to encircle the two. What would happen? Harsh scolding? Beatings? Ethan's mind went to the worst-case scenarios. But watching the faces of the outer circle, Ethan saw no hostility or discord but rather each man had a look of tenderness and love. A few of them began to hum, slowly, softly, the sound ever-building. Different melodies than Malachi's and yet somehow similar. Soon all the men in the outer circle, including Malachi, were humming. Then together they opened their mouths and began to chant. Ethan's jaw dropped. Never had he heard anything so beautiful—a dozen men, each singing their own melody, and yet it swelled as one triumphant symphony of voices. Slowly, beginning in whispers, the two in the middle lifted their faces and joined the throng. First one, then the other more hesitant one. By the time the voices crescendoed to a final, mellifluous note, Ethan realized that all of nature had returned to its character istic Edenic state. The circle opened as the two lay down their scythes and walked to the edge of the field to stand in front of Ethan, the left one's eyes fixated on him. Not wanting to appear weak, Ethan held his stare. Finally, Malachi used words.

"Ethan. These pupils, if you will, have something to say to you. However, you require some background information first." Malachi looked at Ethan and then at the two men. Ethan, still entranced by it all, said nothing. Malachi continued. "These two are still in the knowledge stage of life here, the pre-epiphany stage. I could offer you their names, but names are irrelevant, for soon they both will enter epiphany and their names will change for eternity. However, you deserve an explanation for their behavior. Before epiphany, the darker sides of personalities are more prominent, thus Melody's voice can be squelched by the sour voice of incongruity. Is that an acceptable explanation, Ethan?"

Ethan turned to Malachi. "Maybe." Ethan straigtened up and raised his chin. "I think so." He didn't want to look ignorant.

"It is the responsibility of the sagacious ones to come alongside these men, not only to teach them physical skills but also to teach them spiritual skills."

"Spiritual skills?" The term was foreign to Ethan.

"Training the mind to know Melody's song of harmony. And to listen for her sweet voice over other voices. Not a familiar concept to you?" Malachi had not taken his eyes off the one on the left, the one still staring Ethan down with steely grey eyes under a furrowed brow. Finally, this one shifted his eyes to Malachi.

"Not exactly." Ethan could now look at Malachi. "But I do get that whole voices-in-the-head thing. Been dealing with it for years."

"Yes." Malachi turned to Ethan with eyes of tenderness. "And perhaps that is why you needed to come with me today."

"What? Why?" Ethan shook his head.

"Because these two are more like you. More divided in their minds, more questioning of the music, the greater musical symphony, not born out of rules, but born out of love." Malachi kept his eyes on Ethan.

"You mean there's a lesson for me here? Great. Just great."

He looked down and kicked the dirt lightly, sending up a spray of auroral confetti. He watched it slowly sift down back into the earth.

"Do not fear the learning, Ethan. It might give us all insight into why you are here in Eden, though it is *not* to deceive."

"You know that how?"

"Melody prepared us for your arrival. She knew, which means you are here for good."

"What? For good? You just said I was visiting. How ... ?"

"I meant for the good of us all. Sorry."

Ethan didn't reply. *So many unknowns, so much to comprehend.*

"Peace." The word was uttered like a blessing, then Malachi turned back to the two. "Please offer Ethan your words." Everyone now looked at Ethan.

The one on the right spoke first, free in his use of words. "I am sorry. It is not for us to question the Composer's ways, nor Melody's ways. We welcome you to Eden." He walked casually over to Ethan, stuck out his hand, and grinned.

Ethan, though surprised at the action, slipped the thermos back in its pocket and took the hand, focusing on the face of the man for the first time. "Janus?" He gasped, wide-eyed, his mind racing through his memories of Janus. He hadn't even realized that he'd voiced the name.

"Umm, no." The man's grin widened. "Baldwin, at least for now. Maybe ..."

"Thank you, Baldwin," Malachi said.

Baldwin bowed his head slightly and stepped back.

"I too am sorry." The other man took a step forward, though his hand remained at his side—an honest but reluctant apology.

"Thank you." Malachi smiled, looking at both men. "You

may now return to your day of tutelage. May the music guide you." The two picked up their tools and returned to their posts, the left one giving Ethan one last glance before cutting a wide slice through the stalks.

The image of that swift blade stuck with Ethan the rest of the morning as he followed Malachi around, inspecting fields, though he couldn't tell if the anxiety lingered from the confrontation or if it came because he was sure he was being watched. He kept scanning the fields for something unusual. Nothing.

"Did you see ..." Ethan began his question but then held his tongue as he and Malachi began walking back to the house for lunch.

"Did I see what?" Malachi's eyebrows arched.

"Oh nothing." Ethan felt stupid. "It's been a tough morning." He thought again about the two young men he'd met. The one, much like Janus, his friend, and the other like a nemesis. *Is he the one who's been spying on me?* The thought made him jittery. He snickered at how ridiculous he sounded.

"Are you well, Ethan?"

Ethan stopped, bent over, and took a few deep breaths. "No." He straightened up. "I should've listened to my gut and stayed at the house. That's all." He picked up his pace.

"Nonsense." Malachi lengthened his stride. "And Melody agrees with me."

"Well, I did sense that, at least at first." Ethan surprised himself with his own words. *I sensed that? I sensed her? Yes, I guess I did.*

"Oh?" Malachi's eyes smiled. Ethan pretended not to notice.

"Not like she was feeding me information or anything. More like a gentle progression of notes." Ethan laughed again.

"But, well, I don't know how to describe it really, though I'm sure you know. I was at peace. At first. Like I said." He shrugged his shoulders.

"And then you were not?"

"With that unsettling showdown out in the field? That was anything but peaceful."

"Showdown?"

Ethan looked at Malachi, eyebrows raised. "Yeah, you know. With those two guys. That was definitely confrontational. Even nature seemed to think so."

"Confrontational." Malachi pronounced the word slowly, as if in a foreign tongue.

"Well, what would you call it?"

"An opportunity for learning."

Ethan laughed. "Some opportunity." He rolled his eyes. "All I learned is that those two *really* didn't like me, like I was disrupting their lives. What did the one say? I'm here to deceive?"

"Did Melody offer *you* the same assessment of your presence here?"

Ethan took a moment to think. "No, not Melody. But Melody's just in my head. Those two, they're real."

Malachi slowed his pace, forcing Ethan to follow suit. "You present an argument that, to be honest, is beyond my imagining. Your premise is so inharmonious to our world where the unseen is as real as the seen." He closed his eyes but somehow kept walking.

What a preposterous idea. Ethan stared at Malachi but said nothing.

Malachi opened his eyes. "In reference to 'those two' as you called them, they are still learning and thus questioning is not wrong." Malachi shook his head slowly. "No, they only needed some simple guidance in knowing how to respond to change."

"Change. Like a *farang*." Ethan spit out the word. "A stranger in a strange land. Now *that* I'm familiar with."

Malachi looked at Ethan, as if examining his soul. "Are you looking for change?"

Refusing to answer that question, Ethan switched topics. "So, your simple guidance—can you offer it telepathically?"

"Of course. Remember, telepathy encompasses more than words but also intent, history, and underlying emotion, particularly emotion that is discordant. It encompasses, as you would say, 'Reading between the lines.' Plus, it is actually Melody that uses different styles of music and musical notes to do the guiding. Those of us in the wisdom age only follow her lead in offering restoration."

Ethan shook his head. "I'm having a hard time getting my head around all this. So bizarre."

"Getting your head ... ? Oh, trying to understand." Malachi paused. "Yes, difficult." They walked on in silence. Malachi began to hum, reminding Ethan of the chanting—that symphony of perfection. He considered asking about it but changed his mind. Another time. He had no desire to spoil that part of his memory. He turned his face up to the sun, shutting his eyes, allowing the sun's fingers to massage his taut face. *I'm ready for some time alone. Time. There it is again.* He opened his eyes and smiled, thinking he had discovered a seeming discrepancy in Malachi's talk of time.

"By the way," Ethan said, as they polished off the water in their thermoses on the back patio before lunch. "What's with all the talk about the knowledge age and the wisdom age? Don't those terms contradict your previous statement about time being irrelevant?"

"I know what you are implying." Malachi gave a boisterous laugh, wagging his finger at Ethan. "You are sharp, young Ethan. Melody gave me those terms, just for you. I use them only to help define pre-epiphany and post-epiphany."

"Just for me, huh? Became I'm *so-o-o* important." Ethan began fingering his thermos.

Malachi's voice turned serious. "Yes, Ethan. Both here and in your world. You matter."

Ethan looked down, and impulsively plunked "Take Me Home, Country Roads" on his leg. He swiped his hand over his leg to erase the tune and returned to the previous subject. "So, you're part of the wisdom age, right?"

"Yes." Malachi nodded. "One of the older ones, if we used your way of measuring. One or two of the men you met this morning only became part of the wisdom age recently."

"Recently? You mean like last week or something?"

"No." Malachi paused his familiar pause, his head cocked slightly to one side. "No," he repeated. "But what I tell you now may bring discord to your peace."

"Peace. I'm pretty sure those two guys chased the peace away." Ethan leaned back, trying to hide behind his wall of self-protection. "Anyway, shoot."

"Recently, for your time-driven mind, means within the last two hundred years."

"What the ..." Ethan's mind quickly jumped to some of his recent reading about someone eating from the tree of life a long time ago in this world. How long ago he still didn't know, but the remembering helped him control his agitation.

"Your acceptance is commendable." Malachi peered at him. "I thought perhaps you would be raising your voice, speaking unfamiliar vulgarities. But you are maintaining harmony. You too are learning. That is good."

"Yeah. I can't explain it either." *Is this Melody's doing?* Ethan shook his head. "So, let me get this straight—if someone who's two hundred years old is young, then you must be really old. How old?"

Leaving the question unanswered, Malachi rose and stoked the coals noisily.

"Anyway, the whole concept," Ethan puffed out his cheeks. "It's just mind-blowing."

"Mind-blowing." Malachi grinned. He stepped over to the ice chest, pulling out multiple toppings for the flatbread, their lunch staple. He placed the items on the table and looked at Ethan. "But then, so is your world to me. At least, from what you have said." Unwrapping more flatbread than usual, Malachi tossed it on the coals. The smell of freshly baked bread wafted over, waking Ethan's taste buds.

"Right." Ethan paused. "Guess I'm not the only one with questions." He got up, grabbed a glass, and poured himself some water, relaxed in the routine.

"Remember that until this morning you had not been much more than a mythical beast to most of the men working in the fields."

"Thanks."

"Do not take offense. Your presence has been a topic of conversation for most people in the area. But I assure you, there is no harmful intent. They desire to know why you are here." Malachi flipped the bread and took down two water glasses, placing them on the table.

"Well, I'm not sure about your 'harmful intent' comment. I think the ringleader this morning definitely wanted to jump me in a back alley."

"By ringleader you must mean Reece. That is his name, Reece. Yes, he is definitely a leader, though the ring part of that word does not compute. Reece is a tenacious young man." Malachi sat back down across from Ethan.

"Tenacious? That's what you call him?" Ethan ignored the 'ring' comment.

"Remember, your arrival here is unprecedented. To have these young men question the unknown, to fight it if necessary, is not erroneous. That is why we as wise ones needed to come alongside them and re-harmonize them, if you will."

"Even the leader? Reece? He still looked at me funny."

"Funny. Yes." Malachi sighed. "It is true. His determination does need extra molding. But it will be worth it. It always is."

"Determination, huh?"

"Does it remind you of anyone?" Malachi half-grinned.

"My daughter?" Ethan smiled. She was never far from his thoughts.

Malachi did not hesitate. "I meant you. You have strong leadership qualities."

"I do? I think maybe Melody's feeding you lies 'cause anyone who knows me would beg to differ. My mother for instance. She …"

"Melody cannot lie," Malachi blurted out. "Nor would she have reason to. She looked at those two young men this morning and saw potential. She looks at you and sees potential. Leadership potential."

Ethan remained silent, embarrassed by the compliment.

Malachi leaned over the table. "Ethan, my heart grieves when Melody attempts to share with me the pain in your world, how it needs healing. It is the most sorrowful song I have ever heard. Dissonance searching for resolution."

"Forget it, man." Ethan dropped his eyes.

"No, Ethan. I will not forget. Coming alongside you to change your perspective is possible. Potential, remember?"

"Ha. Sometimes you're full of it." Ethan hoped Melody wouldn't explain that vulgarism.

"And, in an attempt to do so," Malachi said, ignoring Ethan's last words, "I have asked one of the young men to join us for lunch today." Malachi rose from the table, looking at the corner of the house in expectation.

"What? Uh-uh." Sweat began to form on Ethan's brow. "Who? Reece?" He jumped up from the table, suddenly losing his appetite and wishing only for the security of his bedroom.

"Hi, Ethan." The friendly voice stopped Ethan in his tracks. He turned.

"I am Baldwin. Remember?" The young man sauntered over to Ethan and, once again, stuck out his hand.

CHAPTER NINETEEN

Enter or do not.
Locked or un, revolvings call
For action. Exit
Passivity, fear, and shame;
Handle with character. Doors.

While Malachi and Baldwin carried on a lively-looking conversation through lunch, their dialogue more telepathic than verbal, Ethan picked at his food in silence, watching the young man who reminded him so much of Janus, comparing and contrasting physical features, speech and mannerisms, hoping the initial similitude would diminish and then disappear. However, the lunch hour only solidified Ethan's first reaction to Baldwin. For even though Baldwin's eyes were blue, not brown, and even though Baldwin had a few inches on Janus, that same olive-brown complexion and muscular build, that same quirky confidence and easy smile, that same impetuous excitement, only served to strengthen the resemblance.

"You okay?" Malachi peered at Ethan.

"Yeah, man. No problems." Ethan kept his eyes down, not willing to discuss his insights, or to explore the explanation. *Is "doppelgänger" even a word in this world?* He missed his world and all its actual talk. A curious revelation since he remembered all the times he wished the women in his life would stop talking. Oh, to hear Jill's voice again, or even his mother's. The longing weighed on him like a heavy yoke. He was glad Malachi didn't pry.

"Are you really from another world?" Baldwin seemed oblivious to Ethan's inner turmoil.

Ethan swallowed hard. "Yes, I guess I am." He mumbled, not looking up. "And so are you it seems." He hated himself for saying it, but the words spilled out like toothpaste oozing out of the tube, squeezed by an unseen hand.

"Huh?" Baldwin frowned. Both he and Malachi looked curiously at Ethan and then turned to each other. Ethan let them converse in silence. Eyes downcast, he spied a glimmering guitar pick beside his chair. His curiosity getting the best of him, he picked it up. It wasn't a pick at all, but a triangular-shaped pebble, similar to pink quartz yet infused with slender veins of gold. Smooth and cool to the touch, he caressed it in his fingers, distracting him from his anxiety. *Maybe if I rub it hard enough, it will grant me three wishes. Ha! Don't I wish?* The idea somehow reminded him of *Alice in Wonderland,* which reminded him of the rabbit hole he was in, which then brought him right back to where he started, thinking about Janus, Janus of his past and now Janus of his present. *I wish I were home—home, back in my world.* A stream of expletives bubbled up and overflowed in his mind.

As if in response to his unspoken vulgarities, both Malachi and Baldwin turned to look at him. Their stares unnerving, Ethan sought serenity in the touch of the faux-guitar pick.

"Our apologies. The song of your emotional condition startled us." Malachi's eyes were expectant.

Ethan leaned forward and placed his crossed arms on the table, still clutching the smooth stone. "And what kind of song would that've been? Black metal? Death metal? Tell me, ple-e-e-e-ase." Ethan warbled the last word in a minor key.

Baldwin's eyes widened. Malachi's expression didn't change.

"Ethan's a musician in his world," Malachi said, in his same calm voice.

Ethan looked at him, mouth wide open. *Why doesn't he react?*

"Me too." Baldwin grinned, looking at Malachi, then back at Ethan. "I mean, we all play at least one instrument here. I am learning to play a number of them. Added gifting, I am told."

"Huh." It was all Ethan could say, still frustrated with Malachi's unflustered demeanor.

"So what do you play? A type of drum is my guess." Baldwin's smile grew, as if he knew something Ethan did not.

"A drum? Why a drum?" Ethan thought maybe it had something to do with his emotional condition. *Melody's doing, I s'pose.* "No, don't tell me." He yelled up at the sky, winging the pebble high into the air, hoping to hit this invisible being who knew so much about him. "Thanks, Melody."

"No, Ethan." Malachi's usual smile turned down. "Baldwin's response is not Melody's doing. Let me say again that she does not speak specific information. No, she comes through music, though the melodies about your world are difficult to … to translate. We simply do not hear noise like that here. We do not know your fear."

"Why not? Why don't you?" Ethan squeezed the arms of the chair, his fingers trembling. "Why is your world immune and mine isn't?"

Malachi did not rush his one-word answer, but he spoke it with authority. "Choice."

"Choice? Just choice? Life's not that simple." Ethan slid his hands forward and bent over.

"Long ago, the first man and first woman of our world made a choice. You read about it in the book I gave you, did you not?"

"Yeah, I read about it, but still don't get the connection," Ethan did not look up. *Why do I even attempt to converse in this world? I wish I had the ability to speak telepathically. Do I really? No.*

Malachi paused as if he knew he needed to choose his next words judiciously. Baldwin, however, was not so prudent.

"We are not immune to ..." Baldwin stopped and looked at Malachi, who had his hand raised toward Baldwin, then slowly lowering it.

"Nobody in this world ever ate the fruit from the tree of the knowledge of good and evil, as they did in your world. Do you realize the repercussions of that choice?" Malachi looked at Ethan, eyebrows raised.

Ethan lifted his head. "I told you, I'm not that familiar with the Bible." He hoped that would end the discussion. He didn't want to talk about God or religion or about good and evil, and all those myths and their secret meanings. "All I know is, that I've lived a life of 'discord,' as you say, thanks to all the people in my life who fed me lies. They said they loved me and then they left me." Ethan clenched his jaw, speaking the next three words clearly and carefully. "Not. My. Choice."

Malachi remained silent. Baldwin, however, proved to be as impulsive as Janus.

"The tree of the knowledge of good and evil is gone, out of our reach. But temptation still lingers, especially for those of us who have not yet experienced epiphany. The temptation to allow the dark side to take over our minds is real. That is why we need Melody, and why we need each other. You witnessed that in the event of this morning."

"The event of this morning?" Ethan laughed at the absurd wording. "Which part? The eerie shift in the atmosphere? Or the crazy, er, flash-mob chanting? Or your scornful stares?"

"Not sure." Baldwin frowned again. "I guess I did not think …"

Ethan interrupted. "There it is. You did not think. Not surprising, because … because, well, you wanna know what really bothers me about this morning?"

"Yes, I do." Baldwin seemed undeterred by Ethan's rudeness.

Ethan took a second to consider the answer, toying now with the bread on his wooden plate. He resigned himself to the conversation with a sigh. "You, Ja … , Baldwin." He stared right at him. "You bother me."

"I do?" Baldwin returned Ethan's stare with a curious grin.

"Yes. And do you know why? Did Melody tell you why? She should've, so I don't have to." Neither Baldwin nor Malachi replied. "It's because you remind me of someone, of a friend, back in my world. That's why I've been watching you." This time both Malachi and Baldwin looked surprised. "Unfortunately," Ethan continued, "the more I watch, the more you are like him. You, your presence, it just gives me the creeps." Ethan's right leg twitched erratically. Pressing it down, he began to plunk random notes on his thigh.

"Unpredictable." Malachi's voice was unruffled. "Melody did allude to simple connections between our worlds, but she did not expound on the extent of the affinity."

"Tell me more about this friend in your world who looks like me." Baldwin leaned in, his open face captivated by the prospect. "Sounds fascinating."

Ethan stopped plunking. "Fascinating? What world do you live in?" Blank stares. Ethan realized the absurdity of his question. "I'd rather not talk about the comparisons. I'm weirded out by the whole idea."

Baldwin's eyebrows flew up. "Weirded out?"

"You know. Nervous. I'm nervous about what it means, this overlap of people." Ethan wanted to run upstairs.

"Nervous? Why?" Baldwin's inquisitive nature would have kept hounding at Ethan had it not been for Malachi's intervention.

"I think Ethan has had enough questions." He put his hand on Baldwin's shoulder, gave Ethan a small nod and turned back to Baldwin. "I do believe your tutelage harvesting grain continues this afternoon, does it not?"

With carefree deference, Baldwin rose from his chair, and put his hand out to Ethan once again. "I hope we can be friends in this world, too." His eyes twinkled.

"Umm." *Get ahold of yourself.* "Whatever." Ethan rose and took the hand, not wanting to make an enemy of this young man, but also knowing that friendship passed through his fingers like fine prairie dust.

Baldwin turned to Malachi and nodded. Ethan watched them psyche-talk for a minute and then Baldwin gave Ethan one last, large, grin, before disappearing from his dream.

"Thanks for coming to my rescue." Ethan's words of gratefulness came easily. He half-grinned.

"There was a disruption in your heart and mind, was there not? Baldwin was simply being Baldwin. I think the word I would use to describe him would be passionate."

"Passionate?" Ethan laughed. "I would've said impulsive, but I guess passionate works, too, just like Janus in my world."

* * *

It wasn't until Malachi returned to the fields that Ethan

realized the topic of musical instruments with Baldwin had been sidelined. The thought made him melancholic. He went upstairs, curled up on the bed, and lay there, trying to empty his mind, waiting for sleep. Even when he woke from a short nap, however, he was still out of sorts. Knowing physical exercise to be good medicine, he went for his walk. This time he forced himself to smile at all the passers-by, though he still couldn't bring himself to open his mouth, his general distrust of people still controlling his actions.

By the time he got to the pool of water, now dubbed by Malachi's family as "Ethan's pond," the exhaustion returned. He removed his sandals and waded in, the healing water beckoning him further. Looking around, and not sensing the intrusive eye, he yanked out his hair tie and shook his head. He unloosed his sash with a smile, threw off the weightless tunic, and dove recklessly into the cool water. The tiny effervescent bubbles trickled up his body, a tingling freshness. How he wished the water would wash through his mind, clearing away all the confusion, filling in all the whats and wheres and whys.

Coming up to the surface, a little children's ditty filled his head. "Running over, running over; my cup is full and running over." He couldn't remember the rest of the words, only that it was another one of those choruses that Jill would sing to Cassie, along with the actions, making her giggle. He began humming.

"I am here. You need only open the door and let the music in." Unspoken words. Consoling words. He'd always let music into his life. Why not now? And with that, he let down his inner guard and relaxed, letting the water buoy him under the friendly eye of silvery clouds that sashayed through the

iridescent sky. He held his breath. There was something about Eden, the purity in creation, free and untortured, not like on Earth. And somehow Melody danced in and through it all with music. He closed his eyes to hear her song but none came. Just more words: *"Silence, stillness, is the song."*

"Ethan."

Jolted from his dreamy state, Ethan flailed around in the water. In all his walks to the pool, only Malachi had ever shown up. But now, a female voice was calling his name, the water in his eyes preventing him from identifying whom.

"Ethan." There it was again. *Cassie? Is that you?* It took Ethan a minute to realize the voice was not Cassie's, but Gimmel's. *Why? Why is she here? With me naked?* He wanted to blame Melody but realized the idea was stupid. Finding the control he needed, he treaded further out from the pond's edge, hoping Gimmel didn't have some sort of telepathic vision as well.

"What're *you* doing here?" he yelled, now far from the shore.

"Usually you are back at the house by now. Daddy is already preparing food. He sent me out to look for you. Thought you might be here. He was right." Gimmel seemed completely unaware of the awkward situation. However, when Ethan noticed his tunic and sash hanging down from her small arm, he wished he could tie a concrete block to his feet and disappear. As a dad, the whole scene disturbed him. *How do I explain this to Malachi? What will he say? Or do?*

"A swim sounds like fun. Maybe another day?" Gimmel's words did not give away any embarrassment or fear. "I have your tunic so come on, we should go." She held it up in one hand, beckoning him in with her other, the bright smile never leaving her face.

"Why don't you just leave my clothes and head on home, Gimmel. I'll hurry and catch up with you." It took all of Ethan's focused energies to remain calm.

"Don't be alarmed. She's not. Nor does she find this awkward." The thought drifted into his mind on that same children's tune. He knew it was meant to help him, but the comment sounded ridiculous.

Gimmel tilted her head. "Daddy said to bring you back with me." Ethan could see her downturned face and though his arms were tiring, he couldn't bring himself to swim to shore.

"Don't be afraid. I'm sending someone to help." This time Melody's words alleviated some of Ethan's angst.

"Help." Ethan said the word softly.

"Hello, friend." The boisterous voice of Baldwin had never been a more welcomed sound. "Enjoying the pond I see." Baldwin chuckled, waving robustly. "You can go, Gimmel. I will make sure Ethan gets home."

"But that's not …"

"No worries, Gimmel." Ethan tried to sound as convincing as possible. "We'll be right behind you."

"Okay." Gimmel dropped the tunic in Baldwin's arms and bounded off.

Ethan thought of a sprightly gazelle that just missed the hunter's snare as he watched her disappear down the trail. He dove down and came up on the water's edge. "Man, how awkward." He waded out, squeezing excess water from his hair.

"If you say so." Baldwin handed Ethan his tunic and sash. "I came only at Melody's request. But why?"

"You kiddin' me?" Ethan pulled the tunic over his head. He looked at Baldwin. "Did you not see me? Swimming butt-naked?" His voice rose with each word. Baldwin just gave Ethan a confused "so what" face and then laughed again.

"Oh, wow. Your world is comical." Baldwin shook his head. "But maybe we should walk and talk. After all, I promised to get you home." He turned, heading up the trail.

"Comical?" Ethan put on his sandals as he hopped along, trying to keep up. "Our world is comical?" He didn't like Baldwin's inference. "What the heck's so comical about me being naked around Gimmel? I should never be displaying my junk around her." Still ashamed, Ethan yanked the sash tighter around his tunic.

"*Peace, Ethan. Peace.*" Melody's gentle song broke into his thoughts, this time on the soft notes of "Moonlight Sonata." "*Release your anger to me. Make that choice.*"

"I am sorry." Baldwin gave a slight bow. "The tunes in my head about your world? Well, I simply found humor in how you view the human body."

"Yeah, hilarious."

"I heard words like 'shame and embarrassment.' Foreign words to us. Even Melody's explanations are difficult to comprehend. I only have Eden's perspective. Is that suitable?"

"Suitable? Oh, I'm sure." Ethan didn't hold back the mockery in his voice. He sighed, ever the *farang* when not even Baldwin could read his sarcasm.

Baldwin shrugged. "In our world, the human body is beautiful since we are made in the image of the one who made us. Nakedness is neither good nor evil, it just is."

"Okay?" Ethan said it slowly, trying to wrap his head around Baldwin's words.

"There is nothing unsound about the look of our bodies. From what Melody has told me, in your world, viewing the naked body can lead to temptations that cannot be resisted.

We take delight in the differences between male and female of all living things. Together we make a beautiful song." Baldwin closed his eyes and spread out his arms.

Ethan expected him to burst out in some country music love ballad, but he returned to their conversation.

"Is it true that in your world you desire each other in a way that is injurious? Disrupting the light? That the song of harmony in all of life is somehow broken by your own wants and choices? So you cover yourselves?" Baldwin paused. "Is this right? I do not know." Baldwin's happy grin had turned into a perplexed grimace.

Ethan took a minute to think. "That's not always the case." Then he thought of all the wrong, the darkness and discord, not just in his own memories but also in Earth's history: wars, genocide, infanticide, and hate-crimes. Finally, he had to agree. "Yeah, I guess. A lot of disharmony." He did not look up. Baldwin remained silent.

Ethan rubbed the edge of his tunic between his fingers. *The tunic; it's a paradox.* "So if nakedness is okay, what's with the tunics? Aren't these coverings?" He patted his chest. "And you still haven't really explained Gimmel's actions at the pond."

"Bear with me, Ethan. I have never needed to explain any of this to anyone, although part of me finds the whole discussion intriguing." Baldwin peered at Ethan, a slight grin returning to his face. Ethan, however, did not reciprocate and Baldwin went back to his explanation. "The tunics are all the same, worn for service, mostly, but the sashes are different. The pre-epiphany ones wear light-colored sashes—lavender for the girls and turquoise for the guys, like yours, and mine. Did you notice?"

Ethan looked at his sash and shrugged. "Guess not."

"Then once a person has gone through epiphany, the sash color depends on a person's job-related giftings. Take Malachi—he oversees work in the fields, so his sash is indigo. Seshat is an artisan teacher so her sash is burgundy."

"I get it. But where does nakedness fit in all this? I have yet to see anyone naked here."

"You need to ask Malachi about this, but I think Melody asked him and his family to wear their tunics around you all the time, so that you would not be discomposed."

"Discomposed?" Ethan remembered Gimmel's actions at the table the first evening of his arrival. She had continually twisted and turned in her chair. When Seshat put her hand over Gimmel's, Gimmel had said aloud, "Wearing it at home isn't fun." Seshat kept her hand on Gimmel's for a minute or so and then they returned to eating.

"You mean if I weren't there, they'd be walking around naked? That's f … that's messed up." Ethan began envisioning the scene but then he forced it to stop, fearing the lingering image.

"This is normalcy for us. Again, neither good nor evil." Baldwin seemed nonchalant. They reached the gate to Malachi's house and Baldwin turned to Ethan, a glint in his eye. "I think … I think that since you are becoming part of the family, Gimmel did not consider your nakedness to be peculiar. You should actually feel honored."

"Honored?" Ethan almost choked on the word.

"Yes. It means she has accepted you as family. I think she likes having you around, sort of like a big brother."

Ethan had no reply, his thoughts already on what was going to happen next. *Now I have to go into the house and pretend like nothing happened. Maybe they'll be sitting at the table, naked.* His body tottered at the thought. *I need time.*

"Peace." Baldwin turned his head. "Is that what you are looking for?"

"What?"

"Peace," Baldwin repeated. "It is the word I thought of in the song Melody just gave me."

"I've heard that a lot in the last week. In my world peace is hard to come by." Ethan realized he wasn't even sure what peace felt like.

"Then I will ask that you hear the song of peace, my friend." This time Baldwin put one hand on Ethan's shoulder and grabbed Ethan's hand with the other, shaking it wildly, all the while beaming like a little boy after discovering a chest full of treasure. "But now I must go. I hope we will see each other again." Baldwin dropped Ethan's hand, and before Ethan could contest his departure, Baldwin had sauntered off down the path, leaving Ethan alone to face the family on the other side of the door. Petrified, he watched the lively figure of his new friend until it disappeared down a side path. He turned and dragged himself up the path and up the steps to the front door. Forcing his thumb onto the latch, he pressed down.

CHAPTER TWENTY

Announcing her presence with
Seductive curves and sways,
She lures the
Unsuspecting traveler with
Dazzling dance,
And flirtatious tales of
Deep, hidden treasure.

She beckons,
"Drink from my cup.
Taste my wares.
Surrender to my opulence."

Yet—shrouded by her beauty, beneath
Her scintillating surface lies
A powerful passion for
Control—
An insatiable Charybdis,
Sucking and churning,
Swallowing the innocent.
Swallowing the dreamer.
Swallowing life.

Beware the River's beckoning call.

Upon entering the house Ethan found that nothing had
changed. Each family member sat in their usual spot, in their

now-accepted tunics, their smiles offering him the same welcome, seemingly unaware of his neuroticism over his skinny-dipping. They were, however, already eating.

"Our apologies." Malachi dipped his head. "I have a gathering tonight and cannot be delayed." Ethan slipped into the chair across from Gimmel as Seshat placed a generous helping of spicy rice and chickpeas surrounded by roasted vegetables in front of him. For the first time Ethan realized he hadn't had a decent cut of meat since, well, since Canada. But no craving for one either. Surprising.

"Thought you would be hungry." Seshat smiled. "Gimmel tells us you went swimming. Sounds refreshing." Seshat turned to Gimmel. Ethan imagined them both giggling telepathically, but he saw no indication of it. Either Gimmel hadn't divulged the whole swimming story or the situation at the pond really had been inconsequential.

"Next time I want to go with him." Gimmel turned to her father. "Can I?"

"Maybe," Malachi replied, "if you are not at artisan school." Gimmel gave a little squeal of excitement. "And, that is, if Ethan agrees." He offered Ethan an easy smile.

Ethan had to think fast. He had no intention of taking Gimmel swimming, at least not until he could process the ethical non-issue of male/female nakedness. Could he ever accept such a disparity in belief systems? "I think, Gimmel," he said quickly, hiding his fears behind a big smile, "I think what I would enjoy is visiting your music class. I know we talked about it, but we never set up a day or a time."

"Yes. Yes!" Gimmel cheered, wiggling about in her chair.

"Actually," Ethan said, another idea suddenly popping into his head. "I'm thinking that I should be going to school too." He looked at Malachi. "Seems I have much to learn."

Gimmel clapped her hands together and let out another squeal.

"Is that copacetic?" Ethan turned to Seshat, hoping for a readable reaction. "I mean, I could be here for the long haul." *What?* The admission surprised him. It vocalized a disturbing resignation emerging from his subconscious. He was here to stay. He swallowed hard, wanting to cry, Gimmel's happiness only feeding his heartache, a stark reminder of Cassie's vitality and the relationship his heart ached for.

"That is definitely possible." Malachi beamed. "Good idea." He reached out to put his hand on Ethan's shoulder.

Ethan pulled away, the human touch only feeding his pain. "Good idea." He mumbled, pushed away from the table and stood. "Please, excuse me. I think I'm too tired to eat." He did not look up or wait for a response, but almost sprinted to the stairs, taking them two at a time, hoping the family hadn't noticed his watery eyes.

* * *

By the time morning arrived, Ethan had processed enough, was composed enough, to apologize for his rude behavior and move on. "Gimmel reminds me so much of my daughter, Cassie. I miss her, yet I find my dreams of her lessening, the images blurring." That was the explanation he gave Malachi as they sat down for breakfast.

Ethan took his usual spot. "Did you know this is my first real breakfast with all of you?"

"Yes. We are aware." Malachi poured Ethan a coffee. "We thought that perhaps sitting down to a breakfast meal was atypical for you. Is it not?"

"Atypical? Not usually. Guess I've been a lazy bum."

Ethan chuckled. No response.

Malachi finished slathering a soft cheese on his bread and looked up at Ethan. "What did you dream of last night?"

Ethan coughed, choking on his eggs. "What?"

"It is our tradition to share our dreams at breakfast. You spoke of dreaming about Cassie. Would you like to share your dream?"

"I … No. No specific Cassie dream."

"Then another one, perhaps?"

"Oooo yes, tell us a dream." Gimmel's eyes sparkled. "A dream from your world."

Ethan gulped. The dream from his world included Gimmel. Was he ready to share *that* dream? "A dream from my world." He smiled at Gimmel, not wanting to disappoint her. "Maybe another time, Gimmel?"

Patting Gimmel's leg, Seshat nodded at Ethan. "I think Ethan needed some warning. Am I right?"

"Warning. Yes. So, I now consider myself warned," Ethan joked, trying to hide his fear, though he noticed the slight pout of Gimmel's bottom lip.

"There will be other mornings, Gimmel, now that Ethan's going to school with you." Malachi gave her a wink and she dug into her eggs. The topic switched.

Malachi had already made arrangements for Ethan to go to school. Telepathy made that easy, Malachi had said. He accompanied Ethan to the artisan school, introduced him to the students in Gimmel's training group, and then returned to his own duties.

Thus began days of Ethan trekking off to school with his new little sister, the newfound connection with Gimmel a blessing in disguise. For even though her similarities to Cassie made him pine for his daughter, Ethan perceived a bond with Gimmel and the other pre-epiphany students that he'd been needing—that unashamed questioning spirit, that seeking to understand Edenic ways. Part of him wondered if they dealt with inner turmoil as he did, that perhaps Melody's song had less influence on their thoughts.

Fortunately, Ethan didn't have to "show and tell" his ukulele prowess for the first eight days, though Seshat informed him of the class's building anticipation.

"You'll probably discover a whole set of instruments you have never seen before," she said, the night before his "debut." He smiled, knowing his only focus would be on a guitar.

The next day Ethan came down the stairs anxious and unable to eat, not so much because of the performance ahead, but more because he was beginning a new training session. The day without Gimmel made him vulnerable. He didn't like it.

"Come to the music room right after your session." Gimmel chirped as she danced around him on the way to school. "And do not forget."

Ethan laughed. "Don't worry. I won't forget. As long as this new rotation doesn't kill me, first."

Gimmel stopped, the brightness in her eyes now gone. "Kill you? What do you mean?"

"Don't worry." Ethan gave Gimmel a hug. "It's just a stupid expression. It just means, I hope I can make it through the day without you by my side."

Satisfied, Gimmel's playful countenance returned, though that look in her eyes troubled Ethan. Or perhaps what troubled him was the returned notion that someone was watching him from a hidden vantage point, a thought he'd blocked out.

He didn't like that either.

Upon arrival for his new training, he relaxed, his fears needless, for there, on the edge of the circle of young men and women sitting in the grass under a large oak tree, sat Baldwin. As if in the know, Baldwin motioned Ethan to the spot beside him.

The teacher, standing on a small rise, acknowledged Ethan's presence with a slight nod, a nod that drew unwanted attention. Those around Ethan turned their heads, Reece being one of them. Only after Ethan nodded, acknowledging his stares, did Reece turn back. Ethan was sure Reece still doubted his appearance in Eden. Ethan couldn't blame him.

After a brief orientation on watermills, the group picked up their knapsacks and without directions, headed across the field to a wooded area.

"Where are we going?" Ethan half-whispered to Baldwin.

"To the watermill. Our first day of hands-on learning. We all know the mill but have not had opportunity to work the system ourselves." Baldwin sounded excited. "You ever worked a watermill?"

"A watermill? You mean like a waterwheel? I know framing. I know how to drywall. I kinda know concrete. But working a watermill? Sounds primitive."

"Primitive?" They walked in silence for a minute. "Perhaps you are right." Baldwin shrugged. "Other areas of our world are more industrialized. We do make use of some machinery but generally our community has chosen to remain agrarian."

"You chose this?" Ethan wondered why anyone would choose such simple living.

"Yes. Our elders did. An uncluttered society. From your reaction, it sounds like your world is not like this?"

"Ha. Not even close. I can't even compare the two. Perhaps it's like my world before the Industrial Revolution. Funny, I just assumed your whole world was slow."

"Slow?" The voice came from behind them. Ethan turned and stared once again into Reece's brooding eyes. Ethan found his tag-a-long position unsettling. Baldwin, on the other hand, didn't seem startled.

"Hi Reece." Baldwin gave him a quick nod. "Ethan was just explaining …"

"I heard," Reece interrupted. "Our society is slow." At that point the teacher intervened, picking up stride alongside Reece. He did not speak but when both he and Reece stopped, Ethan knew the teacher had initiated a telepathic conversation.

"What's his problem?" Ethan asked Baldwin. When Baldwin didn't respond, Ethan saw that he too was far away in conversation somewhere, perhaps even in the same one occurring now twenty feet behind them.

"He is okay," Baldwin said. "Just questions things more—like your presence here."

"Yeah, I got that from our first encounter. And," Ethan added, "from what I remember, you were on Reece's side in all that. Or have you forgotten?"

"Oh no, I remember." Regret resonated in Baldwin's voice. "I will just say that Reece can be very persuasive and leave it at that."

"Well, if it's any consolation, I question my presence here, too."

"I believe you, since you do not have the music to guide your thoughts with peace. Melody's song is good. Her ways are good. And she gives us the means to counteract the voice that says otherwise. She offers resolution. Reece just struggles with the choice."

"What? You hear other voices too?" Ethan picked up on that immediately.

"Voice. I said another voice. And yes, we do encounter a darkness here, though Melody gives us the means to dispel it. Her music is our instrument of light."

"Let me get this straight. You hear a negative voice in your head?" Ethan couldn't let the idea go. In this, he wasn't alone.

"It is especially prevalent in those of us who have not entered epiphany, since we are still in training."

"In training? You get mind training? As in mind control?"

"You do like to twist things." Baldwin laughed, but stopped when he saw the seriousness in Ethan's face. "Is that what you think Melody does? Control our minds? If anything, she gives us more freedom to choose than we deserve."

"I've heard that idea before, from someone in my world, someone who was close to me and then left." Ethan thought of Jill talking about a greater love than human love, a love so pure that it offered people the freedom to choose it or not. At the time Ethan thought it all just words, empty drivel. Nobody had ever loved *him* like that.

"No, Melody's music comes from the Composer and the Composer is compassionate and loving. He does not want anyone to turn from the light." Baldwin seemed to almost read Ethan's thoughts. "That is why we have Melody."

"Yeah, Malachi's talked about Melody, quite a bit actually. Sad to say there's no Melody in our world," Ethan countered.

"Are you sure? I thought you said you had music."

Ethan remained silent. He needed time to think.

"Artisan school is not just for learning how to run mills or harvest grain or play musical instruments. We also learn inner skills. I think you call it discernment."

"Discernment? For what?" Now Ethan was really confused.

"Well, I guess the big one would be discernment in knowing the difference between Melody's voice and the voice of darkness. By the time we are at level one—er—my age, the choice is not too difficult for most." Baldwin paused and looked back at Reece, now trailing the group on his own. "Getting back to Reece … he still hesitates to trust in Melody's music and voice, as you can tell."

"Reece. Right." Ethan had already forgotten about him.

"But there is no need to fear him, Ethan." Baldwin looked at him. "You were experiencing fear, were you not?"

There goes Melody reading my mind again. Ethan wanted to argue but knew Baldwin was right.

"With the help of the elders, and Lyric," Baldwin continued, "I am sure Reece will make the right choice when the time comes."

Ethan wanted to ask about Lyric, but noticing Reece's glaring eyes, lost his train of thought. Those eyes followed Ethan's movements into the afternoon. Ethan didn't like it, but neither did he want to be the wimp, and whine to Baldwin about it. Ethan did notice, however, how Baldwin discretely stationed himself between them. Either Baldwin sensed the tension or Melody had asked him to intervene. Relieved, Ethan turned his focus to the watermill.

Taking the steps up to a perforated metal mesh platform, he studied the massive, steel-framed waterwheel towering above him. The wheel was at least twenty feet in diameter, the blades about four feet wide and yet it turned with ease. Looking a few feet down, he watched the blades grabbing the fast-flowing water that followed a narrow channel heading to the river.

"Impressive." His comment was directed to no one in particular.

"It's an undershot watermill." Ethan hadn't noticed the girl who had quietly sidled up to him. When he turned to acknowledge her presence, he sucked in a quick breath. Not a girl but a young woman. Had he seen her before? He was sure that somewhere in his jumbled mind, he had a memory of that long, ginger-colored hair, that slight ribbon of freckles along her nose and upper cheeks, and those inviting green eyes, like lustrous jade. Those eyes. Where had he seen those eyes before? Ethan realized he was staring when she turned away. He did the same, suddenly back in junior high.

That's when it happened. Someone elbowed him hard in the ribcage. Ethan let out a groan, buckled over and looked up to see Reece. Somehow, he'd circumvented Baldwin's intervention.

"Reece!" The girl's voice was stern.

Undeterred, and with his eyes fixed on Ethan, Reece moved in again. But this time, his sandal caught on a prong jutting up from the metal floor. He tripped, and in his attempt to gain control, his body contorted into the railing and then twisted over the low guard rail and down into the churning water. The indifferent wheel continued its scooping and catching and turning.

Though Ethan heard no spoken words, everyone around him jumped into action. Two of the millworkers dove into the stream on the other side of the waterwheel as the teacher and students raced to either side of the canal. Were they surprised? Or just concerned? The millworkers remained below the swirling water's surface for a long time. Ethan remembered it later like a slow-motion film, one he felt somewhat responsible for. As the water continued to churn, the teacher and some of the students started a slow hum, reminiscent of the one he heard in the grain field. The cadence of the song built and with it a peace in the notes that enveloped Ethan's doubts and carried them away. Seconds later one of the men came up, his arm girdling a breathing, conscious Reece. Ethan could see a mix of blood and water dripping down the side of his face. The two workers supported a stumbling Reece up the grassy canal bank and the teacher wrapped a gray woolen blanket around his shoulders. Relaxed smiles spread across everyone's faces. Ethan let out his breath, unaware that he'd been holding it in. He waited for the expected outburst of cheering, or clapping, but none came, their celebrations all hidden from him in their telepathic synergy.

"He'll be okay." The silky voice had a slight, foreign-sounding lilt. Ethan found it enticing but he knew better than to look at her, keeping his eyes on Reece, still slumped over in the grass lining the canal. "The music guided his actions," she added.

"And what actions were those?" Ethan held back the desire to swear at the once-again bizarre world he found himself in.

"To swim down, deep enough to avoid the blades. Easy for one so athletic." Her voice carried a lightheartedness, as if she completely miscalculated the severity of the situation.

He turned his head, drawn once again into those strangely familiar eyes, even though they were set on Reece. Ethan's memory failed him. He blinked a few times to regain composure. "What about the cut on his head?"

The girl's delicate lips curved slightly. "His head hit bottom, but it'll heal."

Ethan let out a nervous chuckle. "Guess he listened a little too well."

She turned to Ethan and gave him a perplexed look. Her mesmerizing eyes tunneled into his thoughts. It made him feel naked. He looked away.

"Hey, Ethan." Baldwin's ebullient voice broke her spell. Ethan turned as his friend marched up the canal bank to the base of the platform. "Our session here is over. Did you not hear me calling?" He didn't acknowledge the girl that had Ethan so spellbound.

"Guess not." Ethan dropped his eyes, embarrassed by his boyish infatuation. "Sorry, man."

"Well," Baldwin continued, a twinge of anxiousness in his voice, "we should probably catch up to our class." He turned abruptly, motioning for Ethan to follow. "Besides, a few of them went with Reece to the healing center," he yelled back without looking. Not wanting to be left behind, Ethan scrambled down the metal stairs.

As the two of them hustled back to the school, Ethan took one last glance back at the watermill and the girl. The wheel continued on, its perpetual motion undisturbed by the nuances of life, but the girl was gone. A wave of disappointment came over him. *How stupid.*

CHAPTER TWENTY-ONE

Secret motives, curtained agendas,
hidden deep behind cool windows,
stained in deep opaque colors;
paned in obscurity,
vague in expression.
Soul or no soul—
beyond those
jaded
eyes?

"Will Reece be okay?"

"Reece?" Baldwin sounded surprised. "Without a doubt." When Baldwin's eyes became blank reflectors of the air shimmering around them, Ethan knew he was once again telepathically engaged. Ethan tagged it the "psyche glaze," though he had no one to share the term with. They walked in silence through the trees, the forest resonating with bird trills and small creature chatter. How quickly he had lost that initial awe and wonder of walking through rainbows of color and vibrancy. *What had happened?*

Baldwin returned to Ethan's question. "Sorry. Your question about Reece's physical well-being was like a heavy dirge. I needed Melody's wisdom."

Ethan had already moved on from their conversation, so he remained silent.

"Melody answered. Introduced me to your funeral song with its imperfect intervals. So foreign to me. Words like death, dying, ephemeral. We do not experience any of that here. As immortals, we never need to process the prospect of dying, for ourselves or for others." Baldwin shuddered slightly and shook his head. "How sad your world must be. And, to be honest, I would rather not talk about it. The topic disturbs my peace."

Ethan gasped at Baldwin's words. "You mean *none* of you die? Ever?" The idea was so foreign, so absurd, to Ethan. Death was impossible. He thought about the number of times in the midst of abuse and drowning in pain, he'd wanted it to end. Here, that would never, could never, happen.

"Malachi can answer your questions, Ethan." Baldwin gave a quick nod. "He is much wiser, much older in time-measurement. And you can ask him about the girl. I know you have questions about her too." Out of respect for Baldwin, Ethan stopped the questioning and their conversation became minimal.

Reaching the entrance to the school grounds, a group of excited young boys surrounded Baldwin, begging him to join their impromptu game of soccer. Ethan watched Baldwin's demeanor shift instantly, his infectious joy and love for life spreading through the whole, noisy pack. Ethan forgot about his questions, too, leaning up against one of the large wooden gateposts, a smile crossing his face as he watched the pandemonium. But then his smile turned down in jealousy, remembering his own inability to play team sports because of his knee injury. He switched his thoughts to looking for Gimmel. *Gimmel. I need to get to the mu—*

"Do you want to join them?"

There she was, the "ginger" girl, leaning casually against the opposite post. *When had she arrived?* Poof! All thoughts of Gimmel vaporized out of his mind. The woman's full lips curved up, though she didn't look at him.

"Sorry?"

"Do you want to join the soccer game?" She glanced at him, turning her body his way, sliding her petite hands behind her hips.

How can such a simple move be so enticing? Ethan blinked a few times, switching his thoughts to her question. "Don't I wish." He bent down and rubbed the side of his knee. "Have a bum knee. Hockey injury. I'm afraid if I …"

"C'mon." She waved for him to follow her away from the entrance. Ethan followed, his eyes drinking in her perfectly proportioned body as she swayed from side to side. Another familiar action. Yet in trying to pinpoint a connection to his past, his mind went blank, like wandering in doldrums of nothingness. He looked down at the goose bumps on his arms.

She turned around, sweeping the hair from her face with one twist of the head. "You're not like the others, are you?" She walked backwards with ease.

"Wha … what makes you say that? It's that obvious?"

"Mmm, a woman's intuition, I guess. I mean, you mentioned pain in your knee. That's not the norm around here." She smiled and turned forward again.

Ambling up beside her, Ethan couldn't help but notice her speech. He still heard the slight accent, yet her words were colloquial and easy. Even her use of contractions surprised him. He hadn't noticed until now. *Maybe here is someone I can really talk to.* "You're right. I'm not from around here. But I'm guessing neither are you."

She grinned. "So, where're you from?"

Ethan noticed she had ignored his comment. "Not this world. I guess. Sounds freaky. Not sure if I believe it myself. I thought I was in a dream. Now, I have no idea." Ethan waited for a response, all the while watching for a sign of understanding in her enticing eyes and perfect mouth. "Sorry," he said.

"For what?"

"For talking gibberish. Guess I don't know how to answer your question." Ethan was so charmed by her ways that he didn't realize she was leading him back to the waterwheel. He froze. "Why are we headed this way?"

"Thought maybe you were looking to face your fears."

"What the …" Ethan felt under attack. "My fears?" *Had he misread this girl?*

"C'mon," she persisted.

He didn't move.

She looked back, slowed but didn't stop. "Don't you trust me?"

"Trust?" Ethan laughed at her choice of words. *She obviously can't read my mind, or she wouldn't have used that word.* Yet, unable to control his actions, he ran to catch up.

She didn't say anything more until they reached the river's edge. "Your fears." She dropped her chin and looked up at him. "They're pretty strong." She turned, giving him her full attention. "They're, how would you say, captivating?"

"Captivating?" Ethan couldn't pull away from her mesmerizing looks, and voice.

"Yeah, you know, intriguing. You're so candid about your negative emotions." She leaned into him slightly, seemingly oblivious to Ethan's enthrallment. Then stepping away, she walked on, following the riverbank.

"And you like that?" Ethan followed, like a puppy with his tail wagging.

"I like fear." They reached the base of the platform. She motioned to the top of the platform with her eyes, reaching for Ethan's hand as she began climbing the metal steps.

"Wait." Ethan pulled his hand in, grabbing the railing to steady himself. "Why would you go back up there? After what happened to Reece today?" He looked up at her, hoping for acceptance. What he saw, however, was something like a storm drifting across her face, making her eyes wild and threatening, but only for an instant.

"Reece was an idiot. He hesitated when …" She stopped and pursed her lips.

"When what?" A reflex question. *Do I really want to know?*

"Oh nothing," she said.

The cloud lifted and Ethan's attraction returned. He breathed a sigh of relief.

"Don't you want to face your fears?" She placed her hand on his, her bottom lip in a sensual pout.

Ethan's body tingled at her touch. "Yeah," Ethan remembered. "But what I said earlier, about being afraid, I wasn't referring to the fear of returning here."

"Oh?"

"No, it had to do with my knee. I was afraid of straining my knee. Doing more permanent damage. At least right now I can still go hiking. That's what matters." Ethan knew this was merely his immediate fear, but it seemed to satisfy her.

"Oh," she whispered. "Guess I misunderstood." She stepped off the stairs. "Is that a fear lingering from that other world you mentioned?"

Ethan nodded.

"You *are* intriguing." She smiled and caressed his hand.

"Yeah, that other world." Embarrassed again, Ethan slowly pulled his hand away, wishing he had pockets. *Stupid tunic.* He clasped his fingers behind his back.

"Well, maybe I could help you with that? If that's what you want." She slid up into his personal space and turned her face to his, her breath sweet like ripe cherries.

Control, Ethan. Control. He cleared his throat and stepped back a foot. "Really? Are you in the medical profession because my doctor ... ?"

"No," she blurted, tension in her voice. Then, almost in the same second, she calmed herself and continued. "Not medical. Not really. But I have certain abilities I can offer. Favor for a favor?" She moved in again, her smile sweet, her bewitching eyes a swirl of green shades.

"Ethan."

Ethan heard the voice, but it sounded muffled, distant, like a voice from his old world. *Janus?*

"Ethan." The voice was stronger.

A solid hand came to rest on his shoulder from behind. Squeezing his eyes shut, he shook his head. Baldwin's voice broke through the cold fog that had settled on his mind.

"Baldwin. I ... I ..." He couldn't even form words.

"Where did you go?" Baldwin asked, forcing Ethan to turn, his back now to the girl. "You were there and then you were gone. I wanted you to join our match." Reeling as if in a drunken stupor, Ethan gripped Baldwin's arm. Gaining some control, he let go and sidestepped away from both him and the girl. Baldwin looked at the girl, their eyes locking. Out of the conversation again, Ethan slunk down and shut his eyes. He needed water.

"Here is water," he heard Baldwin say. "And we should return to the school, try out that knee of yours." Ethan opened his eyes to a full bottle of water, mere inches from his face. He took a long drag, not caring that the water dripped down his chin and on to his tunic, wet with nervous sweat.

Baldwin grinned and stretched out his hand. Ethan accepted the help, unsure of his physical state. He stood up, keeping his eyes closed. The wooziness passed.

Baldwin's last comment finally registered. "My knee?" Taking a few steps, Ethan paused, realizing the girl had disappeared, once again. "Wait. Where'd ..." He didn't even know her name. "Where'd that girl go?"

"That girl." Baldwin's voice dropped. "She is gone. For now."

"Good. I think."

"What did she want?"

"She ..." Ethan had to think about that. "She kept talking about my fears. She said she liked them?" Ethan realized how bizarre that sounded. Alice in Wonderland bizarre. "What a mad world, indeed." He shook his head, his thoughts still hazy.

"Such unusual words." Baldwin chuckled. "You are unique, but I think naive as well."

When Ethan opened his mouth to respond, Baldwin kept talking. "I do not think you are in a position to argue at this point. And I really do not want to discuss it. I am pre-epiphany, remember? Best you talk to Malachi." Baldwin looked at the sun beginning to drop toward the horizon. "We should return to the school. Come."

Ethan obeyed, hearing the sincerity in Baldwin's voice. Different than the redhead? Maybe. And yet her face still filled his mind.

"You should really try out your knee though, play some

ball with us," Baldwin said as they approached the school entrance.

"Really? Back to the knee thing? You don't know anything about it." They walked up to the sideline of the soccer pitch.

"I know what Melody has told me. I know that this world is not your world, remember? Things are not the same here." With that, Baldwin re-entered the fray of boys, leaving Ethan to make his own choice.

Ethan looked around. *Wasn't there someone else I was supposed to meet up with today?* His foggy mind wouldn't engage, so he returned to the action in front of him, wondering if this world really could heal his injury. Should he give it a try? Knowing the physical activity would help clear his brain, he inched his way across the white line and into the game, playing on the periphery at first, fastidiously guarding his knee from knocks and jolts. However, when a few of the older boys showed up, Ethan's competitive spirit took over and he soon forgot about being cautious. The ability to run freely up and down the field without pain energized him. Such exhilaration. At one point he wanted to just stop and laugh. He forgot about the highs and lows of his day, about Reece, about the girl, about the waterwheel.

But worst of all, he forgot about the promise he had made to a little girl.

CHAPTER TWENTY-TWO

Life's idioms—
Catchy quips,
Leading to
Lifeless clichés,
On lazy tongues,
And minds.

"The good life"—
"A fat lot of good it does"
To believe that
"Good outweighs the bad"
When hidden,
Silently stalking,
The sweet scent of good
Explodes!
Revealing
The sickening stench—
Of bad.

"E-e-e-than."

Ethan stopped in mid-stride. *Gimmel! Of course!* He looked over to the sideline where Gimmel sat cross-legged on the well-worn grass, her head propped between small fists, her eyes downcast. Even from the field, Ethan could tell she'd been crying.

Asinine me! How you gonna fix this one? Ethan left the pack and walked over slowly, considering his options. "Hey there, Cutie." Option one: make light of the situation. He joined her in the grass and ruffled her hair. When she pulled back and turned her whole body away from him, he knew that option wouldn't work.

"Sorry, Gimmel." He bent around her hunched body and gave her his biggest grin. "But did you hear what happened to Reece at the waterwheel? He fell in and …"

"That was hours ago." She glanced up at him with red, disappointed eyes, her bottom lip quivering. "I asked your teacher. How?" She sniffled. "How could you forget? You promised to come to my music class." She turned away, pulling at the grass. "You promised."

"I know. I said sorry, didn't I?"

"But did you mean it?" Not waiting for his answer, she jolted up, brushed off her tunic, and walked away. "I am going home."

"But Cassie … I mean, Gimmel, wait up." Ethan jumped up to follow, walking a few steps behind, waiting for her drooping body to perk up and dance like it always did on the way home from school. Not today.

Memories flooded Ethan's mind. He knew he'd done this before. Many times. To Cassie. He'd make light of his mistake with a brief apology. But was he ever sincere?

When the house came into sight, Ethan watched Gimmel run up the back stairs and slam the door. Once again, he didn't know what to expect when he went inside. His confidence shattered, he sat down on the top step, needing time to think. His eyes came to rest on the words of his tattoo once again: Come As You Are. *Come as I am? It's others who've made me who I am. I do what I do because of others. Reece. The red-haired girl. Their fault. Not mine. They both distracted me.* He slouched over, knowing his excuses were like howling winds blowing down from the Arctic during winters back home … bitter, dangerous, and unstoppable.

Help. It was a voiceless plea, but he was learning that it wouldn't go unheard. In that moment, he was counting on it.

* * *

The evening meal began in silence. Ethan had managed to slip into the house and sneak upstairs unnoticed, giving him time to process. He really did want to make things right this time, for all the times he hadn't. New world, new opportunity. Plus, Melody's gentle ways had reminded him of Malachi's words. He was in Eden for a reason. If helping Gimmel was part of that reason, and hopefully the way to get home, he didn't want to miss the train.

"I screwed up big time today. Need to get that out in the open." Ethan kept his eyes on Gimmel as they passed around the platters of food, hoping she'd look his way. She didn't. Malachi and Seshat said nothing, but when Seshat gave him a smile and a nod, he kept going. "Other people have let me down all my life, especially when I was a child like you, Gimmel."

"Hmpfh." Gimmel stabbed a piece of potato and stuffed it in her mouth. Seshat gave Ethan a little shake of the head.

"Guess what I'm trying to say here, is that I wanna be a better person than I used to be, Gimmel. Really, I do. So, I'm sorry for failing you today. It's my fault. Nobody else's." When Gimmel glanced up from her plate, if only for a brief second, Ethan knew he had her. "I wasn't a good dad to my Cassie. I let her down. A *lot.*" Ethan swallowed hard, trying to keep down the lump in his throat. "I believe you're giving me a second chance to change. Even …" Ethan dropped his head and closed his eyes. Finishing the sentence might make it come true. The three continued eating in silence, letting him work through his internal debate. "Even if it means I never see Cassie again," he finally said. He wiped wet cheeks with both hands, not even aware that he'd started crying.

Gimmel slipped silently off her chair to Ethan's side, and wrapped her warm, soft arms around his neck, her head on his shoulder. "I forgive you," she breathed, and then quietly returned to her seat.

Ethan couldn't remember the last time he'd known such peace, as if an 80-pound bag of cement had just slid off his back. Rotating his shoulders in disbelief, he looked up at Malachi, whose whole face beamed like a child's on Christmas morning.

Ethan smiled back. "I'm ready to share my dream, breakfast or no breakfast," he blurted out, without thinking.

"Your dream?" Seshat looked up from her plate, her eyebrows raised.

Ethan laughed nervously. "You sound surprised. Me too, honestly." Ethan put his fork down. "But … but I think I gotta do this … that there's a reason." All eyes were now glued to Ethan. "Maybe because it's a dream that includes Gimmel."

"Me? Really?" Gimmel squealed with delight, almost knocking her plate off the table.

"Hush, Gimmel." Seshat put her arm around Gimmel and pushed her plate forward. "I do not think this is a celebration." She turned back to Ethan and nodded. "Am I right?"

"I … I'm not sure." Ethan splayed both hands over his thighs to stop the twitching. "I don't know what kind of dream it is. That's why I haven't shared it. But …" He looked up. "I'm hoping you three can help."

Malachi leaned in. "We will try, Ethan. Helping another

to interpret a dream is foreign, but since you too are foreign, perhaps we can help."

"That's me, ever the foreigner." Ethan closed and opened his eyes slowly. "Okay. Here goes." When Malachi nodded, Ethan released a long breath. "I'm giving the short version. Hopefully that's enough." Ethan cleared his throat. "I had a dream back on Earth. Twice, actually. Both times, I'm running from an evil creature. And I come upon this beautiful pond … like the pond I landed in here, in Eden. And then this girl comes floating down from the sky and talks to me. Well, it's all telepathic, but what she says is lost on me. I mean, I understand the words 'n all, but the meaning … well, I didn't get it until I got here." Ethan looked at Gimmel. "And this is where you come in, Gimmel. 'Cause the girl in my dream was you. I'm sure of it."

Gimmel sucked in a breath. "Ooooo."

"Exactly." Ethan smiled at her. "Exactly my response when I saw you come around the corner of the house that first day. I was *totally* freaked out by you. I'd started calling you 'Ebony,' because of your long black hair. But there you were. Not Ebony but Gimmel."

"And what did this girl say, Ethan?" If Malachi was surprised, his voice didn't let on.

"That's just it. I can't remember her exact words. I wish I could. I've tried. But she said something about needing help."

"I was needing help?" Gimmel's eyes bulged out like big glass marbles. "Why?"

"Not sure if it was *you* needing help or me, Gimmel, though it was probably me." He laughed awkwardly. "Yeah, it'll be me. But … I have no clue." He offered Gimmel a crooked smiled. "That's not all, either. You also said to come. Again,

I don't know why. Then something about making a choice. And hope. I don't know." Ethan shook his head. "After that, you just disappeared up into the sky." Ethan flitted his hand up in the air.

"I did? I flew up into the sky?" Gimmel started flapping her arms. "How did I do that?"

"Gimmel." Seshat turned to Gimmel, brought the waving arms down tenderly, wrapped her hands around Gimmel's, and looked into the sparkling amethyst eyes. "It was a dream. Remember?"

"Your mother's right. Just a dream, Gimmel. But one I wish I could understand." Ethan looked at Malachi. "Can you help me?"

"Well," Malachi looked at Ethan solemnly, "from what Melody has shared with me, I can only tell you two general things."

"Of course." The angst began its slow swirl in Ethan's stomach. "It's 'cause I'm a foreigner, isn't it?"

"No, Ethan." Malachi's eyes took on the usual glaze, but only for a second. "It is Melody alone who illuminates dreams, even for us."

"Ri-i-i-ght. Melody. Who else?" Ethan shivered as a sudden chill passed through the house, and then it was gone. He slumped over in his chair.

"Be encouraged, Ethan." Malachi nodded. "Do you want me to continue?"

Ethan straightened up. "If it'll help, then yeah."

"Your dream guided you in your world, though perhaps you were not aware."

"Huh." Ethan pressed his lips together. His brow wrinkled. "Can't say that I was."

"I cannot answer to that." Malachi smiled. "But I can tell you that your dream also has meaning here."

"Yeah, yeah, part of my purpose." He sat back and sighed. "Not much help."

"Do not be sad, Ethan." Gimmel offered Ethan a huge grin. "You *are* helping me by coming to music class. Remember?"

"So true, Gimmel. But I believe there is so much more." Malachi pushed his empty plate away, leaned back, and burst out laughing.

"You think this funny?" Ethan slapped his hands on the table. "Is my life a joke to you?"

"No, Ethan. Not at all." When Malachi reached out his hand, Ethan pulled away, and put his hands in his lap. Malachi's smile held firm. "Again, I wish I could share with you telepathically the conversation I had with Melody today. It was about you."

"Nothing new there, right? You're *always* talking about me." Ethan wanted to leave.

"Ethan." Seshat's mother-love tone calmed Ethan down.

"I am sorry." Malachi's rich voice softened. "My intention was to encourage you. You see, all our discussion this evening has been moving toward a request of Melody's earlier today. Again, I questioned her timing, but not now. Now I understand. That is why I laughed." He grinned wildly. "Excitement bubbled up inside of me, and I had to let it out."

Ethan stared at Malachi, shaking his head. "What the heck're you talking about? You're making my head hurt. Can someone please explain?" He looked at the girls.

"Firstly, you made reparations with Gimmel, did you not?" Malachi continued.

"Reparations?" Ethan looked at Gimmel. "Yeah, I guess so."

"And an overwhelming peace came over you. Correct?"

"Yes, it did. I'm sure you know. What was that?"

"That was you, my friend, changing your tune."

"I did what?" Ethan looked at Seshat and Gimmel. Both were smiling, with Gimmel almost dancing in her seat. Ethan didn't smile. "You're all excited but I'm still lost."

"Okay." Malachi's perpetual smile returned. "At birth, we are all given the beautiful gift of a song. I believe I have mentioned this in past conversations. You heard a chorus of them out in the field the other day."

"And today too." Ethan nodded. "When Reece fell in the river."

"Yes," Malachi said, responding to Ethan's addition. "We will need to discuss today's events. But now I am talking about your song, the song you came to Eden with. To us, incomprehensible. Melody had to explain the sour notes and unusual chord progressions."

"The devil's interval." The term spewed from Ethan's mouth. And for the first time since arriving in Eden, Ethan's words caught Malachi off guard. He turned his head to look at Ethan, mouth open and eyes wide.

"Is that what you call the dissonance? An untranslatable term, it seems." Malachi's face relaxed. "The word I would use is 'lament,' though that is still not precise."

"A lament? Is that like a dirge?" Ethan mocked.

"Of sorts, I surmise." Malachi's eyes twinkled. "But just now, your song began to change. A shift started. It was unexpected. And I laughed with joy."

"Joy?" Ethan's brow furrowed. "Joy. Okay. I get it. But what does that have to do with my dream, or your conversation with Melody?"

"The girl in your dream …"

"Gimmel."

"Okay. Gimmel was talking about coming and helping, whether to offer help or to receive help, correct?"

"Yeah, so-o-o?"

"The elders of our community are in the midst of dealing with an issue that has arisen that is in need of help."

"That's gotta be me, right? I'm the issue? The problem? C'mon, spit it out." Ethan pushed his hair back off his forehead with both hands and rested his head in his hands. Always the problem. *That* he was familiar with.

"I will assume that means you want me to proceed so I will. The truth is, Ethan, you are part of the solution. Part of the help. Not the problem."

Ethan lifted his head in surprise. "What? Me? How?"

Malachi chuckled. "Honestly, I do not know. What I do know, and want to obey, is Melody's request that you come with me to an elders' meeting tonight. As I said, I questioned her timing, but after all that has transpired here, I see again that her ways are perfect."

Ethan's mouth gaped open. He stared back and forth at all three. "What? Join you? I'm not an elder. Heck, I'm a nobody, really. You know that. I'm just a visitor trying to get home."

"Meaning and purpose, Ethan. Remember?"

"Sh—shoot. You're right." Ethan leaned back in his chair and closed his eyes.

Seshat joined the conversation. "Peace, Ethan. Peace in all your questions."

"*All* my questions?" Ethan sat up, curious as to what she meant. Malachi looked at Seshat and put his hand over hers. A gesture Ethan hadn't seen before. She looked at her husband with raised eyebrows, and then turned back to Ethan.

"About the red-headed girl. You had …"

"You know about her?" Ethan practically jumped out of his seat. "How?"

"Come, Ethan." Malachi stood. "Let us talk on our way to the meeting. Out in creation we will find the fine-tuned harmony we will both need for the meeting." He got up and headed for the back door, not waiting for a response. Ethan looked at the girls. When neither offered any additional information, he stumbled out of his chair to catch Malachi, leaving his meal behind.

* * *

Mostly out of fear, Ethan kept his mouth shut, his jumbled thoughts like lightless tunnels of confusion. After a couple of minutes, Malachi veered off the usual path, cutting a fresh trail through a field dense with tall, soft grass. In silence, he stopped in the center of the field, turned toward the setting sun, and closed his eyes. Ethan parted his lips but the urge to talk melted away. Instead, he too, turned toward the western horizon. The sky began to dance in vivacious hues of blue and green. Bright shards of reflecting icicles bobbed up and down in the ultramarine sky. Then subtle flames of pink and purple appeared, lighting up the shards in bursts of little rainbows, like hundreds of mini sun dogs shimmering over a Canadian winter landscape.

Ethan's apprehension floated away on an invisible arc of white light. In its place a happy memory emerged. He saw Cassie at three years old, twirling about in her ballerina tutu to a tune that sounded almost like Tchaikovsky's "Dance of the Sugar Plum Fairy," the fine netting of her tutu swirling and swishing as she spun throughout the house. Though

Ethan knew the image to be but a memory, Cassie's presence was so real that he put his hand out to touch her. She continued to flit about unaware of his presence and, overcome by an unexplainable quiet, he laughed. The image faded. Yet, the joy lingered. He put his hand down, a smile still on his face. They stood there, the two of them, watching the spectacle in the sky fade into a quiet indigo.

"Thank you," Ethan whispered.

"You're welcome," came a whispering lilt, dancing on lingering celesta bells.

Malachi finally spoke. "Are you composed?"

Ethan looked at Malachi curiously.

"Are you good? At peace?"

"Yes. Are you?"

Malachi smiled and returned to walking through the field, fireflies now rising from the earth, lighting their way. Then the path widened, allowing the two to walk side-by-side through a sparse grove of trees. Malachi spoke. "I had thought your involvement in these meetings would be at a later date. But unforeseen circumstances have changed that, as I said earlier."

"Unforeseen circumstances? Is there such a thing in this world?" Ethan was curious, his mind still quiet.

"Humanly speaking, yes. To Melody, no. You must remember, in her wisdom she reveals what she deems necessary for us to follow her song, to make right choices."

"Huh."

"Anath's arrival. That is the unforeseen circumstance. Her presence is somber because we know so little about her."

"Anath?"

"The red-haired girl, as you call her."

"Ah. Anath."

Malachi half turned to him. "Tell me about her."

"I don't know anything. Not really. But then, maybe the little I know will help." When Malachi said nothing, Ethan continued. "I met her at the waterwheel. Fascinating, the waterwheel, I mean." Ethan did not want to confess his real attraction.

Malachi kept walking. "The waterwheel is run by Yuval. He is a millworker, born and raised in this community. I have been told that Anath is Yuval's relative, a niece, or cousin-niece, or however you describe relations. Yuval had never heard of her before, but she came with a letter of introduction from Yuval's cousin."

"Really?" That sounded suspicious to Ethan. He wondered if Malachi even knew what the word meant. He doubted it. "Well, you seem to know who she is."

"I know *about her*, that is true, Ethan, but I have never met her, so I do not *know* her. You, however, spent time with her today. I need to hear about that."

"Oh, well, we didn't talk that much." Ethan tried to sound indifferent.

"Do you remember anything at all? Did she ask you questions? I need to know."

Malachi's police-like tone startled Ethan. His heart raced.

Be at peace. The words floated in and his body relaxed.

"Yes, she asked me questions. Weird questions."

"About?"

"Mostly about my fears."

"Your fears?" His voice sounding agitated, Malachi stopped mid-stride, closed his eyes, and took a deep breath, letting it out slowly.

"Did I say something wrong?"

Malachi looked at Ethan. "If I asked you to repeat your

conversation word-for-word, could you?"

"Huh? I … I guess I could. Does it matter that much?"

"Good." Malachi picked up his pace.

Ethan tried to equal Malachi's stride. "You've lost me."

"It means her power to cause discord is still minimal."

"Her what? What the he … heck?" The ground quivered under Ethan's sandals.

"We are here." Malachi ended the interrogation.

They arrived on the edge of another field, this one well-manicured and dotted with mere outlines of picnic tables and barbeque pits, their long shadows stretching out from a central building—a large, round pavilion supported by eight thick logs. Bright lamps hung from the rafters and Ethan could see a few men milling about, arranging benches in a u-shaped fashion. Malachi stretched out his arm, preventing Ethan from advancing. "I need to tell you something else before we enter the meeting." Malachi spoke with quiet intensity.

Ethan straightened his back like a soldier waiting for orders.

"I have not explained about the cacophony in this world," he said.

"Caco …" Ethan tried to interrupt.

"Just listen." It was almost a command. He looked at the building and then breathed out, slowly. "Our world is good and harmonious, but we do have an enemy. And sometimes our enemy enters communities through outsiders, disguising himself in some form of attractive means, depending on the situation."

Ethan shuddered.

"Sometimes in female form." Malachi stared into Ethan's face, as if waiting for Ethan to understand what he was saying.

A cold sweat formed on Ethan's skin. "Are you talking

about Anath? She is the enemy? How?" Ethan lowered his eyes and shook his head. "Then what am I? As an outsider?"

Malachi put his hand on Ethan's shoulder. "We have talked about this before, Ethan. Anath's appearance was not like yours. And lack of information about her causes us to wonder."

"But aren't you being hasty in …"

"Listen, Ethan. Information, or lack thereof, is not the only guide for us. Wisdom from past experience. Unsettled minds. Plus, a certain shift of discord within nature. These are all signs as well." Malachi looked straight at Ethan. "Did you experience any of that? When you were with her?"

"I don't think so." But then Ethan remembered his unease with her advances. "Well maybe," he admitted.

"Speaking truth is good." Malachi patted Ethan's shoulder. "Also, the fact that she contacted you reinforces our suspicions."

"What? Why?"

"Because of your vulnerability as a newcomer. The enemy is not stupid. Is never stupid."

Ethan's head throbbed. The weight of the whole day pressed in. His fingers began to twitch along his tunic. He needed to sit down, or lie down. "I can't … I gotta go." When Ethan tried to turn around, Malachi pressed his hand firmly on his shoulder.

"No. You must stay."

Surprised by such a strong rebuttal, Ethan complied without question.

"It is not in my nature to be so forward." Malachi's voice quieted. "Melody has asked that you be here tonight, remember?"

"Do you know why yet?"

"I only know that it has something to do with your experiences from your world. An area unfamiliar to me. But again,

Melody assures me you are ready."

Ethan had no idea what experiences those would be, but from the dim reflection of pavilion lamps, he could see in Malachi's face the tender look a father might give his son.

"Remember what happened at the table this evening. Your song is changing." Malachi lowered his arm. "Do not fear, Ethan. Melody will give you strength."

"I don't know about Melody. But I see and trust you, Malachi."

Do I really? Trust? Is that part of my changing song?

"This is not the first time we have had to deal with evil, nor will it be our last." Malachi lifted his chin. "For those of us who have returned from epiphany, the power to defeat and eject such a threat is always with us and in us."

"No sh … seriously?" Power. Ethan liked that. "Well, if that's the case, then what's the issue? Why the concern?"

"The concern, as you put it, is for the pre-epiphany ones, you included, who have not yet been given the lyrics to their tune. They are still learning discernment. I think Baldwin mentioned discernment to you, right? In discussing Reece?"

"Reece. Right." Ethan sighed. Then he stepped back from Malachi. "Wait. You mean that's why he was in my face? Because of Anath? And why he fell in the river? Was she creating discord?"

Malachi shook his head. "Not creating, but definitely waking a sleeping restlessness. Reece has always had a propensity to question things, which is not wrong. With correct guidance, his voice will add a fuller sound to the community's harmony. But it seems Anath is taking advantage of his inquisitive mind. At least that is what we think."

"Creating discord." Ethan began pacing in front of Malachi. "I admit. I was uneasy around her. But I thought the issue was me, not her." He pressed his thumb into his chest. "She had this concern in her voice. Like she really cared about me."

"Hmm." Malachi seemed surprised, though briefly, by Ethan's assessment of Anath. "Sometimes our eyes betray us, prevent us from hearing the underlying babble."

Ethan stopped his pacing and clenched his fists. Malachi responded with a look of fatherly devotion. "I do not mean to offend, but as I said, this is not a first. I believe the fact that she sought you out, and talked to you, is why *you* are here tonight, Ethan. That is all I know." Sensing Malachi's sincerity, peace returned to Ethan's mind.

Malachi turned to the pavilion. "Looks like the meeting will commence soon. Perhaps begin by just listening." He began walking toward the light, motioning with his hand for Ethan to follow. "Because you are not from this world, some of the elders questioned whether you were of the darkness. But be assured, I have explained your circumstances. Not like Anath's. Melody has confirmed my words."

Ethan had no idea such deliberations had been going on behind his back. He frowned. "Should I be relieved?"

"Again. We can discuss more later." Malachi whispered as they kept walking toward the light. "Our concern tonight is Anath, and perhaps her effect on you as an outsider. We are entering the unknown."

"That's encouraging." Ethan didn't like this one bit.

"Ethan. Remember that even in this world, we all make our own choices."

"I …"

"No more discussion." Malachi stopped behind one of the posts at the edge of the building, hiding briefly in the shadows. "We will take seats on a peripheral bench. Normally I am up front, but tonight is an exception. They all know I am accompanying you."

Ethan didn't know if he should be thankful or not. He didn't know what to think. He didn't want to think at all.

Malachi put both hands on Ethan's shoulders this time. "Remember. Melody has promised you her euphonic peace. Listen to it and trust her." He put his hands down. "Come." He nodded toward the front. "The meeting is starting." The two of them slipped in seemingly undetected.

Ethan sat silently alert, a whirlwind of mixed emotions racing through him. He felt like a spectator sitting in the Roman Colosseum, waiting to be thrown into the ring, a victim in a blood-lust gladiatorial game.

Both men and women were present, about fifty, and when they all stood up and began humming, Ethan was grateful that this was not his first encounter with such actions. As expected, the humming built into the final crescendo of a beautifully harmonic song, the words all foreign to Ethan. Nonetheless, the blended tune seemed to settle on the meeting. Sensing Melody's immediate presence riding on the music, Ethan relaxed his tense muscles and his clenched jaw. As they all sat down, Malachi gave him a bright smile.

The meeting continued, in silence. From the specific gestures and body language, Ethan knew he was witnessing a vibrant telepathic discussion, though their faces showed no anger or misdirected confrontation. At the head of the u-shape sat three men and one woman, and when one of the men finally rose, the gestures stopped, and people relaxed on their benches.

Malachi turned to Ethan and leaned close to whisper.

"Are you ready?"

"Ready? Ready for what?" Ethan half-mouthed, irritated at the personal exclusion.

Malachi cocked his head and, with his eyes, directed Ethan to look over to the far aisle. *What now?* A hesitant Yuval entered the building. Then, from out of the shadows, a strutting Anath followed. Ethan cringed.

CHAPTER TWENTY-THREE

Churning tornado
Howls—descends from the heavens;
Boastful touchdowns of
Unbridled pow'r. Chase not the
Designed foray of fury.

"Anath." Her name spilled out of Ethan's mouth in a voice loud enough to turn heads. He leaned forward, trying to hide his presence. *Control, Ethan. Control.*

As Yuval and Anath sat down on the edge of the front row, one of the men addressed the group. "Due to the nature of this meeting, we will be vocalizing our discussion from this point on. I realize this is an anomalous request, but the situation is also anomalous." He looked directly at Malachi, who concurred with a nod. "And remember," he continued, "the telepathic undertones behind your words will also be noted."

When he called Anath to the front, she rose, immediately turning her head, fixing her eyes on Ethan with a bashful innocence, at least to him. Instantly, his mind wandered. First, to a courtroom scene, not the empty courtroom that he knew from his custody case over Cassie, but the typical scene from a television courtroom drama, crowded with the jury and lawyers and detectives and witnesses and observers. *How overwhelmed Anath must be, all alone up there.* An animosity toward the crowd of elders germinated in his mind.

Then a more powerful daydream dethroned the first. He was back in Northern Myanmar on the edge of a trail, Cassie beside him. With her small hand in his, she looked up at him, her eyes wide with anticipation. He smiled at her as together they began a hike. Then, out of nowhere, Janus and Barnabas appeared, joining them on the path. Their steps were light, their conversation peppered with laughter, as they followed the wide, level path. The bright sun shone down on them in perfect warmth. Upon reaching the white-sand beach of a pristine river, they dropped their gear. Cassie giggled over a flock of opaline egret-like birds whooping quietly beside the sleepy waters as Ethan breathed in the tantalizing scent of steak on the barbeque. His mouth began to water. He hadn't had steak for so long. A grinning Barnabas handed Ethan not just a medium-rare rib eye but also a frothy mug of beer. Beer! Ethan took a long swig of the cold, golden brew, his taste buds dancing at the back of his throat. He chewed each bite of the succulent meat slowly, relishing the rich flavor. He let out a small groan of pleasure.

"Ethan." Malachi's whisper shook him from his dream. "Ethan." Malachi nudged him lightly on his forearm.

Ethan blinked. "What?" He was completely unaware his mind had drifted off far away from his body, far away from the present encounter. Part of him longed to go back to his "perfect day" daydream. Malachi motioned for Ethan to follow him as he slid off the bench and out into the shadows. Ethan complied.

Malachi continued in a low whisper once they were out of earshot of the meeting. "Where were you?"

"Whaddya mean?" Ethan's mind was still in a fog.

"Melody informed me that you lost focus."

"Umm, maybe. What does it matter?"

"Do not be deceived." Malachi looked back at the scene under the bright lights.

"What?" Unable to concentrate, Ethan squeezed his eyes shut.

Malachi took hold of Ethan's upper arm and shook it gently. "She is toying with your mind, is she not? Distracting you from seeing who she really is?"

"She's doing what?" Ethan's whole body tingled, like it had fallen asleep. He shook himself, trying to unchain his stupefied mind. He could swear the lingering taste of steak still clung to his taste buds. He was glad Malachi gave him a moment to gain some control, though his mind was still a box of scrambled puzzle pieces. "Is that why my daydream felt so real?"

"Yes. I actually had no idea, but Melody did." Malachi again placed both his large hands on Ethan's shoulders. "Between Melody's presence and the harmony of the group, you are safe. Remember that." Malachi's fatherly voice was fast becoming a still point for Ethan. "Are you okay now?" Malachi peered at him.

Ethan closed his eyes and concentrated on his breathing, checking his emotional state. *One deep breath in; one deep breath out. And again.* "Yes." He opened his eyes. "I'm good."

"You are good." Malachi repeated with a smile. "Peace, Ethan. Melody's peace. Rely on it." He put his hands down. "Come. We need to return to the meeting." He beckoned Ethan back into the pavilion.

"But ..." Ethan tried to contest, still slightly unhinged. He stood in the shadows for a minute, a war raging in his mind between two choices: trusting Malachi or succumbing to Anath's utopian daydream. *Where is the peace Malachi mentioned? Melody.* His inner voice spoke her name. Instantly, the daydream lost its attraction. His body and mind fully engaged, he slipped back in beside Malachi. Malachi didn't turn to acknowledge Ethan's return, but Ethan saw the corner of his mouth curl up slightly. Content, Ethan shifted his eyes to the front action.

Not trusting his own strength, he delayed looking at Anath. And yet he knew he had to eventually confront her hypnotic gaze. When he gathered enough courage to meet her eyes, he gasped. For there, standing at the center of all the attention, appeared not one but two outlines of Anath. *Another doppelgänger?* He grabbed the edge of the bench with both hands, trying to steady himself, questioning the reality of everything. But the form and frame of everything and everyone else stood firm. The only aberration in the whole scene was Anath. He released his grip. Malachi looked at him with questioning eyes. "All good." Ethan nodded and whispered. Malachi mouthed the word "peace," his eyes returning to the action up front.

Ethan fixed his eyes back on Anath, this time scrutinizing her bizarre appearance. He again saw two distinguishable outlines. The first, the familiar one that she presented to the whole group, began to fluctuate from solid to phantasmal, like the pulsing of his heart. Though her coquettish eyes had been replaced by black holes, he could tell that she was staring at him again, trying to bore back into his thoughts. At each attempt, Ethan's fallacious dream faded, her hold snapped in two, her power extinguished. The other outline hovered an inch or two above her. Initially diaphanous, Ethan watched this second image solidify, but not completely, as if still desiring obscurity. And though it carried the same body frame, it lacked the vibrancy of the first, seemingly covered in a lifeless, gray gouache.

Puzzled but no longer under her spell, Ethan remembered. He remembered where he'd seen Anath before. *Hers* was the face at the bottom of the pool when he splashed into this world. It was *her* bewitching beauty that had swirled into a hideous mutation, shocking him up to the water's surface. His body prickled with the awareness, as if just escaping from her lair.

In that moment of clarity, Ethan realized that in truth, it was the colorless "creature" who had the controls. He watched Anath's form mimic the posterior one, its lifeless eyes somehow affixed to her once bright green ones, now black hollow pools. Despite his new-found awareness, it still took all of Ethan's energy to look away, his body now covered in cold sweat, his twitching legs shaking the whole bench.

Breathe Melody in. Slowly, his body relaxed. Another memory entered his thoughts, a more recent one from his time with Janus and Barnabas. He remembered the night he heard about Khimsha ghosts. His emotions then were the same as now. He recalled the ghosts' choice of forms, their cunning ways and unsuspecting arrivals, their desire to instill dread, their insatiable hunger for human flesh. He also remembered Barnabas's lack of fear, countering it with words of love floating on soothing notes from his bamboo flute. Ethan had no flute. But he knew what he had to do. *Give me strength.*

Almost instinctively, he jumped up from his seat. "You!" He looked directly at the Anath duo. All eyes turned on Ethan, including the oscillating empty holes. Ethan's knees weakened, the urge to sit back down building in his mind.

Help, he cried inwardly. Courage returned. "You!" He pointed at Anath. "You. Are. A. Ghost." He spoke each word forcefully. Freely. Unexpectedly light-headed, he collapsed back onto the bench.

Anath began to laugh hysterically. "There are no ghosts in this world where nobody dies, you stupid human." The first outline screeched, laboring over the words. But with each word, Anath, the relative of Yuval, faded, her outline losing itself in the emerging creature. Soon all that stood before them was a chalky, charcoal gray form of the hidden Anath, its mouth filled with arrowhead teeth, its eyes still two black holes, though now they darted about frantically. The laughter stopped. Silence.

In quiet unison, the elders stood up. *Strength in numbers. But can they win?* Ethan waited, hoping for swift and decisive action from the Edenites. This *thing* needed to be captured and judged. *How does justice play out in this world?*

As if hearing the question, Malachi sat down. "Justice is not ours to give," he whispered.

"What?" Ethan had no idea what that meant. He looked at Malachi and then stood up and looked again at the hideous monster, its hatred foul. Pure evil. He sat back down. "Do you not see her, it, for what it is?" He tried to maintain Malachi's whispering level.

"Yes. It is our enemy."

"Then it deserves justice. And you're going to let it go free?"

"I did not say that. We will respond in the same way we always respond."

"And how ... ?"

Malachi stood up, ignoring Ethan. Ethan rolled his eyes.

Out of the silence, Ethan heard for the fourth time since

entering Eden, the slow beginnings of that symphonic hum, only this time he detected a new string of bass notes, enriching the hums of the Edenites. The hums grew into chants and, though Ethan thought the chant beautiful, its eerie delivery gave him the chills.

As if responding to a call, Ethan heard a new sound, like a massive, approaching hailstorm on the prairies, gusty and gargantuan. The chanting continued as each elder turned their eyes upward to the rafters. Ethan stood up, curious to see the thing's response.

It darted back and forth, trapped within a four-foot radius by some invisible force. Its haughty eyes were now dull pits and it cackled maniacally as if trying to regain its authority, though the lusty chanting of the group overpowered any likelihood of that happening.

A wind roared. And though the air in the pavilion remained still, it quivered with electricity. Ethan had never witnessed a tornado, but he imagined they were in the eye of one right in that moment. Needing assurance, he looked at Malachi. Malachi's eyes were closed, his face intense as if consumed by his own song. Ethan looked behind him, out into the fields. Nothing. No hint of a violent windstorm. No movement of the tall trees in the distance. Only the howling din. The chanting intensified, as if building toward a finale. Ethan turned back to the creature. Motionless now, it appeared to be howling, its fanged mouth turned up to the sky. Its cry, however, was no match for the whirling, flashing, bright-white tornado of blazing fire that descended through the roof, surrounding it completely. Ethan covered his eyes, though only for a second. He wanted to see, to watch, what was going to happen. *How is this pillar of heat and light not ravaging us all?*

We should all be dead. Instead, Ethan knew only a welcoming warmth within the power, as if they were gathered around an inviting campfire on a cool fall evening. Ethan had no words to describe such a paradox.

He looked around. All the elders had collapsed to their knees, as if in awe, yet not afraid of the gyrating, blinding presence as they continued their cantata. Ethan watched as a man robed in light stepped out from, yet somehow remained part of, the whirling blaze, his face shining like the sun. In his hands he held a double-edged sword, like a guard. Something about him looked familiar—another connection to Earth? Despite the concentrated whirling blaze behind him, he stood firm. In fact, nothing moved outside of the twister. Not the lamps hanging above them. Not the banners tacked to the posts. Not even their flimsy tunics. Eyes still glued to the seraphic swordsman, Ethan shifted to the end of the bench, poised to run if necessary.

The walls of light began to press in, lifting the heinous creature off the floor and then closing in under its feet with what looked like mini bolts of lightning. In utter futility, the creature tried to fight back, like a madman in a straitjacket. He questioned it later, but in the moment Ethan was sure he heard the tumultuous noise of wind shift to even deeper, fuller notes, like the heavy bars of a large vibraphone. He was sure both the tornado and the song slowed their rotations, as if someone had switched a 45rpm vinyl record down to 33rpm. The bass notes gradually took control, steering the elders' voices with such power and intricate harmony that Ethan's skin tingled again with goose bumps that danced with electric anticipation. He inched back, needing to touch the bench with his shaky legs.

The white guardian stepped back, sending the whole tornado into fast-forward motion. In the same moment, the spinning swirl of flames and light shot straight up and out of the building and into the night, taking its formidable voice and the creature with it.

Instantaneous and ineffable power. Ethan didn't know how else to describe the feeling. Around him but also inside of him. The sound of a world stunned into stillness. And peace. In the wonder, and the thought of victory, Ethan pumped his fists in the air and gave a loud whoop. Nobody acknowledged his actions. Still absorbed, the elders continued humming. Ethan, excited, but also mentally and physically exhausted, crumpled down on the bench, forced to simply listen. The elders rose and as they did, the solemn hum shifted to a vibrant laud of celebration, reminding him of an Israeli folksong he had heard, somewhere, as a boy. He watched the faces alter from intense concentration to triumphant joy. That's what Ethan had wanted; his celebration had just been slightly premature.

Still bellowing his jubilant song in bright baritone, Malachi turned to Ethan, his eyes shining, as if still reflecting the pillar of wonderful light. When he leaned into Ethan, gesturing for him to join in, Ethan turned away, unable to comply.

Had Malachi forgotten that the song from his world was a lament? Or was it? What had Malachi said? His song was shifting? Dare he join in? He began humming the melody he'd written years ago, the one full of pain and loneliness. After a few lines, he stopped. Not because the words had changed, they hadn't, but because he couldn't relate to them anymore. *What's that about?* He shook it off, returning to the present celebration.

But in the present, he also had questions. *What kind of tug-of-war had he just witnessed? What was this juxtaposition of bad and good?* Without answers, he listened as the harmonious accolades quieted and then concluded on one single note, the cutoff so precise that Ethan expected to look up and see a choir conductor give his closing hand signal.

Cheering and laughter broke out among the elders, a mystical shimmer on all their faces. Almost on cue, they returned to their psyche-talk, complete with telltale eye contact, hugs and clapping. Ever the foreigner, Ethan looked down at the ground, feeling shunned and alone once again. He placed his head in his hands and waited, wishing for Malachi's signal for departure. Malachi tapped his shoulder. All the elders had lined up single file before him. He gave Malachi a questioning look.

"They want to thank you." Malachi still donned his wide grin.

"What?" Keeping his eyes on Malachi, Ethan squeezed his lips tight, afraid he'd cuss.

"You revealed the enemy when we could not, so veiled was it behind Anath's personality, its hold on her powerful and weighty. You, Ethan, are a hero."

"A hero?"

"Yes." Malachi laughed and playfully slapped Ethan on the back. "And in this, you fulfilled your purpose for the greater community. Congratulations are in order."

A hero? A hero. Purpose. Isn't that what I wanted? Yes. But what just happened? Ethan looked at the elders, all lined up, all eyes on him. Embarrassed, he wished he could sneak away to a private place, to his placid pond perhaps. But he also knew that out of respect for Malachi, he had to capitulate. He rose to respond as the first elder stretched out his hand. Ethan put out his hand, offering a slight nod of reverence as well. He was not worthy.

What began as a painful endeavor for Ethan ended with an encouraging acceptance, for he looked into the eyes of each elder and saw appreciation and respect. He couldn't remember the last time he'd been singled out for a personal achievement, though he still wondered what exactly he had achieved to deserve such gratitude.

With the last handshake completed and standing in an emptied pavilion, Ethan could begin his questioning. "What … what was that?" he blurted out to Malachi.

"That, Ethan, was justice." Malachi's face glowed.

CHAPTER TWENTY-FOUR

"Let us go home." Malachi gave no further explanation. They walked back to the house under the moonlight, Malachi completely engrossed in a telepathic conversation. Ethan wondered who he was talking to, though he assumed the conversation to be celebratory because Malachi continued to hum the melody of the triumphant finale. Every now and then he burst out in gleeful laughter. Ethan sighed, looking up into the night sky. The unfamiliar constellations danced all around them, so 3D-like that Ethan wanted to reach out and touch their falling stardust. The moon, too, appeared fuller, purer, as it rose bright and bold just above the tree line. He watched it follow them along the path.

"I always preferred moonlight." He had forgotten Malachi's preoccupation.

"Pardon?" Malachi shifted his head, as if shaking off his other conversation.

Ethan lifted his chin at the glowing orb. "I always preferred moonlight."

"Hmm. Why do you suppose that is?"

"I don't know." He didn't want to get into a philosophical discussion about light and darkness in his own life. So he lied.

"Well, perhaps your preference will change after tonight."

"What? Why? I don't get it at all."

Malachi halted his sprightly gait, turned, and placed a hand on Ethan's forearm. "You unmasked the darkness and that called down the light. Your actions surprised us all. And again, thank you." Malachi's teeth gleamed in the moonlight.

"Yeah, yeah, I got the thanks." Ethan brushed Malachi's words away with his hand. "But I still don't even get what happened. This whole unmasking stuff? You call it justice? You gotta give me more than that."

Malachi closed his eyes and inhaled. Slowly. "Do you smell that?"

Ethan followed suit. "Smell what? I don't smell anything."

"That slight breeze from the west. Take in the aroma." Malachi took another deep breath. "The world is right again."

Ethan breathed in, slower this time, closing his eyes to concentrate. "Maybe. Maybe there's something there. I don't know. The wind doesn't smell. At least, not in *my* world."

Malachi opened his mouth in surprise. "Again, your world sounds so … so tone-deaf. And sorrowful."

Ethan didn't know how to respond.

"But we should not be sorrowful," Malachi proclaimed, his huge smile returning. "My heart is bursting. I am …" Malachi spread out his arms and looked up. "I think the word would be 'euphoric'." He made a child-like twirl. "Spoken words simply fail me."

Ethan was far from euphoric. Frustrated. Alone. Confused. Was he going to get home now? He knew his questions weren't going to get answered tonight so he walked on in tired silence, replaying the evening's mystifying events in his mind so as not to forget them. *As if.*

* * *

He tossed and turned in his bed, the moonlight now filling his room with such intensity that he was sure the white tornado of fire was still out there somewhere, hovering over him. He shuddered. *Where had the tornado come from? Where did it go? And who was that blazing guardian?* A myriad of questions still ran up and down the passageways of his mind like wild children refusing to sleep. He wished for pen and paper. Jotting down his thoughts might free his mind. He looked over at his bedside table, the gold-lettered title on the mahogany cover of the Eden history book jumping out at him in the moonlight, beckoning him to enter. *Maybe this book has answers. Maybe there's a section on what Malachi calls "justice."* Thankful for solar-paneled electricity rather than hanging lanterns, Ethan clicked on the bedside lamp, its light adding little to the moon's luminous presence. Pulling himself up, he reached for the book. A folded sheet of paper slipped out of the vellum-like pages and down onto the floor. *Where'd that come from?* Leaning over to pick it up, he heard music, the light fingering on an acoustic guitar. He recognized the tune: "Take Me Home, Country Roads." That was all. No added words. But he knew. It was enough.

He leaned back against the cotton-filled pillow, the folded paper in his hands, hoping the lyrics really meant the possibility of getting home. Dare he hope? The thought terrified him, and with it, the bag of cement returned, now pressing on his chest. Eyes closed, he lay there, forcing full breaths, letting time pass, then wondering how time passed in this eternal world.

At some point he must've fallen asleep because in the murkiness behind his eyes, an image of an old, coal steam engine appeared, way off in the distance at first, but then ever-growing, coming at him out of a hole in the black void, like a massive comet careening through space, leaving a smoky tail of soot and decay. He knew what it was—his siderodromophobia coming to haunt him in a familiar dream. He watched it grow, with ever-building screeches and grinding squeals. So many times he'd tried to stop it. So many times he'd failed.

But then something happened. Something new. The engine began to break apart. First the rods and wheels, then the smokestack and cowcatcher. Part after part began splitting off around the slowing engine until nothing was left but hundreds of silenced, impotent pieces. Then a myriad of tiny dazzling stars swooped in, plucking up the pieces and carrying them away, farther and farther until they were out of sight. He waited for their return. None came. Cognizant that his fear had been replaced by peace, he relaxed and opened his wet eyes. Wiping away salty tears with the back of his hand, he looked at the moonlight now illuminating the far wall. The eastern sky would start to show signs of sunrise soon. He looked down at the unfolded document on his lap and, no longer afraid, began to read:

Epiphany Explained

The experience of Epiphany is required by all. It is an individual encounter with Lyric that, for our community, occurs in the mountains outside of town at The Summit of Illumination.

When those known as the "Pre-Epiphany Ones" reach a certain age level and have completed the necessary apprenticeship both in service and in telepathic discernment, they will be sent out by the community to meet with Lyric.

This completion generally occurs at the beginning or the end of the Level 1 stage for the individual, between the thirtieth and thirty-third cycle of the sun.

On occasion, a Pre-Epiphany One may complete his or her training at the Level 2 stage. In this case, the person may enter Epiphany early if he or she so desires and if the community agrees.

In contrast, a Pre-Epiphany One may appear to need additional training upon reaching Level 0. This timing is inconsequential. Melody knows all and prepares all by Level 0 and the person must make the journey to The Summit of Illumination before the thirty-fourth cycle.

The period of Epiphany depends on the individual, the shortest known period being three days, the longest known period being forty. (Though it is unknown for those who do not return.)

Ethan paused from his reading. *"Those who do not return?" What the heck does that mean? And where do they go?* He wondered if Anath and her disguise of evil were somehow connected to that parenthetical comment. He needed a pencil, a pen, something to write down his thoughts, eager to follow up with Malachi in the morning. He scrounged around for one in the bedside table drawer. Nothing. Then he remembered he had a pencil in the small cloth bag that Gimmel had given him for school. Finding it under his bed, he dug for the pencil, then used it to circle the last sentence multiple times and continued reading:

The objective of Epiphany is two-fold:

1. *Personal*

    The individual seeks a personal encounter with Lyric. Lyric knows all that Melody has told him. Thus, he knows each person's story. Lyric spends an undisclosed number of days with each individual, revealing himself and illuminating every aspect of the individual by singing over him or her with joy and love. When Lyric believes the individual is ready, he bestows on each a new name, as well as significant lyrics to the tune given them at birth by the Composer. Both are relevant to the individual's personality and lifegoal. The third thing he gives is a new role in the community. And finally, he empowers each individual, enabling them to live a life worthy of their new name, song, and role.

2. *Societal*

    The name and words given by Lyric to the individual also announce their role in the community upon their return. The goal of the apprenticeship training before Epiphany is to develop an individual's specific gifts and talents. Thus, often the community can ascertain roles and purposes in the Pre-Epiphany Ones and can offer early Melody-directed guidance. As a result, Lyric may decide not to change an individual's name. Nonetheless, he always gives distinctive words to their tune.

    Experiencing Epiphany is not optional. At the end of Epiphany, however, the individual is still allowed to choose between accepting or rejecting Lyric's words and guidance. Those who accept Lyric's ways return to the community. Those who reject Lyric's ways never return to the community but exit from The Summit of Illumination by a different way.

Ethan came to the bottom of the page and turned it over, expecting more, but that was it. "What?" He was tempted to crumple the paper into a ball and toss it out the window. "That's epiphany explained? What a joke. And how's this getting me home?" He doubted the tune he thought he'd heard earlier and scratched a huge question mark across the whole page.

"What are you looking for?"

"Huh?" Ethan thought that's what he heard. He listened. No repeat.

Frustrated, he returned to the document, again reading the last paragraph, circling the contradictory phrases "not an option" and "allowed to choose." Curious words. Until recently, he believed he'd never had a choice in life, that other people and circumstances had forced him to behave one way or the other. But now, Gimmel, with her renewed belief in him, was challenging him to re-think all that. Still, his victim mentality would not go away easily as he remembered that *this* world was not *his* world. Yet Gimmel had somehow shown up in his world too, if only in his dreams. *So many questions.*

He shut his eyes, expecting the fearful return of the train but instead, the melodic soloist chords from "Come As You Are" flooded in with a whole new thought: *Come as you are, today. The past is over. A new day is dawning. The choice is yours.*

"The past is over." He repeated the words aloud. "Is it possible?" Ethan waited for Melody's response, but it didn't come. Instead, an unexplainable warmth washed over his ears. So pleasant yet so peculiar. He tilted his head. Something was happening. Sure that his ears had been reshaped, he touched them, outlining their uniqueness with his forefinger. They were the same, and yet, it seemed as if he was truly hearing for the first time. His life's credo returned: *I've never had a choice.* The words sounded empty. Discordant. And self-pitying. Words of self-preservation and loneliness. Words of fear.

In that moment, he realized he'd falsely blamed everyone in his life for all the bad that happened, when really he was responsible for a lifetime of dumb choices. *Stupid, Ethan. Just like my mother taught me.*

"Peace." Melody broke into his self-flagellation and happily carried away his accusatory thoughts, calming his mind and his body. He closed his eyes, his body slipping down into the covers, and with paper still in hand and lamp left on, he fell fast asleep.

* * *

Ethan awoke surprisingly refreshed. He didn't know the exact time. He never knew, but he did know it was still early since the expansive apple tree just outside his window still screened much of the morning rays of shimmering sunshine. The leaves quivered in a slight breeze and Ethan watched the sifted light dance on his bedroom wall, his mind at peace.

A quiet knock on the door. "Ethan?" It was Malachi. "Ethan, are you up?" Malachi repeated softly, bringing Ethan back to reality. *That's a first. He never knocks on my door in the morning.* He wondered what he'd find at the bottom of the stairs. A room full of elders? He curled up under the blanket.

"Ethan?"

"Uh, yeah. I'm coming," Ethan muttered. Malachi said nothing more, so Ethan pulled back the covers. As he did, the piece of paper flipped up and went gliding down to the floor. He watched it fall, all the memories of the night before flooding back, from the roaring tornado and the Anath-creature's disappearance to his reading of the document now silent on the floor. He sat up and bent down to pick up the paper. His body shivered at the sight of the page marked wildly with circles and scribbles and one big question mark. *When did I do that?* A degree of anxiety replaced the peace. Getting out of bed, he tried to ignore it. Then, with tunic and sash on, he and his list of questions scrambled down the stairs.

The house was quiet. *No school for me.* Ethan liked that idea. He found Malachi relaxing in one of two poppy-red Adirondack chairs out in the middle of the backyard, his eyes closed, his face to the sun. He looked like some prophet of old. All he needed was a staff.

"Have a coffee," Malachi said, his eyes still closed. Ethan sat down, grabbed one of the hot, steamy drinks from off a small circular table nestled between the chairs, and took a sip.

"How did you sleep?" Malachi's eyes remained closed.

"Oddly well." Ethan paused. "That is, once I fell asleep. My mind kept racing with questions about what happened last night. And then …" Ethan wondered if the document he'd found was just a bizarre dream. He pressed his hand against his sash. No, it was still there.

Malachi opened his eyes and looked at him. "I know about the document."

"How …"

"And I see you brought it with you from the room." His voice was unruffled.

Ethan pulled the paper out and tossed it on the table, resigning himself to Melody's ways and her telepathic connection with Malachi. "It's not fair." The pouting child returned. He forgot he'd experienced his own epiphany last night.

"What?" Malachi leaned back, folding his hands on his torso.

"Your relationship with Melody. It's not fair. Sometimes I

think you know more about me than I know myself. That's, that's just creepy."

"Sometimes we do not need full information. We just need to trust. The more we trust, the more she reveals."

"Again, that's …" He stopped himself. Remembering last night, he outlined first one ear then the other with his fingers. "A new day is dawning," he muttered to himself.

Malachi's lips curved up. Rising abruptly, he looked out on the golden fields and proclaimed like an orator: "The heaviness of evil has passed and the morning has arrived with newfound freshness and life. Let us not waste it." He picked up his mug and turned to Ethan, the familiar wide grin back on his shining face. "Come. Follow me."

A stunned Ethan waggled his head and dashed to catch up, leaving his coffee behind. "What's up? Where're we headed? Back to school? Gimmel and I still …"

"Do not fret, Ethan. That will happen, but not now. Now we go to your favorite place." Malachi almost skipped as he walked. They followed the well-worn path that wound along the river, so serene in the early morning stillness. When they took a trail to the right, Ethan knew where they were going. Back to his pond, back to his beginnings in this world.

"There is something Melody wants you to see." Malachi kept walking.

"Huh?" *Now what. Haven't I seen enough in the past twenty-four hours?* Ethan felt like a roller-coaster car, remotely controlled by a power outside himself, but somehow inside him now too. *Am I clicking up to the top or speeding down the track?* He didn't know.

"She fed you thoughts of home, did she not? Through the document?"

"The document." Ethan stopped in his tracks. He had left the paper on the table.

Malachi stopped, too, and faced him. "I know what it says, Ethan. Epiphany has been a part of our world for, well, since the beginning." Malachi continued up the trail. Ethan followed. "I must say, though," he continued, "Melody is creative, and wise, in how she has led you to Epiphany and its meaning."

Ethan stepped in front of Malachi and turned, planting his feet to keep Malachi from proceeding. "Wise?" he mocked, hands on his hips. "First, I'm thrown into a bizarro meeting, somehow forced to play my hand, a hand I'm totally oblivious about. Then Anath turns evil and a freakish tornado with a white knight whisks her away with a song. A song? Really?" Ethan glared at Malachi. "And then, on the way back to the house, you refuse to answer my questions. Instead, you prance around like a lunatic, leaving me to try and fall asleep without any closure."

"I …" Malachi tried to interrupt but Ethan stuck his palm in Malachi's face.

"Don't. I'm not finished." Ethan took a deep breath. "So, I can't sleep, but then I think I hear Melody's voice. 'A new day,' she says, offering me peace. But what about getting home? I'm somehow given a piece of paper. She says it's gonna get me home? There's a glimmer of hope. But it's a document that's just a bunch of … of … I don't know the word. But it has nothing to do with me. And suddenly pfft." Ethan swung one hand up as if in resignation. "Hope is gone." He choked under the emotional strain, unable to go on. "Hope is gone." He collapsed down to his haunches, his head in his hands.

Malachi bent down, putting his arm around Ethan's trembling shoulders. Ethan welcomed the tenderness, and yet loathed how it made him feel. Weak and needy. His mind wandered to a similar time: The day Barnabas had explained to him the presence of ghosts and he had fallen down, overwhelmed with emotion. Without a choice, he'd accepted help then. Could he make it his choice now to embrace the help? On his own? Yes, he could.

"Your song is changing."

Ethan remembered being told that. When was that? Only yesterday? It seemed like weeks ago.

"Especially after what transpired last night."

Completely spent, Ethan let himself go, falling backwards, not even caring about the state of his tunic. The cool earth welcomed him like an old friend.

"The written word really does fail in divulging full information. There is loss of meaning." Malachi sat down beside him.

Ethan lay there, not thinking about words or meaning, documents or tornadoes. "Can you just give me some time? Foreign, I know, but I need time." Ethan heard Malachi sit down beside him on the path and then fumble for something. Bluesy notes from his harmonica rose up to join the twittering birds, a hopeful tune. Ethan didn't recognize it at first. When he did, he shot up from the ground and yelled. "How?"

Malachi stopped playing. Suddenly dizzy, Ethan couldn't finish his sentence. Bending down, he sucked in air, hands on his knees.

Malachi rose and waited.

"How do you know that song?" Ethan lifted his head. "That song from my world? That Barnabas played? That Jill sang to Cassie? How's that possible?"

"Hmm." Malachi looked perplexed. "Come." He motioned

Ethan to follow. "I am as surprised as you, though it does make my heart sing. The restoration of Eden has increased the connections with your world. I did not expect that result."

"Is that a good thing?"

"Yes, I believe so. The strength of this connection will serve you well as you take your next step towards finding that personal purpose and meaning."

"That again?" Ethan wanted to turn and run. "And what's this next step? Not sure if I wanna know."

"How old are you Ethan?"

"What? Why are you changing the subject?"

"It matters."

"Okay." Ethan hesitated, and then thought about it. "Umm, thirty-three. Yeah, I guess I turned thirty-three the day that earthquake sent me down that rabbit hole, down to you and to Eden." He became aware for the first time that his birthday had come and gone. *Not surprising, just another forgotten birthday.* He laughed to himself. So focused was he on his own thoughts that he didn't realize they were coming around the final bend to the pond.

I'm thirty-three. He said it again to himself but this time it hit him. *Thirty-three is significant in this world, significant to Epiphany.* He froze. "Wait," he cried.

Malachi didn't stop. His steps seemed even more determined.

"Does that mean what I think it means? That I have to enter Epiphany?" Ethan was now yelling, his arms outspread, the concept sounding so absurd. Annoyed that Malachi was ignoring him, he started jogging to catch up, still shouting. "That's messed up. I'm not even a part of this world." Absorbed in his own thoughts and hating being the outsider once again, Ethan failed to notice the scene before him.

Malachi, his face beaming, turned to Ethan, then to the ebullient water in front of them, not saying a word. Ethan gasped. A cascade of water surged out from the cliffs high above the pool, gushing forth with intensity. A waterfall. His waterfall.

Malachi giggled with pleasure. "Eden has been restored, once again, and with it, your portal home, through Epiphany."

CHAPTER TWENTY-FIVE

There once came a young man from Earth,
Who'd lost his own personal worth.
They told him his choice
Would give him a voice
And then he'd find home—and rebirth.

The two of them sat in silence at the edge of the pond, Ethan awed by the water bursting from the rocks, then frothing up in the basin below, stirring up life, and Malachi leaning back on a rock, his face to the sun. After an hour of basking in the serenity, he spoke.

"When Anath appeared in the community, her malevolent intentions affected the natural order of things, one of those things being the closing off of the waterfall."

Ethan had laid back, disengaged his thoughts, and was nodding off. He frowned at Malachi's interrupting words. "What?" He kept his eyes closed. The words finally registered. He opened his eyes and turned to Malachi. "You mean it happened *because* of Anath? Really?" He thought about the elder meeting. He remembered how he'd seen Anath's face at the bottom of the pool when he tumbled into Eden, a face of beauty that swirled into a dark and hideous contortion. Malachi's words did make sense.

"Yes." Malachi cocked his head. "Although we did not realize it at first. She was cunning, though still limited in power." He grinned and turned to Ethan. "Remember, our world is not like your world. What you see, the physical realm, and what you do not see, the non-physical, the spiritual realm, if you will, live in harmony here."

"So when that tornado thing came down and took her, or rather it, away, the waterfall returned?" He leaned up onto his elbows, looking at the waterfall. "More rabbit hole stuff."

"Yes." Malachi chuckled, then paused. "But can I ask, what is a tornado?"

"Seriously? You don't know what a tornado is?"

"I could ask Melody, but I thought it time I ask you the questions."

Ethan raised his eyebrows. "That's a switch."

"Do you want …"

"No, I'm more than capable." Ethan sat up, tucking his tunic under his legs. "I guess it's a lot like what we saw last night. A swirling force of powerful wind coming down from the clouds, a force of nature. Once it touches ground it pretty much destroys everything in its path. So, you want to stay out of its way. In our world, anyway."

"A destructive energy?" Malachi sat quietly, lost in thought, in another conversation somewhere. "I cannot comprehend this fear of nature. The enemy must be strong in your world. Again, how out of tune." There was anguish in his voice.

Ethan laughed. "Yup, *really* out of tune. The stories I could tell." Not wanting to dwell on his own story, the natural disasters, or man-made horrors in his world's history, he squinted his eyes, focusing on the waterfall's source in the crags of the cliff.

"C'mon." Ethan stood and shook the grass off his tunic. Malachi just gave Ethan a questioning look. "C'mon." Ethan beckoned. "Let's see if we can hike up to the top of the waterfall. I'd like, no, I need, to know."

"But Ethan ..."

Not looking back, Ethan began to forge a path through the tender reed grass and fiery-red sumac bushes surrounding the east shoreline, hoping to find a way up. After half an hour of frequently snagging his tunic and slipping down on loose rock in his sandals, he realized that his spontaneous decision hadn't been a wise one. Finally coming to a wider ledge, he stopped, listening for Malachi. Nothing. But he was sure he heard something up ahead. He jerked his head around. *Did Malachi pass me somehow? Or is it my stalker? Or even a bear?* He had completely forgotten about wildlife awareness. *Stupid, Ethan.* A cold sweat broke out on his forehead.

"H-hello?" His voice barely audible, he hoped for a response. When he heard the grunting, he exhaled. Human. Not animal. He kept his eyes on the upper brush, waiting for Malachi, suddenly anxious to rendezvous, but when he caught a glimpse of the person behind the voice, he stopped. *Reece.* Facing Reece was too much like a wild animal encounter. But how should he react? Should he stare him down, trying to look bigger, or should he turn and run? He didn't have time to decide.

"Ethan the Alien." Reece smirked, standing on a lip of rock a few feet above Ethan, his arms crossed.

Ethan the Alien? Is that what they call me? His anger rose. He swallowed hard. *Help!* He waited for the anger to slide away. "Hi Reece." He tried to sound nonchalant, not wanting to confront.

"Hmpf." Reece put his hands on his hips. "And what might you be looking for? Wait. I think I know." Reece looked up the steep incline to the top of the cliff.

"Umm." Ethan was taken aback by Reece's sarcasm, a first in this world. "Yeah, well, I won't lie. I'm trying to get home." Ethan cleared his throat. "I think that's what you want, too."

"To get home?" Reece mocked. "That does not concern me. No, you do not know what *I* want. If you did, you would not have sent Anath away." Reece's voice began to build.

"Anath? That's what this is about?" Ethan chuckled under his breath. "Let me tell you a thing or two about Anath."

Reece bent his knees, as if preparing to jump.

"Reece and Ethan." Malachi broke through the bushes from a side path. Startled, Ethan stepped back and turned to Malachi. Reece straightened up but kept his eyes on Ethan.

Ethan smiled. "Boy am I glad to ..."

"Stop. Both of you. Stop what you are doing." Malachi was using his authoritative voice. Reece relaxed his arms and shifted his steely eyes to Malachi.

"Firstly." Malachi turned to Reece. "If you had attended class this morning you would have been told the truth about Anath. She came into our community to cause disharmony and woe." Reece's eyebrows went up at that statement. "Do not doubt my words, Reece," Malachi commanded. "And know that once she was exposed, the Composer's glory came down and carried her away."

"The what?" Ethan blurted the words.

Malachi turned to Ethan. "The Composer's glory. That was the tornado of light you witnessed. I thought ..." Malachi sighed. "I will explain more in a minute, Ethan. I need to finish conversing with Reece, for your benefit as well as for his." Malachi turned back to a still-stunned Reece. "So, Reece, attempting to acquire knowledge without the help of the elders, such as in this little venture of yours up this cliff, is not wise. Remember, learning patience is as important, if not more important, than learning physical skills."

Reece lowered his head. "Yes, Malachi. I am sorry. I …"

"You are impetuous is what you are." Malachi said. Then he grinned. "Come here, Reece." He motioned with his hand and head for Reece to come down. Reece obeyed immediately. Ethan watched Malachi put both his hands on Reece's shoulders just as he had done to him. "Impulsivity can be re-channeled into something great. Stay curious. Stay a visionary." Ethan watched as they seemed to switch to the usual telepathy. As soon as Malachi closed his eyes he began to hum. Reece joined in after a few minutes, merely a whisper at first, but then it built until the two voices sounded as one. Once Reece's whole body relaxed, Malachi closed with one long note. They both opened their eyes and Malachi patted Reece's shoulders. "Go home, now." Reece half-smiled and then nodded first to Malachi and then to Ethan. Without another word, Reece turned toward town and disappeared into the undergrowth.

Ethan didn't speak until he was sure Reece was out of range. "Phew, that was close."

Malachi smiled slightly. "Ethan. You, too, are impetuous."

"Huh?"

"You should not have run off, although Melody did share with me the emotion behind your actions."

"I'm just trying to get home. Back the way I came. Up there." Ethan pointed to the top of the cliff.

"Nature has been restored, Ethan, but up there is not your way home. Do you not remember what you read, and what we just talked about?"

Ethan knew. He just didn't want to admit it.

"Your way home, Ethan, is through Epiphany. There *is* no other way."

"Through Epiphany." Ethan took a deep breath. "I have to be honest with you. The idea scares the heck out of me. Can't I find my own way home?"

"Hmm." Malachi paused. "You must understand. The path through Epiphany is set for all. There are no exceptions, even for you, Ethan. It is there you make eternal choices. And for you, I believe how you choose will get you home."

Ethan groaned, closing his eyes. "My batting average with choices is below zero. You've seen that. Even here."

"Perhaps at first, Ethan, but not now. Remember, and alter your perspective. That too is a choice. You proved to be a hero, firstly for Gimmel in fixing your relationship, and then at the elder meeting. Perhaps your decision to climb up here was not wise, but I do understand your motivation. But did you notice in your encounter with Reece? You chose kindness over anger."

"Huh. I *did* do that, didn't I?" Ethan grew quiet.

Malachi sat down on a flat rock at the back of the ledge. Ethan joined him. "I am also starting to comprehend what it means to live without telepathy, as you call it," Malachi said.

"*Finally.*"

"Yes. I know. A concept so foreign has been hard to grasp."

"Yup, I know. My broken world isn't like this. I mean, men with dazzling swords don't step out from white tornadoes that roar and twist and flash, but don't destroy."

"I also thought you would have recognized that man with the dazzling sword."

"Nope." Ethan wasn't willing to admit that something about the white knight looked familiar. "Should I have?"

"Oh-h-h-h." Malachi moaned and lowered his head. "Your world has lost its ability to see."

"Huh? You lost me there. I can see just fine."

"Enough woe." Malachi slapped his knees and stood up. "Let us return to the joy." The smile back on his face, he turned back the way he came.

"The joy?" Ethan got up and followed, though completely confused.

"To the pond." Malachi chuckled. "The girls are on their way, both of them quite enthusiastic about the return of the waterfall."

"How …" Ethan closed his mouth as he followed Malachi down through the brush. "Guess I need to stop asking that question."

Seshat and Gimmel were waiting for them with a lunch of thick egg salad sandwiches, crunchy vegetable sticks, and fresh apple strudel. With a full stomach, Ethan decided to let the morning questions rest. The four of them stretched out in the grass after eating, relaxing under the restored, shimmering outburst of wonder. Every now and then a gust of warm wind sent a misty spray of water their way and Gimmel giggled with delight. Released from his insecurities, Ethan started a water fight with Gimmel that ended in all four of them getting soaked. Ethan felt happier than he had in a very long time, almost as if an enemy had been lifted up and away from his mind as well, though it wasn't until later that he realized the full impact of that fact. In the moment, he knew only joy.

They walked home in tandem, the men bookending "their girls." When Gimmel took Ethan's hand, Ethan returned to his world and the memory of Cassie's hand in his. For the first time, the connection didn't scare him. He glanced down at her. Her eyes smiled. They sauntered along, content. *I am part of this family.* He liked belonging. *Maybe I don't want to leave. Maybe I should stay.* Unexpectedly, the three began to hum. So peaceful. Ethan listened as words joined the tune, their harmonies as natural as bird trills and sunshine. He remained quiet.

After a while, Gimmel looked up at Ethan. "What about your song? Daddy said you have one, right?" She asked the question with childlike innocence. Both Malachi and Seshat looked at him, eyebrows raised.

Ethan, wanting to please Gimmel, answered. "Well, yes, but it's a lament, remember."

"But can you sing it?" Gimmel pulled on his arm and began hopping up and down.

"What? Now?" Ethan didn't expect that. He remembered Malachi's words: *Your song is changing.* He wondered if the lyrics had changed. And if they had, would they be appropriate? Gimmel coaxed him on with her shiny eyes, now swinging her arm, his following. He repeated the lyrics in his mind. At the last stanza, he remembered a couple of lines that he could tweak to offer hope. He began to hum, singing the words to himself: *"Eyes of hope will seek to find me / to offer rest from loss and pain."* But then the rest. *"The tunnels deep and dark envelope / A guiding light I seek in vain ... Lone destiny I find no home."* How could he tweak that? Not just the words but the melody as well? He stopped humming. He stopped walking. He pulled his hand away. His companions stopped too.

"My song." Ethan dropped his head. "Nothing's changed."

"We ..." Seshat started walking toward him.

"Don't." Ethan cut her off, his voice choked. *I'm so ashamed. I thought I could fit in. What a joke.* He bent over and put his hands on his knees. "Just go on. I'll catch up." He didn't look up.

"Come," Malachi said after a couple of minutes. "He has much to ruminate on." Nothing else said, the three walked away. Ethan hated his song. *Why does this have to be my song? I don't want it to be. But how can I break free from it? Is it even possible?* Ethan decided he needed to take some time to actually write his questions down rather than trying to rely on his memory. And he also needed to get past the self-pity. He straightened up, stretched, and set to walking, maintaining a pace that wouldn't reunite with the family up ahead.

Ethan came to the dinner table that night with a couple of specific questions in his head. As soon as they sat down, however, Malachi started their dinner talk with an unexpected plan that included Ethan.

"A small group of Pre-Epiphany Ones will be entering Epiphany in four days." Malachi turned to Ethan. "Ethan. You should join them. Melody says you are ready."

The soft bread he'd been chewing stuck in Ethan's throat. He grabbed his water, gulping it down quickly, trying to hide behind the glass.

"The timing is right." Malachi nodded, ignoring Ethan's response. "Because Baldwin can accompany you. It is his time as well. His friendship will be an asset."

Ethan put his glass down. "I ..." He looked at Gimmel, thankful for an idea. "How can I? I have a promise to keep, remember? To play for Gimmel's music class?" He relaxed.

"That is still possible, Ethan." Seshat smiled. "I scheduled it for tomorrow afternoon."

"Hurray!" Gimmel shrieked with her usual clapping. "I cannot wait to tell my friends." Ethan could tell she'd forgiven him completely and that made him smile, if only for a second.

"Gimmel, you are delightful." Malachi laughed. Then, looking at Ethan, his face became solemn. "Ethan. I now know the meaning of the term, 'the devil's interval.'"

Ethan laughed. "Yeah, I shocked you with that one, didn't I?"

"I admit you did." Malachi leaned back and smiled. "A tritone. Dissonance. A clever way to express your hurt, I must say."

"Yeah, that's me."

Seshat chimed in. "Expressing yourself through music is poetic … and beautiful. Believe it or not, Ethan, there are tritones in Eden, specifically among the pre-epiphany ones."

"What?" Now Ethan was the shocked one. "You made it sound like only *my* world had them."

Malachi sighed. "Yes. I know. But only because of the unusual term you used. *And* because your world is incomprehendable to me—to us. But as Seshat alluded to, expressing your pain through music was therapeutic, was it not?"

"I s'pose. Though as a kid I was just trying to survive."

"Right." Malachi's eyes glazed over for a moment, but then he turned to Ethan with a large grin. "But now, I hear a new tune from Melody telling me that you are wanting those harsh notes and chords resolved … you are wanting a new song. Is that true?"

"I … yeah, I guess so." Ethan knew by now that lying was pointless.

"Well." Malachi pressed his palms together and rubbed them rapidly. For a second Ethan thought he was going to join Gimmel in her clapping. "Well, what a celebration!"

"A celebration?"

"Yes, Ethan." Malachi laughed and bounced playfully in his chair. "In Epiphany, you will find your song."

"Your song, Ethan." Seshat's eyes sparkled. "Your true song. Just think of it."

Ethan couldn't fathom what that would be. His old song was the only truth he'd ever known.

Malachi looked at Ethan and raised his eyebrows. "Yes, Ethan! The song written for you before you were born. Oh the wonder." He closed his eyes, the smile pasted on his face.

"My true song," Ethan said. He ate the rest of his meal in silence, while the three around him chattered away.

Lying in bed that night, he realized once again that none of his questions had been answered. And now he had a new question: How was his new song going to get him home?

CHAPTER TWENTY-SIX

Birds, insects, whales sing
Truth—creation's rhapsody;
O man! Join this song.

The following afternoon, Ethan headed to Gimmel's music class with mixed emotions, nervous to be given the spotlight but eager to get his hands on a guitar. Gimmel accosted him even before he entered the room, giving him no opportunity to examine the long line of acoustic guitars hanging on the far wall. With ukuleles in hand, the fifty plus students, all similar to Gimmel in age, sat attentively as he played all the ukulele tunes he knew. When the class broke into happy clapping after the first song, Ethan burst out laughing. They were all like Gimmel. When Seshat asked him to teach them a song, he chose, "You Are My Sunshine." Buzzing with energy, the students grabbed their ukuleles as Ethan led them in a ukulele ensemble.

"Wonderful. That was wonderful." Seshat beamed as Ethan waved good-bye to the last student. "You are a gifted musician, and teacher."

"Me? A teacher?"

"Judging from your response, that surprises you. It should not." She walked to the back of the classroom.

"Why? Why shouldn't it?"

"Because gifts and skills go hand-in-hand in knowing your lifegoal." Seshat lifted a guitar off the wall. Even at a distance, Ethan recognized the quality.

"My lifegoal?" Ethan remembered the term from the Epiphany document.

"Yes. Your purpose." Seshat walked over to Ethan and held out the choice instrument.

Ethan couldn't take his eyes off the exquisite craftsman-ship. "For me?"

"Yes. For you when you enter Epiphany."

"What?" Ethan had never been given such an expensive gift.

"There is a reason, and it is for good." Seshat offered the instrument again.

"Thank you." Words *did* fail him.

Ethan spent much of the next two days at his pond, just him and his guitar. His once-favorite heavy metal music had lost its appeal, however, and he returned to the songs of his childhood, tweaking them from ukulele form to guitar form, and then creating his own style from the basic melodies. It was a challenging, yet fun, distraction. At no time did he want to play *his* song, but it was never far from his thoughts.

At noon on the second day, he returned to the house where he found Malachi waiting for him with something hot off the grill and a readiness to answer his questions.

"Finally." Ethan broke off a piece of bread and dipped it in the saucy curried chickpea dish Malachi had set before him. The spices danced in his mouth. "This tastes like garam masala."

"I would not know. But by your facial expression, I sur-mise that is a good thing." Malachi joined Ethan at the table.

Ethan laughed. "You surmise correctly. Reminds me of my favorite Indian restaurant back home." He took another bite and closed his eyes. "M-m-m. So good. Guess I was hungry."

"I enjoy your exuberance for food, Ethan. And I think I will miss cooking for you."

"Yeah, I'll miss this." Ethan paused. "Wait, do you know something I don't? About me getting home? *That's* my main question right now." Forgetting about his food, Ethan stared at Malachi and waited.

Malachi finished his bite and took a drink. Then he reached for a napkin and wiped his mouth, as if he had all the time in the world. Finally, he looked up and smiled. "I will tell you what I know, Ethan, in the hope that you will be satisfied." When Ethan said nothing, he continued. "You have changed. Your song is being re-written. We have talked about this before. I still hear your fear, but it is unwarranted."

"How … how do you know?"

"You are stronger than you give yourself credit for, Ethan. But also, you have begun to trust in others, as well as believe in others."

Ethan opened his mouth to argue, but Malachi kept talking.

"Do not dispute my words. I have witnessed this change and it is good. Trusting others gives us strength, and hope. Your trust in others will help you make good choices in getting home."

"Getting home." Ethan looked down on his now-cold food, but he didn't care. "It *is* what I want." They sat in silence. Ethan thought through Malachi's points. He wanted to believe. *Choose to believe, Ethan.* The words were his words and nobody else's. But could he? He wanted to. The familiar fear began swirling in his stomach. "No!" His cheeks turned red.

"Yes, Ethan," Malachi shouted in response, a wide grin on his face. "Yes! Fight the fear, just as you did against the creature at our elders meeting. Your accusation startled it enough for us to see it in truth, as the enemy."

"Huh." Ethan beamed. "My purpose."

"Your purpose."

Ethan had no more questions. By bedtime, he believed there was a reason why he had to enter Epiphany, as if nothing would ever be the same again, whether in this world or in his home world. For the first time, the anticipation became an adrenalin rush of excitement rather than fear.

He woke disturbed on the third morning, however, from a dream he hadn't had for a few weeks. Jill, Cassie, Ben, Janus, and Barnabas sat silently on nondescript chairs in an otherwise empty room with bare walls, their faces tired and distressed. Again, that one stranger, standing in the corner with his outstretched arms, still emitted a mystical ambience of hope and peace. In his dream he floated closer, ever closer to the man, drawn to some subconscious recognition. And just when it seemed the man was about to speak directly to him, Ethan woke up. Shaken and unrested, he opted to remain at the house on this his last day before entering Epiphany.

Finding the house empty, Ethan decided to go sit out in the backyard with his hot drink. He turned one of the overstuffed chairs to face the eastern sky and cozied in like a lazy cat, hoping to gain strength from the mid-morning sun. He tried, but he couldn't relax. Malachi had refused to keep him company and had gone out to the fields. "It is good for you to be alone," he had said. "To help you fully prepare for tomorrow." *Doesn't Malachi know being alone with my thoughts is not good prep for anything?*

Ethan didn't want to play guitar or read, though he did have the document on Epiphany open on the table beside him.

His right leg began to bounce. He pressed his hand down on it, forcing the fidgeting to stop. Then he put his head back and closed his eyes, hoping a touch from the benevolent sun would calm his nerves.

"Hey."

Ethan jerked in the chair. *Janus? No, Baldwin.* Ethan opened his eyes, sat up, and gave Baldwin a happy nod. "Great to see ya. I'm … I'm feeling off this morning." *Why did I share that?*

Baldwin pulled up a chair and plopped down, resting a curved, black case in his lap. "If that means ready to go, then me too." His face almost glowed wth excitement.

"Well tha …"

"Yes. I am ready." Baldwin rubbed his palms together. "Been waiting to enter wonderland all my life."

"Wonderland?" For Ethan, Baldwin's use of the word connected him further to Janus.

"Huh?"

"You used the word 'wonderland.' What made you use that word?"

Baldwin looked at Ethan curiously. "I do not know. It just came into my head. Why?"

"Never mind." Ethan pressed down on both bouncing legs.

"How is the knee?" Baldwin asked in response to Ethan's movements.

"What?"

"The knee? I noticed you rubbing it."

"I wasn't …" Ethan stopped and pushed into the side of his left knee as he bent it back and forth. A sharp pain shot down his leg. He grabbed it and let out a small groan.

"Ah," Baldwin said casually. "That is the mental preparation."

"What … What're you talking about?" Ethan angled his leg to find relief.

"Melody directed me here to encourage you, though her reason seemed vague. She gave me only two words: 'mental preparation.' I think it is because you are not from this world. You experience pain in a way that we do not. The fact that your pain has returned is relevant information for you in entering Epiphany, particularly when you are required to make choices."

"Choices?" Ethan seized the opportunity. "Do you know what *kinds* of choices? And the random connection with my knee pain?" He rubbed his leg. "I have no control, over anything." He said the words without thinking. Then he remembered yesterday's conversation with Malachi. His past perspective of the world didn't seem to ring true anymore.

"Hmm. Well, do not resist the help." Baldwin stood, and gripped the foreign object's handle. "I cannot stay. My coming here has been unorthodox, at least according to the typical way of doing things." Baldwin nodded. "But you are my friend and have proven your importance to our community. So, I bend the rules." He offered a slight grin and began walking away.

"Wait."

Baldwin turned.

"You come waltzing over, spout off a few words, and then go waltzing off?"

Baldwin tilted his head like a curious owl and stared at Ethan in silence.

"The case. Aren't you gonna tell me what's in the case?" Ethan pointed, raising his questioning eyebrows.

"The case. Huh." Baldwin looked down. "Forgot that you have probably never seen it before." He walked back, placed the hard shell on the table, unsnapped the two latches, and lifted the lid. "It is my—umm—I honestly do not know what to call it."

"Looks like a dulcimer to me, a mountain dulcimer, I think." Ethan reached out and caressed the beautifully carved wooden frame. "I've never seen one before, at least not one I could touch. I've seen pictures. Listened to its sound." He placed his whole palm on the warm wood. "But to see one? Amazing." A gleam in his eye, he bent down and studied the wood grain.

"Okay, dulcimer it is." Baldwin grinned. "Sounds like you know your instruments."

"Oh, yeah. Guess you didn't know. Seshat gave me one of the acoustic guitars from her music room. Not what I used to have, though." Ethan sat up straight. "I had a Lake Placid Blue Fender Jazzmaster." He pictured it sitting on its stand in the corner of his home with Jill. He wondered if Jill kept it, as she promised. Oh how he loved that guitar. "I had my own band once." Ethan laughed. "That was a long time ago."

"Guitar, hey?" Baldwin closed the case. "Well, that will serve you well after you are given your song."

"Huh?"

"Your song. My song. We all get one." He picked up the case. "Does that surprise you?"

"Surprise? No. Just hadn't thought about the inclusive thing. Guess I thought I was the only one needing my song changed."

"Changed?" Baldwin tilted his head. "Not changed. More like defined. Rooted."

"Rooted? I …"

"I must interrupt, Ethan." Baldwin looked at the sun. "I

need to go before Malachi returns." Baldwin gave Ethan one last big smile and disappeared around the house.

Rooted. Ethan didn't understand the use of the word. Needing a distraction, he brought out his guitar. In the end, he didn't do much playing. He'd start plunking and then be distracted by past guitar memories, most of them surprisingly good. More than once his home life, his world, had been a Chernobyl eruption. Yet, his guitar and his ability to release his pain through music, had saved him from quitting altogether. He thought about what Seshat said, about his teaching of music being a gift that had meaning. He thought about what Baldwin said, that his musical ability would be a good thing for the future. He thought about playing silly tunes for Cassie, and Gimmel, and how that brought him joy. Such affirmation hinted at a hopeful future which sustained him through the rest of the day.

The family didn't question his pensiveness over dinner, so Ethan presumed his mood typical for someone about to enter Epiphany. As he headed up to his room, Seshat handed him a large mug of hot chamomile tea with lemon balm.

She smiled. "It will help you sleep."

Ethan smiled back, hoping her words to be true. "Thanks." He nodded. "Thanks to all three of you." A lump formed in his throat. Both Malachi and Gimmel looked up from the silly drawing game they were playing at the table and beamed at him. Jumping off her chair, Gimmel ran over and gave Ethan a long, tight hug, nearly spilling tea all over both of them. "Hey!" Ethan returned the hug awkwardly, too choked up to say anything more. She let go, returning to the table. Scared of his emotions, Ethan darted up the stairs.

* * *

Twelve hours later, Ethan found himself standing on the edge of a clearing on the outskirts of town in the opposite direction of his pond. Jittery, he shifted back and forth on his feet, thankful that only a handful of people had gathered for the send-off. However, as more people arrived, he quickly realized his silent thanks had been premature for soon the whole community mingled around him. Or so it seemed. Even the air seemed electric with anticipation, the colors of light in the air somehow frolicking in and out of the gathering. Ethan even thought he could hear the scintillation of bright piccolo notes and harp strings dancing vibrantly above them. He looked around. Either nobody else heard it or everyone else recognized it as just part of the ceremony.

"A total of seven Pre-Epiphany Ones are about to enter the most important event of their eternal lives." Malachi made the proclamation unannounced from the top of a large flat rock, his voice magisterial. Six Pre-Epiphany Ones came forward and stood in a line, facing the community. Ethan looked up at Malachi. He responded with a slight nod, quietly gesturing with his hand for Ethan to join them. Ethan stepped into the line with head down, embarrassed by the spotlight and aware of his unconventional garb since he'd chosen to wear the clothes from his world, though at the last minute he did decide to wrap his sash around his waist, hidden under his t-shirt. *As a good-luck charm?* He touched his shirt lightly, just for security.

"As a community, let us send them forward in harmony and with our blessing." The humming began. It wasn't until Baldwin poked him that Ethan realized the rest of the group had left to follow a path into the bright forest and up into the mountains.

"Thanks," Ethan whispered to Baldwin, as he turned to shadow his friend's steps into the unknown. He didn't look back, but the communal song gave him strength. It followed them as they hiked up and up, and away from who they once were.

The caboose in the single-file line, Ethan remained silent as the six continued humming quietly, the shimmering rainbow of colors still twirling around them. For a split-second Ethan thought it would be funny if he chimed in with his old song, to disrupt the peace and harmony. *That's not you anymore.* He liked that thought better. His steps lightened.

They walked for what seemed hours, Ethan glad for his hiking boots and the thermos of water Seshat had given him, though he still thought it odd that water was their only provision.

"Lyric will attend to your needs," Malachi had said when Ethan asked about it.

They came up to a large alpine meadow and on cue, the group stopped under the last grove of trees beside a field of bright green grass dotted with red and white flowers.

Ethan nestled down against a mossy rock. "Is this where we find the pot of gold?" Ethan thought a joke would open the conversation. The others looked at him, confused. Ethan planned to respond but then he saw Reece resting on his haunches across from him. He gasped. His gut reaction was to blurt out a rude comment. But before he could, Baldwin slid down beside him.

His friend touched his arm. "Do not fear."

"Huh?"

"Words from Melody, although I still do not understand why sometimes you do not hear." Baldwin spoke in hushed tones. "If you would just listen ..."

"If I would just listen?" Ethan muttered. "Would she have told me Reece would be here? None of you told me."

Baldwin looked directly at Ethan and smiled. "Your past encounters with Reece are irrelevant. Anath is gone, remember?"

"So?" Ethan struggled to make the connection.

"Her hold on him is also gone, no matter what you think. And from what I heard, you had a major part in her ejection." Baldwin's smile widened. "If anything, Reece should be *thanking* you." Baldwin's perspective alleviated Ethan's concern. Peace returned.

Unexpectedly, at least for Ethan, all six rose as one. Clumsily, Ethan followed suit, bending down to brush dirt and twigs off his jeans.

"Welcome, friends." The cheerful yet authoritative voice broke into Ethan's world even before he looked up, resonating with a cognizance that Ethan couldn't account for.

"Welcome. I am Lyric." Ethan just stood and stared, for there before him stood the man from his dream, the man in the corner radiating hope and peace before his friends. Then Ethan remembered something else. Lyric was also the blazing guardian in the tornado, only without his sword. Ethan rubbed his eyes. *How could this be? What's the connection? Or is this just another dream?* Ethan was drawn into the soft brown eyes of this real, physical man standing in front of them. Yet, Ethan was sure he could see a surreal ring of white light reflected off his ordinary features. The man's eyes wrinkled at the corners as he looked directly at Ethan. "I'm glad you're here."

CHAPTER TWENTY-SEVEN

Hear the whistle of the train
Nostalgic flash of joy, then pain
Wooden ties, a forever chain
Of here and there and back again.

The next two days were the ultimate vacation in the mountains for Ethan, fairly rustic, but he liked it that way. The group took leisurely hikes around multiple lakes, many of them a brilliant cyan, reminding Ethan of Peyto Lake in the Rockies with all its glacial flour. Sometimes they canoed, sometimes they swam. Lyric brought a joy and lightness that they all reveled in. Ethan's cares, even his questions about getting home, didn't go away, they just became insignificant in Lyric's presence. In fact, the more time he spent around Lyric, the more comforted he was by Lyric's presence in his dream, as if somehow Lyric was back home with his friends, bringing them joy too.

Baldwin was right about Reece as well. With all hint of animosity gone, Ethan found Reece to be both amicable and adventurous, almost to the point of being reckless, reminding Ethan of himself as a child, before his world began to crumble.

Even their eating habits changed in Lyric's presence. They needed only one meal a day of a mysterious wafer that appeared like dew on the meadow every morning. It possessed a flavor and texture unlike anything Ethan had ever tasted, somewhere between a rice cracker and a protein bar, and yet not like that at all. The wafer touched his tongue and immediately melted in his mouth like delicate shortbread. When he swallowed, Ethan's whole body tingled with surging energy. Their first morning, Lyric sat back and watched as the seven of them collected their breakfast, all the while trying to describe the unexplainable. "Pleasurable sustenance for your body." He laughed like a child. And it was, for between the wafers and the prolific plants and trees, they sustained vitality all day and late into the night, their need for sleep also less.

On the first evening, with the sun sinking behind the distant mountain range, and the fire beginning to glow, each one took their turn walking down a short path and returning with a case. Ethan didn't think much of it until Baldwin returned with a case that Ethan recognized as his mountain dulcimer. *What about me? Is there one for me?* Ethan's excitement began to build.

"Yes."

Ethan looked around. Lyric was looking right at him. "Your turn." Lyric nodded. Ethan almost ran down the path. There it was. Seshat's guitar. And with it, a memory of the day his mother had given him a case with a large blue bow. Inside was his ukulele. She was so excited that she opened it for him, immediately giving him his first lesson. It had been a good day.

By the time Ethan returned to the circle, everyone was all tuned up, ready to play. They all sat around a fire and welcomed him to join. The instruments blended perfectly, as if all orchestrated. All the while, Lyric just sat back, eyes closed, soaking it in. Sometimes he'd hum along or pretend to conduct but mostly he just sat, a wide grin never leaving his face.

When the coals began to lose their glow, they put their instruments to rest and watched a myriad of stars flicker opalescent colors from their soft, mossy beds. It was then that Lyric began telling captivating stories about his other home, where he would go when not on the Summit of Illumination. Soon everyone was sharing happy childhood stories. Ethan remained quiet. He had nothing to share.

Before the instruments came out on the second night, Lyric directed his attention to Ethan. "Do you have a story to share tonight, Ethan?"

Do I have a happy story to tell? Help! He gulped. But a story came to him, one he had long forgotten, buried under the weight of soiled pain.

"Yeah." Ethan nodded. "From when I was six or seven. I don't quite remember." He paused, all eyes now focused on him. "My dad worked as a CN locomotive engineer and so as a child I loved trains, especially the sound of the train horn, its distant strain calling to me as I fell asleep at night. The sound soothed me, at least, at the time."

"What's a locomotive engineer?" Baldwin blurted out from the shifting shadows.

Lyric held up his hand. "You may ask questions later, Baldwin." He turned back to Ethan. "Continue, Ethan."

"Well, this one and only time my dad took me with him to the rail yard. He became a different person as we stepped into his diesel engine. 'Like a kid in a candy shop', my mom used to say. *Where'd that come from?* He showed me all the controls. So many buttons and gadgets. He even let me blow the horn, something he said wasn't allowed inside the yard, but he let me do it anyway. I think he got in a bit of trouble later, but he just laughed about it. And it made me happy because in that moment he cared more about me than he did about anyone else." Ethan choked up, thankful for the night, the memory unlocking doors to all sorts of emotions. "That's all, I guess."

Ethan's small revelation about life on Earth prompted a stream of curious questions from the others, from train workings and family relationships to space travel and time measurement, all reminding Ethan again that the Edenites had just as many questions about his world as he had about theirs. Even as they settled in for the night, they continued talking, and for once Ethan enjoyed being the center of attention.

On the third morning, Lyric began all-day one-on-one sessions. Ethan felt snubbed at first, though it seemed none of the others did.

Baldwin tilted his head when Ethan asked what he thought of Lyric's non-presence. "Lyric's not here, but Melody still is. Their voices are as one."

"Right." Ethan nodded, though Baldwin's words didn't alleviate his slight angst. His doubts returned. "Nice for you. You've been talking to Melody all your life." Ethan didn't wait for Baldwin's response. He walked away, deciding he would spend the day hiking on his own, hoping to clear his head.

Ethan took an unexplored trail, anticipating another beautiful lake at its end. It did not disappoint, though just as he approached a rock pinnacle overlooking a narrow lake within a vast valley, his knee began to throb. *Funny, with all the hiking we've done, this is my first pain.* Sitting down, he began massaging the pain away.

"Hi."

At the sound of the voice, he jerked up and turned. He slid on the loose gravel and, in correcting his footing, he found himself a few feet from the cliff's edge. He swallowed hard and looked up. His jaw dropped.

"You." Ethan blinked multiple times in disbelief. *Anath? How's this possible?*

"Hello Ethan." Anath swept up to him, her auburn hair flittering in the breeze. "Guess I've surprised you?" She smiled shyly and bit her bottom lip.

Ethan had nowhere to go. Somehow under her spell again, he was a defenseless animal caught in her trap. Attempting to gain composure, he straightened up. *Help! Help! Help!*

Seeming to enjoy his fear, she simply fluttered her lashes, her eyes fixed on his. Her mind began to burrow into his. "It's just you and me, no others around to support you. That's been your life story, hasn't it? 'Lone destiny to find no home'?" Her voice sounded smooth as Thai silk, her eyes saintly as a monk's.

"You're quoting my lyrics? How?" Ethan stammered, as if forced to engage in the conversation. "How do you know anything about my life?"

"I know many things." Her smile reminded Ethan of someone, but his neural networks wouldn't compute. "For instance, I know your knee pain has returned." She glanced down.

Ethan followed her gaze and rubbed his knee. "How ..."

"Come." She tried to take his hand. "Let's go over to the grass and talk."

"No." Ethan was surprised at his own fortitude as he remembered her soft touch. For a brief second, he noticed a look of frustration on Anath's face, and then it was gone.

"Very well." She shrugged and smiled innocently once again.

Then Ethan recognized the smile, and the voice. They were Jill's, not the recent belligerent Jill, but the Jill he remembered from their first encounter, the Jill with the bright eyes and welcoming smile that Ethan had not been able to resist. *How had he not noticed it before?*

"But don't you think it odd that nobody else has pain in this world except you?" Anath closed in, her voice from his past so alluring, her body movements so compelling. "Don't you think that if Lyric cared about you, that he would take away your pain?"

"I … I don't know. Maybe." Ethan struggled to refuse her charms. He remembered Malachi's words: Trusting others gives us strength. *I will choose to trust.*

"Hasn't Lyric betrayed you by not giving you what you want?" She reached out. Ethan watched her hand touch his forearm, almost as if he were watching from above, powerless to respond. Ethan closed his eyes in an attempt to block her influence. It gave him just enough courage to pull his arm back from her grip, though his feet remained stuck.

"I … He …" Ethan had no argument for her logic. He knew what he had to do. *Help!* A feeble cry. But it was enough. In swooped the recent memory of that elder meeting. Eyes still closed, Ethan relived it all over again in his mind, how Anath had turned into some hideous creature and then disappeared through the roof in a tornado of light. *How could I have forgotten?* It took only seconds for the whole picture to flash through his mind, seconds that revealed added truth. Anath must've been blocking the memory. She no doubt knew it would give Ethan the ammunition to fight her advances.

He opened his eyes and stared at Anath, her smile now a sneer, her eyes now black empty pools. "You are not real." His voice shook.

"So you say. But your mind still doubts."

Mouth open, Ethan watched her smile and green eyes return. "Stop!" He forced the word out between gritted teeth and put both hands up to block her stares. "Stop toying with my mind."

"Lyric is the one …" Her voice was silvery.

"Lyric is my friend." Ethan kept his arms up, protection from her wily voice and eyes. But he could see her cross her arms.

"Lyric is my friend." She mimicked it like a bratty child.

"Yes. He *is* my friend." He saw that the repeated words upset her.

She dropped her arms, clenched her fists and growled, a deep, throaty growl.

Now what? What's next? Help!

"You are more stubborn now." It was a snarl, her voice raspy.

Ethan finally looked at her fully, though still unsure of his own strength. She looked away, her face scowling. That surprised Ethan, but it gave him added confidence. Yet, she didn't budge. But neither did Ethan. For the longest time, the two of them just stood there, a showdown of wills. Finally, with a resigning "hmpfh," she turned and stomped down the path. And just when Ethan thought he could breathe freely, she turned and screeched. "But I'm not done."

Weak-kneed, Ethan hobbled away from the rocky overhang, his eyes glued to the back of Anath's head even as she disappeared into the brush. He stumbled over to a patch of grass off the path and slumped down, keeping his eyes on her exit long after nature had closed her off. He let out a long sigh.

"*We did it.*" Words whispered like a line of music, a simple guitar rift in the background.

"We?" Ethan said aloud. Of course. He'd cried out for help and Melody responded, providing him with what he needed.

Yes, we did. We did do it. He fell back into the grass and laughed, first nervously, then fully. He laughed until tears rolled down his cheeks. He knew he wasn't alone but it didn't scare him. He recognized Melody's bolstering presence in both his mind and in the surrounding majesty. His heart slowed. His brain relaxed. He drifted off into a dreamless sleep.

* * *

He woke refreshed. The sun had begun to set, the shadows from the mountains stretching across the valley turning the cyan of the lake below to a deep teal. Recalling the events of his day, he half-trotted up the trail to the meadow, anxious to share his story with the group.

Engrossed in his own excitement, he almost missed the quiet conversation going on down a side trail. He paused, wondering if he should sneak up and ambush whomever it was, but after listening further, the hushed tones made him uneasy. He pulled back and hid behind the trunk of a large red cedar, focusing on the two voices. *Reece and Anath.* He sucked in a long breath. *Noooooooo.* A debate raged in his mind. *Can I deal with her again? Twice in one day? Or do I leave Reece to himself? But Reece probably needs help. And he is my friend. Isn't he? Would he help me? Does that even matter? But do I have the ability to stop her again?*

"*Do not forget.*" Melody chimed in.

"I'll try not to." He spoke the words … and a little too loudly.

The whispers stopped. "Who's there?" Reece yelled out. "I heard you."

"Sh … shoot," Ethan muttered, gripping the tree as if it were a fulcrum for his teeter-totter emotions.

"*I am with you.*" Melody's voice was clear, calm.

"Come on out." Reece was not backing down.

Ethan pulled away from the tree, steadied himself, and stepped out from behind his security to see Reece and Anath sitting snuggly between two thick lateral roots that stretched out from an even larger cedar just fifteen feet away.

"Ethan. Hey." Reece stood up and chuckled. "Funny, I went out looking for you and you found me. And look who else I found." He smiled down at Anath. "You remember Anath?"

Ethan looked at Reece, then at Anath, then back at Reece. Ethan's gut reaction was to pass judgment on Reece for his naiveté, his willingness to entertain her seductions.

"*Show mercy.*" Melody's response contradicted his own.

"Mercy?" Ethan whispered. "Mercy," he repeated, realizing Anath had probably blocked her true identity from Reece, just as she'd tried to do with him.

Wrinkles formed on Reece's forehead. "You okay? Your face is … unusual."

"Yeah, sure." Ethan forced a half-smile. "I'm good. But …" He glared at Anath, unsure how to continue.

Anath stood and touched Reece's shoulder. "C'mon, Reece. Let's walk. I don't think Ethan wants to hear my story." She stared at Ethan, curling her lips up deviously. She slid her fingers along Reece's arm and tucked her hand into his.

"Well, that's not true." Ethan kept his eyes glued on Anath. "I'm very *interested* in hearing your story."

"Sure thing." Reece seemed oblivious to the tension. "Come. Sit." He tilted his head at Anath for her to do the same. She didn't comply but turned to face Ethan instead, her hand still in Reece's.

Ethan planted his feet directly opposite her. "I'd prefer to stand, thanks."

"Okay." Reece released his hand from Anath's. "Well, Anath was just explaining to me why she had to leave our community so suddenly. Unfortunate, really." He looked at Anath, his puppy-dog eyes drowning in her jade pools.

"Oh?" Ethan kept his voice steady, but his inner voice was shouting. *Beware the enemy!*

"I guess the elders questioned her family history and her connection to our harmony, so they asked her to leave." Reece was obviously in her grip. She looked at him, fluttered her eyelashes and gave him her pseudo-shy smile. "And, being the girl that she is, she complied."

"And what kind of girl is that?" Ethan glared at Anath.

"Huh?"

An acidic mud pot of anger began to bubble in the pit of Ethan's stomach. "You said, 'being the girl that she is.' What kind of girl is that?"

"Uh, I don't know. A kind one?" Reece took his eyes off Anath and stepped into Ethan's personal space, displeasure swirling in his smoky eyes. "Why are you asking that? Why do you doubt her? She's the one from our world, not you. Or have you forgotten?"

Ethan stepped back and looked down, not wanting to entice Reece into doing something impulsive. "No." He shook his head. "I've not forgotten. But are you sure she's kind?" Ethan watched a sly grin spread across Anath's face, Reece's back to her. Ethan's neck hairs prickled but he knew he couldn't back down. He could relate to Reece's predicament, and he couldn't let him be duped by her charisma. He looked back at Reece. "C'mon, Reece." He gave a jerk of his head. "Let's go back to the meadow. You can ask Lyric about her story, and about her." He tried to put his hand on Reece's shoulder, but Reece pulled away.

"Don't touch me. You are just … I think you would use the word *jealous*."

"Jealous? Me?" Ethan knew he had to stay composed. "You've got it all wrong. I know who, or should I say, what Anath *really* is." Ethan paused, long enough to hear Melody's words. Assured of her presence, he spoke the words she gave him. "Anath is the jealous one."

As if now sensing Melody's presence, Anath stepped to the side and to the edge of the clearing, a hint of hysteria on her face, the green of her eyes muted.

"Anath? Are you okay?" Reece reached out his hand and then pulled it back.

They watched her sway back and forth.

Knowing he had to seize the moment, Ethan continued, a conduit of Melody's imposing power. "She's not okay, Reece. Look at her eyes. They're becoming black holes, revealing who she really is. You will see *if* she sticks around. My guess is she won't."

Reece and Ethan watched Anath begin to tremble, now looking like a trapped animal. "Melody won't let her deceive you, Reece." Ethan took Reece's side as together they watched Anath fight to maintain control, her eyes fluctuating between green and slate gray. "Anath played her hand, revealing her jealousy of your relationship with Lyric, and with Melody. She is probably even jealous of our odd, dare-I-say, friendship." A panic-stricken Anath hissed at Ethan, but he continued. "I don't think friends even exist where she comes from."

Reece's eyes glazed over. Ethan knew he was now conversing with Melody. Meawhile, Ethan kept watch over

Anath's movements. The tension in Reece's body loosened and, after releasing a long, slow breath, he gave Ethan a wide smile. Then he turned to Anath.

"Melody commands you to leave me, to leave us. Go." He pointed to the dim forest behind her. Anath, now looking old and fragile, stumbled silently into the heavy undergrowth.

Ethan relaxed. "Wow." He was lost for words.

"Thank you, Ethan." Reece dropped his eyes. "How, how did you know?"

"Believe it or not, that's the third time I've had to deal with her, *and* her alter-ego."

"Her alter ego?"

"Alter ego. Doppelgänger. I don't know. Malachi called her, called it, an instrument of evil. But, yeah, she's just bad news. I'd like to say it's been easier to confront her each time but, well, the truth is, I'm realizing it has little to do with me at all."

Reece looked at Ethan, his eyes sparkling, almost mischievously. He gave Ethan a big bear hug, pulled back and burst out laughing. "Melody, all Melody." He laughed again. "She is always there to help us make the right choices, right?"

Ethan smiled. "I guess so."

"Ironic that you, as the outsider, had to intervene for me. You are a true friend." He slapped Ethan on the back and dashed up the trail leading back to the main path. "Hurry up," he whooped. "I will race you back to the meadow."

Ethan chased after him, giving no thought to his painless knee.

CHAPTER TWENTY-EIGHT

Wakey, wakey little one,
Wakey, wakey night is done.
Or is it?

That evening, as the eight of them sat around a sprightly fire, an animated Reece sketched a vivid word picture of his encounter with Anath. Ethan remained silent, amused by Reece's zeal, intrigued by his perspective. Ethan had no idea how close Reece had come to running away with Anath, so consumed was he by her charms. At the end of his telling, Reece slid over from his log onto Ethan's and put his arm around him.

"If not for my buddy, Ethan, I would not be here." Reece shook Ethan's torso fervently. "I would be, I would be … who knows where I would be." Reece jumped up and started doing a silly jig around the fire, all the while singing a little ditty about victory.

"Yes but …" Ethan tried to assert his voice above everyone's laughter, his attempt futile. *Does nobody want to hear my side of the story?*

"I do."

Ethan hadn't noticed Lyric shift over to sit on the other side of him.

"You do what?"

"I want to hear your side of the story." Lyric smiled. "Although I'm already familiar with the specific events, not just of Reece's story but also yours."

"Huh?"

Lyric's eyes twinkled playfully. "You must remember, whatever Melody knows, I know as well."

"Right." Ethan relaxed. "Funny that you should mention her. I'm sure you already know this, too, but she's the one who helped me in my encounter with Anath. Couldn't have done it without her." He looked at Lyric. "Can I be honest with you?"

"I'm always looking for an honest heart, Ethan."

Such an archaic answer, but said with such kindness. "I don't get Melody, how she swoops in and out of my mind. Very disturbing, when I first landed in Eden at least."

"And now?"

"Well, I guess now I kinda like it. Yeah." Ethan chuckled. "Believe you me, her voice in my head is a welcomed change. Though …" He paused, suddenly aware that Eden, and Melody's voice, had been changing his thought-world too. His mother's haunting voice was no longer strangling him from the inside out. He closed his eyes, a slight smile on his face.

Lyric burst out laughing. "You've changed, Ethan, both inwardly and outwardly. And that brings me joy." He stood up. "You, my friend, will soon be ready for our one-on-one. But not yet. You have one more choice to make."

"One more choice?" Ethan hung his head. He didn't want to know. Lyric had already stepped away to give Reece a celebratory hug. One of the girls pulled out her flute and Baldwin joined her on his dulcimer. Soon everyone was dancing and clapping and chanting. Ethan's guitar remained silent. Lyric's last words nagged at his thoughts. One more choice. *What in Eden did that mean?*

That night Ethan had a dream, vivid and unsettling, the faces and images sharp in detail, not the faded ones that were becoming a part of his memory from Earth. In his dream, he and Jill were still happily in love, and Frank, his dad, had come for a visit. It was a beautiful summer day and they headed to the river valley for a picnic. Frank, ever the history buff, suggested they visit Fort Edmonton Park, a park that Ethan had never been to. Everyone was game and Cassie, though only three years old, was more than thrilled about a pony ride.

By the time they got to the park, an ominous shroud of storm clouds had begun rumbling in the west. They debated over waiting for another day but Jill, ever the optimist, was sure the typical prairie storm would pass quickly so they decided to go for it. When they got to the entrance, Lyric was there, ready to join them, in his bright white tunic and gold sash, though he said nothing and nobody else acknowledged his presence. It was only after they paid the entrance fee that Ethan realized a train ride was part of the experience. Ethan should've known. Frank loved trains. As they waited for the train's arrival, Ethan's anxiety grew.

"Be at peace, Ethan." Lyric's soothing voice broke in. He said nothing more. Then he was gone.

Ethan breathed in the words and relaxed. As Jill predicted, the storm blew north, skipping them completely, and soon the four of them were hopping up the steps of the old steam train and enjoying the short ride to the old Hudson's Bay Fort like any normal family. Mom, dad, daughter, grandpa, without any chaos. Ethan's arm around Jill, they continued through the fort and on to the different time-period streets, Cassie enjoying the view from grandpa's shoulders. They stopped for ice cream and, as they licked giant scoops of their preferred flavors off sugary cones, Ethan awoke.

Startled, he looked around. The first sign of dawn appeared, the midnight sky softening to ultramarine blue on the eastern horizon. Ethan stared right through it, his mind mulling over his puzzling dream. The dream had been the rewrite of a repressed memory involving a train, but with a different and disturbing ending. Frank had come out to visit and they had gone to Fort Edmonton Park, but then the truth took a nasty turn. In reality, Ethan's first glimpse of the train released his own storm of crazed emotions, setting in motion a huge wheel of negative events that neither Frank nor Jill could comprehend, changing their family forever. Ethan publicly accused his dad of being an evil schemer in trying to get him on the train and then screamed at him to leave Edmonton and never return. The rift in their father-son bond was irreparable. Ethan turned to the bottle for comfort, and his relationship with Jill also began to shrivel and die.

Now Ethan lay silent, grieving over the memory. And yet, the dream offered hope. Somehow, Lyric's appearance had rewritten the events of that day and changed the past. "If only it were true," he whispered. Then he caught himself. *How ludicrous! And not helpful. Think about something else.* He turned his thoughts to Cassie, wondering what she was doing right at that moment. Though not quite sure of the passing of time between Eden and Earth, Ethan figured that she would be enjoying winter, with Christmas right around the corner. Her favorite season, and her favorite holiday. Seeing her in his mind prancing around in the snow, making snow angels and building snowmen, brought a warm smile to his face.

"Are you awake?" Baldwin's bed was only a few feet from Ethan's.

"Yeah." Ethan sighed, not wanting to release the memory of Cassie. "Wakey, wakey."

"Pardon?"

"Oh, nothing." Ethan sat up. Thankfully, Baldwin let it go.

They gathered their daily sustenance and sat in a circle eating their wafers. Ethan heard the anticipation in their voices, the intensity in the conversation, assuming it was over Lyric's pick for his one-on-one time. He didn't clue in until he noticed one of their group missing. Vav, the gal that had spent the previous day with Lyric.

"Where's Vav?" All eyes turned on him, as if he had just said something idiotic. Lyric offered Ethan an easy smile.

"She returned to the community." Lyric had that distinctive glint in his eyes. "I gave her a new name, and a song for her melody."

"You what?" Ethan forgot everything he had been told prior to entering Epiphany. He looked at the others. None of them showed surprise at Lyric's modus operandi. "Looks like I'm out of the loop again. The alien oddball," Ethan joked, surprisingly unconcerned about the others' opinions. He looked around the circle and then at Lyric. "So, who's next?"

Lyric laughed. "Well, Mr. Honest Heart, today it's Reece's turn."

Reece rose abruptly, his eyes big, the airy biscuits on his lap scattering to the ground. "Really? It's my turn?" He glanced around. "I … Am I ready? After yesterday …"

Lyric cut in. "After yesterday, yes, you are ready, Reece. Be at peace." Lyric walked over to him and put his hand on his shoulder. "You are ready," he repeated.

"Yes." Reece relaxed his shoulders. "I trust you." Nothing more said, the two of them picked up their water canteens and trekked off, those left behind watching them cross the meadow and disappear into the dense trees on the far side."

"Huh." Ethan peered after them. "Didn't expect that." Nobody responded so Ethan stood up and stretched. "Well, I'm heading off too."

"Want some company?" Baldwin stood as well. "I promise if Anath shows up, I won't run off with her." He grinned.

"Uh …" Ethan wanted to be alone, but he didn't want to offend Baldwin either.

"Be honest." Melody's voice wafted into Ethan's thoughts.

Acknowledging her wisdom, Ethan looked Baldwin in the eye. "If it's okay with you, I'd rather be alone this morning. Had a bizarro dream last night and need some time to process."

"Sure, no problem." Baldwin dipped his head, a hint of disappointment in his voice.

"Tell ya what. How about you and I go canoeing later. Always more fun with a partner." Ethan liked spending time with his new friend.

Baldwin's grin returned. "Sounds great."

Ethan replied with a thumbs up and turned toward a new trail to the right of the meadow.

After a few hours, the path Ethan took veered up and then shifted horizontally along a barren trail following a mountainside covered in slippery shale. Crossing the ridge would be a challenge, but it would also keep his mind focused on the here-and-now rather than the past. He stepped carefully, keeping his eyes on the loose rocks. Almost across, he heard an unexpected sound. Stopping, he planted his feet to face the canyon below, and listened. *Is that a voice? Who would be out here?* He tipped his head to get his bearings straight against any echo. Yes, it was a girl's voice. And she was sobbing.

"Hello." Ethan shouted, the word bouncing off the vast canyon valley. He waited.

"Help," came a shallow reply. "I'm here. Down here."

Ethan assessed the situation. Seeing no path, he knew he would have to make his own trail down into the canyon. Crouching low and at an angle, he took a deep breath and began what he hoped would be a slow and steady descent. The rock face had other plans, however, for Ethan found himself at the mercy of the unpredictable shale, slipping helplessly at times, then gaining composure, then skidding down again, his hiking boots scraping so loudly against the crumbling rock that he couldn't hear the girl's cries. Almost at the bottom, his boots snagged on some tufted grass and he tumbled down the rest of the way.

Ethan lay motionless, doing a mental body check. No sharp pains. He sat up—some cuts on his arms, a tear in his pants at the knee revealing some scrapes, but nothing serious. He rubbed his head. One bump already forming behind his left ear. He remembered that hit. Otherwise, he seemed okay. He stumbled to his feet and shook sediment dust off his pants, thankful for the protection, still inadequate, but better than a tunic.

"Help."

Ethan straightened his twisted body, attentive to the cry.

"Help me." The voice sounded remarkably familiar, and yet not. Judging it to be close and to his left, he hobbled in the direction of what looked like a small cave in the rocks.

"Hello?" Ethan leaned up against the overhang of rock at the cavity's mouth and peered into the sunless cave. Hearing the sobbing, he entered the shadows. "I'm here to help."

"I think I'm lost. And I hurt my foot." The girl whimpered.

"Okay," Ethan replied, all the while thinking, *I know this voice. But how? And who?* He sat down on the clammy earth beside her, waiting for his eyes to adjust, mulling over what to do next. *If this were Cassie, if this had happened when we were hiking, what would I do?* Then it hit him. *Cassie! She sounds like Cassie, yet not quite. But could it be?*

"Cassie?" At first he didn't realize he had said her name aloud.

"Daddy?" she responded.

"Cassie? Is it really you?" Ethan looked hard and long at the girl, not trusting his eyes, or his ears, and unsure of what to do next. Cassie knew.

"Oh, Daddy!" She put her arms around his waist and buried her face in his chest. "I missed you, so much."

What is this? Ethan froze, unable to wrap her up in his arms. This girl was not six years old. She was more like nine or ten. Ethan's mind raced with questions. *Who is this girl, really? What's she doing here? How'd she get here? Why's she here? What does this mean? What do I do next?* He had to see her in the sunlight, to examine her features for some clarity.

Putting his arm around her, he supported her up. "C'mon. Let me help you out of this cave. It's cold and damp in here and that's not good." She leaned on him, unable to put weight on her right foot, and the two of them shuffled out into the bright sunlight. Ethan put his face to the sun. "Ah, that's better isn't it?" The girl didn't answer. "Over here." He guided her to a ledge in the rock and set her down slowly. "Let me take a look at that foot." He was still afraid to look at her face. *What if it is Cassie somehow? Do I want it to be? I don't know. Help!*

"Nothing appears broken." Ethan turned the ankle carefully. "Does this hurt?"

"No," the girl said quietly, still sniffling.

Ethan kept his eyes down on the foot. "And there's no swelling, so that's good. You've got a nice scrape here though." He fingered an abnormal set of scratches on the bridge. "How'd that happen?"

The girl pulled her foot away and covered it with the other. "I … I don't know," she said. "I got lost. I just want to go home." She started to whimper again. "Can't you take me home, Daddy?"

Ethan finally looked up at the girl, her flaxen hair like Cassie's though cut in a bob, her pudgy cheeks and nose the same though slimmer, her eyes big and blue, and the whites red from crying. Oh, how he wanted this girl to be his Cassie. "You look like Cassie except you're older. My Cassie is only six."

The girl uttered a little surprised "oh" but then her face shifted to a pout. "But I am your Cassie." She crossed her arms.

Ethan laughed. "Well, you do act like Cassie. And yet, it doesn't add up." With everything that had happened since his entrance into Eden, Ethan questioned his senses and his own ability to differentiate between the authentic and the counterfeit. Yet he wanted to believe her. *Oh, how I wish.*

"Maybe … maybe time isn't the same here," she offered.

"That's true." *True but what does a nine-year-old know about time dimensions?* Ethan fought to maintain composure. "But how did you get to Eden? And why would you be three years older? I didn't age coming here."

"I don't know. I'm a child. Why don't you believe me?" She gave a loud hmpfh and looked away.

"Okay. Okay. I don't need answers right now, Cassie." Ethan spoke her name intentionally. He rose from his crouched position and, sitting down beside her, studied the canyon and their options for getting back to the meadow. "We do need to get out of here though. Can't very well climb that slope of shale." He turned to her. "Do you remember which direction you came from?"

"Yes." She pointed to the left and a narrow opening between two tall boulders. "I'm sure I came from over there."

"Really? Hmm." Ethan scanned the mountainside from where he had come, re-calculating the cardinal directions in his mind. "I'm thinking that's the opposite direction of the meadow, and of the Eden community."

"You don't believe me?" Her voice turned to a whine.

"That's not it at all, Cassie." Ethan put his arm around her and pulled her close. "It's just that I'm not sure how we'll get back to Lyric and the others if we head in that direction."

"Why, Daddy?" She sounded irritated.

"Why what?"

"Why do we have to go back to Lyric? What does he know? Can he guarantee the way home?" She pulled away.

Ethan's raised his eyebrows in surprise.

Instantly, her emotions switched. Her lips quivered and she wailed, "I just want to go home."

"You're right. Sorry. We can start that way and hopefully veer back to our campsite at some point." He stood up and reached out his hand, wiggling his fingers. She didn't budge. "C'mon, Cassie." He gave her a smile. "We've always found our way hiking, haven't we?"

"Have we?"

"Of course, we have." Ethan remained calm, yet her question was disconcerting. "Don't you remember?"

"Of course, I do." She said it a little too emphatically. "I remember hiking around Fort Edmonton Park. That was fun." She gave Ethan an excessive grin but wouldn't take his hand.

"That wasn't hiking, and you were only three and spent the whole time on your grandpa's shoulders." *Bizarre. Didn't I just dream about this? But maybe her memories have been altered in this world. This could still be Cassie. It really could.* The prickling hairs on the back of his neck said otherwise. *Stay cool, Ethan. And ask another question.* "How about our last hike of the season last year? Do you remember that one? How great it was?" He squatted now, wanting to read Cassie's expression.

"Yes! Yes!" She giggled, clapping her hands in excitement. "We hiked for miles and miles. That was the best day ever!"

Now all of Ethan's skin prickled. He had to maintain composure, knowing what he needed to do. *Help!*

"Peace, Ethan. I am here." Melody's reassuring voice brought harmony to his thoughts.

"No." He stared into the girl's eyes. "On that last hike we were an hour out of Jasper when we ran into an unpredicted deluge of bitter rain, almost snow. The path got so slippery that it took us three hours to get back to the parking lot. By that time, your lips were so purple that no amount of heat in the car could warm you up." Ethan kept his eyes on the girl's face. With each sentence her expression changed, the delightful smile became a clenched jaw, the raised brow furrowed. "You got pneumonia. Jill was furious and I was sick to my stomach, afraid for the worst." At that point, Ethan took his eyes off the girl and looked down, saddened by his own story. He sighed. "You have no memory of that hike, do you?"

The girl pulled her knees up to her chest and began rocking back and forth in silence, her face between her knees.

"You probably have no memories of our times together, other than those pulled from my subconscious. And even those are wrong." He shook his head. "No, you're not my Cassie." Speaking the truth overwhelmed him. He thought the ache in his heart over missing his daughter would split his whole body in two.

The girl began muttering to herself as if trying to rebuild confidence. Ethan wanted to just run away, but he knew he had to somehow squelch her ability to regain control. *Think, Ethan. What did you do yesterday?*

He remembered and straightened up. *With your help, Melody.*

"You are an imposter, a mutation, though I don't know what to call you." Ethan struggled for composure. "Should I call you Anath? Or some other name?" The girl kept rocking. "It doesn't really matter, does it? You are Eden's enemy which makes you Lyric's enemy."

At the mention of Lyric, a loud hiss came from the girl, her rocking now frenetic.

Ethan took a step back. "Which makes you my enemy."

At that, the girl jerked her head up, her teeth bared, her bright, blue eyes now black empty pools. Ethan hated those black pools.

"Oh, Cassie." Ethan moaned, leaned back against a boulder and slid to the ground, unable to bridle his own grief. "How I had hoped." No energy to continue, he curled his arms around his knees and sobbed.

"Go. And do not return." It was Lyric's voice. The tender voice of authority. Ethan looked up. Lyric had his arm out, pointing for the mutation to leave. The creature had shriveled into something black and unearthly. It shrieked and scuttled away like a cockroach. With five words, Lyric had sent it away. Five formidable words. He bent down beside Ethan, put his arm around him and began to hum a tune so hauntingly beautiful, like the sweetest of memories, the happiest of moments for all of creation. Completely indescribable. The melody hushed his sobs, dried his tears, and turned Ethan's sorrow into peace. He had no desire to move, his heart and mind now at rest. Time passed. When he finally looked up, their surroundings had changed. Somehow the two were back in the meadow, with the sun beginning to set in the west.

"Now you are ready." Lyric smiled.

CHAPTER TWENTY-NINE

The eyes of hope they sought and found me,
I disembarked from loss and pain;
The whistle rests—the sun is shining,
A new day dawns, my travel's done.

Ethan kept his promise to Baldwin, though their canoeing excursion happened by the light of a full moon, the kaleidoscopic colors of the water's surface reminding Ethan of an opal. Though exhausted, Ethan felt a lingering peace as he shared his day with his friend.

"You are ready," Baldwin echoed.

"You think?" Ethan paused. "Wait. Did you just repeat Lyric?"

Baldwin chuckled. "Yeah, I guess I did."

"But how …"

"Melody," Baldwin stated matter-of-factly. "When you did not return by midday, my mind became unsettled. Something inharmonious, painful, was happening. You needed help."

"You sensed my pain?" Ethan stopped paddling from the bow and did a one-eighty to look at his friend. "That's some crazy stuff."

"Crazy to you, I guess. It comes naturally to us, although in this world our emotional state is pretty much positive. We experience the joy of our friends. It is good." Baldwin pulled up his paddle. "Listen, Ethan, you are my friend."

"Gee, thanks. But …"

"When a friend is in trouble, though it is rare, we help. Not necessarily with our physical presence, but in a non-physical, unseen way." When Ethan cocked his head and wrinkled his brow, Baldwin smiled, his teeth also shimmering opals. "Difficult for you to comprehend, I take it. I guess it is sort of like encouraging someone or answering a cry for help telepathically. Melody and Lyric hear our unspoken words, which in turn bolsters the one in need. Not sure how else to explain it." Baldwin dipped his paddle back in the water.

"Huh." Ethan let Baldwin's idea sink in as he shifted forward and returned to paddling. "I had friends back in my world that never helped in that way, if they helped at all."

"You judge people hastily, I think."

Ethan stopped mid-stroke, leaving his paddle to drag in the water. "You know *nothing* of my world. If you did, you might take that back."

"Maybe. Maybe you are right, Ethan. But perhaps you have more people that care about you than you realize."

"Not mincing words tonight, are you?" Ethan said, though in the moment he had to admit he appreciated Baldwin's candor.

Baldwin chuckled. "I have never been a quick learner, but I am beginning to understand your foreign ways, Ethan. Your sarcasm for instance. It is honest."

Returning to his strokes, Ethan smiled to himself. *Someone in this world finally gets my sarcasm. And calls it honest? Honest. Lyric's words, too. Honest.*

Ethan lay on his mossy bed that night exhausted but happy. And as his reality began to sink into the clouds of his dream world, he took one last long breath. For a second, he was sure he could smell the delicate night breeze. It smelled like hope.

* * *

Another breakfast with one less person. After Lyric's words the previous day, Ethan anticipated he would be next. He was right.

"Come, Ethan." Lyric smiled. "Today is our day." Ethan got up and simply followed. As they crossed the meadow, he realized that for the first time in a long time, he didn't feel lost.

"See you on the other side." Baldwin yelled after him, just as the two reached the trees. Ethan turned and waved, wondering if he ever would.

The trail being narrow, the two walked single file through the mixed forest, though soon it became more coniferous than deciduous. "What are you looking for, Ethan?" Lyric asked the question as they hopped a lively little stream.

"Me?" Ethan didn't expect this, not from Lyric. "You mean in today?"

"Today, tomorrow. In the forever."

"Uh." Ethan shook his head in confusion. "Well, what I *want* is to get home, but I don't think I have to tell you that. What I'm looking for? Not sure what you mean. Aren't *you* the one who sets the agenda on these days? Where we go? What we do?"

"I can guide but the choice is yours. Always is, was, and will be."

"You talk very guru-ish."

Lyric laughed, full and hearty. "There's that honesty again." The forest opened on the edge of a lush dell. Rainbows danced off popcorn clouds and streamed down to a small pond on the far side, where long-legged birds strutted the shore, their fluorescent pink heads bobbing in and out of the water.

"Wow." Ethan whispered in awe. "Wish I could bring Cassie here."

"That I can't do." Lyric turned to Ethan. "But if she were here, what would the two of you do?"

Another surprise question. "Well, I guess we'd hike. Search for a larger body of water. Fish maybe. Swim, if the day was hot. Mostly we just liked to hike and discover. Cassie loved—er—loves, birds." Ethan was confused by his own word choice.

"Birds." Lyric looked away and began stroking his well-manicured beard. Then he turned back to Ethan, his eyes sparkling. "Okay, we shall hike and discover. Let's take this wide trail for a while. The trek is easy." He closed his eyes and took a long drink from his canteen, his lips curving up as the water dribbled down his chin. After five gulps he let out a passionate "ah" as if the water were a wine of the gods.

Ethan grinned. "You do love life, don't you?"

"Yes, I do." Lyric spread his arms wide. "Every day is a new adventure, a gift." He looked at Ethan. "And the Composer wants us to enjoy it." With an I'm-letting-you-in-on-a-secret wink, Lyric started down the trail that soon wound between fields of olive-colored grasses and silvery shrubs.

Ethan took his place beside him. "Wish I had your zeal for life. Think it's way easier in Eden."

"The choice is yours, Ethan." Lyric caressed the stalks of grass with his fingertips.

"Why do you keep saying that?"

"I only speak the truth."

"Well then, the truth is, with my past life, some choices are just a farce."

"Your outlook is always up to you, Ethan, but that's not the choice I meant."

"What choice do I have to make now? Why can't I be done making choices?" The whine in his sarcastic tone grated on Ethan. An ugly sound.

"Ethan." Lyric said softly. The playful wrinkles around his eyes disappeared but for a second. Then his whole face lit up. He turned his face to the sky and laughed. "Birds."

What now? Ethan didn't have to wonder long. Soon every bird from the surrounding forest, or so it seemed, flapped into their conversation, hovered over Lyric and landed on his extended arms, shoulders, and head. Lyric giggled like a schoolboy as the birds began chirping and singing and hopping about. Ethan stepped back from the fray. Lyric shut his eyes, obviously enjoying the moment. Ethan took another step back, not wanting the birds to transfer to him. After a few minutes of deafening chatter, the motley crew lifted off and returned to the trees.

"That was frickin' amazing." Ethan watched the colorful wings blend in with the leaves and disappear. "Freaky, but still amazing."

Lyric laughed again. "That was for Cassie because I know how much you love her."

"Yes, Cassie would've loved that. Wait." Ethan stopped short. "*You* did that? How? I mean, I've seen Gimmel with Rufus, but a whole flock of birds?"

"Birds, animals, all of creation hears me and trusts me."

Ethan looked for a place to stop and think. He saw a fairly flat rock beside the path and sat down. "Trusts you? How?"

"I think the question is why?"

"I'll bite. Why?"

"Because I, or should I say we, created it—the Composer, Melody and I."

Ethan could swear a peculiar halo of white light encircled Lyric at that moment, as if he was some kind of Roman god. Ethan pressed his eyes closed with his thumb and forefinger and then opened them again. The halo had disappeared. "The Summit of Strangeness," he muttered. He spread his palms over the rock beneath him. It quivered with an odd warmth. *Was it going to suddenly come alive too?* "This world—it's like a million light years from mine, isn't it?"

"C'mon, let's talk while we walk, or we'll never get to our destination." Lyric took off at a brisk pace and Ethan jumped up to follow.

"Well, is it? Light years away, I mean?" Ethan's spectator curiosity about galaxies and stars and the size of the universe now became personal.

"Whether your world is a day away or a million light years away doesn't matter, Ethan. Time isn't the only thing irrelevant."

"Huh?" It took Ethan a couple minutes to catch on to what Lyric was saying. "You're talking about space, aren't you? And why am I not surprised. After all, space was irrelevant to Alice's rabbit hole too."

Lyric smiled. "Nice honesty."

"I know. I need to curb that honesty, don't I?"

Still smiling, Lyric opened his mouth to speak. But Ethan beat him to it.

"I know. The choice is still mine." When Lyric didn't reply, Ethan continued. "But what about Earth? Where lives are based on time *and* space? I don't ..."

"Even in your world, time and space aren't as important as you think, the temporal things ephemeral. That's why choices are so important."

Ethan stopped. "You talk like you know so much about my world. If so, then where are you? Maybe you only know as much as Anath, just stuff you gleaned from my mind. If that's true, you know little about my world, and its choices." Ethan brushed Lyric off with a wave of his hand and kept walking.

Unfazed, Lyric stepped up and kept talking. "Is that what your subconscious is saying?"

"My subconscious?"

"Your dreams, particularly your reoccurring ones. They have a voice. Listen to them."

Ethan stopped again. He remembered his dream about Lyric standing in the corner of a room with his friends. *What is that dream telling me? About Lyric? About my world? Do they coexist? If so, how? And if so, why wasn't his world like Eden, free of pain and death?* Looking up, he watched Lyric disappear around a bend in the trail. He jogged to catch up but when he got to the bend, Lyric was gone.

"Lyric." He called out, turning this way and that. No response. "Lyric?" Nothing. Ethan thought his best option was to keep moving so that's what he did. When the trail ended at the edge of a heavily wooded area, he didn't know what to do. He spun in all directions, 'round and 'round, calling Lyric's name without an answer. The word "betrayal" entered his mind, like an old friend. But he didn't want that friend. *What do I do?*

Without warning, a ferocious growl punctuated the air. In a panic, Ethan twisted around, sure that the animal was directly behind him, the roar so powerful. Then he saw it, a huge grizzly bear, a hulk of a beast, about fifty feet away. It lumbered toward him with frightful dexterity and speed. Ethan backed up slowly, right into the low hanging branches of a large fir tree. He grabbed a branch, pulled himself tight into the trunk and hoisted himself up, the limb bending under his weight. Knowing the bear's capabilities, he pulled himself higher, scrambling to the next layer of branches, hoping his shaking arms would stay true.

"Ethan." Lyric's voice halted his adrenalin-driven climb.

"Hu—hello? L—Lyric? Is that you? Wh—where's the bear?"

"She's down here with me, Ethan."

"Wh—what?" Ethan heard no fear in Lyric's voice. But he couldn't stop stammering.

"Be at peace, Ethan. You can come down."

"I … I don't know if … if I can." Ethan hugged the tree tightly.

"Yes, you can. It's safe."

"It's safe," Ethan repeated. With eyes pressed closed, he began an inchworm climb down, choosing to believe in Lyric's words, though not sure why. The drumming of his heart lessened with each descending branch and soon Ethan could hear Lyric's humming. He recognized the tune from the day before. That same tune had sent the mutation fleeing. *Trust Lyric. Trust Lyric? Yes, trust Lyric.* He kept moving, but still couldn't look down. Releasing his angst upon touching solid ground, he stepped out of the thick branches, and came face-to-face with the bear, its muzzle close enough to sever his arm from his shoulder. "Wha—" he yelled, falling back into the branches. Only then did he notice Lyric, sitting casually on the back of the bear.

"Ethan," Lyric said.

Ethan took his eyes off the bear's bellowing nostrils and

looked up at Lyric.

"Do not fear. The bear is friendly." As if in response to Lyric's voice, the bear grunted lightly, attempting to nudge Ethan's arm. With all his willpower, Ethan remained motionless, the bear's nose tickling his skin, the warm breath heavy on his goose bumps.

"I think she likes you." Lyric smiled.

Without replying, Ethan inched sideways out of the branches and slowly shifted around the bear's head to be near Lyric.

"She's not dangerous, not like in your world. In fact," Lyric said, rubbing the bear behind her ears, "she's rather playful." The bear tossed her head up and down. "Though it's true that she doesn't know her own strength," Lyric joked.

Ethan stood back and watched in silent awe. Sliding down the bear's back, Lyric gave her a slap on her bulging shoulder hump and she bounded away into the trees, crashing and growling as she went. Lyric laughed. "What a clown."

"I, I don't know what to say." Ethan wiped his sweaty brow. "You're like the lion tamer at the circus."

Lyric chuckled. "Not exactly. No taming necessary. Like I said earlier, creation trusts and obeys my voice. Birds or bears, there's no difference."

"Maybe not to you, but I thought I was that bear's dinner." Ethan looked at Lyric. "Hey … why'd you leave me anyway? And where'd you go? All of a sudden you were gone."

"I took a side path. I thought you'd see it. It led to a field of wild strawberries. Tasty and refreshing. Want some?" Lyric stretched out his left hand to offer Ethan a few ripe berries.

"No." Ethan grunted. "No, I do *not* want some."

"Okay. Your choice." Lyric popped them in his mouth and turned off down a path Ethan was sure hadn't been there a few minutes ago.

"That's it?" Ethan stuck close to Lyric's side. "That's all you're gonna say?"

Lyric tilted his head. "What do you want me to say?"

"Sorry? For leaving me back there?" Ethan pointed wildly behind them. "For endangering my life, maybe?"

"Hmmm. After what I said about the birds, I thought you'd understand."

Ethan looked at Lyric and huffed, puzzling over what he was really trying to say.

Lyric stopped and did a 360. "Look around you, Ethan. Do you think all of this was made simply to decay and fall apart?" Lyric stepped over to a small bush along the path. "Look at this wild rose." He touched the flower's soft petals. "I can tell you right now how many leaves are on this bush." Lyric looked up. "Or look at that mountain." He pointed to a lone peak in the hazy distance. "I can tell you the total number of trees growing on that slope." He sighed. "Nobody really wants to know those things or needs to know those things. But I know. And do you know why?" Lyric's voice cracked. Ethan noticed tears in his eyes. "Because I love them. The trees, the flowers, the birds. I love this created world, including people. I love it all and would do anything for it." Lyric returned up the trail.

Ethan paused. He wanted to trust Lyric, to trust this man who was so much more than just a man. But why did he still have doubts? He didn't want to. Then, not wanting to be left behind again, he ran to catch up.

While Ethan processed, they walked in silence. The sun shone brilliantly, high in the sky, though time-wise Ethan figured it should've been late afternoon. *So unusual. Yet why should I be surprised*? Ethan didn't mention it. He returned to thinking about Lyric's words, his mention of creation and his love for it. He remembered Lyric's comments about Ethan's world and his knowledge of it. *Does he really live in my world? And if so, does that mean he loves it too?*

"Yes." Lyric nodded.

"Huh?"

"In answer to your questions, yes. My appearance is not the same, but I am there, loving your world as well."

"What?"

Lyric stopped, turned to face Ethan, and put both his hands on Ethan's shoulders. "All through this day I've been guiding, simply waiting for you to ask those questions, as a seeker. Because you're a visitor here, I know you've had much to process." He motioned to a patch of soft grass. "Come. Let's sit."

Again, Ethan couldn't move. "Wait. Are you trying to tell me that *you* are the main connection between Eden and my world? That all these other connections stem from you?"

"Me, Melody, the Composer. In a way, yes." The white halo of light around Lyric returned as he sat cross-legged in the grass, his face radiating. This time Ethan was sure the source was Lyric himself. Ethan paced, his fingers dancing against his pant legs. Lyric began humming. The melody struck a memory chord for Ethan, but then his thoughts focused elsewhere.

"In a way? In what way?" He continued pacing. "I'm thinking it has something to do with my choice or choices, based on what you said earlier." Ethan looked at Lyric who seemed to be enjoying the moment. "Am I right?"

"Yes, Ethan. Come. Sit." Lyric patted the grass beside him,

but Ethan didn't oblige. He wasn't ready to relax. Undeterred, Lyric continued. "You've made a lot of choices since coming to Eden. Think about how those choices changed throughout your time here."

Ethan stopped pacing, closed his eyes, and sighed. "Malachi said the same thing. Guess I shouldn't be surprised, should I? I mean, since Melody's always communicating with him, and since you and Melody are one. Somehow?" He looked at Lyric. "Did I get that right?"

"Yes. You've learned much. And grown much in character."

"I … I guess." Ethan sat down and crossed his legs, his misgivings over Lyric's aura gone.

"Even two days ago, when you helped Reece. You chose friendship over fear."

Ethan remained quiet.

"There's something you've discovered, what anyone discovers, when they choose others over themselves."

Ethan turned his head. "Now you've lost me."

Lyric grinned. "Purpose, Ethan. You found purpose."

"Purpose." Ethan half-smiled. He was beginning to like that word. He caressed the soft blades of grass.

Lyric put one hand on Ethan's shoulder. "There's one last thing."

"Shoot."

"You've now started *intentionally* asking Melody for help. That's been your biggest change."

"Really?"

"Yes, because it means you're no longer afraid to accept your own human frailty, and that you're willing to trust others."

"Huh." Ethan closed his eyes. He knew that in the past, such words would've made him defensive, angry. At a young age, he'd vowed to not let others in, to do it alone. But now. Now he was learning to let others in.

"And that's why we're here."

"Here? You mean there's more?" Ethan looked around. *What more could there be? Wasn't this revelation enough?*

"Maybe you didn't notice the precipice we're on. Take a look." Lyric pointed to the cliff's edge. "Believe me, it'll be worth it."

Ethan studied Lyric's face. He sensed no guile or ill will. He stood up. But when he realized it was a long way down, he got on all fours and crawled to the edge, then gasped.

His heart pounded against the rock. He looked at Lyric, then back over the drop, then back at Lyric, pointing to the scene below. "That—that's *my* pond. And *my* waterfall. For real?"

"Yes. Yes, it is. I asked you where you wanted to go, remember?"

"But …"

Lyric laughed, a deep guttural laugh. "I knew, Ethan. You wanted to come here. Here's where it all started and here's where it will end. The choice is up to you."

Ethan sat up now, in shock. He'd come full circle. And yet, nothing was the same.

"Well, not *right* here." Lyric stood. "There's a cave entrance nearby. Come."

"Explain something to me first." Ethan wasn't ready to go anywhere else yet.

"Sure. Ask away."

"I know I'm an anomaly here, that it probably didn't even matter if I entered Epiphany. But Malachi said that Epiphany would be my portal home. Is this choice connected to that?"

"Melody gave him that information, so yes, that's right.

Home. In more ways than one."

"Huh?" An old uneasiness hijacked Ethan's thoughts.

"Again, you, and you alone, have the freedom to choose."

"But can I make the right choice? The one that will take me back to Cassie?" Ethan closed his eyes and put his head in his hands.

"Trust who you've become, Ethan." Lyric sat down beside him. "And remember, there are those who will help you *if* you ask."

"Yeah, right, but …"

"What do you fear, Ethan?"

"Choices. I guess I still fear choices." Ethan kept his head down. They sat in silence for a long time. Ethan knew Lyric would wait.

Lyric sat back and began humming. At first, Ethan paid no attention. But then he listened and remembered. His mouth gaped open, he stared in disbelief. "Tha … that's my song you're humming! The one I wrote when I was thirteen. How? How do you know that?"

With a wide grin, Lyric looked at Ethan and started singing the final stanza. "The eyes of hope will seek and find him; will offer rest from loss and pain."

Ethan couldn't believe it. Lyric was singing his song, only somehow he had tweaked the words and imperfect intervals. Now it sounded like a song of joy, not a song of sorrow. Lyric kept singing the same two lines, Ethan too astonished to speak.

"Are those the only two lines you're gonna sing?" Ethan finally asked.

"For now." Lyric tipped his head. "I can rewrite your song, Ethan. I can give resolution to the dissonant tritones of your past, just like I've done for all the others that have trusted me completely. I can give your life a whole new song. But again, that depends on you."

"My own new song." Ethan thought about how great that would be. "And will that get me home?" He only hoped.

"It's a little more complicated than that, since, as you say, you are an anomaly. For the other pre-epiphany ones, they simply have to choose between trusting me completely or not. If they do, then they return to their community."

"And if they don't, they go somewhere else, right? I remember reading that because I was curious about where they'd go. I thought maybe they turned into creatures like Anath." Ethan looked at Lyric. "Do they?"

"No. That would be unkind. No, I send them to a place where there's still hope, where they can still choose to listen to my voice and trust me. They're not doomed to be like the evil creature behind Anath. However, in the place I send them, there is pain and suffering, and my voice is drowned out by many other voices, and many choices."

"Sounds like Earth." Ethan thought about that for a minute. "Wait. Am I right? They head to Earth? To try and find you there?"

"In a manner of speaking, yes."

"That's … I don't know. Screwed up?" Ethan let the idea sink in. "And yet I guess not so screwed up if there's still hope. And if you're there, like you say you are."

"Your honest heart is also a discerning heart."

"Ha." Ethan couldn't hold back the scoff. "Heck. I've been called a lot of things but never discerning."

"I know. But didn't Jill call you sensitive and tender-hearted once?"

"Did she? I …" Ethan remembered. "Yeah, I guess she did.

Once. She said I was tender-hearted toward Cassie." Ethan's mouth opened wide again. "You … that … that was a memory from my world. How? …" Ethan shook his head. "I know. More bizarro connections."

Lyric half-smiled. "Bizarro, perhaps. At least, for now. But not in the future, I hope. And that brings me to the three-fold choice set before you. Are you ready?"

Ethan stared at the grass, individual blades shimmering metallic greens, silver, and gold. He let out a long breath. "You say that I am. So, I am."

Lyric nodded. "Firstly, you can trust me completely, not doubting Melody's voice, and decide to stay here in Eden, living eternally without pain and suffering, which would include healing of your knee."

"Can't say I haven't thought about it. More than once, to be honest. And a working knee would be nice." Ethan rubbed his strong knee. "What's the second choice?"

"You can decide that you want to keep going it alone, refusing to let others in, sheltering your heart from loving and the pain that it brings, believing that's the only way. In that case you will return to Earth and not remember anything about this world. Your memories, and all you've learned since your arrival here, will be erased."

"In other words, I'll be my own boss again." The thought didn't sound as appealing to Ethan as it used to. Cassie came to mind. *Can I be the father she needs? Can I do it alone? I used to think so.* Ethan released a long breath. "And the third option?"

"Well, this is the unorthodox one. It's a combination of the two."

"Which is?"

"An additional leap of faith. You can choose to trust me

completely in this world, but then opt to return to your temporal world. Much, but not all, of this world, and the things you learned, will be hidden away in your subconscious. Melody and I, we will be there, and you will sense us, but because of the dark presence of evil, how we exhibit ourselves in your world will not be the same as here. But if you listen, and look for us, you will find us."

"Whoa."

"I told you, it's convoluted. But I believe in you. I believe you will make the right choice." Lyric stood up and offered his hand to Ethan. "Come."

"Come." Ethan remembered his dream with Gimmel. 'Come,' she'd said. Was the connection hopeful or disconcerting? Ethan didn't have time to wonder. He scrambled to his feet, not wanting to be left behind. "Where to now?"

"The cave. Your choosing depends on it."

Fifty feet down the path, the two of them came to a large crevasse between two massive rocks.

Lyric cautioned him. "Watch your step. We'll be descending quickly, leaving the sunlight behind. Don't look around. Just keep your eyes on me."

"But we don't even have flashlights. How'll I even see you?"

Lyric grinned. "You need to ask?" He turned and walked into the cave.

Ethan followed right behind, keeping his eyes on the back of Lyric's head as they entered the wide chasm. They came to the steps down almost immediately and soon the light of the entrance was a mere pinhole, though that didn't matter. The further down they went, the brighter Lyric's tunic shone. Lyric moved quickly through the hollow silence, not allowing

Ethan time to ask questions.

They finally reached level ground, deep in the mountain. Lyric's tunic glowed like a floodlight, revealing a wide tunnel that extended in two directions. Ethan shuddered.

"Not much longer now." Lyric settled down on a narrow bench hewn in the rock wall. Ethan joined him, no longer stupefied by random objects like the bench. In the stillness, Lyric sang Ethan's song once again, the first few words unchanged but then, new words:

> *The eyes of hope they sought and found me,*
> *I disembarked from loss and pain;*
> *The whistle rests—the sun is shining,*
> *A new day dawns, my travel's done.*

Lyric sang the stanza over and over. Ethan closed his eyes and began to cry silent tears, soaking in the new words. The words once full of anguish were now peaceful and freeing. Overwhelmed with his own thoughts, Ethan didn't notice when the music stopped. He opened his eyes to complete darkness.

Ethan whispered. "Lyric?" No answer. "Lyric?" He heard something, but it wasn't a person. He stood up, straining to listen. Could it be? Yes, it was the sound of a train whistle, far off in the distance. By the consistent whistle he knew it was fast approaching, and yet within the echoing cave walls, the faint sound's direction remained a mystery. The sound began to build, and when he heard the familiar clickety-clack, his heart pulsed loudly in his chest. He moaned. *Why? Why a train? And where's it coming from?* He wanted to run. But where? All alone, in this black cave? The whistle grew louder and louder, and soon he could see a tiny beam of light from far down one of the tunnels. He began spiraling down into a whirlpool of his own nightmare thoughts, menacing memories, and impending doom. *Not again!* And still the light grew, and the reverberating noise intensified.

With quivering fingers, he felt for the bench behind him and sat back down, no longer able to watch. He wished he could drown out the sound with earphones and Heavy Metal. He hunched over, his body shaking uncontrollably. Then he remembered. *Help!* He yelled the word in his mind. And again. His body relaxed.

The whistle ceased. Ethan knew the train was slowing, coming to a stop. *Why? Why is it stopping? What does it want from me?* He heard the hiss of the engine brakes. He closed his eyes, choosing to not look up.

Silence.

Time stood still.

Silence.

Ethan opened his eyes and half-raised his head to see a beam of light shining out from what looked like the inside of a railroad car. His eyes adjusted and he shuddered at the outline of massive, steel driving wheels and side rods. The light source moved slowly along the car, disappeared, and then reappeared with blinding force outside the car. Ethan shut his eyes, though he knew exactly where the light chose to settle. At the top of the passenger steps.

"Ethan."

He knew that voice, pleasant and kind. "Lyric? Is that you?" He looked, half-sheltering his eyes with his cupped hand. A clash of emotions rose in his heart, like multiple opposing weather systems building into an F5 tornado: gratefulness, because the voice was Lyric's; fear, because of the train and all it represented from his past; peace, at the certainty of Melody's presence in his mind; doubt, at his own ability to choose.

"Ethan." This time Lyric's voice was more commanding. "Come here." The light from Lyric's body diminished slightly as Ethan inched forward. Lyric moved to the bottom rung of the steps and stretched out both his arms.

Ethan caught his breath. In that moment, Lyric stood exactly like he had in his dream. The man in the corner, reaching out to Cassie and Jill, to Ben and Janus and Barnabas. Reaching out into the coldness of the room, offering warmth, and peace, with tears of sadness trickling down his face. Somehow, Ethan understood. Those tears were for him.

"Come. Come without fear." Lyric's voice was so tender, offering Ethan a helping hand onto the train. "You alone own this choice."

Ethan stood motionless. Alone, yet not alone. And now unafraid to make probably the biggest choice of his life.

CHAPTER THIRTY

"Ethan! Ethan?"

He hears the voice of desperation, like someone calling to him through the howling and ravaging wind of a prairie blizzard. He looks but cannot see, the white wall of stinging snow shutting him out, or is it in?

"Baldwin?" His inner voice yells. "Baldwin," it repeats, but the name takes on no face, no image. Nothing. He drifts away from the voices, a weightless cloud saturated with ice crystals, yet not ice. He neither senses the cold nor the wind. He drifts outside of time and space, neither anxious nor afraid.

* * *

"How is he?" A voice, a female voice.

"The same, Jill. Still in a coma." A male voice. Deep. Older.

"Oh Dad. What do we do? Wait? Medi-vac him back to Edmonton? What?"

I'm here. I'm here.

"Shh, honey. It's only been four days. Give him time."

Yes, give me time. Time. What is time?

"Four days, with no idea of what happened in that cave. Was he oxygen deprived? Was it an allergic reaction? Is his brain permanently injured? What?"

Ethan hears the fear but can't connect.

"You're getting yourself all worked up, honey. This is Ethan we're talking about. He's tough, remember?"

"Yeah. You're right. He's tough."

Don't give up on me. I'm here.

Voices vanish.

* * *

Floating, ever floating, in a white sea of emptiness, aware of his surroundings but without a lodestar, everything is meaningless. Unable to speak, he searches for a beacon of light or sound or smell or touch, but he encounters nothing. He hangs in a vaporous void without a past, or future.

* * *

"I'm telling you, it was the darndest thing. When I peered in through the opening in the rocks we finally made, he wasn't there. My flashlight revealed nothing. Nada. I checked the floor. I checked the cave walls. I even checked the ceiling. His body was just not there!" A new voice, the angst growing with each word.

"Shadows and light can play tricks on the eyes." The older voice of reason.

"Yeah, you're right. I'm just on edge. After all, if it hadn't been for me, he wouldn't have been in that cave." Such guilt in that distraught voice.

"Mr. Janus." Another voice. It too carries a tone of worry, but something more. "You revived him. Remember? He had no pulse."

"Yeah, sure Barney, I revived him alright. All he kept repeating in his delirium was, 'Baldwin, Baldwin.' Baldwin? Who's that?"

"Janus." The voice of reason. "You could neither predict

the earthquake nor the avalanche of rocks that sealed off the entrance."

"You're right Ben." The distraught voice.

Baldwin? Janus? Ben? Voices with names, yet Ethan has no recollection, his memory still floating. Still disconnected.

"But it's been a week of him just lying there." The anxious voice again. "He may be brain dead for all we know."

No, I am here. And I can hear you.

"Maybe he will remember this." A melody from a bamboo flute plays in Ethan's mind. A pretty tune but that is all. It stirs no memory.

I hear you. I hear your sweet song. How can I tell you?

Voices again vanish.

* * *

Slowly, a silent blizzard of icy nothingness stirs, shifting from barren white to murky gray. Hazy outlines, and nondescript shapes appear in his mind. He watches his own limp body being disconnected from machines, leaving bleached rooms and buildings, then beaming up, only to find himself in another colorless room with more machines. He is waking. He can tell. But waking to what? And where?

* * *

"Oh Ethan."

It's Jill! Ethan recognizes the voice. Hears the pain. Feels the caress of her warm fingers on his hand. Reality replaces his floating world. He hears the beat of his own heart. Thump. Thump. Thump. *Jill! I am alive! I am here and I am alive!*

Trying to shoot energy down his arm, he attempts to make a fist. Nothing. *It's me. I'm here.* He tries again, this time focusing only on his index finger. It twitches. Jill's hand jerks in response. He concentrates. It moves again.

"Nurse!" She yells. He hears her push the chair away. "Nurse!"

Another female, heavy-footed, enters the room. "Yes, Jill?"

"His fingers. They moved. I'm sure of it." Jill touches his forearm. "Ethan, can you hear me? It's Jill. Ethan? It's Jill."

Her breath warm on his brow, Ethan fights to open his eyes. *Small slits of hazy light and dark outlines of movement. I can see. I can see you.* He struggles to smile. *So much energy.* His eyelids collapse.

"Did you see that?" Jill's breath is erratic now. "He opened his eyes. And I think his mouth moved, even with that tube in it."

Ethan feels her pull away. He wants her to stay.

"Can you get the doctor?"

"I'll see if he's still in the hospital."

Ethan hears the nurse walk away. Now fully engaged, he listens intently to the sounds in the room. *Was Jill still there? And where was that faint song coming from?*

"Hi Dad; it's Jill. I think Ethan's waking up."

Her trembling voice is a beautiful melody to Ethan's ears. He can tell she's pacing the floor. Ethan pictures her walking, talking, and twisting her long hair into knots with her slender fingers—a habit she could never shake.

Pause.

"Yeah, he moved his fingers and then opened his eyes."

Pause.

"No, they're not open now. But the doctor's coming so hopefully—"

Pause.

"Yes. No. I don't know. Do you think she's ready to see

her daddy like this?"

Pause.

"Okay. Could you let Janus know?"

Pause.

"You're right, Dad. Thanks. See you soon."

The call ended, Ethan hears Jill pull up the chair beside him. Her hands sandwich his. *I hear you. I hear your beautiful voice.* He screams the words but only in his head, his body unresponsive.

Jill's breath tickles his ear. "Keep fighting, Ethan. Keep fighting and come back to us."

* * *

Floating—more floating. But now the shifting clouds open at times to reveal a world below, giving him perspective. Blurred shapes become distinct features on the landscape. He sees a glistening river and lush fields. He sees log houses and a waterwheel. He sees a shimmering pond and a dancing waterfall. He longs to remember. He knows he should, but the memories are hidden by a nebula of white nothingness.

* * *

"But I saw it."

Back in his physical body, Ethan hears the frustration in Jill's voice.

"He moved his fingers. He opened his eyes. I didn't imagine it." Jill's voice quivers.

Is that fear or anger? Ethan isn't sure.

"Okay, okay. That's okay." Ben's voice. Ethan would know it anywhere, calming and commanding. He also hears an underlying peace that he never understood. Now he connects to it.

"The doctor took the tube out. That's a good sign, right?

All we can do is wait. And hope. And pray."

"You're right, Dad." Jill's voice has relaxed.

For the first time, a sensation, a need, fills Ethan's mind. "Water." He hears Jill gasp. Then hurried footsteps to his bedside.

"Water," Ethan whispers, his eyes still closed.

"I'll get the nurse."

Janus? Was that Janus's voice Ethan heard?

The voice returns quickly. "I found the nurse and the doctor."

"He … he asked for water," Jill says.

"Please. Let me look." An assertive voice.

Caring fingers open one of Ethan's eyelids. Then the other. He jerks, the light shooting pain into his brain.

"Ethan." The doctor correctly pronounces the "th" sound.

I'm not in Asia anymore. I must be back in Edmonton. I remember! I remember! The others converse around him. *I am so thirsty.*

"Water." This time he opens his eyes.

"Did you see that? He spoke. And opened his eyes." Jill's voice is high. Excited. The room fills with exhuberant conversation.

"Quiet and please stand back." The doctor is commanding. The room is quiet once again.

Someone places a straw delicately on Ethan's bottom lip. He welcomes the refreshing coolness. "Thanks." He mouths the word silently.

"Welcome back," the doctor says, leaning keenly over Ethan's face. "Can you tell me your name?"

"Ethan." Ethan's voice is still barely audible. "Ethan Conrad Adam."

"Very good, Mr. Adam." The doctor smiles and pulls back.

"You are in the University of Alberta Hospital in Edmonton. You've been in a coma for almost three weeks. It was touch and go for a while. But now, here you are." He turns to the others. "He's out of his coma. I know you want to talk to him. Be brief. The nurse will give him a sedative, so he'll be asleep soon. He still has lots of healing to do." He nods to the nurse and walks out.

Without a word, the nurse injects something into his I.V., cranks the front of the bed up slightly, gives Ethan another sip of water, and slips out, leaving the four of them alone.

Exhausted, Ethan closes his eyes, finding gentle comfort in recognizing each voice in the room: Jill, Ben, and Janus. He smiles at the memory. *Someone is missing.*

Ethan likes their presence, being back with people on Earth. Someone takes his hand. He knows it's Jill. But he still can't release the thought that someone is missing. Then he remembers.

"Where's the man?" His voice is still hoarse.

"The man?" Jill says.

"The man in the corner." The words take so much energy.

"The man in the corner? I … I don't know." Her voice shakes. Nobody else responds. Ethan slips into his dreams.

* * *

He's falling. Down, down, down an opening in the earth. It sparkles with fluorescent colors. A rabbit hole? Where'd that thought come from? He slows. The colors shift. A soft thump. He recognizes his surroundings immediately. He's in an old passenger train car. There is a presence with him, but he's not alarmed. It's a peaceful place. He rests there.

* * *

"Ethan." Janus's voice.

Ethan doesn't want to be shaken from his peaceful dream.

"Doc says we need to keep trying." Ben's voice.

"But what if he doesn't respond today? When Jill arrives with Cassie?"

"We can tell Cassie he's on medicine that makes him sleep. She'll be alright."

"Yes. She'll believe that."

Ethan listens, focuses on the word, "Cassie." He recognizes it but his memories are a jumble of obscure images. Cassie in this world. Cassie in some other world. Where's the reality?

"Cassie," he mutters.

"Ethan," Janus blurts out. "Welcome back." Janus touches his shoulder. It's comforting.

"Cassie." He repeats her name, opening his eyes. Less work today. A good sign.

"Yes." Ben steps closer. "Cassie's coming today. In fact, I just got a text message from Jill. They're on their way up the elevator as we speak."

"Water." His tongue sticks to the roof of his mouth.

Janus leans in. "Water? Is that what you asked for?" Janus brings the straw up to Ethan's lips before he can answer. "Anything for my old fri ..."

"Daddy?"

Ethan knows that voice. *Cassie. Oh Cassie.* He turns his head. It takes all his strength. There she is, standing in the doorway with her big, baby blue eyes, her chubby cheeks, her golden hair, and he remembers. He remembers her little six-year-old voice singing silly songs as they hiked through the mountains. He remembers her giggle when she splashed him in the canoe. He wants to grab her up in his arms, but he can't get them to cooperate.

"Daddy!" She runs to the bedside, wrapping her little hand around Ethan's index finger. He watches Cassie's face shift. Her lips droop. The sparkle in her eyes fades under a questioning brow. "Is Daddy okay?" She turns to Jill, who's just coming in the doorway carrying a case. It looks familiar, yet Ethan can't remember.

"He was very, very sick, Cassie. But he'll get better. He just needs lots of time to rest."

Cassie looks back at Ethan. "Can I crawl into bed with you, Daddy? I can rest too."

"I'm not sure if that's a good idea." Jill looks at Ben. "Dad?"

"Your call, Jilly girl."

Say yes. Please say yes.

"But ... ," Cassie tightens her hand, "but I was asking Daddy."

"Well, let's ask Daddy together." Jill walks to the bed, leans the case up against the bedside table, and bends over Ethan. "Ethan? Is it okay?"

Jill's breath is fresh, like peppermint candy. Her hazel eyes shimmer green under the fluorescent lights. *Wait. Green eyes?* He closes his eyes and remembers. He remembers Anath, and her green eyes. He remembers Eden in all its twinkling splendor. He remembers his friends: Baldwin and Malachi, Seshat and, of course, Gimmel. He remembers it all: the hideous creature behind Anath's eyes. A formidable evil. The enemy of Eden. He remembers fighting that enemy, but he wasn't alone. Who helped him? Oh yes, Melody. Melody, and ... and .... Inside he laughs a giant Janus laugh, though in reality it's only a slight parting of his lips.

"Are you okay, Daddy?"

Ethan opens his eyes and sees the guitar case. He looks at Jill first, and then at Cassie. "Yes, Cassie girl," he whispers. "For the first time in a long time, I'm okay."

Jill gifts Ethan with a tender grin, and hoists Cassie onto the bed. "Here," she says. "Let me help you onto the blanket. Just be careful of the tubes 'n things." Cassie curls her small, body into his. The others back away from his bed. Oh how he wants to wrap his arms around his little girl. For now, he simply lays there, listening. When the adults' hushed voices cease, he focuses solely on his daughter's breathing as it slows into her dreams. *Oh my Cassie, my little girl. I've come back to you, back home.* Warm tears roll down his cheeks.

In the silence, the light breeze of a lulling melody flutters into his mind, bringing with it a joyful memory of harmony, and friendship, and hope. The tune grows louder and more beautiful like the unfolding of a sunrise. And just when the notes, like the pinks and oranges and golds in the morning sky, reach their peak, a rich baritone voice bursts out from the corner of his mind, like the first rays of sunlight breaking a flat horizon. He knows the voice. In his mind, he hums along, the melody now resolved. He claims the lyrics, now re-written.

Postlude

Riding the mainline,
Feeling the breeze, the joy of time,
Guided by a voice,
Yet free to make my choice,
The harmony of life.

I've seen the stations
And self-seeking faces
Their ravenous ways can't free
Me.

But I'm free.
Free
From the prison of eternal searching
By the Lover of this world
The melody, the lyrics,
Speak from the given word.
To help me, to save me,
Unlocking my mind's door.

Guided by a voice,
Yet free to make my choice,
The harmony of life.
The eyes of hope they sought and found me,
I disembarked from loss and pain;
The whistle rests — the sun is shining,
A new day dawns, my travel's done.
I'm not alone.
I've found my home.

Acknowledgments

- to Mykal, Kendra, and James—my children—and our years together in Southeast Asia. It wasn't always easy or even desirable, yet you were troopers, willing to be part of the adventure. Thanks for the memories, some of which are now part of this novel. How boring life would be without you, even now as adults with children of your own. Thanks for making life beautiful.

- to the Khimsha people. Thanks for sharing your lives with me, and for allowing me to share your cultural stories of origin and ghosts with the rest of the world so that they can know you in a small way as well. Your lives and perseverance in hope are an inspiration to me.

- to my publisher Colleen McCubbin at Siretona Creative. You are both knowledgeable and wise. To say the last nine months have been challenging for me is an understatement. Thanks for not giving up on me, and for believing in this novel. Thanks also to Charity Mongrain as Siretona Creative's author coach. You go above and beyond. Working with my publisher team has been a joy.

- to Writers' Café—my Inklings. Thanks for listening to me read every chapter of this novel and giving me excellent feedback as well as advice as I moved toward publishing. And for praying me through some difficult times in the seven years it's taken me to get this novel written and published. We've laughed together. We've cried together. We've birthed a book together and we've grieved death together. You are a gift.

- to Angie Abdou, my professor at Athabasca University, who not only encouraged me to write and finish this novel, but also agreed to be my advisor. Thanks for pushing me forward.

- to the people and country of Thailand. I learned so much from living in your world.

- to University of Calgary's Public Archaeology program at the Cluny Fortified Village Site, in co-operation with the Siksika Nation and the Blackfoot Crossing Historical Park. Thanks for allowing me to join a dig and actually "be" an archaeologist for three days with your team in the summer of 2016. You never tired of all my questions about archaeology and survey work. Your passion for the work was contagious.

- to my editor, Marcia Laycock. How many edit rounds did I have? Thanks for making my manuscript better.

- to my daughter Mykal. Thanks for agreeing to paint my book cover art. Your ability to create hauntingly powerful images on a canvas always takes my breath away.

- to Gary Horsman, my book cover designer. Thanks for taking my simple ideas and turning them into an eye-catching cover.

- to Dustin Olson for his ability to take "Ethan's Song," my prelude poem, and turn it into an actual heavy metal song. The way you've incorporated Ethan's journey throughout the novel blows me away—and brings tears to my eyes.

- to my fellow Nestbuilders. How does a random group of

writers become so tight in such a short time period and only via Zoom meetings? Only by the grace of God.

- to my sisters, who've always been there for me. Never judgement. Only love. Thanks.

- to my beta readers who offered great feedback.

- to the Canada-wide InScribe family, who've taught me so much, not just about writing but also living.

- to all those who've supported us and our work with minority language groups for the last 30+ years. I would've never arrived at this point if it wasn't for you.

- to all those speculative fiction authors who've gone before and fed my curious mind.

- to all the musicians who've given me melodies and lyrics that speak into my life, connecting with my emotions and feeding my soul, right from childhood. How dull life would be without you.

- to the Trinity for your gift of creativity, curiosity and imagination. Thanks for calling me to write. I feel Your pleasure. I live in Your hope. And for Your glory!

Connie got to "be" an archaeologist for three days in the summer of 2016, when research for the character of Janus led her to participate in the University of Calgary's Public Archaeology program at the Cluny Fortified Village Site, in co-operation with the Siksika Nation and the Blackfoot Crossing Historical Park.

Learn More

- For more on the theme of hope, connect with Connie through her website, A Curious Hope, www.conniemaeinglis.ca.
- Watch for "Ethan's Song" and the *Rewriting Adam* audiobook. Sign up for Connie's newsletter to get all the news!
- Search for "Ethan's Playlist—Rewriting Adam" on Spotify, YouTube Music, iTunes.
- Connie and her husband, Doug, work as Bible translators among the Khimsha people of Southeast Asia with Wycliffe Canada. For information about this cross-cultural and linguistic work, visit https://www.wycliffe.ca.